# Fated

## A Haunted Story

R.L. Merrill

# Fated:

## A Haunted Story

By
R.L. Merrill

**Fated: A Haunted Story**



Published By: Celie Bay Publications, LLC

Edited by: Kelli Collins, Edit Me This

Cover Design: Elizabeth Mackey

Interior book design by: R.L. Merrill – Vellum

 Created with Vellum

*Bad things do happen to good people. This story is for all of those good people. Don't give up hope. Remember to love yourself.*

# Prologue

*April 2012*
*St. Germaine Building*
*French Quarter*
*New Orleans*

*Jaylene Charles*

We all made our way down to the weight room after quick runs to the bathroom for morning business and teeth brushing. Star and Mage hit the weights, and Jade and I ran alongside each other on the treadmills. Music was blaring from the speakers and we were all just in our own worlds.

I realized I still wasn't used to all the skin. The guys were all shirtless, but it didn't feel as weird after our night of bonding. I felt a lot closer to them, even though I still didn't know Mage and Jade as well as Star. They'd all opened up to me and I was grateful for that.

I worked up a good sweat and then went over to an area with mats on the floor to stretch out. I stifled a laugh when I realized how hard they were trying not to watch me. They didn't look at me as if I was a sister or friend, but they were really trying to. I guess you couldn't take the rock star completely out of them.

Mage took my place on the other treadmill and he and Jade fell into step together. Jade had pulled his long black hair back in a hair tie. Mage's brown curls were sweaty and plastered against his back. Star's short blonde hair was sticking out all over. They were all beautiful in their own way, but they had really won me over with their boyish charms and goofy humor. Part of me was loath to think of them in their real element. As rock stars, they probably weren't this accessible.

"So guys, I have another question." They looked curious but concerned. I laughed at their expressions. "It's not a huge deal. I'm just wondering how different you are when you're doing the rock star thing. Because you guys are so much fun to hang out with, I just wonder if when my contract is up, when I'm done tattooing you, and you guys go back to being big time, how different are you going to be?"

They looked at each other and I thought I detected a note of sadness.

Star spoke first. "I don't know that we're really that different. We don't try to put on an act, I don't think. But we don't really share our nerdy sides. Makes it rough with the fans when they think we are still nerds."

Jade was smiling now. "And if they want to think we're like the songs we play, I guess I don't mind."

I rolled my eyes. I didn't want to know the answer to the next question but I thought I'd better ask. "Do you think you guys will ever settle down with someone or do you still like the chase?"

Mage frowned. "I think what you're really wondering is, will *Devon* settle down or if he's still going to be chasing skirt."

I frowned and shook my head. "No, I don't think I'm asking that. I wouldn't want you guys to speak for him. Only time will tell what happens with me and Devon. No, I'm curious about you guys."

He was still frowning but he looked like he was deep in thought.

Star said, "I hope to settle down. I don't need any more empty relationships. I don't want that life anymore." After what Star had shared the past few days about going to rehab, I could pretty much guess what he meant by empty relationships. He seemed determined to stay sober. I was determined to help him however I could.

"I think you'll have what you want, Star. I'll be here however you need me."

He smiled and winked at me.

Jade sighed. "If I can find the perfect woman, I'll settle down. I just don't really know what I want. I can't see past getting this album done right now so I don't know what the hell is going to happen to me. Or what's going to happen to *us*. To Maggie's Bones."

Mage cut in. "Dude, we're going to be fine. We'll do the album and then we'll figure it out. I don't think we're done yet. The Bones still got a lot of music left in us, we. As for settling down?" He got a sly smile on his face. "My woman is out there. She just don't know she's my woman yet. When it's time, I will grab her up and we'll have about twenty kids together. I can't wait to be a dad."

I giggled. "I can totally see you being a dad. You'll be a good one. But twenty kids is a lot to ask of a woman. I'm assuming you meant *one* woman?"

He laughed. "Yeah, one woman. Okay, maybe ten kids. Is that too much?"

"I don't know, the thought of giving birth scares the shit out of me, so I am probably not the right person to ask."

Jade raised an eyebrow. "Don't you want to have kids?"

I concentrated on stretching. I wasn't sure how to answer that. "I don't know. It's scary. I am only just now doing a good job of taking care of myself. I don't know if I'd make a good mom. I wouldn't know what to do with a baby. I love kids... Other people's kids."

The truth was that I was terrified of ever having kids. What if I screwed up? My own mother couldn't handle it, how did I know if I'd be any better? And with the upbringing I'd had? I didn't ever want to put a kid through what I went through, the constant judgments and the pressures. I didn't think I was that kind of person but I didn't want to gamble a child's life on it.

Jade shook his head. "You'd be a great mom, Jaylene! Just look at how well you take care of us."

I snorted. "Yeah, but you guys are already grown ups with healthy egos. A child? I don't know. They are so fragile. I wouldn't want to screw them up."

They all snickered. Jade said, "You've spent over a week with us and you don't think we're screwed up? Maybe your counseling skills are a little rusty."

He was right about my skills. Before I started wallowing in self-pity, I decided I'd better go shower.

# One

September 2012

*Hollywood, Los Angeles*

*Sammara Gunderson*

When news first came out that Maggie's Bones were working on a follow-up album to their smash from last year, I begged my editor to let me do a feature on them. As a music reporter for *Feedback Magazine*, the premier rock magazine in the U.S., I'd followed their career since the beginning and loved their music. Then, when tragedy struck and they lost their manager in a freak accident, I became even more intrigued. The guys put on a brave front for a bit, then their lead guitarist, D, disappeared and people in their camp were tight-lipped about the rest of the band.

The next thing everyone knew, they were all back in New Orleans working on the album, which they tentatively titled *Haunted*. The rock world was dying for news on what was happening with them. I was in contact with their manager and my good friend from college, Sherry Jordan, and she assured me she would ask the guys to do the interview. I could barely contain my excitement. There was something about their music that called to me, and though I knew I needed to remain objective, I couldn't wait to meet them and experience their magic in person.

That was four months ago. The next thing I heard was that they were back in L.A. with Scott Cross, an amazing producer who had given several bands their masterpieces. I figured I'd never get access while they were recording, but I was hoping for a break. Luckily Sherry called me and invited me to meet her and some friends at the Formosa Cafe on a random late-September afternoon.

"Sammara! How are you, girl?" We hugged and Sherry invited me to sit with her and the two women she was dining with in the back section of the restaurant, which looked like an old railroad dining car. "This is Mackenzie McGowan and Jaylene Charles. Ladies, this is Sammara Gunderson, reporter extraordinaire from *Feedback Magazine*."

I scoffed at her introduction. "Extraordinaire? Please. How do you do?" I asked as I slid into the booth next to her.

I hadn't been to the Formosa in a while and I loved the mix of food here. It was a great place if you could get past the tepid service. All of the servers were bored locals. I'd had several meetings here in the past and actually loved the atmosphere of feigned disinterest.

"Jaylene and Mackenzie snuck out here to visit the guys while mixing is going on, and I promised I would show them the town. What have you been up to?" Sherry asked.

I tucked some hair behind my ear. "I had a meeting with Patricia Gordon about interviewing Blackened. They are about to head into the studio as well and I was hoping to catch them before that."

Sherry and her friends all sighed at the prospect.

"Have you met them before?" Mackenzie asked. When I nodded, she exclaimed, "Oh my hell, Danny Black is so friggin' hot!"

Sherry laughed and said, "Mackenzie, you're a walking hormone."

Jaylene rolled her eyes and sipped her soda, giggling a little at her friend.

"I have interviewed him before. He's pretty damn funny. He's just kind of a dick when you first meet him," I said with a laugh. My first piece on Blackened cemented my position as a features writer with the magazine, and since then Danny only wanted to deal with me. I was grateful for that.

"I wanted to see when we could have you meet with the Bones. They're ready to talk...about everything. I told them you would be the best person to tell their story."

I dropped my suddenly slimy hands into my lap. "Really? That would be... Thank you, Sherry! I would love to work with them. When were you thinking?"

Sherry opened her calendar on her phone and chuckled. "They have tonight free, or Saturday. I think it would be perfect if you came out to the house they're staying in. It's perfect for them."

I checked my own calendar and frowned. I had a work function tonight, and Saturday I was scheduled to see a show at the Whisky. "I can do either. You tell me and I'll make it work." My managing editor, Joshua Freeman, would let me out of my commitment tonight for this. I could catch the other band at another venue.

I wasn't going to miss my chance to interview Maggie's Bones. For some reason I couldn't put my finger on, I knew in my heart I had to do this, that the repercussions of this interview would be massive in my life. When I had "feelings" like that, I paid attention.

"Why don't you come by tonight then? You're always bound to get them at their goofiest at night. They're so serious during the day."

I opened the GPS app on my phone. "Where should I meet them?"

Sherry made a face. "Uh, they're staying at the Los Feliz Murder Mansion."

My phone clattered on the table. "Say what? I thought the owners wouldn't let anyone in that place?" The mansion had one of the creepiest histories in Hollywood. I was definitely intrigued.

"It just so happens," Sherry said with a chuckle, "that one of their kids is a huge fan of Maggie's Bones and she talked her parents into letting the band use the place after they initially refused. They cleaned it all up, only leaving a couple of the rooms untouched. The owners hadn't changed anything since the night in 1959 when the dude killed his wife. Mage was all excited about it. He thought it would be an inspirational place for them to stay while they were in the studio."

Sherry shuddered and Mackenzie barked out a laugh. "That guy is obsessed, I'm tellin' ya. You should have seen the creepy-ass house he wanted to buy in New Orleans. He's even convincing the guys to go ahead and purchase the St. Germaine building where they stayed in the French Quarter and turn it into a club. Club Haunt, he wants to call it."

Jaylene swirled her straw around in her glass and smiled fondly at the mention of Mage's name. "Poor guy. He swears the building is haunted, but nothing happened while I was there."

Sherry turned to me. "Jaylene stayed with the boys while they were writing for the album. She's a tattoo artist."

Jaylene raised an eyebrow in surprise, as if she thought Sherry was spilling the beans about confidential information.

"It's fine, Jay," Sherry reassured her. "The guys are going to give her complete access, so she'll find out anyway. Don't worry."

Jaylene relaxed noticeably. Her eyes darted between her two friends then her phone started buzzing. She picked it up and her cheeks turned rosy.

"Is that loverboy?" Mackenzie asked, peeking over her shoulder.

Both of their eyes went wide.

"O-kay! I didn't need to see that...or maybe I did. Bring that back up!"

Jaylene was trying to respond, her bottom lip between her teeth, while also trying to block Mackenzie's view.

"Damn, he's got a fine—"

"Kenz! He'll be so embarrassed if he knows you saw that, now stop!"

Mackenzie winked at Sherry, then frowned. "How come mine doesn't send me hot pics like— WHOA!"

It was Mackenzie's turn to blush at whatever had just buzzed her phone.

Jaylene peeked over her shoulder and gasped. "He wants you to do *that*?"

Mackenzie got a dreamy look. "I always dreamed I'd date a man brave enough to let me do that. Sherry? When does their tour start?"

Sherry laughed nervously. "Why? You aren't thinking of... Let me see that picture!"

Mackenzie held the phone to her ample bust. "I promise he will be okay to play. Scouts honor."

Jaylene snorted. "Yeah, you're just lucky he hasn't yanked out his nipple rings while playing yet."

"That was so much fun," Mackenzie said with a sly smile.

I thought I was picking up the gist of what this conversation was about. Mackenzie showed Sherry the phone across the table and as much as the reporter in me wanted to be nosy, I really didn't want to be tempted to print something this salacious.

Sherry looked horrified and intrigued at the same time. "How do you even do that? Can't that cause permanent damage?"

Mackenzie shook her head. "Not if you do it right, and I've done plenty. Yes, ma'am, there are plenty of dudes walking around New Orleans with these babies!"

Okay, that was too much temptation for me. "So you do body modification?"

Mackenzie smiled wickedly. She swirled a lock of her teal hair around a manicured finger with polish in a matching shade. "Give me a needle and I can pierce anything," she said with a wink.

I shivered. I had my ears pierced three times on each side and had considered piercing my navel for about five minutes, but anything lower... "Gotcha. Why do people want to pierce their, um, their—"

"Dicks? Adds sexual pleasure. I have yet to actually get to experience it, though. Sadly. I've provided pleasure for hundreds of other women." She wiggled her eyebrows and rested her chin on her hands. "But now, I just might—"

"Kenz," Jaylene interrupted by throwing an elbow into Mackenzie's boob. "You do know she's a reporter? You really want Star's business about his business out there?" Jaylene's eyes bugged out. "Oh God. You won't report that, will you?"

I laughed and shook my head. "I'm off the clock right now, don't worry. I can't say I'm not intrigued, though. So you tattoo them and Mackenzie—"

"Only Star has been brave enough to let me go to work on him. Jaylene's tattooed them, but for some reason they're afraid of little ol' me!" Mackenzie tried to do her best to look demure, but she didn't fool me. "If you're ever in New Orleans, you could come see my portfolio," Mackenzie purred. "Maybe you might want a little something yourself."

I gulped. Since leaving behind my home and strict upbringing, I'd worked really hard to overcome my naiveté about the more eccentric aspects of the world. I encountered a lot of crazy shit while writing about rock 'n' roll, but every once in a while I came across something that shocked me. I'd had quite an education since moving to Hollywood from a bedroom community in the East Bay after attending UCLA's School of Journalism. Luckily, I had a good poker face when faced with something a little out there.

"Then it's settled," Sherry said while working her phone frantically. "Sammara, you'll meet the band out at the house tonight. I've texted you the address and we can touch base after in case you need anything further."

Jaylene frowned as Sherry packed up her things to go. "Will you be there, Sherry?"

The usually poised and self-assured manager for the band looked flustered. "I'm going to pass, I think. I'm not in the mood for a certain person. He's been texting me all week and I just don't want to hear it."

I wondered which "certain person" she was talking about but didn't want to butt in if Sherry didn't want to share. We'd been fairly close since college and had confided in each other many times, but it was obvious this was a detail she'd decided to keep from me. I wasn't upset. She didn't always tell me who she was seeing. Unfortunately, the ones she'd usually kept from me in the past were guys who'd hurt her really badly. I hoped that wasn't the case this time.

"But he really wants to fix things with you," Jaylene pleaded gently. "He's been such a good boy since New Orleans. I'm not asking you to do anything other than talk to him."

Jaylene seemed like a caretaker. She was guarded, or maybe just quiet. I couldn't tell for sure yet, but I *could* tell she didn't know how much she could trust me by the way her eyes darted to me with every topic of conversation.

Sherry exhaled loudly. "I'll think about it. Let's get you two to your spa treatments and back to the house before Devon starts blowing up my phone looking for you. I swear, it's like you're his security blanket or something."

Jaylene blushed, Mackenzie laughed and Sherry winked.

I was already thinking of questions I wanted to ask tonight. "I'm glad you called today, Sherry. I'll be there tonight. About what time?"

Sherry checked her watch. "Around eight o'clock? They should be back from the studio, fed, and will have had time to snuggle up with their ladies for a bit."

Jaylene and Mackenzie groaned and laughed.

"No problem," I said. I wanted the women to feel comfortable around me. "And don't worry. I know they've had a rough year. I won't push."

Sherry's smile dropped. "Thanks, Sammara. I reassured them that you would take good care of them."

I was grateful for Sherry's confidence. It was often hard to earn respect in this crazy business.

Sherry stood from the table and said, "Now, I need to get my lovely guests to the spa."

"Oh, Sherry, can we skip the spa and go to that Hollywood History Museum? Devon said they are finished for the day and he wants to meet up there. He says there's a replica of Hannibal Lecter's cell in the basement!"

Sherry's expression was priceless. "You and your horror movie fascination. You guys are creeps!" She shuddered and shook her hands out as if she'd just seen a big hairy spider in her bathroom.

Jaylene just smiled innocently and bounced on her toes.

Sherry rolled her eyes. "Fine, sure. No problem. Sammara, we'll see you tonight, okay?"

I waved goodbye and gathered my sweater and purse. I had a night with Maggie's Bones to look forward to.

# Two

Skinny jeans, an off-the-shoulder sweater with skulls on it, and black combat boots were the dress code for my evening with the band. My black bob was straight and smooth. I went with minimal makeup and wore my favorite jewelry: silver hoop earrings, onyx ring, and my mother's pentagram necklace. I wore it for her as she couldn't exactly wear it herself any longer.

I rubbed my hands on my pants just before knocking on the door. The mansion was just as creepy up close as it was from the street. What would possess the guys to want to stay here, and why had I agreed to do the interview in this morbid place? I had a tendency to get really affected by places such as this, where there was likely to be unrest.

It didn't help that I was nervous for the first time over an interview. All of my other writing assignments had been exciting and a little bit nerve-racking, but this time was different. I wondered if the feelings I had meant that this piece was going to have repercussions on my life professionally...or personally.

The door flew open as I was about to knock for a third time and I was face to chest with none other than Mage, the bassist for the band. His long, curly tresses were pulled back off his face and his green eyes were wild with excitement.

"Hurry! You're going to miss it!" He grabbed me by the arm and yanked me inside, closing the door behind me. He pulled me down the entry hall and to the entrance to the living room, where the doorway was boarded up.

Just then, a grandfather clock started clanging and chiming totally out of whack. It was so loud I had to cover my ears.

I shouted, "What is—"

"Shhh. Just wait," he murmured close to my ear.

The clanging continued for almost a minute. When it ended, I looked at my watch. It was 8:06 p.m. And Mage still had his hands on my arms.

"That is so cool!" he said excitedly. "It gets me every night!"

I could hear other voices chatting towards the rear of the house. It smelled a bit musty inside the entry hall, and I wondered what was on the other side of the wood.

"So you're the reporter," Mage spoke again near my ear. His breath brought chills to my body. He was around six feet, I'd guess. Much taller than my five feet six.

I turned and looked up at him. I felt like I had marbles in my mouth as I tried to speak. "Mmmm, yes. Mm-my...I'm Sammara Gunderson. You're Mage."

His smile lit up and he took my hand gently. Then his eyes fell to my necklace and he froze. "Do you worship the Mother?"

I felt my cheeks flush and I reached up to touch my pendant. "It's my mother's. I wear it for her. How do you do?" I would have reached out to shake his hand, but he was crowding me. He was standing so close, I could make out the flecks of gold in his irises. He just kept staring until I grew uncomfortable and started giggling. "Mage?"

After a moment, he shook himself. "I'm sorry. You probably want to meet everyone else." Actually, I was in no hurry to leave my current space. Even if I was, the draw between us had me anchored to the spot.

Neither of us made a move until someone shouted his name. Again, he shook himself and then took me by the elbow. He walked us into the kitchen, where people were gathered around food trays and talking. "Guys? This is Sammara Gunderson from *Feedback Magazine*."

The other members of Maggie's Bones came over and said hello.

They were just as incredible looking up close as when I'd seen them perform. That, and they all smelled really good, as if they'd all come home from the studio and showered recently.

"I'm Jade. Nice to meet you." Jade Lambert, their rhythm guitarist, shook my hand and kissed my cheek. I hadn't been greeted that way before and didn't quite know how to respond.

Star Stevenson, the drummer for the Bones, peeled himself away from Mackenzie. She waved and smiled at me from the other side of the bar.

"Hi. I'm Star. Thanks for coming." I did my best not to swoon as he greeted me like Jade had, but damn they were a lot to behold!

Jaylene was sitting on D's lap on a couch and he looked in no hurry to move. He waved to me and Jaylene smiled. Those two definitely were going to require some work to get them to open up. I didn't mind. It wasn't unusual for folks to be guarded around me.

Marcus Lambert, the front man for the band, was nursing a root beer and was much less in-your-face than he had been the first time I'd met him. "Good to see you, Sammara," he said, making his way over with a little less swagger than he'd had in the past. He took my hand gently and lingered a little with his kiss on the cheek.

"You, too, Marcus. Thanks for having me."

Mage was at my side this whole time and for some reason, I felt really comforted by that. I turned back to face him and could feel all sorts of emotions coming off of him. I was still confused about what I'd witnessed when I came in, so I asked him, "What's up with the clock?"

He grinned and took me by the hand. "Let me give you the tour."

As he pulled me out of the kitchen, laughter followed. "Mage, you can't hog her all night," one of the guys yelled.

He ignored them and tugged me down the hall, his eyes studying me. We stopped near a staircase, which I assumed went to the second floor.

"Where are you from, Sammara? Where have you been all my life?"

I barked out a laugh. He didn't waste any time.

"I'm sorry," he said, blushing a little. "It's just... Wow. You wouldn't believe me if I told you."

I stopped walking and faced him. I crossed my arms over my chest, raising an eyebrow. "Try me."

His hand came up to rub his chest and he swallowed hard. "What if I told you I dreamed about you?"

My smile fell a little, but I was intrigued. Mage didn't seem to be afraid to speak his mind to me. It was refreshing.

"Tell me what you saw."

He stepped closer. I dropped my hands to my sides and backed up as he was now totally in my personal space. He took my hand in his, turning it palm up. He traced a finger along my palm as he spoke. "I dreamt of you under a night sky. Stars were falling all around you and there was fire. The moonlight hit your necklace and it was glowing." He reached his other hand up to touch my necklace and I didn't move to stop him. "I couldn't see your face, just your necklace and your black hair. But it was you. I could smell you. You smell like roses."

*Smell me?* I stepped back and hit the wall.

He let go suddenly. "I'm awful sorry. I hope Sherry told you I'm harmless. I am. It's just, I felt like I was supposed to meet you, and now I have, and...Whoa."

Mage stepped closer to me, until our chests were almost touching. I had nowhere to go and waited to feel the panic come on. It didn't. Luckily for him, Sherry *had* warned me in the past that Mage could be a little different, but that he wasn't like a creep or anything. It was also lucky for him that he was ridiculously attractive and I was already quite taken with him, despite my usual response to a man hitting on me this blatantly.

"Why do you think you were supposed to meet me?" I asked breathlessly.

He started to speak, then stopped and licked his lips. "If I tell you, you'll run. I think I'll keep it to myself for now. So you know about the murders? Isn't it crazy?" He took a half step back with that subject change, presumably to give me some space.

I shook my head. "It *is* crazy. It's crazy the owners are letting you guys stay here."

He was still standing close, appraising me. "We were told not to go in the living room, nor the master bedroom that the murder happened in. They're boarded up. Star and Devon and their ladies each have master bedrooms up there," he said, gesturing upstairs with a chin lift. "Marcus has the last bedroom, and Jade and I each took a room in the maid's quarters. We turned the ballroom into rehearsal space. It's got great acoustics. But yeah, there is definitely an unhappy spirit in the place. There've only been a few strange occurrences—the clock banging like that at eight-oh-six every night, and one night we heard banging on the floor upstairs just after the clock started. Jade said he heard children crying a couple of nights. We're just all wondering why the guy went off and killed his wife and tried to kill his daughter, then offed himself. No one knows."

I looked around a little. The place was definitely in disrepair in the front hall, where we were still standing, but the kitchen looked as though it had been renovated. "The owners finally decided to fix the place up?"

He crossed his arms over his chest, pulling his t-shirt tight and smiled proudly. "They couldn't resist their daughter. She loves us. They let us bring a team in here to make repairs before we moved in this past July, as long as we didn't touch the bedroom upstairs or the living room. We had the place cleaned up, restored the hardwood floors in the rest of the house, painted, and repaired the bathrooms so they were usable. We didn't want to disrupt anything, you know. There's a story here."

I smiled and looked up the stairs. "You're really fascinated by this place, aren't you?" I turned back to look at him and his eyelids had grown heavy. He reached out to touch my face.

I know I should have recoiled, normally I would have, but for some reason it wasn't weird that a man I'd just met, this man, was acting so familiarly. Still, I thought I'd remind him why I was here. I figured it might cause him to cool his burners a little. Sometimes people forgot they were talking to a reporter, and when they remembered, they'd be angry with themselves and resentful that they'd spilled their guts. I didn't want Mage to feel that way about me.

"I was hoping to talk to all of you tonight. Is that still okay?" He raised an eyebrow and let his fingers graze my jaw. His eyes were on my lips as though he wasn't really hearing me, as though he was somewhere else. "Mage?" I asked, trying to pull him from his trance.

"Hmmm? Sorry," he said with a smile. "Yeah. We'll talk. But when it's over, when it's done, you and I have some things to discuss."

I frowned, wondering what he could mean by that. He leaned even closer and my heart started jumping around. He grazed my cheek with his nose and lips and breathed once again in my ear. "We're just getting started, chère."

He pulled back with a serious look and started walking back to the kitchen.

What was that all about? Was he for real? His attentions didn't feel slimy, like those of the other celebs I'd interviewed who thought every woman was going to invite them into their vagina. I'd quickly learned to ignore that kind of behavior, turn it back on them, or call them on it outright. I was very careful to never give anyone the wrong impression of me, especially after a few bad experiences.

Back in the kitchen, I was still a little dazed from my non-tour with Mage. I had this feeling, like an intuition, that something really big was happening tonight. I never ignored my feelings like this. I intended to stay on guard.

Marcus was still hunched over his root beer in the kitchen, not at all looking like the dazzling front man he usually portrayed himself to be. The two couples were cozy on the couch and Jade was entertaining them with some story. Sherry hadn't come over, which maybe explained why Marcus was moping. I was incredibly curious and hoped the story would come out at some point without too much prodding.

Mage gestured grandly for me to enter the kitchen before him. He entered the kitchen behind me rubbing his hands together. "Why don't we go in the ballroom, guys? We'll have more room." He opened the fridge and pulled out some more snack trays. "Sammara, can I get you something to drink?" he asked while presenting his backside.

I bit my lip at the sight. He was striking, a real stunner, and obviously paid attention to his body. He wasn't hulked out or anything, but he looked damn good in his black jeans that hugged all the right places. He turned and said my name again before I remembered what he'd asked. "Um, sure," I replied, kicking myself for spacing out while ogling him. "Something cold. Iced Tea?"

Jaylene yelped and hurried over to us. "Better tell him whether you like it sweet or not. These boys like their tea sweet enough to give you a cavity just looking at it."

I laughed. "That's right. Southern thing, right? Unsweetened. Please."

Mage turned and handed me a bottle, his fingers lingering over mine long enough to add to my goose bumps. "Jaylene tried to train us to ask."

I uncapped the bottle and raised an eyebrow at Jaylene. "You local?"

She shook her head. "I'm from the East Bay originally."

"Get out!" I exclaimed. "Me too. I grew up in Fremont."

Jaylene high-fived me. "Hayward. How funny!"

We chatted for a moment about high schools, old hangouts, land marks. It was funny to meet people down here that were from back home. I hadn't met too many Bay Area folks who'd transplanted to Hollywood.

Mage looked between the two of us as Jade joined our conversation. Mage elbowed him in the arm and stage whispered, "Bro, we might be in trouble here," he joked.

Jade looked confused. "Why?"

Mage paused as though he was going to explain his statement, and then decided against it. He shook his head and closed the fridge with his hip instead.

"C'mon. I'll show you to the ballroom," he said to me as he led me from the kitchen.

I could not believe I was walking through the famed Los Feliz Murder Mansion on the arm of the charming and handsome Mage of Maggie's Bones, a band I'd followed for a long time but had never met as a whole group. I had even written their first live performance review for *Feedback* before being promoted to features writer.

I'd grown up listening to everything from Fleetwood Mac and the Grateful Dead to Korn, Slipknot, and Judas Priest. Maggie's Bones, in my opinion, had staying power like those bands. They'd been a tight unit; cousins and friends who'd played together for years, and each album only got better and better. I'd heard the stories of their excesses and I knew they'd been through rough times, but seeing them together tonight they seemed to be in a good place. I couldn't wait to hear what they'd been working on. Getting to hear new music first was one of the best perks of the job with the magazine, and I hoped I'd get a sneak peek tonight.

Mage led me up two flights of stairs to the third level. We entered a large ballroom that had been cleaned, but not fully restored. Faded wallpaper peeled from the walls and the room had a faint odor of mildew and bleach. The hardwood floor, however, had been resurfaced, and new light fixtures were strung from the ceiling. A large leather sectional filled one corner near a bar and instruments and equipment were strewn across the rest of the room.

"Jade," Mage called over his shoulder. "Can you grab those beanbags so we have enough seating?" Mage guided me over to one end of the sectional and gestured for me to sit. Star and D took the other, longer portion of the sectional with their ladies on their laps. Jade plopped down in a beanbag and Mage dragged the other one a couple of feet away from the couch on my right side and sat down, still staring at me. Marcus looked at the couples, frowned, and took a seat on the large matching ottoman.

I took out my recorder and a notebook. I'd jotted down some notes as soon as I got home from the cafe. I liked to keep my interviews organic, though, so I didn't have a list of questions, more like a collection of thoughts. Once I was organized, I looked around to find them all staring at me. Time to break the ice. "So. A blonde and a brunette walk into a bar..." I waited a beat for someone to ask for more.

Jade was the one to bite first. "Then what?"

I fought the urge to laugh at his confused face. "They went to the hospital with concussions."

I heard a snort from D, a snicker from Mackenzie, and then Star started belly laughing.

Jade just looked confused. "I don't get it."

I took pity on him. Sort of. "I'm sorry. Ok, let's try another one. Want to hear a dirty joke?"

Jade laughed. "Hell yeah!" He rubbed his hands together. Marcus muttered something under his breath. The rest of the group waited with smiles.

I cleared my throat for effect. "White horse fell in a mud puddle."

Jade's smile was gone and the confused look was back.

I continued. "How about a clean joke?" He smiled again. I said, "He took a bath."

Star started howling and the others chuckled. Jade still looked confused. "C'mon! I really don't get it. Star? Why is that funny?"

Star kept laughing, holding his belly. "Aw, man. Those were good. Dude, they're non-jokes. They're hilarious? Don't you ever watch YouTube?"

"I'm sorry," I said when I realized Jade was still upset. "I just wanted to break the tension a little. I know being interviewed can be uncomfortable. I hate making people uncomfortable and I suck at telling jokes, so this is my solution." I was also rambling, a habit of mine when I was nervous.

Mage placed his hand on my knee and squeezed. "You can't suck more than Jade at telling jokes. He always forgets the punch line."

Jade gave him an ugly look. "Oh yeah? What about you? You ruin every fucking movie by telling us what's going to happen!" He turned to me. "He does. Even the ones he hasn't seen before. It fucking pisses me off!" He stood up and walked over to the bar to stuff his mouth full of cheese. "I thtill can't bewieve you ruined Theven!"

D and Star laughed along with their band mates, and I guessed by their reactions, Jaylene and Mackenzie hadn't heard this story before either.

"I can't help it, Jade," Mage said. "It just comes to me!"

Jade threw a piece of food at him. "Yeah, well keep it to yourself next time." Mage picked it up and threw it back.

Jaylene crawled off D's lap and bent down to whisper in Jade's ear.

A shit-eating grin lit up his face. "Yeah, at least I'm not ticklish," he said with a laugh. Jaylene winked at Mage, who rolled his eyes, and then she left the room for a minute. D watched her go out the door. There was such love in his gaze. I sighed internally at how sweet they were. My attention was pulled away from watching them by a flying ice cube. The food fight was continuing between the combatants and I didn't want to be a casualty.

"Alright, boys," Sherry called from the doorway. "Enough! Jade, grab a broom. We just cleaned up after the last mess you guys made in here."

Marcus immediately perked up and stood as she approached. She glanced at him, irritated, and made her way over to hug me, avoiding any contact with him.

"Fine," Jade groaned. "Make me clean it up. Mage started it," he mumbled as he left the room.

Mage gave me a repentant smile. "I can't help it. He's my best friend, has been since we were kids, but he's so easy. The dude struggles to detect any subtlety, sarcasm, or innuendo. I have to be careful with him."

Jaylene came back in with a sketchbook in hand and was in the act of sitting down on D's lap as Mage spoke. "Mage," she scolded. "Remember what—"

"Yeah, yeah," he grumbled. "I'll try." Jaylene smiled at him and snuggled up to D, who kissed her neck, causing her to giggle.

I was a little shocked. I'd heard rumors about the stoic guitarist, that he didn't have much time for women. There were even those who speculated he was gay. But he was utterly consumed with Jaylene. Obviously the rumors were false. Seems he just hadn't found the right woman until now. I thought about that as I prepared to ask my first question.

"This past year has been full of trials and tribulations for you as a band and personally. Can each of you share one thing you are grateful for right now? Something that has put you in a good place, whether it be personally or professionally?"

They all took a moment to think about it.

Star was the first one to speak. "My sobriety. Without it, I wouldn't be here right now, able to contribute to the band and able to be next to this lovely lady." Mackenzie leaned over and bit his ear, causing him to shiver. Their looks toward each other weren't necessarily sweet, like D and Jaylene's. Mackenzie looked as though she wanted to eat Star alive. He appeared completely prepared to be the main course.

I nodded in understanding, appreciating his candor. "Thank you. Given what you all have been through, I can imagine being sober is incredibly important to you now." Star gave me a look in return that seemed to bore right into me with its depth. It was as if he was showing me his battered soul through eyes that showed a determination to stay healthy. I felt his pain so tangibly my hands shook for a moment and I dropped my pencil. I had a feeling that as we got deeper into this conversation, their emotions were going to start affecting me deeply. I became a reporter not because I wanted to know the scoop, but because I wanted to tell peoples' stories. The emotional experience was important to me.

Mage reached for the pencil at the same moment I did and our hands brushed. He handed it to me, holding on to it a moment longer than necessary just to make a connection. That touch grounded me and I was able to get it together. Interesting development.

"Thanks," I stammered. Just as Star had projected his pain, I was getting some very different vibes from Mage. He was throwing all kinds of lust and desire my way. He must have realized it, because a moment later, it was gone. I started to speak, to call him on it, but stopped as I remembered we weren't alone.

"I'm just grateful we've got a fucking album to deliver," Marcus remarked.

I turned my attention to the leader of the band. I'd spoken at length with Marcus several times before. I did an interview with him two years ago and had seen him since with Sherry a couple of times. He was way toned down tonight. Everything about him was mellowed out. He'd left off the guyliner and was dressed simply in black jeans and a t-shirt with none of his usual accessories. His hair was kind of flat and hanging around his face. He seemed grim, not cocky. I wasn't sure what that was about, but Sherry's strange reactions to him made it clear she had something to do with the change.

"The writing process this time was plagued with one thing after another," he continued. "D left L.A., we relocated back to New Orleans temporarily, our Uncle Daryl had a heart attack, Jaylene got hurt... It was fucked up for awhile."

Mage leaned forward with his elbows on his knees. "But then the stars aligned for us. Scott Cross was able to reschedule our sessions with him. We did some amazing work with Jaylene that really focused our songwriting. We went back and did the cleansing at D's house—"

"Mage," Marcus said, giving him a stern look and shaking his head, as if he wanted his band mate to shut up.

"What? I think that made a huge difference," Mage said. He looked to D. "Can I tell her?"

D shrugged, let out a tired breath, and then nodded.

Mage seemed determined. "Cool. So. When we got back home, we decided to stay in New Orleans 'cause that's where D was living with his mama, Miss Marie, and it was close to Mr. Daryl and my family. But you know we're from Houma, right?" he asked me. I nodded and he continued.

"So much of our history happened in D's house. Maggie heard us play there the first time, we wrote our first songs there...it was where it all started, dig? So I told my brothers here that we should have a medium come to the house. I thought it might help us and make it a healthy place again. My auntie Babette knew a woman who was supposed to be an expert. Madame Genevieve, a Creole woman from my gran's neighborhood, agreed to meet with us at the house—"

"Dude, Mage, you gotta tell her what happened when you called her," Star said, his eyes wild.

Mage shook his head. "See? You always do that, Star. So what if she said she knew I would be calling? So fucking what? You want to laugh—"

"I'm just saying, bro, that it's an important part of the story!" Star gestured for Mage to speak.

"Fine. When I called her, she said she knew I was going to call her, that our case was going to be a difficult one because Maggie died in California, and that she'd have to consult with her advising spirits as to whether we could even contact Maggie from Louisiana, which would cost us an extra three hundred dollars. I hadn't even told her who I was or anything about Maggie, but she knew."

Jade and Star snickered, Devon smirked, and Marcus continued to mope, shooting looks at Sherry every so often. Poor man. I didn't care that he wasn't always a great guy. He was obviously hurting. He looked in my direction and the sadness hit me like a bucket of cold water. I closed my eyes for a moment and tried to send him some soothing energy. Sometimes I could do it, sometimes it didn't seem to make any difference, but it couldn't hurt to try.

Marcus looked away and rubbed at the back of his neck. I turned my attention back to Mage.

"So you hired the woman? She came out to the house?" I smiled at Mage and his eyes lit up.

"Yeah, we did," he said in a low voice. "I gave her directions to Miss Marie's house and we met her out there on a Saturday evening at dusk. She only worked on Saturdays, she explained, because that was when her powers were aligned with the spirits. When she arrived, she did a thorough cleansing of the house with bay leaves and used some other herbs to make sure the environment was welcoming—"

"It smelled like shit," Marcus muttered.

Jade snorted a laugh and then looked sorry when Mage gave him a frustrated glance. "Bro, I'm sorry, but he's right. Whatever she was burning smelled like hot ass with foot funk thrown in for good measure." Everyone cracked up at that olfactory memory and Mage shook his head.

"I understand for those types of visits it's important to make sure the spirits feel welcome. Did she use burdock root or wormwood?"

Mage blinked hard a couple of times. He moved off of the beanbag to sit closer to the couch, crossing his legs and resting his hands on his knees, almost in a meditative position.

He flicked his ponytail back over his shoulders. "I don't think so. It smelled more like vervain. I asked her what she was burning, but she went into a trance before she would answer me. I always thought vervain was more for sexual energy?"

I set my notepad aside and clasped my hands in front of me, trying to decide how to tell him he'd been had. "Vervain is supposed to bring about love or lustful feelings. It's more used for love spells or—"

"I knew it," he gasped, leaning closer. "I knew she was using the wrong—"

"Dude, she was trying to get into your pants," Star said. "You wanted to think she was the real deal, brother. I know you. She just wanted to get on your good side," he said, dropping his eyes to Mage's groin. Everyone laughed, except Jaylene. She put a hand on Star's arm and gave him a look.

"Mage," Jaylene said. "Finish telling the story. I want to hear what happened next." Mage smiled gratefully at her and I could feel a strong connection between them. Devon whispered something in her ear then and she blushed.

"Anyway..." Mage drawled. "Y'all gonna let me tell this tale?" They all grumbled and encouraged him to continue. "So, we were sitting around the table, except Marcus. His allergies were bothering him." Mage frowned at Marcus like he was a misbehaving child.

Jade snorted, which brought on more chuckles. Marcus smirked and shrugged his shoulder. "Yeah, I was allergic to that woman's sex magick, Mage. I like my sex magick a little more organic, feel me?" The women groaned and Devon kicked at Marcus's seat. Mage just seemed to grow impatient. Poor guy. He probably got razzed like this all the time. I could totally relate to the ridicule.

"Funny, Lambert! See what I have to put up with? Anyway, Madame lit her candles in the middle of the table and it started getting real smoky inside. We held each other's hands and as Marcus rejoined us, lightning cracked almost immediately and the outside lights went out. It started pouring down rain hard and she shouted, 'Don't let go, no matter what happens!' We stopped laughing because shit was getting serious. Jade started to let go, but I held on, not wanting to unleash whatever this woman had conjured. The front door blew open and rain splattered loudly against the windows behind us. Star screamed and fell over in his chair, breaking the circle. Madame shrieked and moaned in this otherworldly voice and then a huge crack of thunder boomed and we heard loud crashes outside. That was it! Everyone else let go and ran to look outside. A whole tree had been yanked out of the ground in the front yard and crashed against the garage."

"Yeah, it was so fucking scary. It did damage, too, huh, D?" Jade was sitting forward and totally engrossed in this part.

"Yeah," Devon said quietly. "It was just a storm, though."

Mage shook his head. "Call it what you want, bro, but after she got pissed and said she'd need more money to reestablish the connection, it got crazier outside and then that window broke, remember? That wasn't all from the storm."

"Sounds scary. Then what happened?" I asked, creeped out and excited at the same time. I'd always been too chicken to attend a séance or any type of attempt to reach the other side. My mother had warned me that I felt things too deeply to get involved with spirits, that I could be overcome.

"Well, we told her we wouldn't pay her anything else, and anyway, the other guys wouldn't come back to the table, so she left. We went about setting things to rights in the house while D ran out to check on his baby in the garage."

Jaylene sucked in a breath. "You mean Rose could have been damaged?" Everyone laughed.

"His precious Dodge was fine, Jay. We just had to have someone replace the window on the house, repair part of the gutter on the garage, and the front doorknob went through the drywall in the entryway so we had to patch that up. But we didn't stay there that night," Marcus finished, shivering a little.

Mage nodded. "Yeah. Madame called something out and she didn't end her ceremony properly. I ended up bringing Auntie Babette out there and we did a more thorough cleansing at the house. I think everything is okay now, but I should go out there again and check."

I wanted to know more, but I needed to get on with the band's story before I lost them.

"Were you able to gain any relief from this experience, or are you still dealing with your grief? And how are you dealing with it?"

The room got really quiet. The guys kind of looked around at each other. Sherry waited for someone to speak. Jaylene pulled Devon's head to her shoulder and kissed him.

"Well, Jaylene tattooed us, and she got us talking. That sort of made it better," Jade offered.

Mage nodded, tugging on his hair. "It's still really hard, but we've pulled together. Sherry really stepped up and made things come together for us when we needed her to."

Sherry smiled at Mage and he nudged her foot with his.

"Sherry, what's been the hardest part, do you think, about picking up where Maggie left off?"

She looked at the faces of her charges around her, purposely avoiding Marcus. "Gaining their trust took some time. Getting the label to stop dicking with them, forcing them to do this album when they weren't ready. There was a lot of flack from the label because of the courts— I'm sorry, Devon."

Our eyes went to Devon and he shook his head, his huge blue eyes sad, but also angry. "It's fine, Sherry."

She breathed a sigh of relief and looked to me, ready to continue. "Because Maggie's husband, Thomas, was also an employee of the label, and his court case was still pending, the band was pressured to not say anything about it and to just shut up and make music. The label was very insensitive."

"Yeah, but you stood up for us, Sherry. You made it right." Jade was such a puppy dog, the way he talked to people. He was incredibly handsome, just like his brother, but had an innocence about him. I gathered the other guys let him get away with more.

"Sherry was instrumental in getting us to where we are now. Without her, we wouldn't have had our time with Jaylene, we wouldn't have gotten Scott Cross, and we wouldn't be getting ready to do this short fall tour," Marcus said. He took a drink of his root beer and watched Sherry intently. She smiled sadly.

I waited a moment, and then Jaylene spoke. "I'm not sure if I'm supposed to talk or not, but these guys worked so hard, not just on the album, but on themselves."

Star smiled at her and hugged Mackenzie tight. "That was your doing, Jay," Star said. "She made us talk to each other again, made us, like, get along again like we used to. She had to shoot us to do it, but it worked."

The room erupted in laughter and Jaylene turned bright red. She play-swatted Star but he caught her hand and kissed it like the rascal he was.

"And the tattoos...?"

"Yeah," Jade said, his voice full of admiration. "The tattoos she gave us are fucking brilliant." Jade jumped up, stepped in front of me, and lifted his shirt to reveal a beautiful black and gray tattoo on the left side of his chest. It was an angel kneeling and cradling a fleur-de-lis in its hands. Some of the feathers were falling from the wings. I leaned a little closer so I could see the detail.

"Wow," I breathed. "You do incredible work, Jaylene. Did you all get the same one?"

One by one, they nodded.

"I'm glad you were able to do this. I understand that you guys are thinking of starting some sort of foundation for victims of domestic violence?"

Star spoke in a firm voice. "Our management firm and the band have begun looking into some options. We want to do something to help people in that situation. My mama was beaten nearly every day of her life, and I just can't stand seeing anyone else go through that. Maggie had been dealing with the threats and the drama by herself, and that was awful. No one should have to be afraid."

Mackenzie smiled down at him and looked very proud.

"That's wonderful. Let me know when things are finalized. I'd love to help with publicity, or however else I can," I said with a shaky voice. I knew this was a tough topic for Star and the band. Their sorrow washed over me. I was near to gasping for breath before I realized what it was. I needed to redirect the conversation.

I asked them questions about the album and the tour and they all shared ideas and concepts they were working on. They even played me a couple of rough cuts from the album. I was blown away. I wanted to ask about some of the songs.

"Can you tell me about the lyrics of 'Heavy'? It's quite a departure."

They looked a little grim, like maybe they were concerned about the reaction from fans.

"D wrote it," Marcus said. "He really should have sung it—"

"Marcus," Devon interrupted in a low warning voice.

"It's true," Mage said. "But the label wasn't interested in 'adding a new voice to our repertoire—'"

"And we have a singer," D interrupted. "I never intended to sing it." Jaylene spoke to him in soothing tones. D was visibly upset. I could tell he had a long way to go until he was really okay. His grief was tangible. It was different from that of the others. I could see it like a dark spot on his aura, as though it was a diseased part of him.

"When D brought us 'Heavy', it was kind of the game changer. After that, we decided to take the album in a new direction, with

Maggie as our focus. Jaylene had us all talk about our most important memories of her, and it just grew from there. I'm really proud of the album. It's very spiritual, very reflective of where we are right now in our lives." Mage's words had the rest of the band nodding.

Then Marcus chuckled. "I should let you do all the interviews from now on," he laughed.

Mage looked down at his lap and grew quiet. He had really spoken from the heart. I was so drawn to him that it was hard not to touch him. His back was now leaning against the couch to my right, next to where I was sitting. It would be so easy.

"I can hear it in the music," I said softly so just Mage could hear. He turned and smiled up at me. There was something so compelling about him. This wasn't just a rock-star crush happening here. I couldn't explain it really, but it felt as if I was connecting with him on a deeper level. Everything he shared, the way he viewed the world...it resonated with me.

I had to get myself together and continue this interview. "It seems like things are changing personally for many of you. What's next for the band, and what's next for each of you, if you care to share?"

They looked around at each other and then looked to Marcus. He cleared his throat.

"I can't speak for personal, necessarily, but for the band, we've got some dates in October, the album drops in December, we'll film the first video in November, and then we go on a world tour in the spring and summer. We're going to play the festivals, starting in Australia, then the European big ones, including Download and Sonisphere and hopefully Wacken. We were asked to do Warped Tour again, but I think we're going to focus on some heavier acts supporting us this time. But we're definitely going to take breaks in between. We'd been on the road almost the entire four years before Maggie died. We were a wreck before that even happened. I think we're in a healthier place, but I don't want us getting back to that again."

Their gazes were solemn. I could tell they'd been through so much.

Mage sat up a little bit. "In addition to the band stuff, we've been talking about buying the St. Germaine building in New Orleans. We'd like to turn it into a live-music venue. Capacity for live shows could be up to a thousand if we do some renovating upstairs. The French Quarter doesn't really have anything like that right now. It's small for us, but we'd like to be able to support other bands and bring something classy to the area. Plus, after the time we just spent there, it feels like ours, you dig? Like we bonded with it. I don't know. There was something really special about that building and what happened there."

"I still say it ain't haunted, dude." Jade was smirking. Mage threw an ice cube at him and they were at it again.

Sherry leaned over to me and said, "I think you're about to lose them. Is there anything else you want to know?"

As a matter of fact...

"Hey guys? I wanted to ask. I heard you were big fans of that Nickelodeon channel band, Big Time Rush? What's the appeal?"

Jade hopped up and looked shocked. "Are you kidding? They are awesome! I don't remember how we found them. Mage?"

Mage laughed. "Yeah, we caught their TV show once while we were stuck on the bus broke down somewhere. It was cold outside, we were bored out of our heads and weren't going anywhere. The show is funny, but we just liked their vibe, man. They had some moves and some catchy hooks. I don't know. We all like to dance and when we was kids we had to sing in the church choir and we learned how to do harmonies and all that."

"Then you guys dragged me to that show when we were in the Bay Area," Sherry groaned, rolling her eyes.

I couldn't help but laugh. "Yeah, I've been to one of their shows. Not bad for pop music, I guess. The show reminds me of—"

"—The Monkees." Mage and I said at the same time.

"Yeah! How did you—"

"I had an auntie who loved all those old seventies shows and being at her house was like a time warp, man. When my mama left my daddy and we moved to Houma, we lived with my auntie Poppy. She was an old hippie."

"That's crazy. I thought I was the only one raised by leftover hippies. Far out!"

I had so many questions for Mage.

"When did you move to Houma?"

He shrugged and looked to Jade. "I don't know. Seventh grade, was it?"

"It was sixth grade, man. You started middle school with us." Jade smirked. "You stood out like a sore thumb in your hippie clothes and long hair."

"What the fuck you talking about? You grew your hair out after you met me, so I'd watch it with the insults." More ice cubes thrown.

"Truth is," Marcus said, diffusing the situation, "Mage was a little lost in Houma. He'd grown up in Tremé and his mama run them outta there when he was just entering his formative years. We took care of the rest."

They all laughed.

"Yeah, they turned me from a stand-up-bass, jazz-lovin' beau from Tremé, to an honorary zydeco-listenin', metal-playin' Cajun. I blame them for my corruption."

"And you loved every minute of it," Marcus said. "We got the other kids to quit picking on him...well, him individually. See, we all kinda stood out and often had to assert ourselves. At least me and Jade and Star did. D was the talented pretty boy and everyone left him alone. The rest of us were looked at as the scourge of Houma. Our mama and Mage's mama both worked nights at the hospital, and we were barely supervised. Star's uncles let us do whatever when we were there. D's mama was working the restaurant until late. As long as we stayed away from Maggie, we were safe to get into whatever trouble we wanted."

"Yeah, but if she caught us, she made sure we got busted," Jade said seriously. "She'd tell Uncle David and Uncle Daryl, and then we'd be runnin' for cover!"

"Now I know you three are cousins," I said to D, Marcus and Jade. "But how does Star fit into this?"

He cleared his throat. "I met Devon when I was in grammar school through my uncles. They helped Devon and Mr. David work on cars, and when I learned Devon was a musician, I started following him around. Then I met these other clowns, who were actually in my same grade, and it just all fell into place."

"When did you guys play together for the first time?"

They all looked at each other and laughed. Jade launched into a history lesson for me.

"Uncle David was teaching Devon how to play guitar, so one day Marcus and I showed up and said, 'We're not leavin' 'til you show us how to play, too'. Our mama was always tellin' us to hang out at their house anyway. Uncle David was nice enough to find us some beat-up guitars and he taught us how to play. We didn't take it quite as serious as Devon, but we were decent after a while. Maggie laughed at us all the time in the garage, until we started to make noise that sounded like music. Then we discovered Mage playin' the stand-up in the band room one day and we told him to come over. Uncle David had a bass he let Mage use, and he was like a prodigy! He could play anything. He was the most knowledgeable about music of all of us at that point."

"Yeah. Then we stuck Star behind the drums and said, 'Learn'. He was just like Animal, man. A true natural talent." Mage lifted his chin at Star, who turned a little red and pulled at his blonde hair, making it stand up all over.

"And that's how Maggie's Bones was born," I said thoughtfully. "Your first gig was in New Orleans, right? You were still in high school?"

"That wasn't our first performance in public, but the first as the Bones, yeah." Marcus pulled at his soul patch.

Devon cleared his throat and the other guys fell apart.

"Okay, what am I missing?" Sherry asked.

Jaylene covered her mouth and started giggling, too.

"Oh, come on! When are you guys going to let this rest?" Marcus put his head in his hands and ran his hands back over his hair. He stood from his spot and walked towards the bar, reaching into the fridge for another root beer. "Anyone else need to drown their sorrows?"

Jade raised his hand and Marcus frowned.

"Should I really encourage your lack of inhibitions? No telling what other stories you will feel the need to dredge up."

I thought of a rumor I'd heard. "Is it true that you guys were banned from playing in Des Moines?"

They all started cracking up.

"It's true? I guess at this stage in your career, one city is no big deal."

"It *is* a big deal," Marcus said, getting more serious. "I mean, none of us were happy about it, but what could we do?"

Sherry agreed. "Yeah, it was really a mess," she said. "The guys had to stick to their guns. On their second tour, they always ended the show with 'Mystikal Stick'. They had a pretty graphic animated video made up for it and it was shown on the screens. A group of mothers from the local Baptist church caught their kids watching it on YouTube and vowed not to let 'that filth' into their city. They even called themselves Moms Oppose Maggie's Bones, MOMB.

"When we showed up, they were picketing outside the venue on one side of the entrance, and a huge crowd of fans were on the other side. They were screaming at each other. The manager of the venue tried to make the guys promise they wouldn't play it and they refused. It was a huge hit for them at the time and they didn't want to be known as a band that would cave to pressure like that, even though they had a lot of teenaged fans. When they refused, there was a near riot. They made a video on YouTube apologizing for cancelling the show, and ended up doing an extra show in Boone the next night, rather than take the night off, and made it up to the fans. It was a huge deal."

"Yeah," Jade cut in. "Some guys showed up the next night wearing shirts they'd made saying 'MOMS OFTEN MOUNT BONERS'. It was hilarious! There were even some hip moms there with their little kids, cheering us on. I enjoy it when the moms come out to the shows. They really—"

"Jade, bro..." Mage was probably trying to save Jade from divulging his sexual conquests.

"You guys were developing quite a reputation here in L.A. before everything went crazy. Any comments on that?"

"It's over, that's my comment. We're not that band anymore," said an irritated D.

"I'm sorry, I—"

"It's okay, Miss Gunderson, I apologize for snapping. It's just that the reason we went back to New Orleans, and why we'll be going back there as soon as we're done with the album, is that we don't want that life anymore. At least I don't." He pulled Jaylene a little closer.

Star cleared his throat. "Yeah. There're too many bad memories here. I mean, it's where we needed to be to record, but our home is in Louisiana."

Mage looked at his band mates and seemed a little conflicted. "New Orleans is my home, yes, and I do want to go back, but Hollywood is my second home. I love it here. There's still a lot to explore."

He turned and looked at me over his shoulder. His smile was inviting. I bet I could have fun exploring with him. I wasn't sure, though, whether he was hinting or not.

"Miss Gunderson, is there anything else you'd like to ask? Jaylene and I have plans..."

Everyone else giggled.

"Oh shut up," he snapped good-naturedly.

Star and Mackenzie were whispering to each other, too. I figured if these ladies had come out for just a few days, they probably needed their alone time.

"If I think of anything, can I check in with you again?"

D nodded. He and Jaylene stood and walked over to me. He offered his giant hand and I took it. "Thank you for making this easy on us," he said quietly.

All I could do was nod. Jaylene shook my hand and thanked me as well. The two of them walked out of the ballroom and down the hall to where Mage had said their room was. Not that I ever really got that tour. Star and Mackenzie excused themselves next. I thanked them all. Then it was just Sherry and I facing Marcus and Jade, with Mage now pressing against my leg.

Jade was looking at me funny.

I wondered if I had something on my face and almost reached up to wipe my nose. "Is there something you—"

"Bro, we are not—" Mage interrupted.

"Oh come on! You know we always—"

"Jade Michel Lambert! You do not always have to play that silly game with new friends!" Marcus chided his not-so-little brother using the French pronunciation of his name. Then Jade whined like a little kid. I had to hold in a laugh.

"But Marcus!" Jade complained.

"I'm game, Jade. What do you want to play?" Their exchange had me curious.

Mage and Marcus groaned, and Sherry whispered, "Be careful what you agree to."

"Oh! It's just like answering questions. No big deal. You asked us a bunch of questions, and now we should get to ask you some. Besides, I don't think Mage is ready to let you go."

I looked down and saw that Mage was not only pressed against my leg, but now had his arm around my calf and his hand resting on top of my boot. I felt my cheeks get hot as everyone started laughing, but Mage just smiled up at me again. He didn't say anything, just smiled that lazy smile of his.

"Fine. Um, what do you want to know?" I had no idea what they would ask me, and I wasn't sure how much I was willing to tell them. I tended to be an incredibly private person. After my experiences and the environment I grew up in? It was better if I didn't share too much or people shied away. I shifted back on the couch, which caused my leg to move and Mage let it go.

"Oh, you're fine," I said to him, but he was already moving. He turned towards me and rested his elbow on the couch pressed between my thigh and the armrest with his chin in his hand.

"Okay, she agreed, Marcus. I'm going to go first. Miss Gunderson, do you—"

"Please call me Sammara. You guys are so formal."

Jade blushed and said, "Sammara, are you married or otherwise involved with another person?"

"What do you mean by 'otherwise involved'? That could mean a lot of things," I laughed.

Marcus shook his head at Jade. "What he means is, do you currently have a guy, or a girl if you swing that way, who shares your bed and your body?"

"Don't be a douche, Marcus! She's our guest." Mage looked pissed. I put a hand on his arm.

Sherry stood up and shook her head. "I've got to run, Sammara. You okay?" She looked like she didn't want to leave me here, but as if maybe she wanted to get away from Marcus. I just knew something bad had happened. I stood up and hugged her goodbye.

"I'll talk to you soon," I whispered to her. "Thanks for setting this up." She pulled back, glared at Marcus and then looked down at Mage.

"Behave," she said, narrowing her eyes at him, and then she strolled out the door like she meant business. Mage cursed under his breath as I settled back onto the couch.

"It's alright, Mage. No, I am not involved with anyone, I sleep in my bed alone, and the only thing I share my body with is my vibrator occasionally. Does that count?" I couldn't help it. I had to dish it out. I'd learned over the years that getting embarrassed or trying to avoid the questions led men to think they could take things further.

"Really? Ah, I mean, okay, um. That's good?" Jade didn't seem to know what to do with my statement.

Marcus gave me an attempt at a sexy smirk. Mage had an eyebrow raised and he looked determined.

"I'll go next," Marcus said, causing Mage to curse again. I patted his shoulder and he frowned.

"Relax, dude. I'll be good. So what are your thoughts on relationships? Are you a friends-with-benefits kinda gal, or a practitioner of monogamy?" His words were playful, but all of a sudden he seemed irritated, as though he wanted to say more.

"I've done both. There's a time and a place for both," I said, leaving my answer open.

"Yeah, but when you agree to be friends with benefits, and the other person decides they want more, would you just say no, or would you consider it? Because you can't help who you fall in love with, you know. You might think you'll be fine just having sex, but then after you spend time with this person and they grow on you and you tell them that they're the only one for you, and then they just walk the fuck away, it really fucking sucks." He was almost shouting as he finished.

Both Jade and Mage stared at Marcus, seemingly dumbfounded by his outburst.

I raised an eyebrow. "Sometimes it's hard to change the path of a relationship once parameters have been set, but if you're honest with each other..."

"Yeah. Honesty. That really got me far." Marcus downed the rest of his root beer, slammed the empty bottle down and glared at us. "I'm done for the night. Sammara? Thank you for coming. I'm sure I'll see you again." He nodded in my direction and strutted his way out the door with a little less sex appeal than usual. Something seemed really broken with him. If I was reading him right, he was hurt and angry. Despondent.

"Alrighty then," Jade said. "That was awkward. What do you think is wrong with him?" he asked Mage.

"Sounds like he didn't get his way for once. He's not used to being told no. It's messing with him." Mage jerked his head towards where Sherry had been sitting. "I just hope he doesn't do anything stupid and fuck things up for us."

Jade just frowned. "What do you mean? What does... Ohhhhh. I get it. Man, that sucks. We finally get D's head in the game..."

The two friends looked at each other and then at Sammara.

"That's off the record, right?" Mage gazed at me shrewdly.

"I'm not here to hurt anyone," I said quietly. "I have no idea what he was talking about, so how could I write anything?" I tried to sound overly innocent. It worked. Mage's lips split into a satisfied grin.

"Okay, well, shall we get back to—"

"Jade, I want to show Sammara something. Can we quit with the questions now?"

Jade frowned and pouted a little. I wanted to laugh at his expression but I had a feeling he'd be offended. Mage stood and took my hand, leading me toward the doors at the other end of the ballroom. I glanced back at Jade, whose expression changed from confused, to understanding, then to admiration for his friend.

# Three

I had a new understanding of the guys in Maggie's Bones tonight. I had a hard time connecting Jade with the sexy rocker he was onstage. All the women I knew who worked in the rock industry thought he was the band member to snag. He rocked the leather pants onstage, the waistband in back barely covering the top curves of his glutes. His long black hair hung down to his waist and flew like a silk scarf in the breeze as he jerked around stage with his guitar. He'd slide his legs out into a deep lunge and pour on the sex god whenever he had the chance, causing girls to scream, cry and lose their panties to the cause. Even tonight, dressed casually in jeans and a t-shirt, his hazel eyes sparkled and those lips of his were just so sexy. He was naturally beautiful in an innately masculine way.

D, the lead guitarist, was also surreally gorgeous. He got the attention of a large majority of the fans, but he was not as interactive. He mostly kept to himself. It was the pure bliss that descended over him when he started to play that defined his performance and made him irresistible.

Marcus strutted about the stage and you could just tell he knew the women, and often the men, wanted him. He flaunted it. His leather pants or black denim fit him even tighter than Jade's pants did, leaving no room to the imagination as to what he was packing. It was almost too much sometimes. He would be even sexier if he didn't pour it on so heavy.

Star was just a spaz. In the same vein as Taylor from the Foo Fighters or Lars from Metallica, Star was in his own world and didn't perform for anyone. He would smile at the audience in between songs and occasionally sing backup, but when he was in the zone, he was all limbs flying. It was easy to respect his skill and tenacity. He was no less handsome than the rest of his band mates, but he seemed rougher around the edges. A little dangerous.

Then there was Mage. I didn't think I could accurately describe what he was like on stage. Mage's eyes never stopped travelling whatever venue they played. Sometimes his gaze would stop on you and his stare was so intense it would unravel you. You'd look around, thinking there was no way he'd be staring at you, then you'd look back and those eyes would burn into your soul before moving on to the next victim. That had been my experience the first time I'd seen them live, and I'd never forgotten it. Mage made music that penetrated your psyche, bathed your chakras in whatever energy he decided to pour out, and left you feeling like you'd had a religious experience.

I'd gotten a much different view of the band tonight and it left me even more intrigued. Mage was still tugging on my hand, leading me through the house, until we came to a room with French doors that opened onto a small balcony. He let go of my hand to open the doors, and then he stepped behind me and put his hands on his hips.

"This is my favorite view from the house."

He pointed towards the hills and the lights from the Griffith Observatory, which sat above the home on the hill. I scanned the area, thinking this view was not what most people thought of when they pictured Los Angeles.

"It's like you could get lost out there," I whispered, taking in the peaceful surroundings. There were few places you could go in L.A. to get away from the insanity, and this hillside was one of them. I took in a deep breath and closed my eyes. I was picking up so many feelings from this house: anger, sadness, love, loneliness...

That one was closer. In the dim light, I turned to see Mage frowning slightly. His green eyes were shiny and full of emotion. I wanted to see if he would open up to me, not as a reporter, but as a woman.

"It always amazes me how we can be surrounded by our loved ones, and even surrounded by the million or so people in this area, and still feel alone. Sometimes I embrace it. Other times I feel like I'll be swallowed up and lose myself," I admitted.

He was way too close to me. It felt almost too intense to look at him. Since I'd entered this house, he had been all over me. Was he like that with everyone? I stepped to the side and leaned my left shoulder against the doorframe. He stepped closer, his body turned toward me.

"Let's not be alone tonight," he whispered, his finger coming up and tracing my neck. "I'm not trying to be crass or forward. I just want to spend the night with you."

Disappointed that he'd go that route and a little unsettled, I turned to face him, my back now against the doorframe. "That's not what I meant by being alone." I raised an eyebrow at him and waited for him to speak.

"It's not what I meant either. Talk to me. Walk with me. We can go anywhere or stay right here. I just—"

He stepped even closer, taking my hands in his. My breath caught at the way he was looking at me. "I just want to be close to you. I can't explain it, and even if I tried, you'd think I was a freak."

The insecurity in his voice made me wince. I squeezed his hands. "Unless you tell me you've got a torture chamber up here somewhere or you're studying to become the next axe murderer of the Los Angeles hills, I won't think you're crazy. Being a freak isn't so bad. I've spent much of my life trying to live with that label myself."

A faint smile touched his lips. "Why do you get me, Sammara? I mean, why are you not shocked by anything that comes out of my mouth when everyone else is? Except maybe Jaylene. She's the first one in a long time who didn't flinch when I started asking her questions. The guys all put up with me, but they are forever giving me shit about my 'feelings' and shit. Why not you?"

I shrugged. "Maybe I'm like you. Maybe I have to keep my freaky side from showing in front of the people in my life, too. Want me to tell you a story?" He smiled and then looked around. He gracefully lowered himself to the floor to sit cross-legged in the doorway. I followed him down and sat in front of him. He didn't let go of my hands. Our knees touched and the expression on his face was like a kid at Christmas.

"I love story time. Tell me a story, Sammara." His voice was like velvet against my skin. Either the sound, or the breeze from outside, or a combination of those and the fact that we were alone in the dark, touching, brought goose bumps once again to my skin. I giggled a little then tried to pull it together. He proved to be a most attentive listener, his fingers playing with mine as I spoke.

"Once upon a time, there was a happy kid who lived in the desert with her mom in a huge hippie crash pad. She was surrounded by musicians and artists and everyone spoiled her. She had a pony and a puppy and chickens and cats to keep her occupied. Life was magical. She learned the ways of the Mother from some of the others, and she learned to read and write and sing songs from her mommy. Everything was perfect, until the day the police came and broke up her happy family.

"Some of the people went to jail, including her mommy for a while. The little girl went to live with her grandparents in another world, where there was no music, no magic, and no pets. Only God. She had to go to regular school with other kids who thought she was a freak. She dreamed of being able to live free again, to be surrounded by music and friends, and to be free to worship the Mother.

"Eventually she realized that was never going to happen. Her mommy came to live with them and became just like her grandparents. She went to church with them, got a job at a bank, and forbid the little girl to do any of the things she loved to do, or else mommy might get taken away again.

"When the little girl grew up, she became top of her class in school and vowed to get away as soon as she was able. She turned eighteen, ran away to accept a scholarship at UCLA against her family's wishes, and the rest is history. She never made it back to the desert, but she could live free once again."

I hadn't told that story for a long time, and never to a stranger. In fact, the last person I probably told was Sherry back in college. Mage's eyes hadn't left me once. His intense gaze made me feel...things. He was firing all kinds of emotions at me and causing all kinds of physiological effects.

"So maybe that little girl needs to go to the desert and heal." It was a statement, not a question. I felt joy at the thought.

"Maybe she should. It's a little scary, though, and there might be people who don't want to see her. She's not even sure she could find the place again."

He frowned. "Scary because it's not safe?"

I shrugged. I honestly didn't know if there were people who were angry with my mother for making a deal to get a shorter sentence. They were probably all gone by now.

"Could be. I don't really know. My mom stayed with my grandparents until I left home, then she got an apartment. We aren't real close, just because she's kind of a shell of a woman and won't do anything to make herself better." *Ha! Pot. Kettle. Black.* Change of subject called for. "Have you been to the desert, Mage? It's very different from your home."

He smiled and shook his head. "I haven't, but I hear it's beautiful."

We sat and stared at each other a long time. I nudged his knee with mine and raised an eyebrow. "I think it's your turn for story time."

He laughed and let go of one of my hands to push a piece of his hair back from his face. His long dark brown curls were heavenly. His hair was a few shades darker than his deep bronze skin. He had it pulled back in a hair tie but a few wiry curls escaped. His green-eyed gaze penetrated, but instead of feeling put off, I wanted to get closer. When he started to speak, his deep voice with the New Orleans cadence had me mesmerized.

"Once upon a time, an only son was born to a seventh son. A blues man. The blues man had married a beautiful lady who bore him this child. The blues man had such high hopes for his son. He taught him everything he knew about playing the bass and about the history of New Orleans's jazz and blues scenes. They lived in Tremé with his large family and all was good with the world. The boy knew nothing but music: how to read it, how to write it, how to play it... It became his life, just as it was his father's life.

"But his mother didn't understand and didn't share their love of music. When an opportunity came for his father to take his music to the next level, he told her they were moving to New York. She refused to go. After a big fight, she ran away in the night to find a new life with stability. She dragged her boy with her even though he begged to go with his father, not understanding what was happening. His mother said the road was no place for a boy. He'd never been to regular school either, and was teased and beaten on by the rough Cajun boys in Houma. It wasn't until he found kindred, music-loving spirits that he began to find his song, and life began to have meaning.

"The rest of the story, I think you know." He looked down at our hands. My pale white ones covered lightly with freckles contrasted with his dark flawless ones.

"Seems as though *I* might have found a kindred spirit," I said, smiling at him. He returned my smile.

After a beat, we fell into easy conversation about being the freaky kids who hadn't gone to school. I found that he and I had read many of the same books as kids and had many of the same favorites. His grandmother and aunties taught him at home and he played music on the street with his father day in and day out. He was a little older than me when he left that life, which probably made it harder to fit in with the other kids. Middle school is the worst time to have to move to a new area and start a new life. I had been eight years old when I had to go live with my grandparents.

He asked me why the police came and I told him about the drugs. Some of the men we lived with at the ranch were manufacturing and distributing hallucinogenic drugs, some natural like peyote, and some LSD. Mom had gotten hooked on drugs as well and instead of a long jail sentence, she spent some time in county jail on misdemeanor charges and then went to rehab before she came to live with us. She found God in rehab and that put her back in the good graces of my grandparents. Mage asked me how I made it through that part.

"It was hard. I'd get in trouble for asking questions at Sunday School and my grandmother would make me sit in my room and read the Bible for hours at a time. I begged my mom to let me stop going, but she was afraid. She'd say, 'If I don't go along, they might take you away from me for good. Besides, you need to forget about the ranch and our life there. It was wrong, Sammara'. I never agreed with her, though. Christianity just never felt right to me."

"Me neither. Mama tried to make me go with her to worship, but it was like her preacher knew I shouldn't be there. I did the choir thing with the guys, but tried to avoid church otherwise. I spent all my time with the guys once I got to know them. That's when we really started to play together."

He smiled at that thought and I found myself wondering what they were like as kids.

We talked about so much over the next couple of hours, never letting go of each other's hands. It was as though we were communing, our souls reaching out to make deeper contact. I remembered my mother sitting with friends like this for hours when I was a child. I had a memory of a man with her...

"Sammara? Do you believe in fate?"

My eyes found his. "As in everything happens for a reason, like destiny? I don't know. Sometimes I do, but I war with the idea that we don't have free choice or free will. Why do you ask?"

He cleared his throat and looked as though he wasn't sure how to say what he wanted to say. Then he shook his head. "Nope. Not yet. C'mon," he said, standing quickly and tugging me to my feet. He pulled me into his arms and against his chest. He made no move to kiss me, but I could feel him breathing deeply. I should have been alarmed at his closeness, but his energy was good. I could feel nothing but goodness from him.

"Where are we going?"

He didn't respond right away, he just rubbed his chin against my hair and sighed happily. "Someplace we can listen to some music; that alright?"

"That sounds perfect."

I got my answer soon enough. I let him lead me out the front of the house and to a Jeep with tinted windows. He unlocked the doors and held the passenger door open for me. It was after midnight and after the hours we'd just spent together, I was captivated by this man. The way he moved, the way he spoke...the way he'd finish my sentences, as if he could pick up on what I was trying to say.

I climbed in and he shut the door, jogged around the front, and then climbed in next to me. After he started the car, he held my hand the whole time unless he needed to shift. He even got testy if I moved it out of his range in between shifts.

We drove down North Vermont then he turned into the parking lot behind the Dresden Restaurant. He turned off the engine and then faced me.

"I wanted to hear some jazz. Do you mind? They have great desserts."

I laughed and followed him inside. The restaurant was one of my favorites, although I hadn't been here since the last time I'd interviewed Danny Black. Danny hung out here a lot after his divorce and used to play piano and sing in the bar some nights.

Once inside, the maître d' guided us towards the bar. Mage led us to a table in the corner that was so small we were practically face-to-face. He held my hands while we listened to a woman sing. She was accompanied by a piano and a stand-up bass. I loved the old jazz standards they were playing. When they took a break, I asked a question I'd been pondering.

"Mage? Why are we here? I mean, why am I with you? I'm certainly not complaining. This has been the best night I've had in a long time." I blushed at my admission. He'd probably think I didn't have much of a life.

He linked and unlinked our fingers absently and appeared to be concentrating on what he was about to say. "I'm not sure other than I feel like this is supposed to be, that we are supposed to be here together. It's like I'm supposed to touch you and when I do, I feel grounded. That's all I got," he said, taking a swig of his water.

I laughed at his serious tone, but that seemed to hurt his feelings, based on his expression.

"Mage, I'm not laughing at you. I feel it, too. I felt a connection with you as soon as you opened the door. But see, when that comes out of my mouth it sounds like I'm one of your groupies just trying to fuck you. That's not what I mean." I slurped my beer—making sure to leave a foam mustache—set my mug down hard and said, "That's all I got."

It was his turn to crack up. That is, until he wiped the foam from my upper lip with his thumb. His gaze turned serious. He used his thumb to gently trace my lips as they curled up into a smile. He leaned forward and pressed his lips against my ear and whispered, "I don't fuck groupies, Sammara. Not since our first tour. I don't intend to fuck anyone but my wife."

Startled, I pulled back. "Your wife?"

He locked eyes with me and his tone was serious as a heart attack. "My wife. And then we'll make a whole lotta babies."

I jerked my hands away, nearly knocking my beer to the floor. Instead, I sloshed it onto my sweater.

"Shit. Will you excuse me?" I asked, covering my embarrassment with a mad dash to the ladies' room. Once inside, I used a towel from the attendant to dab at the spot. I used the restroom and took a minute to get my head together. I made sure to tip the attendant after washing my hands. Restroom attendants were always a funny thing, but this lady wasn't invasive.

I gave myself a once-over in the mirror and saw what I always saw. Jet-black hair that was flat and framed my face, curling under my jaw. Makeup that was dramatic around my gray eyes. Lips a dark shade of pink, which was natural. Freckles sprinkled my face and chest; otherwise my skin was so pale it was almost translucent in the pale light.

Mage's words had me panicking. A wife? Babies? I didn't know if I would ever be able to let a man touch me intimately again, much less have his babies. He'd said a lot of things this night that should have alarmed me that didn't. Marriage and babies proved to be the topics to make me run. What was I supposed to say? I told myself I was being ridiculous and started to walk back towards the bar, but my heart was pounding.

Instead of being where I'd left him, he was next to the piano with the stand-up bass in his hands. His fingers lovingly massaged the strings and his eyes were closed in the most peaceful expression. The pianist played softly while Mage created beautiful music. It was a soulful jazz piece, and the way he was playing had my chest tightening and my eyes burning with tears.

Then I remembered his whispered words.

I grabbed my purse, threw some bills on the table, and hurried out the back door. The valet had a cab waiting, and with a few carefully placed bats of my eyelashes, he gave me the cab and called for another. I hoped I would make it back to the house before Mage so I could grab my car and split. My feelings were all jumbled. I was scared and sad. I don't know what I was thinking spending time with him like this. I was in no shape to start anything up with a man like him.

The house was still lit up when I arrived, but the Jeep wasn't there. I paid the cabbie, giving him a hefty tip, and slid into my car, hoping I didn't pass Mage on the narrow road down the hill. Once I hit North Vermont, I knew I was in the clear. It wasn't a far drive to my condo off of Sunset in Hollywood and traffic was light at nearly two in the morning. I pulled up to the gate, punched in my code, and drove carefully over to my spot. Once inside my condo, I ripped off my clothes, wanting to get his scent as far away as possible. It only reminded me of my cowardice.

I couldn't believe I'd run away, but then what was I supposed to do when he got so serious? He'd just met me! He had no clue about the hell I'd been through, and I intended to make sure he never did.

In the meantime, I had to get my mind in a better place before I started writing my piece. I slipped into a cami and yoga pants and grabbed another beer from the fridge. I lit a candle and asked a blessing before tucking into my computer to start writing. I always tried to write as soon as I returned from an interview, while my impressions were still sharp. This time my impressions were all over the place. I took a sip of beer and got to work.

# FOUR

The Follow-Up
*October 2012*
*Four weeks later...*

*Once upon a time, in a small Louisiana town called Houma, a group of talented but vulnerable young men turned to the church of rock 'n' roll to heal their souls. They started out in a garage playing loud and fierce and eventually made their way to Hollywood, with their manager's promise they would be the next big thing in metal. Somewhere along the way, one might presume they sold their souls to the devil in exchange for wild success and excess. That excess led to the circumstances surrounding the death of their beloved manager and sent the band into a tailspin.*

*It took them months to reconvene and get started writing their fourth studio album, but their efforts were plagued by depression, chemical dependence, and misery. It wasn't until they contacted a local tattoo artist to aid them in their time of grief that things started to turn around for the band. Now they are back with their most eloquent and personal album yet.*

*Will Maggie's Bones reclaim their throne? Or will they once again be at the mercy of that devil and the excess that seems to plague them?*

. . .

My managing editor required my presence. I'd submitted my piece on Maggie's Bones a week after the interview and my disastrous night with Mage. Josh told me he loved what I had, but that he wanted more.

"Sammara, this is great," Josh said. "But there's more to the story here and you know it. You barely talked about what happened in New Orleans, or how they ended up with Scott. I'd love more on how the album is different. You barely scratched the surface. Spend some more time with the band. They're finishing up some dates up in San Francisco before they head home to New Orleans. I heard Scott Cross may be up there, too. You can interview him as well. I'll get you in so you can get what you need."

This was a really bad idea. If I explained why, though, my boss would be pissed. I'd gotten too close to the story. It had been really hard to portray them objectively when my heart still hurt from walking away from Mage. I almost would have preferred he just treat me like most men did; like I was a piece of ass. Instead, he'd made me care and made me think there was something different about our chemistry. That made it all the more terrible that I left like that, but I just wasn't ready to even go there.

My editor wanted to make my interview the main feature of the December issue. The cover story. My feeling that the piece was going to make or break my career had been accurate. Since interviewing Maggie's Bones, I'd been given prime assignments, including being the first to interview the lead singer of the metal band Wrath after he'd returned from a Russian prison. Ronnie Blanchard had been arrested there after a fan died during their concert under suspicious circumstances. He spent six months in a Russian prison before our government was able to get him freed. The fan had been stalking him for the previous year. Once the attorneys were allowed to bring in that evidence, the charges against him were dropped. Our interview had been a lively one, as I had been invited to a private reunion party for the band and their families.

That had been the highlight of the past month. But I kept replaying my night with Maggie's Bones—or make that my blunder with Mage, over in my mind. Sherry and I had played phone tag a few times, but I hadn't heard from anyone else.

"So I have to fly up to San Francisco, catch the show, and then get a few minutes with the band afterward. I can hardly wait."

Josh frowned at my sarcasm. "I thought you were a fan of theirs? Something happen? It wouldn't be the first time doing an interview turned someone off a band. It'll be great, though, and the talk is that this album will most likely top the charts. It would be good for us, Sammara."

I agreed to it, but a huge part of me did not want to see them, ever again. I emailed Sherry and told her I would be coming up and asked her if we could meet. This was her response:

*Hey girl! Can't wait to see you. The past month has been hell on me personally. I've stepped back from my day-to-day duties with the band but I will be going up to San Francisco with Jaylene and Mackenzie. We'd love to hook up with you and you're welcome to come with us to the after-party. You can crash with us at the hotel if you need to. I'll make sure I let their road manager know that you'd like to speak to them and see if he can arrange that. Love ya!*

That was an interesting development. I had a feeling it had to do with the weirdness between her and Marcus. I responded that I'd love to see her and the girls, but that I didn't think I'd be up for much of a party after. I just wanted to get my information and hightail it back to L.A. and be done with this band. Sherry and I would always be friends and we'd see each other from time to time. I just didn't want to see Mage any more than I had to.

During my flight to the Bay Area that Friday, I decided to drop in and see my family. I rented a car and drove from the airport to Fremont that afternoon. I dressed sedately in slacks and a turtleneck, knowing I'd need time to change into my "work clothes" before I went to see the band.

My grandparents and I sat down to have tea when I arrived and they asked me about my job.

"I'm doing great. I'm actually going to have the cover story in December. I've been given some really good assignments lately."

They both nodded solemnly at me, the "you're going to hell and we can't save you" vibe coming off them in waves.

"That's admirable," Grandfather said. I smiled at him and sipped my tea. I held on to that teacup like a life preserver.

"Have you found a church to attend? The best way to a peaceful life is through worship."

I hid a smile. *Sure, Grandma, I'd found a church to attend.* It just wasn't her church.

"I worship. I've met nice people. Most of my time is spent on assignment, though. I haven't been home much the past couple of months." They nodded. We sipped our tea. We avoided talking about taboo subjects.

"How is Mom?" I asked. I hadn't talked to her in months, which wasn't odd for us.

Grandmother looked sad. "Sandie moved away from here a month ago and we haven't heard from her. I'm not sure where she went. She got fired from her job, Sam."

I frowned. "Fired? For what?"

They looked at each other, disappointment clear in their expressions.

"Her cash drawers came up short too many times. Her boss tried to help her, but in the end she had to be fired. Sam, dear, if she contacts you and asks for money, you mustn't give it to her. Grandfather and I believe she is using drugs again."

That news was like a kick in the gut. She'd kept it together for a lot of years, but I knew she hadn't been happy. I hoped she was safe. The fact that she hadn't even called to tell me she was leaving didn't sit well with me and I could feel my stomach start churning. I worried the tea was going to come back up. Fear of puking on my grandmother's nice tablecloth was the only thing keeping it down.

We tried to talk to each other for a few more minutes, but after we finished our tea, there were no safe topics left. I loved my grandparents and was grateful to them for taking care of Mom and me when we needed it, but I'd never be the granddaughter they wanted. We hugged at the door and they waved to me as I drove away from their home in my rental car. My tears flowed the whole trip back across the bay to San Francisco.

The valet took my rental car at the Sir Francis Drake Hotel and check-in went smoothly. I had hoped I'd cleaned up my makeup enough to not look a total mess when I got there, but based on the concierge's treatment of me, I'd failed. He went over the top with his efforts to make my stay more comfortable. I assured him I was fine.

Once in my room, I collapsed on my bed. I needed to get it together. Sure, I was going to see Mage, but that didn't mean I could fall apart. I had a job to do. I stripped out of my clothes and scattered them around the stately room. I pulled my black medicine bag onto the bed and pulled out a red candle, some matches, and some cedar oil. I stepped close to the window and located the southern point of the space, where I set the candle. I lit the wick and sat cross-legged before it, anointing myself with the oil.

"*Strength be mine. Courage shine!*"

I sat for a moment, continuing to chant and trying to pull strength from my surroundings. I was picking up on so many emotions in this place. Hotels could be tough sometimes because so much positive and negative energy passed through that I had a hard time sorting it all out.

It was just something I did. I'd heard it called being an empath before, a sensitive, a medium... I just picked up on feelings and energies from time to time. The closest explanation I'd ever read was that of psychometry, or measuring of the soul. I could sometimes pick up impressions from objects, but often it was from places or people. I had no way of explaining it, and I usually didn't talk about it. Friends had always just called me different, others called me a freak because I sometimes knew things or I would call them on their emotions if they didn't match what they were saying. Needless to say it didn't make me popular, but it made me good at my job.

It was time to get ready for the show, so I dressed in a black shimmery tank, slim black pants with raised black velvet skulls embossed on them, and my matching combat boots. I never wore skirts anymore. I felt safer this way. My hair had streaks of hot pink that peeked out from the lower layers and my nails were painted a matching shade. I wore my pentagram necklace; its heat was comforting against my skin. Skull posts, hoop earrings and my onyx ring finished off my outfit, and dramatic black and smoky gray makeup around the eyes polished off my look. I left on the cedar oil, hoping the scent would continue to give me strength.

Down in the lobby, I ran into Sherry and the girls, who were headed over to the theater.

"Come with us," Mackenzie begged. The band had hired a limo to take the ladies to the Warfield, a vintage theater with incredible sound that many of the greats had played over the years. I begrudgingly agreed once they assured me the band was already over at the venue.

I should have known better. Once we were inside, all six eyes stared me down.

"So," Mackenzie started. "A certain member of the Bones is pretty confused. See, he met this amazing woman—"

"Mackenzie," warned Jaylene. "It's not our business to pry."

Mackenzie shot her an overly innocent look. "It is, too, when it comes to our boys. Now let me finish, would you?"

Jaylene rolled her eyes and looked out the window. Sherry just laughed.

"Anyway, as I was saying before I was so *rudely* interrupted, he met this amazing woman, they talked all night, they went out to hear some music, and just when things were getting good? Would you believe she tore off outta the restaurant bar and left him hanging? Who does that?"

"Someone with a good reason," Jaylene muttered. "Look, Sammara—"

"No, I get it. He's your friend. I'm sorry if you are angry with me, but I'm not going to talk about it, okay?" I took a deep breath, wondering where that strength was hiding. I could really use some.

Sherry's eyes were sympathetic. "We all know Mage. We know he's a bit out there. If he said something that offended you—"

"Sherry, I just don't want to talk about it. It's hard enough being here. Can we just pretend that we're not involved with the band, enjoy the show and fangirl like we're known to do? Then I'll do my job and get the hell out of San Francisco? Because I really need things to happen that way tonight."

The three of them burst out laughing. "Oh, no, my sweet. For one, we cannot pretend we are not involved with them. They've grown on us," Mackenzie said.

"Like a fungus," Sherry muttered, and we all laughed, breaking some of the tension.

"True," Jaylene said. "But that doesn't mean we aren't here for you, too. Did something happen, Sammara? He's really—"

"I appreciate it, Jaylene," I said, cutting her off before she even got to telling me anything, or even mentioning his name. "I just can't." The limo pulled up to the rear entrance of The Warfield and Sherry fished out VIP badges for the four of us. The line was wrapped around the building and lots of folks were trying to peer into the window.

"Keep these visible, ladies. Security is tight here and they won't let just anyone traipse around near the band." We climbed out, put on our lanyards, and walked towards the back doors of the venue past hundreds of screaming fans waiting in line to get in.

Then someone shouted, "That's D's girlfriend!"

Picture flashes started going off and the screaming went from fangirl to ugly in a split second. Someone threw a water bottle and it hit Jaylene in the face. Someone else threw a beer and it splashed Mackenzie's stockings. She turned in a murderous rage and started for the crowd before a security guard approached her.

"Ma'am, let's get you inside."

Mackenzie pushed past him and slapped away his hands as he tried to stop her. "Not until I give that bitch a piece of my fist!"

The guard picked her up and tossed her over his shoulder in a fireman's carry, which was comical because his face was now hidden in layers of chiffon, her skirt had ridden up to reveal her shiny ass cheeks and thigh-high stockings. The male bystanders cheered. Then the security guard turned sideways to get in the door and rammed her head into the door. He almost dropped her before the three of us caught her and managed to show off the rest of her teal satin thong.

"Jeez! Hurry, before her tits pop out," Jaylene growled.

Mackenzie continued to scream at the girl who'd thrown the beer.

Security grabbed the woman and escorted her to the San Francisco cops who had just arrived to oversee the crowd.

Venue staff led us upstairs to the women's lounge, which had an outer room with couches and a separate room to the rear with sinks and toilet stalls. Mackenzie got a look at her disheveled self in the large vanity. Her big blue eyes filled with tears and Jaylene held her tight. "We can fix this, Kenzie Kitten. Don't cry."

Sherry opened up her purse and, between the two of them, they had Mackenzie all cleaned up in no time.

Jaylene, on the other hand, was starting to get a black eye.

"Jaylene, let me go get you some ice," I said, turning her towards the mirror.

The other women gasped.

"Oh, shit," Sherry said. "Devon is going to flip the fuck out. You can't see him before the show," she warned. Jaylene shook her head vigorously.

"No way! He'll be out for blood. Remember that time in Florida when those guys cornered us by the bar? I thought for sure he was going to jail. It took the whole rest of the band and Daryl to hold him back." Jaylene shook herself, then winced and grabbed her face.

"I'll be right back," I said.

I rushed out to the bar. "Can you put some ice in a bag for me? My friend was hit by a bottle and she's starting to get a shiner."

The bartender, a gorgeous woman adorned with piercings and tattoos, nodded sympathetically and quickly handed me a makeshift ice pack. I thanked her and was heading for the lounge when I heard thunderous sounds from the stairs and a booming voice.

"JAYLEEEEEENE!"

*Oh shit.*

Once I was inside, Sherry closed the door and instructed me to lock it. "If he gets in here, he's—"

"Sherry, goddammit. Open this door! I need to see my woman!"

Sherry and I panicked, our eyes the size of saucers.

"Shit," Jaylene said in a defeated voice.

There was more pounding on the door.

"KENZ! Let me in, chère! Are you alright? Open the door!"

Mackenzie pulled herself together and nodded to us to let her through.

"Hey, baby," she cooed to Star through the door we opened just a crack. She kissed him and he groaned with delight. Then he got back to the business of being the worried boyfriend.

"What happened? You okay?"

"Where's Jaylene, Kenzie?"

She batted her eyes at D and said in a stage whisper, "She's on the toilet, Devon. Can't you give her some privacy?"

"Mackenzie, I heard there was trouble. You better let me in to see her—"

"Guys! They're letting the crowd in! We've got to get you backstage or there will be even bigger problems." Their road manager tried yanking them away.

"We'll see you guys after the show, okay? We'll be there right after. She's fine, just had a little too much Mexican food at lunch."

Sherry snorted at Mackenzie's attempt to cover up the problem.

D wasn't appeased. "JAYLENE!" he yelled once more.

A toilet flushed and Jaylene stepped to the interior doorway. He could only see one side of her face.

"Baby, I'm fine. Go get ready. I'll see you after. I love you."

He frowned a bit, but he bought it. Sort of. He growled as he stomped away with Star and their road manager.

The four of us ladies looked at each other and breathed a sigh of relief.

"Phew! That was close," Sherry breathed. We all got the nervous giggles.

"Wow," I said, my hand holding my chest so my heart didn't burst out. "I didn't realize a Bones show could get so exciting! Are you ladies alright?"

Mackenzie cursed a string of deliciously vulgar terms, some of which I'd never been privy to. "I'm fine. I just didn't need my ass flashed all over San Francisco. And that asshole security guard banged my head into the door." She winced when she ran her fingers over a bump starting on her forehead.

"Well, shit," Sherry said. "Sammara, go grab another ice pack, would ya?"

I went back out to the bar, which was already getting some business. I motioned to the bartender I'd talked to before and told her we needed more ice. She looked worried.

"We're okay," I told her as she handed it to me. I hurried back into the lounge and found that we had some curious onlookers. Sherry handed Mackenzie the ice and said, "We better get to our seats quickly."

Unfortunately, the Warfield did not have a VIP lounge. We could go backstage, but at this rate, we didn't want the guys any more agitated.

Our seats were in a corner section of the loge, close to the exit, and no one was going to really bother us there. There were two opening bands, label mates Deafening Silence and Scare the Children. They were loud, pretty good but not great, and they did their job of getting the audience ready for the Bones.

Sherry and I made the trips to the bar for drinks and snacks, since we didn't want anyone seeing Mackenzie and Jaylene and recognizing them. During the second band, I wandered downstairs to see if I could get a word with someone from the venue and ran into some associates. By the time I made it back upstairs, Maggie's Bones had begun their intro. I hurried to my seat and slid in next to Sherry. I handed out bags of candy and the women thanked me profusely.

Then I saw Mage on stage—and my jaw hit the floor.

His luscious hair was down tonight and flowing around his face. He was wearing guyliner and had black streaks painted on his face. A ripped-up band tee was open low on the sides and showed glimpses of his pecs and other delicious muscle groups as he moved. Black slim-fit pants and Chucks finished off his stage wear. He was perfection. *Damn did I screw this one up.*

I could not tear my eyes from him the entire performance. He rarely smiled, but when he did, my heart did a dance in my chest. It was so bad, I didn't think I could do this. There was no way I could handle seeing him again without it being totally obvious how much he affected me.

The guys played a helluva show. The Warfield could really bring out the best sound. I was partial to this venue for a lot of reasons. I'd seen so many great performances here, like The Dead Weather, which landed me my first major artist interview, with Alison Mosshart and Jack White. It was that interview that landed me the job with *Feedback* and I believed the magic of this place made things start to happen for me. I just didn't think the magic could overcome the obstacles I had before me now.

As the band went into their second encore, I knew it was business time. The ladies and I made our way backstage so the four lovebirds could be reunited. The crowd roared for several minutes after the band made their way back to us. Marcus was first, followed by Jade.

D went straight for Jaylene like an angry beast. He grabbed her face, looked at the shiner we'd had no hope of curing with our ice packs, and pressed his forehead against hers, whispering apologies.

Star approached Mackenzie with a worried look on his face. "You okay, chère?"

She nodded and tried to cover her forehead with a lock of teal hair, but he wasn't having it. She assured him she wasn't hurt, though, and the two of them and the other couple headed for the dressing room.

Sherry was speaking coolly to Marcus and Jade. I started to approach them when I heard my name spoken in that deep voice that had haunted me for the past four weeks.

"Sammara," Mage called again. I turned to face him and put on a brave face.

"Mage. Good show tonight."

He nodded, gazing at me speculatively. "I see you, Sammara. I see you."

Then he turned and walked away, ripping his shirt off and using it to wipe his face.

"Mage," I called after him.

He turned to regard me with a wounded look on his face. I sucked in a breath for courage, smelling a hint of the oil.

"I see you, too." It was barely above a whisper. He looked as though he wanted to say more, but Jade grabbed me and pulled me over to him and the others.

"I'm glad you came," he said, crossing his arms over his chest. "I wanted to give you a piece of my mind."

Marcus put a hand on his shoulder. "Jade, bro, let it go."

"No! She fucked with Mage and that doesn't go over well with me. He's my best friend." He stared daggers into me, which was actually kind of funny because Jade was so sweet he couldn't hurt a fly. But I could tell he was angry.

I sighed and said, "I'm not going to discuss what happened. Now, I have a job to do. If you choose not to give me any more information for my article, which is going to be the cover feature, that's up to you."

Marcus shot Jade a look. "Bro, go see if everyone is ready and tell them to head over to the Drake. I'll follow with these lovely ladies and give Sammara her story."

Jade started to speak, but then clamped his mouth shut and glared at me.

"Thank you, Marcus," I said as Jade walked away. "Look, I didn't—"

"Whatever happened between the two of you is none of my business, but the band is, so let's talk."

Marcus gave me a lot more information for my article, including details on the record release party. He and Sherry encouraged me to come. He talked to me in more detail about the plans for touring more next spring and summer. He also said they'd be taking some time off at the end of next summer, probably a good length of time, because they needed to slow down for a bit. He kept looking to Sherry and while she smiled and tried to look professional, I could feel her sadness. I silently prayed to the Mother that she guide these two lovers to a better place without all the pain they kept causing each other.

When we returned to the hotel, we went with Marcus to his suite. He played me the final tracks off the album while he showered. He came out in his towel with his hair wet and clinging to his face.

"Did you need anything else, Sammara?"

"No, thank you. I really appreciate you sharing the tapes with me. The album is terrific. Definitely your strongest. You guys have created an incredible piece of music."

He blushed a little and thanked me. "It was the most difficult experience of my life, even worse than when my daddy left, or when Uncle

David died. That was D's father. We had a tough time then, but this... losing Maggie, the guys falling apart, and losing my best friend—"

"Marcus," Sherry choked out. I saw tears fill her eyes and he winced.

"I'm sorry, but it's true. I know I fucked up. I fucked up a lot of things. Just ask D and Jaylene. Did you hear that story yet, Sammara?"

I shook my head, afraid of what he was going to say.

"See, Jaylene coming along brought D out of his stupor, and it was great, but then I realized this could be it, that D might just leave us. He was pissed at me and I had to do a lot of asshole things to get everyone to stay on board long enough for us to put the damn album out. Unfortunately, I didn't watch my mouth, and I said some ugly things to Jaylene one morning when I thought she was going to try to... I don't know. Let's just say I didn't handle it well when they got together. I'm happy as a clam for them now, especially since D stuck around to do the album. I don't know for how long, but he's here for as long as we have commitments as a band. But you, Sherry—"

"Marcus," she warned, wiping at her eyes. He reached out to touch her and she shot up off the couch.

He looked crushed as he lowered his hand. "See? Fucked up." He shrugged and walked toward the bedroom. "I'm going to go drown my sorrows upstairs... Oh wait, I can't do that anymore. That's right," he growled loudly and shut the door.

"Sherry," I whispered, but she just shook her head.

"I can't, Sammara. Not if I'm on the record."

"Sherry," I said, hurt that she'd think that little of me. "You're my friend first, always. I wouldn't do that to you." She patted my hand and stood.

"I need a drink before I tell you any more."

We stopped off at my room so I could dump my purse and catch my breath. Sherry waited patiently while I stood in the bathroom, silently giving myself a pep talk. I was unsettled by the energy in my room. I rejoined Sherry and she gave me a worried look, so I assured her I was okay.

We took the elevator to the twenty-first floor where the Starlight Room had been closed off for a Maggie's Bones special event. The music was loud, the lights were low, and the laughter was pinging off every surface. We easily found the two couples snuggling in a corner. D was holding another ice pack on Jaylene's eye, which she was trying to pull away from. Jade was dancing in the middle of the floor with about five scantily clad ladies, and Marcus was sitting with some official-looking people at a huge booth. He glanced up when we walked in and gestured for us to come over. He seemed much more together than he'd been down in his room.

"Sammara Gunderson, have you met our producer, Scott Cross?"

I shook hands with Scott and several other men I'd heard about but had never met. They were all involved with production and very well known in the business.

"Gunderson... Aren't you the reporter who did that piece on Blanchard after he got out of that Russian prison?" Scott asked. "Glad that whole situation turned out okay for him."

Sherry and I sat at the table and talked business with the producer and his associates. They gave me some good info for the Bones piece and I knew I'd made some contacts I could revisit in the future.

The music changed from house to some '70s funk and people got out on the floor to start dancing. I excused myself from the group and went to get a drink. As I sat down at the bar and looked out the large bank of windows giving a breathtaking view of the city, a feeling of overwhelming aloneness settled in. I saw reflections in the windows of happy couples, obvious friends and coworkers...

Everyone had someone. I had me.

I took a sip of whisky and sighed. Knowing I was a journalist often kept people at bay. They loved you when you made them look good and avoided you like the plague when you were critical. I had been doing this for seven years now, and while I had friends like Sherry, Patricia Gordon and a few others I'd met along the way, it was just me.

I didn't even date much because you couldn't trust people. I'd dated some musicians, but it had to be all about them and their careers. They tended to get insanely jealous whenever I got closer to another band to do my job.

The last guy I'd dated, Rick, turned out to be a greasy slimeball who wouldn't take no for an answer. Luckily, I'd been able to get ahold of one of my pewter candlestick holders and clobbered him upside the head before he could do the deed. I'd pressed charges against him for attempted rape, but the D.A. didn't prosecute. That whole experience just about made me swear off men for good.

And then there were the two times I'd been roofied. Only one of those turned out as awful as you'd think. The other time, someone noticed before the jackass got me out of the bar. I was really careful now. I only accepted drinks from the bartender, and I almost always gravitated towards a female bartender. If I had trust issues, I had my reasons. It seemed my intuition, or whatever you called it, didn't always work when it came to my own safety.

The music changed to some synthy pop stuff and I turned around as the floor cleared. I barked out a laugh when I saw Jade, Mage and Marcus all lined up, starting some sort of dance routine. Star jumped over a railing a second later and joined them. I didn't recognize the tune, but the four of them knew it by heart.

Dressed in their metal gear, the boy band had the whole crowd howling. They all sang lead at some point, including Mage. His eyes found me across the crowd and he just stared. It was unsettling to say the least. He didn't even miss a beat as he took his turn leading the others. His voice soared. He even did some vocal pyrotechnics that most pop stars would kill to have in their arsenal. I couldn't help but laugh and be impressed at the same time.

"Lord, these guys. Thank goodness at least Devon has some sense or they'd be pulling this shit onstage." Sherry plopped on the stool next to me, and by the look on her face, I had a feeling the interrogation techniques were going to be turned on me.

"Sammara, I know it's none of my business—"

"If you're going to ask about Mage again—"

"I just know him and I can't imagine what he might have said or done—"

"Just forget it, Sherry. We had a nice talk. That was it. I don't have the energy—"

"Oh please! Come on, Sammara. I know you've been through it, but are you just going to swear off dudes forever? Become an old spinster? You turn thirty soon."

I turned on her with an eyebrow raised. "You're already thirty! I don't see *you* out there."

She huffed out a breath, downed the rest of her drink, and frowned at me. "It's because I already have someone. Well, I don't, but I'm in love with someone who is a pain in the ass, okay? I can't seem to get rid of him, I can't seem to let him go... FUCK MY LIFE!"

We both laughed at her outburst. Sherry was such a strong woman and had always been a no-commitment kind of gal. She didn't want a relationship—or hadn't wanted one. I guess she'd found someone to change that.

"Marcus," I said.

She turned away and nodded. "He's an enormous jackass, but I can't seem to help myself." She snuck a look at me and we both started giggling.

"Tell me why. Off the record."

She nodded and blew out a breath, her eyes following the goofballs on their second number. "Sammara, under all that swagger and manwhore attitude is a really insecure guy. When we're together, he is very attentive and wants to please. He's never disrespectful, and Lord, can that man... Sorry. But seriously, we've had so much fun together, and then he almost fucked things up for the band. He came out to see me after fighting with Devon, and...it was awful. He accused me of playing him and I kind of let him think that because I wasn't ready to go there with him. That was back in the spring. Now when he's around me, he's either sulking like you saw the other night, or he goes out of his way to pour on the sleaze, trying to get a rise out of me, so I just stepped back. I still handle a lot of stuff for the band, but I don't tour with them. I've hardly been to any of these shows. But I'm still thinking about him all the time and it just plain sucks." She downed another glass of something brown and coughed.

"Take it easy, girl," I said quietly, putting my hand on her back. Sherry was always so tough. I'd never seen her like this. The alcohol wasn't going to help.

"Have you tried to talk to him? Tell him how you feel?"

She rolled her eyes. "Please. Take a look at that. Would you want to bare it all to someone like that?"

At that moment, Marcus was on his knee before some young woman crooning all the *baby babys* and *ooo ooos* in the song. I turned back to Sherry and fake gagged.

"But when you're alone?"

Sherry's smile turned wicked. "Staying power. Oral talents. Generous and playful. Pretty much the perfect lover."

We both sighed.

"Yeah, well, I'd just like someone to talk to," I muttered.

She nodded. "And Mage is really good at talking." She elbowed me and I frowned.

"Ladies! What do you think of the show?" Mackenzie asked as she plopped on Sherry's other side and ordered a Shirley Temple. Mackenzie whistled at Star, who did an extra spin and dropped into a disco split. We all cracked up at his execution. He was really showing off for the crowd. He didn't get to be in the spotlight often, being the drummer. I had no idea he was such a ham.

"He better not hurt himself," Mackenzie pouted. "I've got plans for him later. He should be all healed and it's time to give it a test run—Oh!" She blushed when she looked at me, probably forgetting I was even there.

"Off the record, Mackenzie. Don't worry. I don't think *Feedback* readers would... Hmmm. Actually—"

"You can't!"

I laughed at her shocked expression. "I wouldn't dare. But I hope it's as good as you think it will be."

She visibly relaxed and we watched the guys finish up their act. It was my turn to tense up as they approached the bar to get sodas.

Star headed straight for Mackenzie and they wrapped around each other in a deep kiss. "You ready to go, darlin'? I need you bad."

She sighed and nodded. He scooped her up with her legs wrapped around his waist and made a break for the door.

"Great, another one down," Jade mumbled. "D and Jaylene already left."

He looked over to see Marcus trying to talk to Sherry. He had a serious look on his face and a moment later, they stood to leave.

I was now alone with Jade and Mage, who was glaring at me. I needed to get out of this.

"I heard we're going to be on the December cover," Jade said, his voice a bit more civil than it was earlier. "I'm interested to read what you wrote about us." He looked nervously at Mage. "Can we read it before it's in print?"

I pulled out my phone. "I don't have it finished yet. I wanted to add something about the show tonight and the new songs being played live. I also spoke a bit to your producer and I want to include all the great things he said about you guys." I opened the file of my draft and handed it to Jade. "You can read this much."

He smiled excitedly and took my phone, leaning against the stool next to me. Mage read over his shoulder, sneaking glances at me.

I turned to finish my drink and I felt a gnawing sadness growing in my belly. I wanted to get out of there before the tears started.

He wouldn't even speak to me. Of course, he was probably pissed. And why should I even want him to? It's not like I...

I could tell myself that, but it didn't change the hurt. I wished he'd never talked to me, told me—

"Wow, Sammara! That's really what you think, huh? That's...just, wow! Thank you."

I smiled at Jade and went to take my phone when Mage snatched it.

"I have questions," he said, turning back to the screen so he could keep reading.

Three women came up and tried to drag the two of them off. Jade went happily but then frowned when he noticed his wingman was staying behind.

"Mage?"

Mage just looked up at him and shook his head. Jade hesitated, but then one of the women shoved her hands down his pants and he smiled from ear to ear. The women obviously planned to have their way with him.

"I hope he's careful," I muttered.

"He always is." He hadn't looked up from my phone. I just wanted him to give it back so I could leave.

"Right here. You wrote, 'One can only hope the Bones find their happy ending. For some in the band it seems as though life has taken a turn for the better, while others continue to search for their muse.' What did you mean by that?"

I groaned. "Mage, I—"

"Why did you leave the Dresden?"

He was obviously still pissed. The intensity of his stare, which wasn't warm and welcoming like last time, had me nervous. I stumbled back off my stool and made a grab for my phone.

He was too quick. He shot out an arm to steady me against him, but held my phone over his head.

"I'm not letting you go until you talk to me. You ignored my calls, you wouldn't let Sherry—"

"What calls?" He hadn't called me.

"I called your cell phone a million times. I left you messages. You had to get them."

I shook my head and then rolled my eyes. "Where did you get my number?"

He frowned. "From the magazine. I told them I had more information for you on your article and they gave me your cell."

I relaxed a little, but he didn't let go of me. My chest was pressed up against him and his arm was around my lower back.

"They probably gave you my old work cell number. I had to change it because, well, I had some problems. But why would you call anyway? It's not like we had anything to say to each other."

He pulled me tighter to him and frowned. "Why did you leave, Sammara? That really hurt. I thought—"

"Give me that." I stepped on the spindle at the bottom of the stool and used it to push up enough to grab my phone out of his hand.

He let go of me in surprise and I practically ran from the room. I heard him calling my name. I climbed in the elevator and as the doors closed, he came running up. The hurt on his face was the last thing I saw and it brought on the waterworks.

I hurried to my room, shut myself in, and started to pace. I didn't think I'd be able to rest knowing he was this close, so I decided to pack up and leave. I'd drive my rental car down to Hollywood and hide in my own bed. Cry myself to sleep. I started throwing things in my bag without taking care. Wrinkles were an annoyance I could live with if it got me far from Mage.

I cleaned out my toiletries, took one look around the room, and opened the door—crashing into Mage.

"Shit! You scared me!"

He grabbed me by my arms and pushed me backwards into my room. My heart started pounding and I panicked. *No, please. Not again. Not Mage.*

"Sammara, I just want to talk to you."

"No. Please, don't do this." I started shaking.

He must have noticed how scared I looked. He let go and I pushed away from him, putting the bed between us.

"Sammara—"

"I will scream if you touch me. I just want to leave."

He frowned and held out his hands. "What's wrong? Chère, I would never hurt you! What has happened to you?"

I shook my head. "Please. Just let me leave."

He paused and started to say something, then crossed his arms. "Can we go somewhere and talk? Sammara, I—"

"Please don't do this." My voice came out just above a whisper. "Just let me go. Please don't hurt me."

That startled him enough to move.

"I'm out, okay?" He held out his hands again like he was dealing with a crazy person and backed toward the door. I flinched when I heard him fumble with the lock, thinking he was just going to throw the deadbolt, but after a second, he got the door opened. He stepped out in the hall, still with his hands out.

I rushed the door, grabbing my bags, and tore off down the hallway. I heard him call my name once as I climbed into the elevator, but luckily he didn't follow.

The front desk clerk seemed confused when I checked out at two in the morning. "But ma'am. You're paid up through tomorrow. We thought you were staying for two nights."

I couldn't help the tears that sprung from my eyes. "I just want to go home," I said.

"Are you okay, Ms. Gunderson? Did something happen?"

"No! I just want to go. Can you please just give me my receipt and let me go?"

She hurried through our business and I thanked her. It took forever for the valet to bring my rental car, and then I sped away from the hotel, praying I'd make it home in one piece.

# FIVE

Two weeks later
October 2012

I sat staring blankly at the proofs for the next issue in Josh's office. I had avoided the photo session with the band. I didn't think I could ever look any of them in the face again. I even avoided Sherry, letting her calls go to voice mail and not answering her emails.

I hated to do it, she was my good friend, but I couldn't have anything else to do with the band. I felt bad about what happened with Mage, sure, but I could only imagine the humiliation of having to answer her questions. He probably hadn't meant to do anything other than talk to me, but he'd pushed my fucked-up button and I'd lost it. I hadn't left my house in two weeks, but my editor called today and demanded I come in and look over the proofs.

"Well? Do you like the layout? Do you see any issues with the article?" Josh was a great guy to work for. He wasn't a hothead, but he did demand excellence. I hoped he was pleased.

"It looks fine. Do you like it?"

He regarded me with concern. “Of course I like it, Sammara. It’s some of your best work. Frankly, I’m worried about you. You’ve never taken time off like this before. Did something happen in San Francisco?”

My eyes went wide. “Why would you ask that?”

He frowned and rubbed at his chin. “Well, I didn’t want to tell you over the phone, but I’ve been getting calls from the band’s rep, Sherry Jordan. She said you haven’t been answering the phone and she was worried because you left so abruptly in the middle of the night. What is going on?”

How did I explain to him that I was having a nervous breakdown? That my mother’s disappearance, reminders of my prior assaults at the hands of men, and my feelings of disconnect had me hiding in my apartment and afraid to come out? I’d even resumed cutting myself, a nasty ritual I started as a teen when things didn’t go well for me.

As I sat there, unable to speak, I felt everything around me start to go dark around the edges and I knew I had to get out of there.

“Sammara?”

I heard a familiar voice and turned to see Sherry. My eyes shot to Josh in alarm.

“Sammara, I know she’s your friend. You can trust us.”

I buried my face in my hands and let him lead me to his office with Sherry right behind me. He closed us in, closed the blinds and guided me to his couch. The two of them pulled up chairs as if to say they weren’t letting me out of there until I talked.

“Sammara, Mage told me what happened in your room. He was frantic when he came to find me. We rushed down to the lobby, but you’d already left. I’ve been calling and calling... What’s wrong, babe? What happened to you?”

I wished I could fold back into myself. “When?” I asked with a humorless laugh. “Which time? Please tell Mage I’m sorry. I don’t think he meant to scare me, but he just...” I took a deep breath, feeling the panic come back on. If I were at home, the sight of blood might calm me. It was taking more and more these days to get me focused.

“Sammara, did someone hurt you?” Josh looked pissed. He and I had been close, but I’d never told him about any of my past.

"Yeah. But I'm fine," I said, and then laughed when I looked down at myself. I'd thrown on two different Chucks, a pair of old sweats so threadbare you could see through them in parts. My shirt had holes in it. I couldn't remember if I'd washed my hair or even brushed it.

My laughter turned to tears. Sherry sat next to me on the couch and held me. I don't know how long we sat there, but when I finally got myself together, I heard Sherry telling Josh she'd take me home with her.

"No, Sherry, I don't want to put you out."

"It's not up for discussion, unless you want me to call your grandparents."

That shut me up. I shook my head. The two of them walked me out to the parking lot and over to Sherry's car. I gave her one last pleading look.

"Grandparents."

I shook my head, groaned and climbed into her car. She talked to Josh for a minute and then climbed in next to me.

"I'm going to call Jaylene and have her come over. She flew in last night because the band is in rehearsals. She's good at this stuff."

"I don't think getting tattooed is going to help me right now," I joked half-heartedly.

She rolled her eyes. "She was an intern therapist before she moved to New Orleans, didn't you know that? She was doing an internship. She's almost got enough hours for her license. If you won't talk to me—"

"Sherry, it's not like that. It's not you. I just can't." The tears completely took over and I sobbed the whole rest of the way to her place off Melrose. She got me inside and put me in her bed. I was too weak to move. I hadn't eaten in a few days and my whole body hurt. I heard her speaking on the phone as I fell asleep.

# Six

I slept for a long time and felt really groggy when I woke up. I heard quiet voices in the other room, which probably meant Jaylene was here. I peeked my head out and saw not just her, but D and Marcus, too. I tried to slip back into the room, but Marcus must have seen me from where he was perched at the island.

"Sammara," he said, standing up. The others turned and their expressions were concerned. Sherry hurried to the door, followed by Jaylene.

"I was just going to ask if I could borrow some clothes and use your shower. I know your clothes will be small on me, but—"

"I already set some things out for you in the bathroom. Let us help you."

It was horribly embarrassing for me, but I let them help me undress.

Sherry gasped. "Oh, fuck me, Sammara! What the hell?"

I tried to cover my cuts with my hands. "I've got this. If you could just wait by the door in case I need help?"

I turned to look at Sherry before I shut the shower door and she was crying. Jaylene whispered something to her and they both walked out into the room, giving me some privacy.

I wanted to crawl in a hole and die. I looked down at my wasted body and wanted to scream. I'd obviously lost weight, as I could see hip bones sticking out, but I thought my ample ass was still as big as ever. I'd made several groupings of cuts on my stomach, figuring no one would see, and since it was a sensitive spot, I got the pain rush as well as the blood I needed to release the pain and frustration. A couple of the cuts looked really irritated. I'd probably given myself an infection. *Great.*

I showered and washed my greasy hair. I was able to get myself dry and into the yoga pants and sports bra she'd left for me before there was a knock at the door.

"Sammara? Can I come in?" Jaylene opened the door a crack.

"Sure," I said, feeling defeated. I didn't feel uncomfortable around Jaylene. I could sense she was trustworthy and I could feel the empathy coming off her in comforting waves. Maybe that's why she had been so helpful in getting the band back on their feet. She walked over to me and handed me a white tube.

"It's bacitracin. It'll help with infections. I had some extra in my bag."

I stood there with the tube in my hand just staring at her.

"Would you like me to put some on for you?" she asked.

I nodded and handed it back to her. She was all business as she washed her hands thoroughly and then accepted the tube back. She spread the ointment generously with a Q-tip all over the cuts I'd made just above my waist on the left side. Shame filled me at having my secret nightmare exposed.

"I don't think these will scar too badly if you continue to use this. I'm going to leave it with you." She stepped back, washed her hands again, and wiped them on a towel before popping up to sit on the counter. I guess it was her turn to try to talk to the crazy person. I grabbed the man-sized t-shirt Sherry had left, giggling softly when I figured out it belonged to Marcus.

"You absolutely don't have to talk to me. I know you wanted to distance yourself from the band, and after hearing what happened with Mage at the hotel, I can totally understand. I just want to tell you one thing and then you can decide whether you want to talk or you want me to leave."

I shrugged, figuring it couldn't hurt. She smiled at me, blushing a little.

"When I first met the band, I knew nothing about them. I was asked to go live with them for seventeen days and help them design memorial tattoos for Margaret Boudreaux. I had no clue about what had happened to them, but Marcus's Uncle Daryl can be very persuasive. We had a rough few days as I was getting to know them, but then Devon and I..." She blushed a little. "Well, when we got together, some things happened between the guys and I ended up staying with just Star, Jade and Mage one night. We talked about a lot of things, including a very weird game of twenty questions Jade insisted on." I smiled a little remembering I'd gotten the same treatment.

"I had a long talk with Mage the next morning. He told me how much he couldn't wait to find his wife, that she was out there, she just didn't know she belonged to him yet." She gave me a look to see if I got what she was saying.

"Okay," I said, realizing he must have told her everything.

"He also had some crazy idea about wanting like twenty kids. I told him he was nuts, that one woman having all those babies was a pretty insane idea." She swallowed and laced her fingers together. "Mage told me he said something to you about that the night you met him. He figured that might be what made you run."

I gave her a sad smile. "That started it, I guess. I'm not really sure I ever want another man to touch me. I mean, I didn't feel weird about things until he said that...And then in the hotel, when he kind of pushed his way into my room... I know he didn't mean to scare me, but... I'm so embarrassed." I hugged myself and took in a shaky breath.

"Sammara," Jaylene continued. "I think Mage was a little overzealous in his pursuit of you, but he has only the best intentions. He thought he'd found someone he'd been looking for a long time and, well, he got all *Mage* on you." She laughed softly. The sound made me relax a bit.

"I know I blew it by leaving, but he just overwhelmed me."

"Oh no doubt! I'd freak the fuck out if Devon ever said he wanted me to have twenty babies!"

"Why did he say those things to *me*?"

Jaylene bit her lip and smiled at me. "That's not really my place to say, but I can tell you that he can't stop talking about you or thinking about you. He's been a mess since San Francisco, worried sick about you. He feels terrible thinking he hurt you somehow. I'm guessing he didn't, but that his actions brought up some bad memories for you. Is that what happened?"

I nodded, wishing I could just tell her everything. "He scared me, but I wasn't thinking right. I'd had a really bad day and my emotions were all a mess from visiting my grandparents and being in that hotel."

She quirked her head to the side. "Did something happen there?"

I shook my head, hoping she didn't call for a psych eval when I told her the next part.

"I pick up feelings when I'm in certain places. Hotels are particularly difficult because there's a lot of residual energy."

She nodded, and thankfully didn't seem to think I was certifiable yet. "You're like an empath? I've heard about people who are like that. I bet that's hard to live with sometimes."

"It can be. It's worse if I'm in a bad place and, well, I have been lately. I went to see my grandparents before going to the hotel and they told me my mother is missing. I still haven't heard from her. I'm assuming she's okay. I just don't know. And seeing the band was hard because, well, I thought..."

"You thought you and Mage clicked. So did he. He was devastated when you left him at the Dresden. He and I talked about it a lot. He kept going back over the night and couldn't figure out why you would leave, not until he told me the babies part, which I told him would make any woman run. I'm not telling you this so you'll feel bad about it. I totally understand what you did. I just want you to know where I think his mind is at."

I felt a little lighter knowing that he'd felt like I had. I just didn't know how to fix my present predicament.

"Jaylene, are you really a therapist? I mean, have you talked to, um..." *Just spit it out, Sammara.* "Have you worked with rape victims before?"

Her eyes flared and I saw her swallow hard. "I have. Did you want to talk to me?"

I really did.

She led me into the bedroom and we curled up on Sherry's bed. Sherry came in as I was about to get started and said, "I was going to send the guys to pick up food for us. Is there anything you want?"

I nodded. "Can you ask Marcus to come here?"

She looked surprised, but she called his name and spoke softly to him. His head popped into the room above Sherry's.

"You okay, darlin'?"

I nodded and smiled. "I think so. Can you do me a favor?"

He nodded and put his arm around Sherry in the doorway.

"Can you please tell Mage how sorry I am? I just... I've had a lot of bad stuff happen...Yeah... I just thought..."

"I'll tell him. He'll be glad to hear it was a misunderstanding. He's really worried. Can I tell him you'll see him? Soon?"

I looked to Jaylene and she smiled encouragingly.

"Yes. I don't know when. Um, I kind of don't want him to see me like this."

Marcus walked toward the bed and sat on the edge, not too close, but close enough to take my hand in his. He brought it up to his mouth and kissed it, acting like the total gentleman. His hazel eyes were bright when he smiled at me.

"You look beautiful. He will wait until you are ready. Probably. Maybe not. But he'll be pleased you'll see him." He kissed my hand once more, then stood and walked to the bedroom door. He opened it wide and I saw D and Sherry hovering there. D asked Jaylene if she needed anything and she looked down at me.

"Pizza and ice cream?" she asked.

I nodded and smiled, curling up farther into Sherry's fabulous bed.

"Pizza and ice cream, boys. You know what to do," Sherry said. Marcus bent down and kissed her cheek before the guys left. She turned back to us with a questioning look in her eyes. "Can I join the party, too?"

I laughed and waved her to come in. She sat on one side of me with her back against the headboard and Jaylene was on the other side. I turned my body to face Jaylene and Sherry curled up to my back and started running her fingers through my hair. She was taking such good care of me. I couldn't believe I'd shut her out the way I did.

"Where should I start?" I asked Jaylene.

She took my hand in hers and said, "Wherever it starts."

I blew out a breath and launched into my tale. The two women held me and cried with me as I told them about being violated, not once, but several times. "Each time I thought, 'this won't happen again. I'll be fine. I'll be safer next time'. But then it would happen again. Being raped and then almost raped again really put a damper on my social life. In my mind, I know it's still possible to fall in love and have a healthy relationship with a man, but I'm pretty gun-shy."

"God, Sammara. You are so brave! If that happened to me, I would have curled up in my house and never came out again— Oh. Oops!" Sherry was so funny, trying to be helpful but obviously out of her element.

The three of us laughed to break the tension. The guys came back in then with Mulberry Street Pizza, Ben and Jerry's—and the rest of the band.

*Oh no.*

"I hope you don't mind," Marcus said from the doorway to the bedroom. "I couldn't keep him away when I told him you were in a bad way."

My heart was pounding. I didn't think I could talk to him in my current state. I sat up in the bed, feeling my hair that dried all wonky after my shower. I had no makeup on and felt weak, but damn if I didn't want to see him.

"It's okay, Marcus. Thank you for bringing food. Can you guys give me a minute?"

Jaylene stood from the bed and walked towards the door.

"Sammara," she said before she opened it. I looked at her and smiled. "You're incredibly brave. If you want to talk more, if you want me to work with you, I'd be honored. You have a family here that wants to see you well."

Her words comforted me more than I think she knew.

"I'd appreciate that, Jaylene. It's time to deal with it, I think."

She nodded and stepped out the door, leaving me with Sherry. She pulled me into a tight hug.

"I feel so terrible! I never knew. You kept that all inside. I don't want you to do that anymore, got it? I love you and I'm here for you, okay? We'll get you through it."

I believed Sherry when she said that. She was so good at managing people. I knew that now that I was in her tractor beam, she wasn't going to let me out of it until I was ready.

"I love you, too," I whispered to her and hugged her back. "Now, can you help me look presentable?"

She led me into the bathroom and put some product in my hair. "You've got natural wave, I've got out-of-control curls. This stuff will probably tame your waves into something manageable." She gave me some cream to help with the puffy eyes, even though it wouldn't work right away. I didn't want to put on any makeup or anything. We'd see what Mage thought when faced with this disaster. He'd probably run for the hills.

I walked into Sherry's living space and tried to look brave. Everyone stood and smiled worriedly at me, probably thinking I might break down in front of them. I smiled at Jade, Star and D before making my way over to Mage. He was wringing his hands. I stopped in front of him and took a deep breath.

"Hi," I finally said.

He didn't smile.

"Sammara," he said in a low voice. "I'm so sorry."

Tears pricked at my eyes and I blinked them back hard. "I'm the one who is sorry. I shouldn't have run."

"No, I shouldn't have said all that to you. I just...you really affected me, chère. I kinda lost my head."

I smiled shyly at him and his worry seemed to melt a little. "You affected me, too."

He reached for my hand, but then hesitated. "Can I?"

I stepped closer and tentatively put my hands on his waist, pressing my face to his shoulder. I felt strong arms come around me and pull me tight against him. I felt him sigh and kiss my hair.

"Can we *please* eat now? I'm starving over here!" Jade bounced on his toes next to the huge pizza boxes.

"Oh for fuck's sake, Jade," Marcus scolded.

"It's alright. You guys go ahead," I laughed. I inhaled Mage's delicious scent and huddled closer.

"Here," Sherry said, handing Mage a plate for me. "Don't try to fight me. You are going to eat all of this pizza and have ice cream for dessert. My yoga pants shouldn't be baggy on you."

I coughed out a laugh and pulled away from Mage to look down at myself. "Huh. You're right. I didn't know." I looked back to him and he handed me the pizza.

"I don't want to smother you, Sammara, but can I sit by you?"

Smother me? I didn't want him to ever let me go. That connection I'd felt to him at the Los Feliz house was back and I wanted to bathe in it. It felt so good to be with him. It was soothing. He was throwing off waves of sorrow, worry and protection. My psyche was eating it up.

Mage led me over to the couch. He sat first and then pulled me down to sit with my back to his chest. He fed me pizza, not eating until I was finished. I only had a small slice. My stomach was off after not eating right for days. He ate the other two pieces Sherry had put on the plate. I leaned back against him and felt way more at ease than I should have with a man I'd only really had one evening of significant conversation with. The voices of the band members and the two ladies lulled me into a relaxed state. At one point I felt fingers in my hair and I closed my eyes, surrendering to the peace.

When I woke up next, I heard lots of heavy breathing and snores. I looked around to see Jade and Star asleep on the other couch, all sprawled out. I could see into Sherry's room and it looked as though she and Marcus, and maybe Jaylene and Devon, were all piled on her custom king-size bed.

Breath tickled my neck and I snuggled closer to Mage, who had fallen asleep behind me. I turned a little in his arms so I could see his face, which roused him from sleep.

"Are you okay? Do you need anything?" he whispered.

"I just need to use the restroom."

He nodded and let me up. He stood behind me and placed a hand on my shoulder. "Sherry said when you woke up that I should tuck you into the bed in the guest room. She set out toiletries for you to use. I was supposed to remember that." He rubbed sleepily at his hair and rolled his head around on his neck.

"Will you come with me?" I asked him.

He nodded with his eyes half closed and followed me up the stairs and into the guest room. Sherry lived in a two-bedroom condo not too far from mine, but way more upscale. I had a single-story one bedroom that could fit twice into this place.

I went into the bathroom and peed, then brushed my teeth. When I came back out, Mage was leaning against the doorjamb with his eyes closed.

"Mage, will you stay? I can't be...intimate. I'm not—"

He placed a finger against my lips. "How could you think I'd even ask that of you, chère? I know you're hurting, just not why. I want you to trust that I'm not going to hurt you or ask more from you than you are able to give."

My eyes filled with tears, but I was too tired to cry. I took his hand and led him to the bed. I crawled in and watched as he slipped his shoes off, removed his belt and wallet with chain. He pulled off his shirt, but left his pants on. He paused for a minute and then started to lie down on top of the blankets.

"You can cover up, Mage. It might get cold."

His expression showed me just how hard he was concentrating on not scaring me. He lifted the blankets and then slid into bed stiffly. He left a lot of space between us. I tried not to giggle at how rigid his body was. Instead, I closed the gap and put my face next to his on the pillow.

"Mage? Was I just imagining things that first night?"

"I wanted you. I still want to be near you. Something about you touched something in me and I haven't been able to get you out of my mind since then. You're in my blood, just circulating through me all the time, and it just plain hurts to not be able to see you. When you left me at the Dresden, I was wrecked. I thought I'd found something really special with you. I can't explain it. Then after San Francisco, I went a little crazy. The guys forbid me from hunting you down and showing up at your house after what happened. They said I'd freak you out. If

Sherry wouldn't have been able to get you to leave your house, I was going to bust down the door and make you talk to me. I probably would be in jail right now if that happened, so thank you for coming out."

I laughed softly, trying to keep the noise down so I didn't wake the others. Mage wasn't laughing.

"I know we don't know each other that well, yet, but dammit, Sammara, please don't disappear like that again. It hurt worse than anything. I don't want to scare you, chère, but what I was trying to tell you that night..."

He was quiet for a minute, and then he shook his head. "I'll scare you for sure. Just say I can be with you, that I can be near you as much as you'll let me? I've got it bad for you."

I smiled against the warm skin of his chest. "I'm glad. I feel for you, too, but I can't go deeper. Not just yet. And I can't share my body with you. I don't know for how long. I just know I need to get better. I can't fall apart like that again. It was so bad." My heart was racing at the thought of going back to my house and never coming out again. I was so alone there.

Mage's arms cradled me gently to him. "I'm in no hurry for any of that, Sammara. I'll wait for you. I'll stand by you and hold you together if you start to fall apart until you can do it on your own, feel me?"

Boy, did I. How the hell did I get so lucky? Mage of Maggie's Bones was holding me, in a bed, and saying he would wait for me.

"Mage? What's your real name? Can I ask you that?"

He laughed. "You can ask. Are we off the record?"

"Pretty much if I'm in a bed with someone, it's off the record." That didn't sit well with me. "I mean, if we're like involved—"

"I know what you meant. But tell me, chère. What happened to you? Who hurt you? I can't tell what's wrong, but I can feel it. Are you with someone? Have you—"

"God, no. No. That was months ago. He finally stopped bothering me about a month before I met you. We dated a few times, things got bad, and then, um, I pressed charges on him. The D.A. said there wasn't enough to prosecute so the case was dropped. He kept harassing me until I got a new number, that's why you couldn't get ahold of me, I guess. I stopped using my work cell. That was probably the number they gave you. Then he'd show up at the house or near the office and I had to get a restraining order. I had him served in August, but I never told anyone. I should have told my boss, but I was afraid of anything coming back to hurt the magazine or jeopardizing my job."

I felt Mage stiffen under my hands. "When I think about someone hurting you, Sammara, it makes me violent. I want to fucking kill him."

"Get in line," I laughed. "I thought for sure that since I'd decided to come forward this time, that finally someone would pay for what they did. I was wrong."

"What do you mean, 'this time'? Did he do it more than once?"

"No. It was other people."

"PEOPLE?! Sammara!" He sat up and looked down at me. His eyes were way too intense. *He* was too intense.

"I don't think I can go through it all again tonight. Can we just not talk about it right now? I'm going to talk to Jaylene. She offered to help me. I promise I'll talk about it, but I can't do it now, and I can't do it with *you* if you're going to get upset. It's not yours to be upset about."

He started to argue and had to literally bite his lip to be quiet. He settled back in next to me, but this time his hold was much more protective. I was just grateful he didn't run after I'd told him that, but I had to know.

"Mage? Does it make you want to be with me less, knowing that I'm, well...damaged? I would understand if it did."

"Like hell! Sammara, I'm going to forget you asked me that question. You are not damaged, do you hear me? You have a beautiful soul. Nothing that has happened to you can touch that part of you. It can't touch your soul unless you let it, and you haven't. You have such light coming from you. It's irresistible. Hush now, beautiful, and get some sleep. I'm not going anywhere."

I breathed a sigh of relief and tried to sleep. Mage held perfectly still while I fidgeted. I listened to his breathing, trying to determine if he was asleep. I looked up to his face and his eyes were closed, but his forehead was drawn together in a scowl.

"Mage," I whispered finally.

He spoke with his eyes closed. "Have you finished wiggling yet?"

I laughed at his admonishment and then it was all over. I giggled until I got the hiccups and my side got a stitch in it. Mage got up and shut the door so we wouldn't wake anyone. He came back to the bed and lay down facing me. I tried to be still and quiet, but he was staring at me, which made me giggle even more.

"Your hiccups shake the whole bed," he scolded.

I held my breath, trying to get the hiccups to stop. I blew out a breath and then hiccupped even harder.

"I can't help it," I whispered back, hiccupping loudly.

His lips split into an amused grin. "Maybe I can take your mind off things."

My smile fell a little. He looked worried and shook his head.

"Let me sing to you."

*Oh.*

He sang me the most sensual lullaby. I couldn't quite place the words but the music sounded familiar.

*Hush now baby girl*
*Don't you cry no more*
*Baby's gonna catch you*
*You can be sure*
*Hush now baby girl*
*Let's try and pretend*
*All of that sadness*
*Has come to an end*

*Your cradle done rocked*
*The bow is now broken*
*Let me catch you*
*The past left unspoken*
*And when you feel ready*
*To let love in*
*Let me just hold you*
*Let love begin*

. . .

*Hush now baby girl*
*The dawn it approaches*
*The sun will come up*
*The color of roses*
*Hush now baby girl*
*The clouds will disappear*
*The rain will not touch you*
*When you're with me my dear*

*Your cradle done rocked*
*The bow is now broken*
*Let me catch you*
*The past left unspoken*
*And when you feel ready*
*To let love in*
*Let me just hold you*
*Let love begin*

He sang through it twice. His gravelly voice mesmerized me. He was magical. Just beautiful. I felt honored he would share such a sacred moment with me.

"That was incredible. What is that?"

He shrugged. "I don't know. It just happened."

I pushed back a little. "It just happened? Songs don't just happen! Did you just make that up?"

He put his arm behind his head, his biceps flexing. In the dim light of the room, the shadows played across his face, accentuating his full lips and strong jawline. I could stare at him forever and never get my fill. "It got your hiccups to stop."

My hand flew to my chest and I realized he was right. My eyes grew wide. "How did you do that?"

He chuckled quietly. "I didn't do anything but take your mind off of them for a minute."

"Sing it again, please?"

He frowned. He hummed for a minute and then stopped.

"It's gone. Sorry." He smiled meekly at me.

Frustrated, I put my hands on his chest and gave a little shove. "Gone? It can't be gone! It was so perfect!"

He squirmed under my hands and made a face at me.

I pulled back. "What's wrong?"

He grew dramatically serious. "Nothing's wrong. Nothing. I'm just fine."

I raised my eyebrow and moved my fingers a little against his rib cage. He jerked and moved back.

"Mage, are you ticklish? For real? I thought Jaylene was making it up."

He growled and looked away. He spoke from between clenched teeth. "They are never going to let me live that down."

I laughed and then looked closer at his tattoo. I ran my fingers over it lightly, making his skin rise up in goose bumps. He shifted under my touch and growled again.

"Really," he said. "Now quit that! Roll over, I want to hold you so you can't mess with me."

I giggled and turned over. He pulled me back against him, careful not to yank my hips too close to his. He pressed his chest to my back and sighed happily just before he started humming that tune again. He really was a musical genius to be able to spout out a song that good on the spot.

"Wish I had my recorder. That song was special."

"Thank you," he said. "It was inspired by a beautiful woman. Now go to sleep, beautiful woman. I want to hold you all night."

I couldn't believe, after everything that had happened, that we were here together. I was grateful. I listened to him breathe and then start humming again. It soothed me so much I was able to forget about everything but him, and fall asleep.

# Seven

I woke more rested than I'd felt in weeks. I turned over and frowned when I saw the empty pillow next to me. Empty except for a note.

*Sammara,*

*I wanted to stay and talk to you, but we have rehearsal and then we're getting on a plane tonight. I hate that I have to be away. Such is our lives. I'll be back in L.A. after Halloween and I want to see you. I want to see a lot of you. You and me have unfinished business. I hope you don't mind, but I got your correct number from Sherry and I'm going to call you. Like every day. At least once. I've got it bad for you.*

*Mage*

. . .

I giggled through his note. He was so sweet. Strange, but sweet. I rolled onto my back and stretched. I said a silent prayer to the Mother that she give me the strength I would need to deal with the drama.

A soft knock sounded at the door and Jaylene poked her head in.

"Hey, I brought you some breakfast. The guys left earlier and Sherry's still asleep."

I peeked at the clock. It was noon.

"Thank you. I *am* pretty hungry."

She put the plate of food on the bedside table and sat in the chair next to the bed. "I hope you rested well. Did Mage behave?"

"He really did. He was a complete gentleman. You were right," I said, sipping on the coffee she'd brought along. Black, just a little too strong for me, but I appreciated the gesture. "This is perfect."

"Don't thank me. Sherry has one of those Keurigs. I hate coffee myself. I wouldn't even try to make it except it's pretty easy in that thing."

She watched me so closely, I was a little nervous.

"What was I right about?" she finally asked.

I thought for a minute. "Oh! You were right about his ticklish spot. Man!"

She dropped her head back and laughed. "Yeah. He was a pain in the ass to tattoo. He took the longest. I even had to do his in two sittings." She pressed her lips together. "I probably shouldn't be telling you this."

"Off the record," I said, drinking the last of the coffee.

"Phew," she said. "Anyway, I just wanted to check on you. I'm leaving in a bit for the airport. But I wanted to say that I'm happy to talk to you whenever, by phone, Skype... Just because I'm going home doesn't mean we can't still talk. If you want."

She would never know just how much her words meant to me. "Thank you. Other than Sherry, I don't really have any girlfriends that I talk to."

"Me either. Mackenzie and Sherry are really the first girlfriends I've ever had. I was kind of a loner growing up."

"Me too! My grandparents were very strict. I wasn't allowed to see friends out of school or go anywhere. No music, no movies, no TV. Just the Bible."

Jaylene sucked in a breath. "Whoa. That's rough. You seem to have made up for it though."

"Yeah," I said with a smile. "I snuck a radio into my room and listened to local rock radio whenever I could. In college I went a little crazy. I'm living the dream now."

Was I? Yes, I had a prime job as a reporter and got to travel all over to interview my musical heroes. But was I truly happy?

I was last night. In his arms...

Jaylene looked at the clock and then peeked out the door. "I'm sorry to bail..."

"Thank you. So much, Jaylene. I just might take you up on the phone calls. For sure I'm going to see about going to a therapist. I thought I was doing a good job ignoring everything—"

"And that's usually when it comes out to bite you in the ass. I know. Even bodies weighted down with concrete shoes resurface most of the time. Remind me to tell you about me and hospitals sometime."

Her words resonated with me. Even after we said goodbye later that afternoon, I thought about what she said. I needed to get well. I had something, and someone, to get better for.

The next day, I dragged myself into Josh's office. I told him everything.

Everything.

"I'm sorry I never told you. I promise, if you'll let me keep my job, I won't fall apart like this again."

He pulled me into a hug. "Sammara, honey. Why didn't you tell me? I thought we were friends? I thought you trusted me."

I patted his back when he refused to let me go. "It has nothing to do with you. I know I could have trusted you to care and to be there, but I didn't want to get the magazine involved. I'm telling you now because I want to do a feature on sexual assault for the magazine. I want people to know what is happening out there. I don't want other women to go through what I did. To blame themselves and fall apart."

I'd decided on this upon meditating when I returned to my condo after leaving Sherry's. After spending the night with Mage, where I felt safe for the first time in so long. There was something bigger I needed to do. For myself and for every other woman out there who had been hurt and didn't have someone to make them feel safe.

# Eight

November 2012

The next few weeks were hectic. I finished up the article on Maggie's Bones and had it ready by the first week in November for the December issue. I also made a phone call to a therapist that Sherry found for me and had my first appointment. I liked her. She was a no-nonsense Jewish woman who called me on every trick in the book I tried to use to cover up my anxiety. She had me sign a pledge to not cut myself, and so far I'd been able to honor it. Mostly. I still had my kit. I put it away, out of sight, but I couldn't bring myself to get rid of it yet.

The cuts had all healed to faint red lines. Thankfully. At one point the scars were important to me. They reminded me of what I'd been through. Now I just wanted to move on and let go of the past. It's hard to let go when you have visible reminders.

I still hadn't heard a word from my mother. I checked in with my grandmother and she had no new information. I was worried she was in trouble and hated feeling helpless to do anything about it. I debated hiring a private investigator, but I almost wondered if maybe she didn't want to be found. That hurt, a little. I understood the need to run away from the life my grandparents expected.

Jaylene and I talked about once a week. Our conversations had a dual purpose. I could talk to her about what had happened to me in a way I couldn't with my therapist, and she filled me in on the band's antics. The ones Mage conveniently left out of our phone calls. Like the night the guys, minus Devon and Star, got into a fender bender in some guy named Rudy's Hummer because they were reenacting the Bohemian Rhapsody scene from *Wayne's World* and Jade's foot slipped off the brake. No one was hurt and there was no damage to the Hummer, of course. But Devon walked around for a week humming the tune to them, which led to a challenge at the paintball course in Houma. Jaylene went along to make the teams even, and, she assured me, she won.

Their life in Louisiana sounded like so much fun, and I missed being around their energy. Work made me feel fulfilled. The rest of my time was empty.

Mage made good on his promise. He called me every day. Sometimes he'd only have two minutes to ask me a question, and those calls were the weirdest ones. He knew shit that I don't know how he knew unless he was having me followed. Like when he asked me about the dinner I had that night, if the salmon was cooked just right. Or the time he told me not to drive on Sunset that evening because he "just had a bad feeling about it." Or—and this one was downright creepy—he asked me one night if I always took off my rings before I took a shower.

"I wouldn't want one to slip off in the shower and go down the drain is all," he replied when I asked him if he had cameras installed in my bathroom. If I were any other woman, his knowledge of my routines would have triggered stalker alarms all over. Only I knew the difference. I'd had an actual stalker.

I decided I needed to tell Mage a little about some of the things that had happened to me. I thought it was only fair since he was only getting a half of a woman in this budding relationship. It was a tough conversation to have over the phone, so he suggested we FaceTime. He was quiet for a long time after I finished telling him what happened with my ex.

"And here I've probably been creeping you out with my phone calls. I'm sorry, chère. I wish I knew."

I assured him I was fine.

"I know you're the real deal. I only feel safe knowing that you see the things you do, never threatened."

He looked away from the screen and sighed. He pulled his hair back into a hair tie and then leaned forward, his face closer now, so close I could see those gold flecks.

"I don't like keeping those bad feelings to myself, especially when it comes to people I care about. Did I tell you I had a really bad feeling the day Maggie died?"

He hadn't talked to me about her other than on the night we first met at the mansion. "Do you want to tell me?"

He paused, looking down. I could see his eyelashes fan out over his cheekbones. He hadn't shaved in a couple of days, I surmised. He also had dark circles under his eyes. I wanted to ask him if he was eating right and getting enough sleep, but I could feel he needed to get this off his chest.

"When my feelings come, sometimes it's because of a bad dream, but the really bad ones come on like a cold sweat, you know? Like when you've got a fever? And that day I actually went so far as to take my temperature because I thought I had the flu or some shit. I dreaded going to the club that night, so bad."

"It's like your skin is crawling and you can barely put one foot in front of the other and force yourself to do anything..."

"Yeah," he answered, staring straight into the camera. "That's exactly it. Oh, chère. I really wish—"

"I know. I do, too." Being apart felt wrong to both of us. He was so brutally honest. It helped to know he felt some of the same weird things I did.

It was also really good to be able to talk to him about my mom missing. It was really frustrating to not be able to just call her, or to know she was ok. Mage offered his help. I thanked him but assured him that if I needed, I had resources that could help me.

"I'm here for you, Sammara. Don't forget that, feel me?"

I did feel him. I was so grateful for him.

After Maggie's Bones had finished their dates in October at the VooDoo Experience, the band had stayed in New Orleans to do some business instead of coming to L.A. Mage was frustrated. They were in talks to buy the St. Germaine building and Mage told me he was looking at real estate for himself.

"I don't like being homeless. I need a home base that's not my gran's, feel me?" He asked me to come out there to spend Thanksgiving, but I wasn't ready to be away from my safe zone. We agreed we'd see each other in December at the release party for the new album. The space did wonders for my confidence. I loved getting to know him like this. When I was near him, other things influenced how I felt...like his magnetism, his scent, his...

Yeah. I needed to be out of his sphere of influence right now, as much as I missed his touch, and his scent, and the safety of his arms.

# NINE

I brought the proposal for my article to Josh the week after Thanksgiving and waited patiently to see what he thought.

"Wow. I'm not sure what the boss will say about it, but I think it's fantastic. I'll stand with you every step of the way."

I got to work that day on the sexual assault article. I dove into my research, only coming up to trade a few texts with Mage. They were really curt, not playful like I'd grown used to. He reminded me about the release party and I assured him I'd be there. It was being held the same week of the anniversary of Maggie's death. I knew it would be tough for all of them.

And then I fell into a rabbit hole.

I didn't come out for days. I made calls and set up interviews. I got so many women to tell me their stories, women I'd known professionally who agreed to come out with their tales of abuse and nonconsensual sex. Instead of being afraid, I was invigorated. I shut out the rest of the world while I worked my fingers to the bone writing my greatest article yet.

The day of the release party, I had an opportunity to interview one last woman, who was a crucial part of my own story. I got in touch with the bartender who took care of me the night I was drugged for the second time. I told her I wanted to ask her more questions about that night and she invited me to come to the bar before it opened so we could talk. I checked the time and sent a text to Mage telling him I'd be there a little later than expected, just in case the interview went long.

Which it did. The woman, Joy, filled in a lot of gaps for me about that night, and then told me she'd been raped in the parking lot after work one night.

"I never told anyone. Not a soul. I kept coming to work like nothing was wrong, but it was eating me inside." I noticed she chain-smoked while we talked, but her words kept me riveted.

"It wasn't until six months or so later, a musician who hung out here a lot, I won't name names just because, yeah. Kind of embarrassing. I knew he wanted to hook up. I'd seen him with women and I'd heard plenty enough to know that he'd be fantastic in bed and wouldn't want any ties after. I thought it would be perfect. Unfortunately for him, I wasn't quite ready for any of it. I took him home with me one night and...I kind of beat the shit out him," she said, laughing at herself. "Fucker had no idea what he'd gotten himself into. I spilled my guts, told him the whole damn story. He was so awesome about it. Let me get it all out. After that? I got myself into therapy and decided to quit my job here."

I frowned at her. "And yet you're still here?"

She took a long drag on her cigarette and gave me a sly smile. "The owner? My boss? He wouldn't let me go. Ha! Like for real. We're married now with two kids, isn't that crazy? I just needed to let it go, you know? And Bron—I mean, that guy—he was so cool about it. It was what I had to do. Now I'm great."

Her story hit so close to home. All I could think about was how much I needed to see Mage. I glanced at my phone and saw that not only was I totally late, but I'd had two missed calls from him.

"Shit. Joy? You are such a peach. I'm so sorry to be insensitive and leave right after that story? But I have my own 'guy' I gotta see."

She laughed and assured me I wasn't being insensitive. I would always owe her a debt of gratitude for stepping in and assuring that I didn't fall prey to another rapist.

# Ten

I flew down Sunset to the Key Club for the party. The security guy at the door gave me some flack until I could get ahold of Sherry on my phone. She appeared at the door and frowned.

"Where the hell have you been? They're almost finished playing!"

She grabbed my arm and dragged me inside and through a crowd of people to be close to the stage. The music was loud and I'd forgotten my earplugs. I could barely move through the ridiculous crowd. And someone spilled a drink on my back. None of that mattered, not the bodies pressing against me, or the sweaty heat in the club, once I saw him.

Mage was wickedly handsome and completely immersed in the music. He had on a white dress shirt and charcoal-gray slacks. I would have thought he'd look out of place dressed like that, or awkward even, but he owned it. He devastated me. He couldn't see me, or didn't anyway. I recognized the tune as one Marcus played for me in his hotel room in San Francisco. Mage kept the heavy rhythm with Star, occasionally playing some complicated bass lines that made me shiver. He was brilliant. I watched them play another song and then Devon stepped up to the mic.

"Before we finish up here, I have one more song to sing. It's called 'Branded', and I would like to dedicate this to my beautiful Jaylene."

I heard Mackenzie squeal behind me and turned to see her and Jaylene hugging each other. When the heartfelt song was finished, he called for her to come up on stage. Sherry and Mackenzie pushed Jaylene forward and she stumbled towards him. Marcus held out a hand to help her ascend the steps to the stage.

Devon spoke some emotional words to her and got down on one knee. The crowd gasped, but my attention was fully on Mage. He watched his friend get engaged with his lips pressed firmly together. When Jaylene accepted, Jade and Star comically played the wedding march. Mage quietly set his bass aside and left the stage.

I pushed my way to the stage and called out to him, but he kept on walking. Frantic, I tried to get backstage but was held off by security. I growled at the guy, literally, but besides looking at me like I was crazy, he wouldn't budge. I shoved people out of my path to find Sherry, but she was surrounded by people.

*To hell with not making a scene.*

"Sherry!" I shouted at her and she turned to face me, her smile slipping. She looked around.

"He's gone!" I felt my heart pounding. I desperately needed to see him. She excused herself from the group.

"He can't have gotten too far," she said in an irritated tone. "If you would have been here on time—"

"I know, and I'm sorry. I've been working on something and—" She waved off my excuse as we pushed past security and made our way to the back area of the club. No one had seen him. No one knew where he went.

"What do I do?" I asked her.

She frowned and turned toward the stage. Marcus was smiling at Devon and Jaylene but as soon as he saw Sherry, that smile turned sly.

"Hey, chère," he said as he pulled her to him and kissed her cheek. She put her hands on his chest.

"Where's Mage? Where would he have gone?"

Marcus finally noticed me, and then frowned.

"No clue. Come on." He grabbed Sherry's hand, Sherry grabbed mine, and we ran out the back door. Marcus lifted Sherry up and into the Jeep and then helped me into the backseat on the driver's side. He climbed in, told us to buckle up and hold on.

Marcus drove like a maniac down Sunset with Sherry yelling at him to slow down.

"I'm not having my brother out here alone on this night." He calmed down, though, and the three of us looked around frantically. We figured he was on foot.

A block ahead, we noticed a cab pull over and saw Mage get inside.

"Follow that cab," I shouted, thinking Marcus hadn't seen him.

Marcus gunned it, running a red light, and fishtailed through the intersection. Suddenly there were flashing lights behind us.

"NO! No no no no no," Marcus said. He cursed and yanked the wheel over to the curb. He pulled up the emergency brake and opened the door.

"STAY INSIDE THE VEHICLE," the officer shouted to him.

"But officer, our friend is getting away—"

"PUT YOUR HANDS WHERE I CAN SEE THEM."

*Oh shit.*

Marcus swore loudly as the officer approached. Another police car pulled up behind the first and two more officers got out, guns drawn.

"Driver, put both hands outside the window and open the door from the outside."

I couldn't believe this was happening. Marcus calmed down, shot a worried look at Sherry, and then did what he was asked. The two other cops made their way around the passenger side and told Sherry and me to put our hands up.

"Driver, step away from the vehicle and kneel with your hands behind your head."

Marcus moved slowly and did what he was told. One of the other officers opened Sherry's door and pulled her out, her hands behind her head. He walked her to the sidewalk and told her to do the same. Kneeling was a bit awkward for her in her dress, but she complied.

"You. Miss. Climb out with your hands up." My heart was threatening to jump out of my chest. I tried to get out but I couldn't climb out without using my hands. I stumbled and started to fall from the cab.

The third officer grabbed my arm and dragged me out of the backseat straight onto my knees on the asphalt, cutting my legs all up in the process.

I could hear the first officer asking Marcus questions, and goddess bless him, he kept his cool. He explained to the officer what happened. The officer shared that our vehicle matched the description of an AMBER alert in the area, which explained their intense response. When the officer had his ID out and saw his license was from Louisiana and, unfortunately, not current, he placed him in handcuffs and sat him on the curb where Sherry was.

"Sir, I'm his manager. My ID is in my purse on the floor of the passenger side." They checked her ID and mine and called us into the station. After many long minutes, they received a call back on the radio.

"Mr. Lambert? We're going to need to search the vehicle. Do we have your permission?"

Marcus clenched his jaw and agreed. He shot an ugly look at me and then nodded. Dammit. This was all my fault.

It took the officers forty-five minutes to clear the vehicle. Since Marcus's license was expired, and Sherry couldn't drive a stick, I drove them back to the Key Club. Thankfully nothing worse had happened, but I still felt terrible. The worst part was that we still hadn't located Mage. He was out there all alone on this night full of horrible memories.

"What the hell happened to you, brother?" Jade was in a jovial mood when we got back to the club, but he took one look at Marcus's and Sherry's pissed-off expressions and got serious.

"We lost Mage," Marcus said.

"Yeah, and Mr. Band Leader here didn't get his damn driver's license renewed. Jesus, Marcus! How could you have been driving around like that?"

"I haven't been driving, Ms. Manager, since I've been here, and I haven't exactly been able to take care of it! I planned on doing it after the release. I was going to get a California ID."

"Why the hell would you do that? It's not like you plan to stay here!"

Sherry was not her usual businesslike self. The two of them squared off, unaware that the rest of their friends were now watching.

"I would if you would just quit pretending you don't want me here! Dammit Sherry, how many times do I have to tell you I love you before you quit fighting with me?"

Sherry's eyes went wide, along with those of the rest of the spectators. She looked around at everyone and froze. I heard Marcus curse.

"I'm sorry, chère," he said quietly.

Sherry grabbed my arm and said, "Get me out of here."

I let her pull me towards the front entrance, looking apologetically over my shoulder at Marcus, whose sad eyes watched us leave the place. I'd parked a block away on a side street and struggled to keep up with Sherry's long strides.

"Son of a BITCH! How could he just blurt that out? In front of everyone! God! I'm going to lose my fucking job." Her words were not matching her emotions.

"What are you really angry about, Sherry?"

She pulled up short in front of my car and turned her fiery gaze on me. "What do you mean, what am I angry about? You were there! You heard him—"

"Tell you he loves you. And you're afraid. You're not upset with him or worried about your job. What's really the problem?"

She narrowed her eyes. "Fuck. I forgot you're weird, too. Jesus. No wonder Mage is a mess." She put a shaky hand up to her forehead.

"Let me take you home. I'm so sorry about all of this." She let me lead her into the passenger seat of my Escape. I got behind the wheel and drove towards her condo.

"That was fucking scary. I thought we were going to jail. Or worse. I can't believe—"

"Yeah, that's not the kind of interaction I'd prefer to have with L.A.'s finest." I'd actually been treated decent by LAPD when I went through my situations, but I'd seen a lot, especially as a journalist. And I knew that pretty boys with tattoos like Marcus often didn't fare well. Neither did people of color like Sherry.

She glanced at me and barked out a nervous laugh. "I've never had a gun pointed at me before. That was awful. And Marcus was so brave, and so good! He didn't mouth off or anything. Oh, I was so mean. Why do I keep pushing him away?"

"You tell me. How do you feel about him?"

Sherry dropped her head into her hands and I watched as her shoulders started shaking with sobs. "I love him, the rat bastard! Why did he make me fall in love with him? He's just going to fuck up my whole world and then leave me holding the bag while he goes out and bangs half of the women on the continent."

"They're touring overseas. At least it won't be women on *this* continent," I joked, hoping to break the tension a little.

It worked. Sherry snorted. "You're right. As long as it's not American pussy I guess I can live with it." She reached for some tissue. "Dammit, I'm a wreck. And fucking Mage! He's been so withdrawn this whole week. What happened with you two?"

I shrugged. "I don't know. We've been talking, not as much this past week... I'm doing a huge feature article on sexual assault, Sherry. Josh supports the idea and is going to run it by the bosses. It's going really well, and I guess I kind of fell off the face of the earth, I've been so wrapped up in it. I left him a message that I would be late, and then my interview went long. He's been so patient."

I pulled up to her complex and turned to face her. She was looking at me like I was a lunatic. "What? I told you I was sorry I was late tonight. I feel terrible. I wanted to see him—"

"Well you had a funny way of showing it. Tonight was going to be tough anyway, but for you to not be there... That doesn't sound like you're crazy about him."

"I didn't mean to, I just...this piece for the magazine is really important to me. It's helping me deal with my shit, as is that therapist you recommended. And I talk to Jaylene. I'm trying to do what I'm supposed to do. I want to get better. I told Mage I needed to heal and..."

"Yeah. Huh. Sounds like you both have some stuff to work out. All of us do. Except Jaylene and Devon. Why can't it just be all roses and love and fucking happy shit like it is for them?"

I laughed humorlessly. "Fate. You can't mess with it. It seems like you're fated to be constantly butting heads with Marcus, and Mage and I are fated to keep passing each other like two ships in the night. I really want to find him."

Sherry smiled sadly at me. "Go to the Dresden. He goes there a lot. Maybe you'll find him there."

I nodded and sighed. "You ok?" I asked her, praying I hadn't screwed things up with my best friend.

She cussed again. Poor Sherry.

"Yeah, I'm fine. I guess I better call Marcus and fix things. God, he has the worst timing. I love you, girl. I'm glad you're better, but don't disappear on us again, ok?"

I nodded, hugging her and kissing her cheek. "Promise."

She waved to me as I pulled away then I drove carefully to the Dresden, not wanting another run-in with the cops.

# Eleven

It was nearly one in the morning by this time, but the bar was still open. Only a handful of folks sat around the grand piano. Danny Black was playing a sad tune and singing along. Mage was playing the stand-up with his eyes closed. The bass wept under his fingers, a completely different vibe than he had just created at the Key Club.

I watched from the end of the bar until the song was finished, then Mage opened his eyes. He shook hands with Danny. Then he saw me. We both stood there, staring. Neither approaching the other.

Danny said something to him and when he didn't answer, he turned and saw me.

"Sammara! Hey girl! How the hell are you?" Danny stood and gave me a hug.

My eyes didn't leave Mage's. I saw his feathers get ruffled and his expression said he didn't know whether to tell me to fuck off, or to sock Danny in the mouth for touching me. Before the night got any uglier, I pulled away from Danny and smiled at Mage. Danny looked puzzled and then turned to look at Mage. Then back at me.

"Oh. You two apparently know each other. Awesome. I'm just going to play some piano here." He looked between the two of us again and carefully sat down at the piano as if he were trying to avoid breaking his grandmother's china.

Tired of this face-off, I moved into his space. "You were great tonight. I'm sorry I was late."

He frowned and stepped away from me to put the stand-up bass back in its case. I stood there feeling dumb.

Mage handled the instrument with so much care. He wiped down the wood and frets with a cloth and then placed the bow lovingly inside before closing the lid. He snapped the closures and then paused, taking a deep breath.

He walked right past me.

Even though he hadn't spoken, I followed. I intended to stick with him, whether he wanted me there or not, until I had a chance to talk.

He gave a wave to the valet and then walked toward my car. He still didn't speak a word.

"Mage?" I couldn't stand it, even though I knew I needed to take his silent treatment.

"The others are staying at the hotel tonight. I want to go back to the mansion. Will you come with me?" He still wouldn't look at me. I was beginning to believe words weren't going to fix this.

"I'll go anywhere with you."

He nodded and walked around to let me into the driver's side, and then he took the passenger seat. He reminded me how to get up to the house and then fell silent. I drove cautiously up the narrow drive. I pulled up out front and followed him inside. He led me up to his bedroom, which was a simple room in what he had told me used to be the maids' quarters. There was a comfy chair in front of a window and a double bed in the middle of the room. By this time I was so tired, it was all I could do to keep putting one foot in front of the other. He seemed just as weary.

He shut the door behind him and walked past me, unbuttoning his shirt. He sat in the chair and kicked off his shoes. He unbuttoned his slacks but made no move to remove them.

"I'm all over the place tonight," he said quietly, his stern green-eyed gaze burning through me. I felt awful that he was so unsettled because of me.

"That's okay. I can go if you want—"

He stood quickly, as if he wanted to say something important, but the words wouldn't come. Then he just scowled. His expression might have caused me to flee, if I couldn't sense that inside he was hurt and angry. I sensed he felt rejected, and that a huge injustice had been done. He really was all over the place, and I couldn't do a damn thing about it except...

"Can I just...?" I remembered what he said to me our first night together. "Just say I can be with you, that I can be near you as much as you'll let me? I've got it bad for you." I smiled nervously and prayed he'd remember.

He studied me for a long time before he grunted. He slid his slacks off, revealing silk boxers. He lifted the covers and slid across the bed to the side nearest the wall. There, he just stared at me.

"Do you want me to explain?"

He shook his head and closed his eyes. "Just get in here." He had a crease between his eyebrows from frowning. I could feel his anger slowly begin to dissipate. I was still standing in my leggings and blouse and wanted to be comfortable if I was in for it. I started to peel my pants off and sucked in a breath when I remembered my cut-up legs.

"Mage? Do you guys have any Band-Aids or anything?" I winced at the feel of my skin coming away with the shredded material.

"What the fuck happened?"

"Oh this? Just a run-in with the police. No biggie."

He threw the covers off and jumped out of bed. "Are you ok? Chère?" He swung me up in his arms and carried me down the hall to the bathroom. I squealed the whole way.

"Put me down! I just fell, that's all! I'm fine."

He sat me on the counter and knelt in front of me. He playfully slapped at my hands when I tried to take a washcloth from him. He pulled out a first-aid kit and then thoroughly cleaned my scrapes, carefully placing a large bandage over the parts that were still bleeding.

"Thank you," I whispered when he'd finished. He stood and wrapped his arms around me, pulling me to his chest. I melted against him, so happy to be close to him again.

"I missed you," he said against my hair. "My heart hurts when I'm away from you, but dammit, chère. What happened? What did I do?"

I pulled back. "It wasn't you. I've been writing. About what happened. And then my mom... I'm trying to—"

"I know. I could feel you were dealing with something heavy. I'm trying to be patient. I'm just not. I mess with Jade all the time because he's Mr. Instant Gratification. Now I get it. Since I've found you, I just..."

"I can feel you, too. I know. I'm sorry you found me and I'm such a mess."

His hands came up to my face and his thumbs caressed my cheekbones. There were so many things I wanted to say to him. I just couldn't find the words. Somehow he knew. He inhaled deeply and let it out, resignation on his face.

"Somehow, someday, we are going to meet on solid ground, chère. It's going to happen. Just not tonight, I'm afraid."

I hated this! I hated all of this strife that was still messing with my well-being. I wanted to be free to give myself to him, not held back by wrongs done to me by other men. I was better, but not there, and Mage, with all of his intuition, could tell. He was trying to be patient with me, but neither of us liked it.

He carried me back to his room and set me down on the bed. He handed me a t-shirt and said, "This might be more comfortable." He crawled back into bed, his weariness visible.

I thanked him and turned away to slip my blouse off and pull his shirt over me. It was long on me, falling almost to my knees. When I turned back around, he smiled up at me.

"If I can't swallow you up, I can let my clothes do it for me."

Relieved his playful side was making a showing, I crawled under the covers and curled up next to him, his arm coming around my back. My cheek fit perfectly in the depression between his pec and his shoulder.

"How did you feel about tonight?" I asked him. I knew he was tired, but I wanted him to release any stress he could before sleep.

"I really missed Maggie. I tried to feel whether she was there, but I got nothing. She was almost always with us before a show and she'd talk to me and help me get my head straight if it wasn't. I get weird about performing sometimes. If I get any sort of a negative vibe about a place, sometimes I can't shake the bad feeling. Maggie always listened to me and would take what I said and would try to fix whatever she could. I miss that. Sherry is good, but she looks at me like I'm crazy half the time, or treats me like I'm on a day pass or something."

I laughed. "Oh, I'm sure she doesn't mean it like that."

"I know she doesn't. But of all people, I would think you'd understand how it feels to have a feeling about something and those around you don't get it."

"I can totally relate. I've known Sherry for a long time. Since college. There were plenty of times when she would roll her eyes at my 'feelings'. She'd tease me when I insisted we not go to a certain place. Or when I would pick up some residual energy someplace and tell her what had happened there before, she'd tell me I was giving her the willies. I wouldn't go to the apartment she lived in right after college because there had been a horrible person who lived there before her who did things..." Ew, I totally didn't want to relive that one. I shuddered and Mage pulled me closer.

"You and I are so similar, but I'm often drawn to those negative places, not creeped out by them. I feel like if I'm there, I can kind of counteract that negative energy. Does that sound dumb? I don't know. I've never been able to explain it before. Like this place. All the noises and freaky shit that goes on, I kind of process it, I guess. I get excited by the feelings I get from the spirits, or energies, whatever you call it. I like to make it better. Does this place bother you?"

"I guess not. It's like a cleansing almost, with you. You think?"

I looked up at his face, so close to mine. I forgot what I wanted to say and desperately wanted to...

"I see you, Sammara," he whispered, his eyelids going heavy. When he spoke those words to me, I felt them. He was telling me he could see what was in my head and heart.

I refused to wait a second longer.

The moment our lips touched, I could feel him in my bones.

Something shifted in me, vibrated through me, and my fear was replaced instantly with a passion I'd never felt before. It was as if I were standing in front of a fire while someone squirted an accelerant right into the heart of the flames.

The heat rushed up around me and licked at my skin. I gasped as Mage moaned against my lips, obviously feeling it, too. Our eyes opened and so much passed between us. Communion. Understanding. Wonder.

Our bodies connected all the way to our toes. I let him know wordlessly that I needed his touch. I craved it. He knew not to take things too far, but we explored each other, bringing on something akin to a spiritual orgasm. His long curls brushed against me, making me feel more alive than ever. His strong fingers grazed the sensitive skin along the curve of my bottom before pulling my hips against his, allowing me to feel every inch of him. Flashes of our bodies entwined, naked and joined in the most intimate way, fueled my desire. I knew when we finally came together, I would completely give myself to him. I could see it happening, and though I desperately wished it could happen tonight, we both knew this wasn't our time.

We had more wounds to heal and he had commitments that would keep us apart geographically. But after tonight, there was no doubt in my mind that all he'd been saying, all his talk about finding his wife, he knew what he was talking about.

I just hoped I could be everything he wanted me to be.

# Twelve

I tried to sit up but something was crushing me. I wiggled my shoulders, trying not to panic. I didn't know where I was, and when I heard moaning behind me, that was it. I shoved hard and then dove off the other side of the bed. I heard a grunt as a body hit the floor on the opposite side.

"What the fuck?"

I peeked over the top of the mattress and saw Mage rubbing his head.

"I'm so sorry," I said. It started to come back to me: the show, chasing after Mage, the police—

"You ok, chère? You have a bad dream?" He was so sweet and looked so worried.

"Just disoriented. I'm sorry. Did you hit your head?"

"Yeah, but this skull can take a lot of damage."

I smiled, but still didn't move. I could only see his eyes on the other side of the bed and the top of his head. His curly hair was wild this morning, his eyes puffy from sleep. I knew I looked a fright. I tried to smooth down my hair.

"Did you sleep at all?" I asked, trying to diffuse the awkwardness.

"I slept great until an earthquake knocked me on my ass. Or was that you?"

I giggled. "I'm sorry. I woke up and didn't know where I was. You were kind of squishing me." He rested his forearms on the side of the bed and laid his chin on top.

"Squishing you? I thought we were cuddling," he said with mock seriousness and a big pout.

"Um, cuddling is cool. As long as oxygen is involved. I wasn't exactly getting any." I was totally teasing, just peeking my eyes over the bed. He smirked deviously at me.

"Oxygen is overrated, chère. Can we get back in bed if I promise to let you breathe?"

I raised an eyebrow at him and he laughed.

"I feel like I'm talking to a severed head," he said. "Come back to bed."

I shook my head, feeling a little vulnerable. "Mage?"

"*Oui, mon chère*?"

Ok, that made me blush.

"You never told me your real name."

He grinned at me from across the bed. "If I tell you, will you come back to bed?"

I shrugged. "Maybe."

He frowned and that just made me laugh harder.

"Maybe, huh? All right. My real name is Mage. I had it changed legally."

I rolled my eyes at him. "Well, what was it before?"

"Are we off the record?"

I nodded, hoping I could get some more information out of him. For my own personal use, of course.

He cleared his throat. "My given name at birth was Martín LeRoy Dumas, the second. Now can we get into bed?" He sounded irritated, but he was still smiling at me, so I shook my head,

"How old are you?"

He raised an eyebrow again. "Aren't you supposed to know all this already? Where's that journalistic ambition? Don't you want to find out on your own through, like, research and stuff?"

I giggled and shook my head. "I want *you* to tell me. I want you to tell me more about you. Then it feels real, not like work."

His expression grew serious. "Then I'll tell you whatever you want to know. But can we *pleeeeeeease* get back in bed? I'm freezing and my tushy is sore from falling off the bed."

He started to stand up, so I mirrored him. We lifted back the covers at the same time, then moved in synchronicity until we were lying on our sides facing each other with about two feet between us. We were quiet for a few beats before he said, "Hi."

"Hi. This is better."

He smiled and it made me want to just melt into him. He was stunning. His bright green eyes were wide with curiosity. "What else do you want to know?"

"You didn't tell me how old you are."

"Why do you want to know that?"

I shrugged. "I don't know. Because when you get to know someone, you ask questions like that." All of the phone calls we'd had were short and usually about what we were doing, some strange questions and just silence. We hadn't had the time to get to know the little things about each other. I intended to go no further without knowing more of the basics.

"There're no rules here, sugar. We can do whatever we want. Don't nobody know what we're talking about or what we're doing in here." Mage slipped into his New Orleans accent, which was different from the boys' Cajun drawl. I knew he was biracial and suddenly I had so many questions about his formative years.

"Did you prefer living in Houma or in Tremé? I mean, where does your soul call home? Where's your happy place?"

Mage rested his head on his hand. He looked like a damn model with his ludicrous sensuality. His dark brown curls spread around his shoulders. His chest was bare—*really* bare, as in he wasn't wearing a shirt and he had no chest hair. He didn't seem to have much body hair at all. His eyes were droopy and a lazy smile played on his full, dark brown lips.

"Houma was fun because it was me and the boys. It was about making my own thing, you know? I wasn't in my daddy's shadow no longer and I could make music how I pleased. But as far as my home? It'll always be New Orleans. The bulk of my family is there. I learned how to make music, how to live it, from my daddy, my uncles, and others we played with. It was in my blood growing up. I had no choice. It wasn't like I wanted to fight it neither." He rubbed absently at his chest over his heart. I got distracted by his long fingers...

"Where is your daddy? Do you talk to him? Are you close?"

He swallowed hard and I watched as his Adam's apple bobbed. "Not really. I didn't see him for a long time after we moved. Years. He knew where I was but he was so pissed at my mama for not coming with him when he left, he stayed gone. Then when the band got big, he got a little competitive with me, said I'd never be the musician he was. Put down our music. It really bothered me because that's not what our family is about, feel me? It's about loving each other and supporting each other no matter what path the person decides to take. My gran, his mama, she's the one I stay with when I go back. She's the best. I spent most of my time with her as a child. Until we moved."

"How about your mama? Is she still in Houma?"

He laughed. "Yeah. She still works as a nurse, busting her ass taking care of people. She's one of those people who's never quite happy and thinks everyone else should be bitter like her. I visit her when I'm back and I send her money, but she has a hard time congratulating me on my success. She thinks what we do isn't work and therefore isn't being productive, make sense?"

It sure did, but it sucked. "I hate it for you," I muttered, but he shushed me.

"Nah, chère. It's all good. I had my gran and my uncles and aunties all around showing me what's right. My boys and I are doing what we are meant to do. It's in the cards. This is what I was born to do and I wouldn't change a thing. Well, maybe I'd be in Hollywood longer than a couple of days this time..."

I didn't want to think about being away from him. If we really made a go of this, we were going to have to deal with being apart for long stretches potentially. The space would be good for me, but I'd go through withdrawals every time he was away. I loved his energy, got drunk on it being this near to him.

Forgetting myself, I reached for him and kissed him like last night. The energy exchange was so hot, I thought we'd set the sheets on fire. We pulled back, panting, and giggled like teenagers in the backseat of the car doing some heavy petting. If we kept this up, we'd fog the windows!

Mage smoothed my hair back and stared into my eyes, as though he was reading me. "Where does *your* soul call home?"

I felt myself frowning. "I don't know. I've felt like a drifter, like I didn't belong, ever since I left the desert. I love Hollywood, but that has more to do with the legacy of the place, of the residual energies and pure talent that has come from this place than actually enjoying living here. When it comes to people, it's so empty sometimes. I wish I had a rich cultural home like you do. I've only been to New Orleans once on an overnight. I don't know it well, but it's produced so many amazing things."

He smiled and reached for my hand. "I want to take you home with me, Sammara. I want to take you somewhere you'll feel safe. Let's go somewhere together."

My eyes went wide with panic. I was certainly more comfortable with him and where we were going, but what was he asking me for? I wanted to be with him, but I wasn't ready to take—

"I see you, Sammara. I can feel an epic freak-out coming on, but just listen to me. I feel connected to you and I care about you. I thought at one point you might feel the same for me and then everything got in the way. Give me another shot, darlin'. Let me help ease your pain."

Could I run away with Mage? Would he be as gentle with me? Would he tolerate my "stuff"?

"What are you thinkin'?" he finally asked me, seeming a little impatient.

"I'm thinking this is crazy...but I want to. I'm just afraid."

"No, Sammara. No being afraid. I just want to spend time with you. Nothing has to come of us taking a trip together except spending time together, getting to know each other, and exploring this connection. Maybe we'll turn out to be the best of friends. Maybe we'll fall in love. Maybe you'll leave me on the side of the road because I drive you crazy."

I couldn't help but laugh, thinking if I didn't trust him like I did, his crazy talk *might* just make me leave him on the side of the road.

"So where do we go? When? How?" I asked, laughing nervously. "I don't know that I can just pick up and leave. I do have a job."

"We can go anywhere you want, darlin', and as much as I want to take you home with me, I'm thinking that trip to the desert might just be what you need. Get in touch with your inner child. Maybe we can find that place you grew up. Let's just go!"

His expression, and his charisma convinced me.

We hurriedly dressed, he threw some things in a bag and we left a note for the guys so they would know Mage made it back ok and wouldn't worry. We planned as we went: Swing by my place long enough for me to pack a bag, call the magazine, telling them a slight fib, that I had a story I was working on, and hit the road.

The trip would take about two and a half hours, according to the navigation system in my Ford Escape and it was nearing noon when we left Hollywood. I called my grandmother to ask once more if there was any word from mom. She told me my mother had sent a postcard from Indio. It could have either been a diversion or she was really here. The card had simply said, "I'm fine. I'm not coming back. Please tell Sammara that I love her." Mage let me drive, but he insisted on being the DJ. I got quite a musical education as he played me everyone from Allen Toussaint, to Dr. John, to the Rebirth Brass Band from his iPod. He talked about how his daddy played with all of them at one point.

"He was a street musician at the start, and I was gonna be just like him. Mama wasn't havin' it. I still resent her for taking me away sometimes, but it was meant to be."

"I resent a lot about my childhood, but what's done is done. I just had to deal with it until I was old enough to get out of the house. My grandparents were super strict fundamentalists. They don't approve of my ways. I'm okay with that now. I don't need their approval, but it's hard to be around them. And my mom..."

I told Mage more of the story about my mom and the ranch. He seemed just as puzzled.

"Did she ever talk about finding anyone from her past? Do you remember any names? Do you think it's possible she connected with someone in Indio?"

I shook my head. "I only remember the name of the place. The desert rose oasis." Mage frowned when he heard the name, but didn't say anything.

We arrived late in the afternoon after hitting some traffic. Just as the sun was starting to fall over the Santa Rosa Mountains, we pulled up to the small inn Mage had found online. It looked clean from the outside and relatively uninhabited. I pulled the car into a spot near the office.

"I'll check us in. Do you want me to get two rooms, chère? I'd like to sleep in a separate bed in a shared room, but if you would rather—"

"One room is fine. Two beds, please." He was being so thoughtful. I hated that I couldn't just give in to my wishes, but I didn't want whatever might happen to be tainted by my past.

Mage strolled casually towards the door of the office. I watched him in the rearview as he held the door open for an elderly couple. The woman smiled at him and he nodded back. I loved watching him interact with other people, and especially their reactions to him. He was so polite, so handsome, and everyone he came in contact with seemed to pick up on that, despite his rocker appearance.

I was a little weirded out about going there, but he thought we could cruise by, see what was going on, "do a little recon", and then go back tomorrow if need be. Then we could look around for my mom

Our relationship was strange, mine and my mother's. I bore no ill feelings for her. I learned soon after she came to live with us that she was not going to be a loving, doting mother, and I accepted it. She refused to talk about the Mother. While she was supportive of my writing, she would caution me to be careful. "*There's so much sin and temptation in that work, Sammara. In that lifestyle. Be careful it doesn't overwhelm you. Forget your past. It can only hurt you.*"

I strongly disagreed. My worship of the Mother had been the only thing to keep me sane over the years, and as an adult, I took pleasure in being able to practice freely.

I told myself I just needed to see her in the flesh and make sure she was okay, but I had a feeling that seeing her again after several years was going to bring up new issues.

When Mage returned to the car with our room keys, he suggested we have a late lunch and then drive out to the ranch where I'd grown up. He led me down to the end of the row of single-story rooms. The place looked like it had gotten a fresh coat of paint not too long ago and the landscaping was maintained very well. I was relieved the room didn't reek of mildew or cigarette smoke. We dropped our bags on the floor and looked at each other.

"You ready?" He must have picked up on my hesitation. I smiled up at him, enjoying the way the sun shone behind him, illuminating his skin. I wanted to touch him but I needed to not send him mixed signals. Too much touching would do just that.

# Thirteen

We opted for Mexican food, his favorite since spending time in California, and we both ate until we were ready to burst. The older woman who ran the place was determined to stuff us to the max. She kept bringing more chips, guacamole, tortillas... Mage finally put his hands out and begged her to stop, groaning in pleasure and pain.

A lone guitarist came strolling through the place, singing and strumming his guitar. His voice was so tender as it soared to hit some powerful notes. A young girl followed behind him with a bucket filled with roses, stopping at each table and offering them for purchase.

Mage waved her over and handed her a wad of twenties. "I'll take the whole bunch of them."

Her eyes bugged out as she reached for the money with a shaky hand. She put it slowly into her pocket, watching Mage's reaction the whole time. He winked at her and then she started giggling. She handed him an armload of red roses wrapped in plastic.

"Thank you, chère," he said with a drop-dead sexy smile. She picked up her bucket and skipped back over to the man playing guitar, who smiled and nodded to us.

"That was very sweet of you. I hope you like roses," I joked.

He shrugged. "I thought I would spread the petals all over my bed tonight and roll around in them."

I burst out laughing so hard, every patron in the restaurant turned to stare.

"Sorry," I squeaked out, and then covered my face. Mage gave a good belly laugh and then pulled my hands away.

"Red roses look beautiful against your skin. Maybe we'll put them in *your* bed."

I shivered at the thought of being bathed in rose petals. It might seem cliché, but I could imagine the scent and the feel would be—

"Sammara? Did you hear what I said?" He was trying hard not to laugh.

"I'm sorry. I was swimming in rose petals."

"Yeah, well, I couldn't resist her cute little face. Isn't she cute?" he asked, resting his chin on his hand.

"I guess. I didn't realize you liked such younger women. It's a shame I'm older than you."

"Are you now?" he asked. "That's interesting. Not settled down yet, though. You want kids, Sammara?"

I tried to mask my shuddering. "Kids? Kids scare the hell out of me. They're kind of creepy."

His dreamy look was gone. He actually looked disappointed.

"What's wrong?" I asked him, confused.

"Nothing. Just not the answer I was hoping for."

I raised an eyebrow at him. "What do you mean? Kids? I don't know. I haven't really been in a position to consider them. It's not like I want to be a single mom, you know? That didn't work out real well for my mother." I looked out the window, disturbed to be talking about this.

"Yeah. I wouldn't want that for you. It was real hard on my mama. C'mon," he said, standing from the table. He held his hand out to me. "Let's get out of here while we still have light. I want to watch the sun go down with you."

Could he be any more romantic? His mood had shifted from gloomy to excited, just like that. I hated to think that I'd disappointed him, but we were honest with each other. That's what we agreed on, and that's what I needed.

He paid for dinner despite my insistence that we split this trip. I sulked out to the car, but it was hard to sulk when the aroma from the flowers invaded my senses. I held them to my face and breathed in the scent.

"Do you like them, chère? Really?"

All I could do was nod up at him. He stepped close to me and brushed my hair back behind my ear.

"I love them. Thank you."

His eyes searched mine and then he nodded. "Let's go."

The drive to the ranch was quiet. I'd done some research and located where I thought it might be. It was quite far outside of town, about an hour's drive. We passed horse ranches and date palm fields until we were driving into nothing. The sunset was breathtaking. All of the colors tumbled down the mountainside onto the sand dunes, making it look like small fires dotted the landscape.

"I think we just turn up ahead," he said, looking down at the map on my phone. We drove down a barely paved road and bumped along for about another quarter of a mile before seeing a large cinderblock house sprawled out behind some brush. The sign said, "desert rose oasis."

I stopped the car about a hundred yards from where a few others were parked. It took a few beats before I was completely overwhelmed with memories. They hit me like a warm breeze, taking me so by surprise that I gasped.

"Mage," I breathed. I looked at him and his eyes were intense.

"This is the place, isn't it? Makes sense. Your scent. You always smell like roses to me..."

I nodded, blushing slightly.

He gazed out the windshield and blew out a breath. "I know this place. It's a recording studio now, Sammara. Scott Cross told me about it. Is this the place you grew up?"

"It has to be. Why else would I be feeling these things?" He took my hand in his and I breathed in deep. Beyond the rose scent coming from the backseat was the smell of smoke. By this time it was getting later and the sky was starting to reveal the glittering stars from within the deep blue. I opened my door and climbed out, wanting to feel the last of the day's heat on my face. Mage got out on his side and walked around behind me. He wrapped me in his arms and brushed his chin against my hair.

"It's amazing here. Desolate, but not lonely. Sammara?"

I turned in his arms and looked up into his face. "Yes, Mage?" I felt safe in this place. Close to this man. He smiled down at me and did that thing again where he nuzzled my cheek with his nose. I relaxed against him.

"Let's go check this place out."

I glanced up at him, still a little unsure about this idea. "Okay. Hold my hand?"

He took my hand in his, raised it to his lips to kiss, and said, "Always, chère."

I wanted to just stay there and get lost in his eyes. The dramatic desert sunset and his handsome face were intoxicating. Before I could stop myself, I pushed up on my toes and pressed my lips against his.

Mage pulled back, startled. "Sammara—"

"Come back here. I'm not done yet." I snaked my hand into his hair and pulled him closer to me. His hand braced against my hip as he let me explore. His full lips were so luscious. I sucked the top one into my mouth and nibbled, causing him to groan. I think he cursed, but I was too involved in my activity to care. I was bombarded by all kinds of emotions I assumed were coming from him. Lust, frustration, excitement, concern...

And love.

I pulled back as that emotion came to the forefront. It caressed me like the warm desert breeze that skirted my shoulders and tousled my hair.

Mage's breathing was shaky as I smiled up at him. "I'm sorry, but I'm not sorry. I needed to do that." I felt like a doe-eyed girl, full of wonder about this man.

"I'm not sorry, either. It was nearly perfect."

"Nearly?" I asked with a frown.

"Nearly. Perfect would have been like this." His arms came around me and crushed me to him.

I surrendered to his passion and released my fear. Nothing could hurt me while I was in his arms. He kissed me desperately, moaning softly. He maneuvered me against the car and pressed his body to mine. His lips devoured then caressed gently, the sensation a bit like what I imagined his lovemaking would be. His tongue demanded my compliance. I frantically pulled at his hair and pushed up on my toes to get even closer. His hands slid down to grip my hips tight, pulling me against him...

Then he grunted.

"Sammara," he whispered. We were both panting, completely overcome by the magic surrounding us. Only the slightest wisp of pink lingered in the sky. Stars were visible everywhere. The world around us was silent but for a dog barking somewhere in the distance and the approaching clop-clop of a horse.

Mage's gaze darted towards the side of the sprawling house and he smiled. "We've got company."

An older man dressed in flannel plaid and jeans approached us on a huge black horse.

"You kids lost?"

Mage had a sudden look of recognition. "Actually, no," he said. "I'm here to see Robin? Scott Cross said he might be out here."

"I'm Robin. Who might you two be?"

Mage approached him, leading me by my hand, and stretched his other out to the man.

"Mage. My band is Maggie's Bones? We've been recording with Scott and he told me about this place. We just wanted to come by and check it out. This is Sammara."

The man smiled as he shook Mage's hand and nodded to me. "Why don't you two follow me? We were just about to have a BBQ. My partner and I have some friends over, but you're welcome to join us." His eyes lingered on me a little, almost as if he was trying to place me. I clutched Mage a little tighter and let him lead me towards the house. I tugged on his hand, trying to communicate my confusion as to how he suddenly knew this place.

"It just came to me," he whispered. He just shrugged with a goofy smile and kept on walking.

Robin tied his horse to an old fashioned post out front that resembled something out of the old west. In fact, the whole outside of the house looked like the set of a Spaghetti Western. A wagon wheel with succulents planted all around it stood next to the iron gate. A bare tree had bottles hung from its many branches and they tinkled faintly in the breeze. Robin gestured for us to follow him inside the house.

My heart thudded to a stop in my chest as I crossed the threshold.

I was overwhelmed with memories. Running through the house in a patchwork dress someone made for me. Leaping over guitars and microphone cords. Hiding inside cabinets while men and women danced and sang and had sex with each other. Following the rituals to worship the Mother with my own mother under a starlit sky like the one above us right now. Being happy. Being at peace. Then being frightened.

"Sammara," Mage whispered worriedly.

I turned to him, my eyes wide, and swallowed back a sob. "I'm scared," I whispered.

He watched me closely and I prayed the man wasn't paying attention.

"Young lady, you look like you've seen a ghost," another man said as he entered the room to stand next to Robin. "Babe, you didn't tell me we had guests."

Robin smiled at him and kissed his cheek. "This is Mage, he's a friend of Scott Cross, and his lady friend is—

"Sammara."

I thought maybe her voice was a hallucination. I turned toward the doorway leading to another part of the house and gasped when I saw my mother. I couldn't believe she was really here. I was sure it was just another memory, and I didn't want the men to think I was crazy if I responded to her.

"Sammara? Darling? How did you find me?" It was then I noticed her mostly gray hair and the different clothes. Mother in my dreams dressed like a hippie—long wavy black hair past her breasts, crocheted halter tops, floral corduroy pants or long peasant skirts. This vision before me had shorter hair and was plainly dressed in jeans and a tank top.

"Mom," I squeaked out as she approached me. She placed her hands on my shoulders and smiled before pulling me into a tentative hug.

"Sammara, you look so beautiful. How did you find this place?"

"I thought...I mean, I remembered."

"Sandie?" Another man, this one a giant with a bushy gray beard and wild hair, stepped up behind Mother in a leather vest and dirty jeans. Mom smiled at him and let go of me. Luckily, Mage pulled me back against him so I didn't panic.

"Oliver, this is my daughter, Sammara. Do you remember her?"

The man stared at me, his eyes narrowed. "She looks dead-on like my mother, Sandie. But you never said—"

"Oliver—"

"How about you all come out back and have some food? Sounds like there's a lot to discuss. Sandie? Will you help me bring out the trays?"

She looked to Robin and his partner and smiled. "Yes, of course, Laramie. Sammara, why don't you and your friend go out back with Oliver? I'll be right there."

Oliver was staring at me with a curious smile. Mother had never said who my father was. All I could gather from my grandparents was that it could have been any of the men living at the commune at the time. But Oliver seemed to think I belonged to him. I could feel his excitement growing at the thought I just might be his daughter.

My feet refused to move. Mage stumbled when I stopped walking and bumped into me.

"You okay, chère?"

I felt the edges of my vision go a little dark and I freaked out, thinking a panic attack was about to come on. I shook my head to clear it and took a deep breath. I was not about to lose it now that I was so close to getting some answers.

"Not really, but I need to do this," I said quietly, just for his ears. He turned me to look at him and lifted my chin with a finger.

"I'm here for you, Sammara. If you want to leave at any time...if you feel uncomfortable..."

"Thanks." I took one more deep breath and tried to smile for him.

He nodded and pulled me in for a hug. "I'm so proud of you," he whispered against my ear.

Oliver cleared his throat. "I'm sorry if I upset you, Sammara, it's just—"

"Yeah," I answered him with a shy smile. "It's a lot to take in."

He smiled and I searched my memory to try to place him. I didn't remember anyone looking like him, but that was so long ago. We followed him out to a terrace that had different furniture than I remembered. I was hit with a memory of riding a tricycle back here.

"You used to tear up this yard, little one," Oliver said. "You damn near ran over my feet several times with that little trike."

I stared up at him, wide-eyed. "How did you know I was thinking of that?"

"I can read you, darlin'. Where do you think you got your gifts from?"

Whoa. This just kept getting weirder. I glanced at Mage. He was staring coolly at Oliver, as though he didn't know if he could trust him.

We sat down around a fire pit on some worn outdoor wicker furniture with faded cushions. Robin, his Laramie, and Mother came out with trays of food. It looked like Oliver was manning the grill.

"We're making chicken and tofu burgers. I hope you two are hungry." Mom was so different. Her shoulders didn't hunch over and she didn't seem afraid of her shadow. The last time I'd seen her was when I'd gone home to visit for my grandparents' $50^{th}$ wedding anniversary. Her hair had been stringy and flat, she'd been too thin, and she'd been so quiet. She'd only given one-word answers when spoken to, and had hidden in her room as soon as she was no longer needed for the party.

This Sandie was playful with her male friends. She smiled lovingly at Oliver. He was very gentle with her, touching her affectionately and laughing when she spoke. We each doctored up our plates and went back to sit on the cushions. Mage pulled me in close to him and Mom sat on Oliver's lap. He kissed her briefly and she stuck a chip in his mouth.

"How did this happen, Mom? Why did you just take off?"

"Oliver found me. He'd been out of prison for a few years and was waiting until he was off parole to come find me. You know I didn't have any kind of life with your grandparents, Sam. I'd been lost for so long. Oliver convinced me to come back here with him. Laramie inherited this place from his uncle. Do you remember Uncle George?"

"I think so," I murmured, feeling so overwhelmed. "But what about the bank?"

Mom's smile faltered and I saw Oliver squeeze her hand. "I don't know what you've been told, but I was fired. I didn't do anything. Which is *why* I got fired," she said with a humorless laugh.

"Her boss was sexually harassing her," Laramie growled. "That bastard. He told her if she didn't have sex with him, he would fire her."

"Mom! Is that true? Did you report him?"

She shook her head and smiled sadly. "No. I'd been short on my drawer once and he told me they'd bring me up on criminal charges if I told anyone. I didn't want to go back to jail. I was lucky they'd even hired me at all."

Goddess, the two of us had both been victims of predators. Sadly, Mom's history put her in a very difficult place to complain. It just wasn't right.

"How did you get hired at the bank with your record?"

Oliver looked irritated that Robin was asking the question. It pleased me to see him being protective of her.

"They cleaned my record when I agreed to testify. I got time served and they said as long as I met with my probation officer regularly for a period of time, they'd wipe it off my record." She looked down at her hands. Oliver squeezed her.

"You did what you had to do, love. None of us here blame you."

"Yeah, but what about Rhoda and Barb? Frank and Gary? They spent a long time—"

"Because they chose to bring drugs into our home. We had something beautiful here," Laramie said. He appeared to be only a little older than me, but I couldn't be sure. I didn't remember him from my childhood.

"Laramie was away at college when you were a child. He grew up here, too."

Okay, Oliver was creeping me out a little. Now I could see how others felt around *me*.

"You knew she was thinking that?" Mage asked, surprised.

I turned and looked at him. "You, too?"

He shrugged. I knew he was really attuned to me. I just wasn't used to being around others like me.

"Okay, kids, let's let Sammara relax and get used to us a bit," Laramie said kindly. He was very handsome and well-built in his stark white t-shirt and jeans. Robin appeared to be a bit older than him, but was equally good-looking, if a little more rugged. The two of them sat together, always touching somehow.

"Robin? Were you here before? When I lived here?"

He shook his head. "I met Laramie in college. We came back afterwards, after everyone was gone. It took us a long time to fix the place back up. We invited some of our musician friends to come stay here and we rebuilt the studio Uncle George had set up. We stay pretty busy now. Oliver came to stay with us and helped out. Now he's our sound man, handyman...well, pretty much our manly man," he chuckled.

"Yeah, because I certainly can't swing a hammer," Laramie joked. "But I can produce the shit out of some amazing music." He and Robin had finished eating and were now cuddling on their section of the couch.

Mage started asking questions about their studio and I got a little lost listening to his voice. I sank back against his chest and his arms came around me. I had so much to process, but for now, I intended to bask in the warmth he was sending my way.

Mom kept glancing nervously at me. I offered her a tense smile and she looked away. I knew this was hard for her. She never meant for my childhood to turn out the way it did. It was just unfortunate. Life was good for her, until it wasn't, and then she was tied to the situation when it went bad. I had to remember she was young, too. She'd only been seventeen when she became pregnant with me.

"Sammara, will you take a walk with me?" she asked, bringing me out of my thoughts. Mage gave me a protective squeeze. I smiled at him, so happy he was here with me and curious as to why he had been put in my life at this particular time. The Mother was certainly looking out for me.

Mom stood and I followed her down some steps leading away from the terrace. It was really dark out here, but she seemed to know where she was going. I could hear the men talking behind us, their voices growing fainter and fainter.

About a hundred yards from the house was a clearing with another fire pit in the ground, this one not lit. There were benches around. Five of them. They surrounded a pentagram made of stones with the fire in the center. My breath caught in my chest as I stepped closer to the star. There was a strong presence here, one that tickled my memory.

Mom opened a box and took out a lighter. The fire pit had already been prepared. She lit the tinder and it ignited rapidly. The warmth from the flames rushed over me and I felt my body relaxing. It was so good to let go of some of the awful tension I'd been carrying around. She walked to each of the five corners and lit candles at each point. Soon the area was brightly lit around us. Mom chanted as she moved from corner to corner, burning sage.

"Will you pray with me? It's been a really long time." She held out her hand to me. It had been so long...I felt a pull towards her. She began to disrobe and I followed her lead. We set our clothes outside the star and knelt before the fire, holding hands. I let Mom lead us. My heart swelled. Tears streamed down my face as I listened to her familiar voice. Prayers said together like this as a child were some of my best memories of our time here. She spoke to the Mother of peace and forgiveness. I let the spirit flow through me and tried to let go of all the pain and hurt I felt about our history together.

"Mom," I whispered to her when she was quiet. She turned to me and held out her arms.

"Sammara, can you ever forgive me for the life I cursed you to? I never intended for our lifestyle to affect you as it did. And I'm sorry I wasn't braver when it came to standing up to your grandparents. I was so afraid they would take you away from me if I didn't obey their wishes. I didn't want to lose you, baby."

"I think I knew that. I was never angry, just confused. Mom? Is Oliver my father?

She smiled at me with a faraway look in her eyes. "I'm not a hundred percent sure, but I've always hoped so. There were a couple of other men I was intimate with around that time... You remember what the nights were like."

Boy, did I. It wasn't until I went to regular school and started hearing kids talk about sex that I understood what I'd seen. It just seemed so natural. No one ever touched the kids at the ranch. There were a couple of others around my age, and we would just sleep all together when the adults were "worshipping."

"I don't know how to feel about all of this," I whispered aloud.

Mom smiled and squeezed my hand. "Oliver sure seems to think you're his daughter. He's a good man, Sammara. He wasn't involved with the bad stuff. When the others came and brought the drugs, Uncle George was too old and sickly to do anything about it. Laramie's other uncle, Drew, was the ringleader. He and his partners moved onto the property in trailers and ran electricity from the house out to their lab. When the cops came, they didn't care who was living where. Oliver and I were pretty exclusive by then. We talked about leaving, but Oliver was trying to save up enough money doing odd jobs in town. He kept us away from the drama for the most part, until it was too late."

I had wanted to ask her about what happened for so long. I hoped now she would give me more answers and it seemed like she was willing to talk.

"I never regretted how you raised me, Mom. I only had good memories of this place. Until the police came. That was scary. It was hard pretending to be what Grandma and Grandpa wanted me to be, but I knew I just had to hold on until I could leave for college."

Mom wiped at her eyes and smiled. "I'm glad you held on to what was important to you. I was a shell for so long. I was weak."

"You seem happy now," I offered, hoping I was right.

"I am. I worried Oliver hated me. But when he found me and made contact, it was like a day hadn't passed. We're planning to stay here for a bit, and then we may travel. He's an electrician and can get work anywhere. We're thinking about it."

I thought that sounded sweet, the two of them living like bohemians on the road.

"I just want you to be happy, Mom."

"I want the same for you," she said. Her eyes looked toward the house. "Does this young man make you happy?"

How did I explain this so it made sense? "We've had a bit of a rocky start, but I care about him a lot. He sure has some wild ideas, though. He seems to think we are fated to be together. He says he's been searching for me, that he dreamed about me. I don't know how I feel about that. What if I'm not what he's looking for? I don't want him to realize that someday and then bail." I had so many reasons to be afraid of being involved with him. They went away when he held me, but when I was out of his hold, I worried.

"The Mother wouldn't have made your paths cross without a purpose. Let go of your fear and trust. It's all you can do, really, when Fate sets her sights on you."

"I'm glad I found you."

She smiled at me and pulled me into her arms. "I'm glad you found me, too."

We were still holding each other when the men came down to check on us. "Everything okay, girls?" Laramie and Robin took their shirts off as they approached.

Unsure, I moved behind Mom.

"It's okay, honey. We come here to pray often. No one will hurt you." She must have sensed my fear. She squeezed my hand against her arm and smiled at me.

"Sammara," Mage said, coming around to my side. He didn't enter the star until Mom nodded to him. I went into his arms and allowed him to support me.

"Do you want your clothes, chère?" I saw that the other men had all disrobed and were doing their own prayers to the Mother. I looked into Mage's eyes and let go of my fear. His warmth bathed me along with the heat from the fire. I felt at peace, more so than I thought possible.

He must have seen or felt the shift in my emotions. He smiled back.

"Why don't you join me?" I asked. He paused for a moment, then stood and pulled his shirt off slowly, his eyes never leaving me. I was stunned by his movements, all sleek like some sort of predator, but I didn't fear him. He unfastened his pants hesitantly. The emotions coming off of him were more determined than lust-filled. I appreciated that, but it wasn't necessary. He didn't have to worry about keeping himself in check for me. I trusted him.

Boots kicked off, he slid his pants down his legs and stood before me in the moonlight, smooth and lean. His body was as beautiful as his soul. I held my hands out to him and he entered the sacred area to stand before me.

"Mage? Do you worship the Mother?" Mom smiled at him and gave me a knowing look.

"In a manner of speaking, Ma'am. My people practice Voodoo. I'm kind of open to it all. I've done a lot of reading on Pagan religions. I find it fascinating. It's kind of like home to me."

I smiled up at him and squeezed his hand. The six of us joined hands around the fire and let its power warm us. Robin and Laramie let go first and one of them turned on a boom box. Bluesy tunes echoed through the valley as they started to swing and sway around each other, gradually disappearing into the dark around the firepit. Mom and Oliver laughed and danced together. I turned my attention back to Mage, who had a smirk on his face.

"Dance with me, pretty lady." He wrapped his arms around me and picked me up, spinning me around in circles. I laughed and threw my arms out, basking in the magical night. Our bodies cast shadows on the ground. I was riveted watching them gliding, orbiting, and swaying together. He set me down and we began to dance together. Mage's hands never left my body. I felt like the one being worshiped.

Everything else drifted away from my consciousness as I focused on the beautiful man beneath my hands. Hours passed as we talked and laughed, touched each other and danced. We reveled in the magic of the night. At some point the other couples were enveloped in the spirit and we heard hushed sounds of them making love passionately under the stars in the darkness. Mage just danced with me until our legs could no longer hold us, then he held me on his lap on a bench as we talked and talked about our dreams. I learned that Mage loved traveling best of all in his line of work. We talked about our favorite places we'd been, and the places we desired to see. I also learned that he wrote his own music, separate from the band, and planned to one day join up with some of his New Orleans family and jam together, maybe even record. He hadn't spent much time with them over the past few years, but once this album and tour cycle was finished, he was going back to Trème to recharge his batteries.

"I want you to come with me, Sammara. I want to share my home with you. I want—"

"That's months from now. We'll see where you are when that happens. I've got to get my head together and get serious about work before I lose my job. I fought hard to become a features writer and I don't intend to lose it because my mental health decided to take a little vacation."

Mage frowned at me and smoothed my hair back from my face. "Chère, your mind was just telling you it was time to stop running. Channel that pain, darlin'. Turn it into something positive, like this article you're writing. But don't throw yourself back in and forget to take care of yourself. I don't ever want to feel your pain like that again. I'll do it." He looked down at the scars on my stomach and his lips turned down in a frown and trembled. He ran his fingers lightly over them and for once I didn't feel ashamed. "I'd do anything for you, but please take care of you. You're so precious to me."

I was straddling his lap and he leaned forward and brushed kisses along my collarbone. My head fell back and I melted against him. He was being so careful with me, but I had to know...

"Mage, what is happening between us?" He kissed me once more before looking up into my eyes.

"We've made a connection, chère. One I intend to let grow between us until you aren't afraid of me. Of this. I'll wait until you can come to me freely and share yourself, body and soul."

In the light of the fire and under this magnificent sky, I felt like I could do just that, but out of the safety of this sacred place, I didn't know...

"I want that, too, Mage. But then what? What did you mean when you said you were looking for your wife? Is that what you want? A wife?"

He was trying to read me. I could feel it. He sighed heavily and I watched some very heavy weight descend on his shoulders.

"Nope. I'm not ready to go there with you. Not—"

"Come on, Mage. I want to let you in, but you need to tell me what you want."

"That's not how it works, chère. When you let me in, none of it will matter anymore. It will just be what it's meant to be. If I tell you what I saw, then you might change your mind or decide you can't live with it. I just want things to progress how they're meant to, dig? Or not. If you can't go there with me, that's okay. You're always going to hold a piece of my heart, though, woman. Whatever you decide."

My head started to spin. I suddenly felt completely drained by the past thirty-six hours. I slumped against Mage and rested my cheek on his shoulder. His arms came around me protectively. In the waning firelight, I faintly heard the others find their release together and then the magic seemed to dissipate from the night. The four of them spoke softly of their love for each other and praised the Mother.

I felt Mage shift beneath me and I sat up. "This bench has to be murder on your skin," I whispered and he chuckled.

"I may need you to pull a few splinters out of my ass." I burst out laughing, then tried to shush myself so as not to disturb the other lovers. I sighed as I noticed them getting dressed. I eased myself off of his lap, sad to lose our connection. Mage handed me my clothes and I was sorry that the night was ending like this. I wanted to be basking in post-coital bliss with him, not putting on our clothes clumsily in the dark with heavy thoughts weighing on us.

I walked over to Mom and hugged her tight. "Thank you," I whispered as she squeezed me.

"I love you, Sammara. Thank you for finding me. I hope we can talk some more. When are you leaving?"

We walked up to the house together, the men following behind and talking loudly and jovially with each other. Once inside I gave Mom my cell number and got hers.

"We haven't really made plans. I'll call you tomorrow. I mean, later today." It was already after one in the morning and the exhaustion was really beginning to hit.

"You go rest, darling. I hope you'll come and see me again." Mage hugged her goodbye as well and I heard her whisper to him to take care of me. He smiled and pressed a hand to his heart. The chivalry this man exuded was unbelievable.

I handed Mage my keys and asked if he could get us back to the hotel in one piece. "I don't think I can make it." He got me settled in the passenger seat and the next thing I knew he was him shaking me awake at our inn.

We trudged inside the room, stripped hurriedly out of our clothes and collapsed together in one of the double beds. It was a little short for him, but he curled himself around me. As soon as I stopped fidgeting, he started humming sweetly in my ear. His voice was the most soothing balm for my psyche.

My lips curled up in a smile and I kissed his bare chest where I could reach and tucked in for some much needed sleep. I faintly recalled our plan for the rose petals, but it would have to wait for another time.

# Fourteen

The next morning, I woke to find Mage sitting up on the edge of the bed staring out the window. He was motionless, his body tense. I picked up all kinds of negative thoughts and feelings coming from him. I sat up and pulled the sheet to my chest.

"What's wrong?" I asked him.

He didn't answer for a few beats. "I don't know. I just have this bad feeling."

"What did you dream?"

He looked to me sharply and frowned. "Why?"

I shrugged my shoulders. Why did it feel like he was all of a sudden wary of me? "When I wake up feeling like this it's usually because I dreamed something. Tell me."

He sighed heavily as I ran my hands down his back. I'd learned to help unblock the chakras, and I thought I would try to draw away some of his tension. I pressed my hands on the top of his head and whispered an incantation as I made my way down his back, trying to focus on drawing out his negativity. By the time I reached his root chakra, he was much more relaxed and breathing easier.

"How's that?" I asked him, leaning in to kiss his shoulder. I couldn't help it. He was so beautiful.

"You feel so good," he murmured huskily, looking over his shoulder at me. "I love how I feel when I'm near you, Sammara. But I think I need to go back. Something's not right."

We hadn't made a set plan other than visiting the ranch last night. "That's fine. I don't want to keep you," I said as I leaned over the bed to grab my shirt. As I sat up, he reached for my hand.

"Sammara, last night...this morning... Being with you here has been really special. Thank you for letting me experience it with you. I hope we can do it again. I just can't help this feeling that I need to go back." He ran his thumb over my wrist and tugged me closer. I let him pull me into an embrace, wishing we had all the time in the world.

"It's okay. I need to get back, too. I want to finish my article. Josh, my editor, he was able to get me some face time with our publisher to see if they'll pick up my story. It's not a common topic for the magazine. We're not as big as *Rolling Stone* and we haven't really had many issue-related pieces up until now. I want to push for that. My assault—well, the first one—was directly related to my job working around the music industry. And like you guys discussed, Maggie's death and her relationship with her husband...you were talking about wanting to do something for domestic violence victims... I think *Feedback* should become more aware of the issues affecting its readers."

Mage tilted his head and smiled. "I love your passion about this. You're right. There's not enough being written about those things where typical music fans are going to read about them. I think it will be great. *You'll* be great. I'd love to see this work out for you." His smile drifted off a bit and he turned back to look out the window.

"But..." I said, encouraging him to speak his mind. He seemed hesitant.

"But...I don't know. It's not the time...I shouldn't... I need to let things take their course—"

"That doesn't sit well with you."

He shook his head sadly. "I'm sorry. I shouldn't even—"

"You have to be honest with me. I'm going to know if you're not. What I don't know is what exactly you're afraid of?"

He turned to look at me and his bright green eyes had gone dark, almost hazel. His expression was heartbroken. When he spoke, his voice cracked with emotion.

"I'm afraid you're going to slip away. I'm afraid to be away from you because I want your energy. I've tried not to need it, but it's intoxicating. You make me feel whole, Sammara. And knowing I have to be away, and you have to do what you need to do...I just worry our paths are going to forever be leading away from each other. That's not what I imagined my life would be like, you know? I always just felt that when I found... I mean, when I, well...we'd just be together and that would be that. Stupid, huh?"

His attempt at a laugh just made me hurt more for him. "This connection, this whatever we have, is stronger than that. I feel you even when we're away from each other. And yes, our lives are going to keep us apart, sometimes for quite a while. But that doesn't mean we can't—"

"I know," he said softly. He reached for me and cupped my jaw in his strong hand, rubbing his thumb across my lips. "I know. Perhaps this is just a lesson for me."

"For us both." I didn't want him to think he was the only one hurting at the thought of being apart. I had always been comfortable living alone, although I wished to have a familiar. Traveling as much as I did meant that I had no right to bring an animal into my life. I just hoped I had the right to ask Mage to wait for me.

"Something is changing," he said, looking back out the window.

I felt it, too. I just hoped it was for the best.

# FIFTEEN

We cleaned up, made a stop for some breakfast, which we ate quietly, and then made the trek back to the mansion. When we arrived, Mage made no move to leave the car. He linked his fingers with mine and brought my hand up to kiss it.

"I really want to take you home with me. Will you think about coming to New Orleans? For a few days? I want to show you my home. My hometown, anyway. I'm still looking for a house. It's time for me to buy a place. I'm twenty-six years old. I should have a place to call my own, don't you think?"

"Aha! I've been *waiting* for you to tell me how old you are!" My shit-eating grin made him belly laugh.

"Huh. You got me. But I'm not allowed to ask you how old you are. I got in trouble for asking Jaylene."

I laughed. I could see that happening. "I'm not one of those women who have an issue with it. I will be thirty on the winter solstice."

His eyes flared and it seemed a bit of the darkness left them. "Blessed be, chère! I'd love to spend it with you."

The solstice was a week away. "But how will that fit into your plans? I thought you were going to New Orleans?"

"Meet me there. For the weekend. Let's celebrate you. You can stay as long or as short as you need. Just let me celebrate with you. It's a special day."

I hadn't spent my birthday with anyone since I'd left home. I hadn't made plans for this year. I had no idea what would happen if I went to New Orleans to meet him. What would he expect?

"I don't expect anything from you, Sammara, but faith. Have faith in me. I won't hurt you, and I won't let you down."

# Sixteen

## You Can't Snuff This Light

*I've always been at war with Fate. I was raised to believe first the Mother, then the Christian deity, had a plan for me. I wanted to believe things like there is someone meant just for me, that I have a purpose in this life, or that I am destined for greatness. But so many things have happened to make me question Fate. How is it possible, in any theology or spiritual belief system, to explain the horrific things that happen to good people? I've tried to live my life in the Light, therefore I was taught to believe that positive things would happen to me. After being sexually assaulted on more than one occasion, I began to hate the idea of Fate.*

*I was simply doing my job. Watching a brand new artist play at one of the hottest clubs on the Sunset Strip, I sat at the bar where I had a great view of the stage and the band's set. I did not have a great view of my glass. When a man in a suit sat next to me and introduced himself as an A&R rep for a label I was very familiar with, I thought nothing of chatting with him in between sets. After two beers, I was feeling really sick and figured I was coming down with the flu everyone at the office had succumbed to lately. A&R offered to help me out to my car, and the last thing I remembered before waking up in the parking lot at dawn the next morning was his confident, easygoing way of saying, "how much fun I'm going to have getting to know you."*

*I was so out of it when I came to, I opened the car door and vomited repeatedly onto the asphalt. He'd somehow managed to get me into the driver's seat and even took the time to belt me in.*

*I don't know exactly what happened, I don't know how long I was with him, and I never saw him again. It wasn't until I got myself back to my condo that I realized my panties were gone, my stockings had been ripped up the middle, and there was semen all over the seat.*

*I panicked. I did what every woman is taught not to do when they have been sexually assaulted. I showered and scrubbed my body down for at least an hour, I spent the rest of the weekend in bed, and I never told a soul.*

*I somehow convinced myself it hadn't happened. I was a good person. I lived my life in harmony with the earth as the Mother teaches us to, and I decided it was all a bad dream. I went back to my normal life, dating, interviewing the hottest musicians around the country, and paid my respects to the Mother daily.*

*A year later I was sitting at another bar, seeing another promising new artist, and chatting with a group of executives from another label. Just part of the job, nothing out of the ordinary. One of the men was very interested in an article I'd written the previous month for this magazine, and I was having a wonderful time rehashing the trip I'd taken to London to write the piece. When he asked me to step outside with him so he could have a smoke, I agreed, thinking I could use some fresh air myself.*

*As soon as I stood from the bar, I stumbled. The man told me to lean on him to get me outside but I felt faint. I grabbed the bar to steady myself and thought this whole scene was feeling eerily familiar. The bartender, a woman I'd met several times, came around the bar and grabbed me by the arm. She dragged me to the back office.*

*"You've been roofied," she said to me, and started to call 9-1-1. I stopped her.*

*"I have no idea who it could have been," I told her. "I don't want to*

*cause any problems," I said, feeling foolish that I'd been victimized again. I thanked her profusely for stepping in. By this time I was so woozy I knew I couldn't drive. She had one of the bouncers carry me to her car, she drove me to my house, and she stayed with me that night to assure herself that I would be okay. I've seen her several times since that night, but we never talked about it again.*

*After those two experiences, I got smarter. I never accept drinks from anyone but a female bartender. I always hold my drink in my hand in front of me, and I limit my conversations with people at the bar. I figured I must have done something wrong, something hurtful, to have been victimized not once, but twice. I chalked it up to some bad karma and continued putting one foot in front of the other.*

*People often say "the third time's the charm." For me, it was more like "enough's enough."*

*When a man I'd been dating a short time showed his true colors and didn't want to take "no" for an answer, I was clearheaded enough to fight him and got away with only scratches and bruises.*

*This time I called the police and told them firmly that I wanted to press charges. They took pictures of my injuries, of the bruises on my neck, forearms, and thighs. They took hair and skin samples from under my fingernails and documented the scratches I'd inflicted on my violent paramour as evidence. I gave them my ripped clothing and the pewter candlestick holder I'd used to hit him over the head, ending his assault. I did everything right this time. I felt stronger, no longer like a victim. Until they let him go. And then he began stalking me.*

*I filed for a restraining order and had him served. They told me I was safe, that he couldn't hurt me again. However, by now, you can imagine my trust and belief in Fate is bruised and battered.*

*I still want to believe there are good people out there and not every man is a potential rapist. I want to believe in true love and destiny. I just happen to live in a world where bad things happen to good people and those good people must fight back and grow stronger. Perhaps by making me a journalist and endowing me with ambition and drive, Fate put me here to fight back on behalf of others who have been victimized.*

*Fate doesn't cause bad things to happen to people; it gives us the power to turn that ugliness into strength and courage. It doesn't make us victims;*

*it empowers us to fight for what we believe to be right and true. And that is where I begin...*

"Jesus, Sammara," Josh said, wiping his eyes. His chin trembled as he enfolded me in his lanky embrace and held me for a long time.

"You are the strongest person I know," he whispered, kissing my hair.

I leaned back and smiled at him. "Do you think they'll print it? Will they accept it?"

He frowned down at me. "We're about to find out. Come on."

He grabbed me by the hand and clenched my masterpiece in his fingers. We went down the hall to the office of the publisher and Josh spoke briefly with his assistant. She phoned his office and hung up with a confused stare.

"He'll see you both."

Josh thanked her. My head was spinning. I didn't think we'd be presenting it today!

Josh pushed through the double doors and into the sleek office of Norman Brantley.

"What do you have for me that's so important it can't wait until our next meeting?" he asked Josh, barely covering his irritation with our interruption.

Involuntarily, I stepped behind Josh and peeked over his shoulder. I'd met Mr. Brantley before in meetings and such, never like this. He was intimidating, but a damn good editor, and I was proud to work for him. I just hoped he would be willing to take the next step with *Feedback Magazine*. Since I'd been here, the magazine hadn't really focused on or advocated for any social issues. It was time we did.

Josh shoved my précis and the body of my article in front of him. He raised an eyebrow at me and then began to read. Josh and I stood there fidgeting in front of him, our fingers still clutching at each other behind his back. My hands were sweating so much he had to hold on tight.

Mr. Brantley didn't just read the précis and toss it back to us, like I was afraid he would. He sat back in his chair and read the entire body of my article. His face turned red a few times, he frowned deeper and deeper as he went on, and when it was over, he set the pages down on the desk in front of him and spread his hands out on top.

Without looking up, he spoke in terse sentences with his jaw clenched tight.

"You mean to tell me, Miss Gunderson, that these things happened to you right under my nose? You were working for me this entire time and you never, ever told anyone here at the magazine? You have delivered incredible work for me while hiding all of this?"

I gulped hard and froze. I couldn't get my mouth to form any words. My voice box was paralyzed. Brantley was in his early fifties and always seemed to me like a guy who'd lived a hard life. He dressed in band t-shirts from the '60s and '70s mostly, with pressed Levi's and Chucks. His steel-gray hair was cut short like a punk and his tattoos covered him from neck to wrist. He barked commands and had our staff fairly intimidated.

In his office, I was beyond intimidated to petrified.

"Answer me, young lady," he ordered impatiently. Josh gave my hand a tug and attempted to extricate me from my hiding spot.

"Y-yes, sir. I apologize."

"Don't you dare fucking apologize for anything other than not telling us right away. That completely confounds me and pisses me off. How in God's name have you...? Nevermind. This is brilliant journalism, and it's a story that fucking needs to be published. I really fucking wish I knew who these fucktarded douchebags were so I could slice their fucking pricks off myself, but that's beside the point. You are going to clean this up; it's going in February's features, that should give you enough time, and from now on, you are going to report directly to me. You and me, Gunderson, are going to start a new department here writing about shit like this that really fucking matters. Josh, you get to work on this layout. I want pictures, I want..."

The edges of my vision went dark and I heard "blah blah blah" from Brantley for the next five minutes until Josh tugged on my hand once again. I shook myself and met Mr. Brantley's gaze.

"Thank you for writing this. This kind of shit is why I never want to let my daughters out of the house. You and I are not finished discussing this matter. Finish this up, and then I expect to see you back here next week to talk about what we're going to tackle next. Consider yourself promoted."

"Thank you, sir. I'm very—"

"Don't even fucking say it. Get out of here, both of you, and get to work." He went back to yelling at people on the phone before we were out the door. Josh walked me back to his office, where I sat on the couch and tried to stave off a panic attack.

"What the hell just happened?"

My editor, my very good friend, was laughing at me. Bent over at the waist, belly laughing at me.

"What the fuck?"

"Girlfriend, you just got promoted to Features Editor! Damn, I'm proud of you! This is amazing!"

"Yeah, but what does that mean? No more bands? No more travel? What?"

He stopped laughing and knelt in front of me. He took my hands in his. "What this means is I'm no longer your boss. We're partners. It means you will still write for the magazine, but you will also be making decisions about what stories are covered, what direction your...well, I guess new department is going. You're going to be a trailblazer. I hope you're up for the challenge."

"So do I," I muttered. A promotion? Less time traveling, more time here... More responsibility meant less flexibility. Less Mage. Oh, that made my heart hurt.

"Josh I don't know if I can handle this. What if I can't—"

"You will be great. I will be here for you every step of the way." He talked more about my article and what needed to happen to get it polished and I numbed out. All I could think of was Mage and his earlier words.

*"I just worry our paths are going to forever be leading away from each other. That's not what I imagined my life would be like, you know? I always just felt that when I found... I mean, when I, well...we'd just be together and that would be that."*

Maybe this is what he meant. Maybe he saw that we would be apart.

I refused to let that happen. Somehow, someway, I would find a way for us to be together, because as much as my career was important to me and I felt I had a lot of important things to say, having Mage in my life was vital to my happiness, to my wholeness. I wanted *him*.

When I returned from the desert with Mage, he asked me to come to New Orleans. I asked him to give me a day to think it over. He had to leave today and wanted my answer before he left. I dialed his number on my way home from the office.

"*Ma cherie.* Tell me you're okay, cuz I've been freaking out all afternoon. What's wrong?"

"When should I fly in?"

There was silence on his end of the line.

"Mage?"

"You'll come? You'll meet me? Oh, thank God. I promise I'll behave, I just need you—"

"Mage? I...I need you, too. I have things to tell you."

He let that sit for a few beats. "I see you, Sammara. It's okay. I just want to touch you. I mean...God that sounds so wrong. I—"

"Don't you know by now I trust you? Mage, you've held me, you've slept next to me. Hell, we danced naked by the fire! I know your heart."

He was quiet for a long time. "I haven't been with a woman in a very long time. Not since I dreamed of you. When I'm next to you, it's hard."

I heard him swearing on the other end of the line and I couldn't hold back a laugh.

"God, that sounded horribly wrong. What I meant was—"

"Don't you think I feel it, too? I curse my fucked-up panic buttons every time you touch me. I wish I wasn't bringing that baggage into what we have. I don't ever worry you will hurt me. I just worry I won't ever be whole enough to let you in."

"Sammara, I will wait for you until the end of time. I know that *I'm* whole with you as a part of my life. That's all that matters to me."

We made plans for me to fly out on Thursday afternoon. I told him I had to come back Sunday because I already had an email from Brantley's assistant scheduling a meeting with him first thing Monday morning and a contract for my new position. I was shaky all over and couldn't wait to be back in Mage's arms, the only place I felt at peace.

The next few days flew by as Josh and I finalized the layout for the article and decided it needed a few more details and statistics. I met with a photographer named Tally to discuss what I thought would be good shots. She was totally on board with my ideas.

"This is so important, Sammara. I could tell you stories..."

She and I spent a long time talking about our shared experiences working with bands and the shit we'd both seen. I looked forward to working with her. I thought we could collaborate on some really important subjects.

My mind was working overtime plotting my next moves. I wanted to take this beyond rape and sexual assault. I wanted to push the envelope and touch on all the sensitive issues that needed to be addressed. Our rock community had a strong base of people who spoke out about issues that were important to them. I planned on calling in a few favors. By the time I was ready to board my plane to New Orleans, I had six months' worth of features planned in my brain.

# Seventeen

Mage had told me he'd meet me by baggage claim, but I wasn't prepared for his welcoming committee. He was dressed in a black suit with a bright green dress shirt open at the collar and his hair pulled back, one strand of curls hanging in his face. He stood with a five-piece brass band that was playing a jazz standard I couldn't quite put my finger on. Clutched in one hand, he had a huge bouquet of red roses.

His other hand was holding on to a tiny little girl that had his very same green eyes and curly hair.

I approached him nervously, a little overwhelmed. His eyes tracked me cautiously as his lips fought splitting into a Cheshire grin. He let go of the little girl's hand just long enough to take mine and pull me in to kiss my cheek. He pressed his forehead against mine and murmured, "I've never been so glad to see a person in my entire life."

I exhaled with a huge grin on my face. "I missed you, too." I gazed up into his beautiful face and our eyes held for several moments—until I heard a very determined "ahem".

"My apologies," he said with a smirk. "Sammara, please meet my niece, Josephina. Josephina, this lovely lady is my very good friend, Sammara Gunderson. Can you say hello to Miss Sammara?"

Josephina had her little fists balled up against her hips. "Finally you got here! *Parrain* Mage was all worried about you."

Her little lips pursed together and I felt her wrath. She didn't trust me one bit. Her suspicion that I was a bad person was not going to be easily overcome.

I crouched down to be more on her level and offered my hand. "I'm sorry, Josephina. My flight got delayed in Dallas. If I would have known Mage had all this waiting for me, I woulda made those pilots fly faster!"

She narrowed her eyes at me, obviously unconvinced by my words.

I glanced up at Mage. "I don't think I've passed muster."

He quirked up an eyebrow and said, "Not many do, *ma cherie.* You got any bags?"

I shook my head. "I always pack light." I gestured to the flowers and whispered, "Are those for later?"

His eyes bugged out and then he laughed, remembering his previous threat.

"Yeah. I never did get a chance to roll in them last time. I thought I'd try again. Maybe I'll even throw a couple your way."

He laughed as he handed the huge bouquet to me, slipping my bag off my shoulder so he could carry it for me. The band followed us out to a limousine, where they finished their song. I clapped enthusiastically, unsure what the protocol was. Mage hugged the trumpet player and thanked him as they kissed cheeks, then he bent down and kissed Josephina on top of her head.

"I'll see you later, *mon petit.* You be good for Tante Lulu. Tell her we'll be over for dinner Saturday."

She blew him a kiss, gave me one more suspicious glance, and then took the hand of the trumpet player, who Mage introduced as his Oncle Joseph.

"It is a pleasure to meet you, chère," he said as he shook my hand and kissed my cheek.

"Thank you so much. You all sounded amazing!" He bowed to me and winked at Mage. The driver had the door open for us. Mage handed him my bag and then took my hand to help me into the car. I slid into the car as gracefully as possible. Mage sat next to me and took my hand in his as the door closed.

"You are so lovely, Sammara. I swear, my heart stopped beating when you came through that doorway." He kissed my hand as he gazed into my eyes. "I don't even think it's started back up again." He held our hands against his chest and indeed, his heart had started beating again. It was pounding under my touch. Intensity was coming off of Mage in waves, suddenly making me very nervous.

"I don't know what to say," I whispered. "I dreamed about you every night since L.A. You're in my thoughts always. I can feel you even when we're apart."

His hand came up to my face and he closed his eyes as his thumb traced my lips. The car pulled away from the curb and out into traffic. I don't think I caught one glimpse of Louisiana on the short drive into town from the airport. Thoughts and feelings passed between us without any words.

When the car stopped and I looked out the window, I squealed with excitement.

"What is this place?" We were parked in front of a hotel. The car door opened and I looked back at Mage.

"I booked us rooms here at the Maison Dupuy so you could stay someplace nice. I know you've been working hard. I wanted to pamper you, chère. I figured you'd be more comfortable here than my gran's or the St. Germaine."

I giggled at his sincerity. "I'd be comfortable anywhere as long as you were with me."

He looked so unsure. I couldn't figure out why. He paused before he spoke, taking his time to choose his words. "It's very important to me that I do this right. I want you to fall in love with my hometown as much as...as much as I love it. I want—"

"As long as you are here, I will love it. I can't wait to learn more about you." His eyes darted back and forth between mine, and I could feel the tension in his body. "Relax! Why are you so worried? You already know I'm crazy about you."

His eyes bugged out. "Do you mean that? No matter what?"

"Of course I do! Have you been worried about that this whole time?"

He shrugged and we heard a polite cough outside the car. We turned to look at the waiting bellman.

"I'm so sorry. Do you need a minute, madam?"

I giggled and turned back to Mage. "Are you ready?" He still didn't move. "Hey," I said, taking his face in my hands. "You don't have to do anything but be here with me. I have almost three days to spend by your side and I intend to do just that. Now come on!"

I tugged on his hand and as I climbed out of the car, I heard him mutter to himself, "Please, God, don't let me screw this up."

Mage took my bag from the bellman, and then tipped our driver. He placed his hand at the small of my back and led me and my giant bouquet of roses into the lobby.

"Good evening, sir. You have a reservation?"

"I do. Two rooms. Name's Dumas."

I frowned up at him. "Two rooms?"

He looked down at his hands on the counter and waited for the clerk to finish up and give us the keys. He thanked the clerk and took my hand, leading me down the hall. We took the elevator to the third floor and walked down the hall towards the end.

"I got us two rooms next to each other. They both have balconies. I—"

"But Mage..."

He opened the first door and gestured for me to enter ahead of him. Once I was inside, he came in and set my bag down. The room was cozy and charming, with a king-size bed. The sky was dark outside. I was excited to sit on the balcony but the problem was, I wanted to share this with Mage, who was acting really weird. He stood near the door with his hands in his pocket. He'd make a delectable picture, if he'd just relax.

"Why two rooms, Mage?"

He kicked at the edge of the bed with his foot. "I want to do this right. I don't trust myself with you, like horizontal. Not anymore. I'm sorry. I'm not trying to be crude. I just can't be in bed with you."

I figured I could play this one of two ways. I could be coy and pretend like I didn't know what he was talking about, but that would insult whatever connection we'd been building. I knew exactly what was going on. He was sending out completely conflicting emotions. He wanted to touch me, but he wanted me to feel safe. He wanted to make love to me, but he was afraid he would scare me away. I had to respect his wishes since he was trying so hard.

"I understand. I do. Do you feel this?" I approached him and put my hand on his chest. I closed my eyes and attempted to open myself to him.

I felt him inhale before he stepped back.

"You want me, but you're afraid. You're... You're afraid. But not of me. Why? What scares you?"

"You can tell it's not you, right? It's not you. I have things to tell you. I—"

"No. If it's bad, don't tell me now. I just want to have this time with you, chère. No pressures, no worries. Just us. Let me show you my home."

I smiled at him, looking so nervous. "Okay. But you have to relax, too. Don't be afraid to touch me. I'm not afraid of you."

"I'll try. Do you need to rest, or are you ready to start your tour?"

"Give me a second?" I just needed to freshen up and collect myself. My flight should have landed by nine, but it was after ten thirty when we arrived at the hotel.

He said he was going to go next door and make sure his bag made it up. He'd dropped it off earlier in the day. After he stepped out, I hurried into the restroom and checked my makeup. Thankfully my trip hadn't been too horrendous. I knew this city was a long way from sleeping and I couldn't wait to start my New Orleans experience with my very own guide.

I met him in the hallway and his eyes perused my outfit. "You going to be warm enough, chère?"

I had on black crushed-velvet leggings, a stretchy long-sleeved top also in black, and a warm cardigan. "I think I'm okay."

His eyes kept traveling my body.

"What?" I finally asked, trying to get a sense of what he was feeling. All I could get from him was determination. That could mean a lot of things.

"I'm just trying to remember all the things I promised myself about your trip, but you're so damn beautiful, I could almost forget my name."

Coming from any other man, that line would make my eyes roll so hard I'd have to run to catch them. But he was so sincere. I'd never accuse him of being a cad. He held out his arm hesitantly and I gladly accepted, pleased as punch to be walking through this amazing place with such a good man by my side.

Once we were outside the hotel, he pointed out the sights and chatted in a loving voice about people he knew still living in the city.

"Where does your family live? Are they in the French Quarter?"

He shook his head, keeping a watchful eye on our surroundings and the comings and goings of folks as we walked. "You saw the main street just past our hotel?"

"No."

"You didn't? It's just past the hotel."

"I didn't see it."

"Really? Well if you—"

"Mage, the only thing I saw was you."

He stopped walking and the streetlights illuminated enough of his face for me to see him blush.

"It's true. It happens a lot when I'm with you. I don't really see anything else, which is weird. You know, reporter? I kind of have to be observant for my job? But when I'm with you, all I see, hear, smell...is you. You overwhelm my senses."

He frowned down at me, his expression confused. "I'm sorry. I don't mean—"

"Why are you sorry? I'm not sorry. I'm only sorry that not all five of the senses get a workout." I smiled wickedly at him, aware I was crossing that line and unable to stop myself. It had been so long since I'd felt comfortable flirting with someone that I was rusty. Awkward. But I felt quite wanton being on his arm in this exotic place. There were so many shadows we could step into and be swallowed up to catch a few kisses. Suddenly that's all I wanted to do, and he must have felt the same.

"Sammara, you're playing with fire," he spoke against my lips as he backed me up to a building out of the light. His hands gripped my waist hard as his tongue plunged into my mouth, no longer holding back the desperation he felt at having me near him again.

I clutched at his shoulders to keep from sliding to the ground in a pool of desire. He was a damn good kisser. He was a total-body kisser, and my body responded enthusiastically. His hands roamed eagerly. He pressed me against the wall using his hips. I imagined how delicious his weight would feel without any clothing in the way.

He cursed and pulled back, breathing deeply with his eyes closed. I continued to nibble on his jawline as he collected himself.

"I'm sorry, Sammara," he said, his voice cracking. "I didn't mean—"

"Don't apologize. Don't. I want this. You'll know if I'm not okay."

He regarded me cautiously. "I see you. Something's changed, though. You feel different."

"Different good?" Did he know how worried I was?

"I'm not sure. You have something to tell me. Maybe you should tell me."

"It's kind of mixed news. I'm not sure what you will think about it."

I paused to let him consider my words. We started walking slowly, his arm around my shoulders. He started to speak in a deep voice.

"I dreamed of you exactly two years ago on the solstice. It happened one night after I'd been partying with the guys. We'd just done a show in Pittsburgh. I remember it was Pittsburgh because we got into a bit of a bar fight over a Steelers/Saints thing. Anyway, that night when I climbed into my bunk, the whole bus was spinning. We had to drive all night to get to the next gig and the other guys planned to stay up and sleep when we got there. I was too wasted. I was missing home, missing Louisiana... Life on the road was exciting most of the time, but lonely nights? They were getting tired, feel me?

"I fell into a fitful sleep. My whole body hurt. Then I saw you. You stepped out of fire. I saw the stars and the necklace. My soul was healed, chère. I just knew I had to find you. That's that. I found you. You're it for me." He stepped back and offered his arm to me. "Whatever it is you got to tell me won't change how I feel."

His belief in his dream, and that I was his fate, could have been overwhelming. But this man had told me on many occasions that he believed in me, believed in us. I wasn't so sure, but I was going to trust him. I'd learned to trust him more than any man in my life.

"I told you about my article, you know, about what happened?" He nodded, still looking around, keeping an eye on a group of drunken partiers headed our way. Once they'd passed, I continued. "The boss loved it. Like really a lot. So much so that I got a promotion."

He stopped and pulled me to him. "I know how difficult it was for you to write that," he said, kissing my hair. "I'm so glad."

I pulled back and continued walking. "So that's all great, but my promotion means less flexibility. I've got my own department. Brantley wants more social-issue pieces and he wants me in charge. I'm not sure how I feel about it other than I'm scared as hell, mostly because I don't know what this means for *us*."

Mage kept walking and didn't talk for a long time. He rested his other hand on mine against his arm and I could feel tension in his grip.

"Now I understand. I thought it might be something like this. When I saw you away from me, I assumed it was something bad. I never thought it would be this. You feel conflicted about it."

"I do feel conflicted. I'm excited for the opportunity to get the magazine moving in a good direction, one that means something. I'm scared as hell, and disappointed because I hoped..."

"What do you hope for, *ma cherie*? What do you want?"

I exhaled harshly. "I want to have my cake and eat it, too! I want this opportunity and I want you. I want to be where you are," I said, surprising myself at how candid this conversation had become.

"I want that, too. We're just going to have to make it happen."

His words were encouraging, but I wasn't getting the feeling from him that he was as confident as he sounded. I'd have to give him time.

We made our way through the Quarter, past the wild scene on Bourbon Street and on towards Jackson Square. There were groups walking around huddled together against the brisk air, and there was still a line outside Café Du Monde. "You want a coffee, chère?"

"Boy, do I! But no powdered sugar. I'm totally not dressed for it."

He smiled at me and we crossed the street to get in line. A few folks stared and giggled when they saw Mage. He was certainly not dressed like his Maggie's Bones persona, but he was so incredibly gorgeous, even if you didn't know who he was, you'd look and drool. I felt proud to be on his arm, but also fascinated by the attention he got. He said hello to a couple of the servers and shook hands. I wanted to ask so many questions.

"Cousins," he said quietly to me. "I've got cousins all over. Most of them are in food service, a few even run restaurants around here. Being the son of a seventh son means lots of family."

"That's wild. I don't have any cousins, at least not first cousins. I was an only child and my mother was an only child. I guess I may have other family on my father's side." I had only spoken to my mom once since our visit to the ranch. I wanted to go back out and talk more with Oliver. I was still working up the nerve.

"You're going to have a lot to learn from him. He's got some mad Sight. He wants to know you."

"You amaze me, you know that? You pick up a lot more than I do. But then I've always been more in touch with places and energies than the living."

He rubbed at his chin and smiled.

A server came by and took us to a table. We sat on the outside edge of the patio near the bridge. My skin was tingling from all the energy here. I hugged myself and had a little shiver. Mage started to take his coat off and I held up a hand.

"I'm fine. Just a lot going on."

He smiled knowingly. "Yeah, you're probably getting overloaded here."

We talked about how we first knew we were different from others. I told him how when I started school with other kids, they all gave me a wide berth because I would just say anything. It took me a long time to realize I was making them uncomfortable. Then I just closed up and kept it to myself. Eventually I met other kids who were just as socially awkward and we banded together.

"Luckily for me, my boys took me under their wing and schooled me on when it was ok to let my freak flag fly. People in Houma all knew each other and were suspicious of new folks. Except for Jade. He loves everybody and he grabbed on to me the first day I showed up at school in my funky-ass clothes and said, 'We're going to be best friends'. He has the purest energy I've ever known. He's authentic. Always. What you see is what you get. He's an open book. Totally accepting of everyone. I love that guy like a brother. I owe him a lot. Him and D, man."

"I love watching you guys together. I can still see the teenage boys." He smiled and tangled our fingers together.

"I guess," he said with a chuckle. "In some ways we're still innocent. Some. We've seen a lot of shit, been through a lot of shit since we started this gig. I tell you what, these boys are my family, chère. They mean everything to me, above and beyond the band. I know even if the band were to end tomorrow, they'd still be my brothers."

We ordered coffee and Mage bravely ordered beignets with extra powdered sugar. "I guarantee you won't get any powdered sugar on you if you let me feed you."

"Really," I said with a smirk. "That's just not possible. I'm a slob enough as it is. It'll never work."

"Oh, it's on now. Just you wait." I loved playful Mage. I was so excited he was making a showing tonight. His green eyes were so bright. The gold flecks seemed to glow. He licked his lips and grinned.

"Mage? From Maggie's Bones?" A couple of emo boys with cute, flippy hair and dressed all in black with band tees on stood next to our table.

"And who might you boys be?"

They looked at each other and smiled earnestly. "We're, like, sorry to bother you, but could we, like, have your autograph? We're huge fans of Maggie's Bones. We saw you guys in L.A. last year."

Mage accepted a pen from one of the boys and grabbed a napkin off the table. He signed his name in a very cool-looking design and then signed another one for the second boy.

"Y'all here visiting?" Mage was such a good sport.

"Yeah, um, our parents brought us. Our father is on business here. We're from Los Angeles."

"That's cool. You like it so far?"

The boys nodded enthusiastically. "It's awesome! We went to the cemetery today." They were kind of blushing and hiding behind their long fringe. They had to be maybe early teens? Both were skinny with some acne on their excited faces and they both had mouths full of braces.

"You guys gonna catch the Haunted tour?" They nodded enthusiastically. "You play?"

"Yeah," the spokesbrother said. "Not like good or anything, but we're learning. We've been teaching ourselves your stuff. My brother Isaac here, he plays bass, and I play rhythm. Hey, are you guys ever going to do any clinics?"

"Sure. Jade and me do them occasionally at the Guitar Center on Sunset. Make sure you sign up for the mailing list and when the registration starts, just tell them I said to let you in, that you met me at Café Du Monde."

"No shit? Oh, sorry. I mean, cool. Thanks, dude." The boys both shook hands with Mage, who nodded to them, and then they left us as the server brought our order.

"That was incredibly adorable," I said as I sipped my coffee. "Wow, this stuff is strong. I'm kind of a coffee wimp." He chuckled at the face I made.

"Allow me," Mage said, grabbing the crème and sugar and doctored my coffee for me. We clinked our cups together and I took another sip.

"Mmmmm," I breathed. "That's heavenly!"

He nodded and put his coffee down. He took off his suit coat and draped it over the back of my chair. Then he meticulously rolled up his sleeves, displaying his heavily tattooed arms. The black-and-gray collages were done beautifully. The line work was very delicate. I wanted to spend hours tracing them with my fingers, exploring every inch of his body.

"You ready for this?" He had broken off a piece of the confection while I was lost in my salacious thoughts. He held it a few inches in front of me over the table. "It's important to catch all the powdered sugar on your tongue. You gotta suck the fingers clean."

Oh my. He said suck and tongue and fingers. I was a goner. "Um, maybe you should demonstrate?"

He smiled at me, leaned forward and wrapped those luscious lips around his thumb and forefinger up to the knuckle, dragging them slowly out of his mouth for emphasis. His cheeks hollowed before they popped out, and then he licked the underside of his finger for good measure.

That's all it took for my panties to be drenched.

"Easy does it, chère," he drawled, carefully pulling off another piece of the beignet. He waited as I leaned forward slowly, trying not to press my black top against the table. It had been wiped clean before we sat down, but was undoubtedly still contaminated by the evil white powder.

I stopped a couple of inches from his waiting treat and opened my mouth.

This time, he was the one who lost composure. His eyelids grew heavy as my lips closed over his fingers up to the knuckle. I paused for a moment and watched as his pink tongue darted out to wet his rosy lips.

"There you go," he said in a low, gravelly voice. "Now suck, chère."

I did as he instructed, hollowing my cheeks as I slowly slid my mouth down his fingers in retreat, taking care to swirl my tongue over the pads of his fingers as I hooked the piece of pastry from between his fingers and brought it further into my mouth. The sweet sugar became one with the taste and texture of his skin: smooth over the length of his finger, tough on the pad from years of playing his instrument. As I slid my lips off the tip of his fingers, a slow groan sounded from deep in his chest. I released him with a pop and licked my lips for good measure.

"How'd I do?" I asked demurely.

Mage sat speechless for several beats before he shook himself. "Sammara? You mind if we do the rest of this tour tomorrow?"

I blinked, surprised by his changed demeanor. Gone was playful Mage. In his place was desperate Mage.

"Whatever you think is best," I said, licking my lips again, delighting in the way his eyes tracked my movement. "Did I get any sugar on me?"

He actually growled.

He stood up hurriedly, grabbed some bills from his wallet, reached for the bag of beignets on the table and then held out his hand for me. "I think what I need to show you next is better viewed in your hotel room."

I took one last sip of my coffee and stood slowly from the table, milking this moment as much as I was preparing myself mentally for being alone in a hotel room with him. I wasn't afraid of him; rather, I was afraid of what might happen if we remained in public. We'd managed to get ourselves in quite a state from just some simple powdered sugar delights.

Mage's long strides had me running to keep up as he hailed a carriage in front of the square. He took my hand to help me into the carriage and I thought to myself, *How romantic! A carriage ride!* But I was consumed with desire as soon as he sat next to me and his thigh pressed against mine. I vaguely remember him telling the driver where to take us before his lips claimed mine. They remained there for the several minutes it took the driver to take us to our hotel. I'm sure he paid him, but my focus could not leave Mage's lips.

We hurried to our hall and then he stalled out. He looked between our doors and cleared his throat. "Sammara, I want you to know that whatever you—"

"I know. Just open the damn door."

He laughed and pulled out our keys. "Which?"

"Doesn't matter. Mine," I said.

He nodded and used the card to open the door. Once inside, he set the white paper bag down on the table beside the bed.

"I decided it would be more fun *not* to keep this sugar off of you."

I laughed as he took me in his arms and spun me around. We undressed each other clumsily and fell on the bed. I couldn't get enough of the feel of his skin against mine; his smooth over hard muscle and mine soft, the stark contrast between his powerful frame and my rounded curves. He broke away from our kiss with a smile and reached for the treats from Café Dumond.

"Are you still hungry, *Monsieur Dumas*?"

He raised an eyebrow tauntingly, and then proceeded to dump the contents of the bag onto my torso.

"Very much so." He ran his tongue under my breasts in long swipes. "Powdered sugar tastes so much better on you."

I laughed—until he sucked a nipple into his mouth and worried it between his teeth and lips.

Nothing had ever felt so right as his mouth on me. There was nothing predatory about his touch. It was as if he were worshiping my body, caressing it like a priceless artifact, proceeding with care and wonder. I arched into him, encouraging him to take his ministrations further, which he did. South.

I kept waiting for my panic button to activate. I'd never had a man with any skill attend to my lady bits quite like Mage did, but as he made his way down to what he called "the best place to taste sugar", all I felt was our connection growing stronger, our love growing deeper.

That's right. Love. I recognized it for what it was as he poured all of his emotion into me, knowing I would feel it. He whispered as he worked, words that I didn't need to hear to understand, bringing me to the most powerful orgasm I'd ever experienced.

I knew it was love by the careful way he held me to him as I came down to earth from the most magical place I'd ever been. I knew it was love as he kissed me tenderly and whispered, "I see you, my beloved." I knew it was love as I fell asleep in his powerful arms and felt safe as could be.

# EIGHTEEN

I came awake suddenly to darkened skies. I sat up and looked around, my heart pounding in my ears almost drowning out the sound of Mage breathing peacefully next to me in bed.

I gazed down upon his handsome face and allowed myself to finally take the time to study him thoroughly. The white sheet had slid down his torso in the night and he'd kicked a leg out from underneath. His left arm was above his head and his hair fanned out around the pillow. An artist couldn't ask for a more perfect subject. I decided to do a little art of my own.

I stood from the bed carefully so as not to disturb his sleep. We'd placed the roses in the ice bucket the night before with some water from the tap. I inhaled their magical scent as I crept quietly to the bed. Careful not to drip water on him, I pulled the petals from the roses and sprinkled them all over my sleeping love. I started at his feet, and with the last of the two dozen buds, I wove them into his hair and placed them around his face.

I wanted to take pictures, but I knew he'd kill me if they ever got out. I would just have to make a mental picture. I wanted to remember this for always, how incredibly attractive he was.

I watched him sleep a little longer and then I grew restless. I wrapped myself in the blanket we'd kicked off the bed sometime in the night. The sky was beginning to lighten with the dawn and I wanted to experience it firsthand.

Quietly, I slid the door open to the balcony and sat on one of the bistro chairs just outside. I still had a perfect view of Mage's sleeping, rose-petal-covered form, and I could watch the French Quarter wake from its slumber on this Friday morning. The solstice. My birthday. It was a perfectly peaceful morning. Letting myself sit alone with my thoughts in an incredible place with an incredible man. I knew in my heart I wanted many more of these moments.

Sometime later, when the sun was fully in the sky, I watched as Mage began to move restlessly and stretch. I giggled as he wiped at his face, where his movements had caused some of the petals to fall against his nose.

"What the—?" He looked down at himself and then saw me on the balcony. He frowned. "Your flowers. Why—"

"They looked so good on you. I couldn't resist." He was still frowning as he pushed up onto his elbows, his sleepy face so adorable I couldn't stay away a moment longer. I walked to his side of the bed and sat on the edge. His serious face was cracking me up.

"How long you been awake?" He reached up to touch my face and let his fingers trail down my arm.

"I don't know. A couple of hours? I watched the sunrise. It was amazing, Mage. I can understand why you love this place so much, and I've barely seen anything. It just feels right."

"Sammara... Last night? I didn't mean—"

"You better have meant last night," I said, afraid he was going to put space between us. "Please don't say it was a mistake."

"God no, chère! How could you possibly think I'd say that? I know you felt what I felt."

"I did. I just... Don't say it was a mistake. When you touched me like that...the way you held me, I could tell."

His smile was as bright as the sun coming through the window. "I'm glad you can tell. I want you to feel it, too. You need to be there with me before we can take this thing where it's meant to go." His lips split into a lazy grin as he pulled on my blanket. "I tell you what else feels right. Get your sexy ass back here in this bed with me. I want to share my petals."

He yanked a little harder, removing the blanket from me, and pulled me on top of him. I giggled as I sprawled across his chest and ran my toes along his legs. He jerked as my fingers found purchase on his rib cage and soon we were wrestling and covered in smashed rose petals.

"Mercy! Oh God, mercy, chère. I can't take it anymore."

I straddled him and held his arms above his head. He wasn't trying to fight off my hold so I leaned down and kissed him softly.

"Good morning," I whispered as I rubbed noses with him. "I hope you don't mind being lazy for a while. I kind of like these rose petals. What a great idea you had."

We remained in bed together, talking and laughing for several hours until we could no longer ignore the growling in our stomachs. We agreed to split up to shower. I was already having a really hard time not taking things further, and a naked, wet Mage in the shower would most likely prove to be even more irresistible than naked, rose-petal-covered Mage in bed.

After I cleaned up, I knocked on his door. He answered in a towel with the phone to his ear. He motioned for me to come in.

"We hadn't decided yet... No... No, I was going to... Oh, come on, I wasn't trying to hog her. Well, yeah, I guess that's what I was doing... Of course I wouldn't leave the shop off of her tour." He looked at me and mouthed the word "busted". I giggled and stepped around him to the bathroom. I saw he had a wide-toothed comb on the counter. I grabbed it and then turned to find him sitting on the edge of the bed. I crawled around behind him and began slowly combing the tangles out of his thick hair. I could do this all day, I thought to myself, and be completely satisfied.

"Alright! Alright. Damn. No, don't do that... No! Aw, man... Fine. Let me feed her and— Dude, don't be disgusting! Lunch, you idiot. Fine. We'll be by later. Stop bothering me! I love you, too." He ended the call and threw the phone across the room to land in the armchair on top of his bag. He exhaled on a groan.

"I take it someone doesn't want you keeping me all to yourself today?" I was torn. I really enjoyed his friends and their ladies, and to be honest, I'd been thinking about what Mackenzie said about letting her stick me with a needle. But I was also enjoying having Mage alone. I could be with him all of the time, day and night, never seeing another soul, and I'd be perfectly content.

"That was Jade. He wants us to all meet up at the shop later and then go hang out. He's, uh..."

"Hard to say no to? It's okay. I want to see Jaylene's and Mackenzie's tattoo and piercing shop anyway. I was going to ask if we had time." Mage started to turn to face me but I stopped him with my hand. "I'm not finished yet. Let me have fun. I've never let my hair get very long. You have so much of it. Do you mind if I play?"

He gave me a sultry glance over his shoulder and said, "You can have fun however you want, chère. It's your birthday."

I smiled so wide my cheeks hurt, so excited to be sharing my special day with my special man. He kissed me softly and then let me continue with my task while we discussed what I wanted to do on "my day."

I really wanted to stay in and explore more of Mage, but I was also hungry. I took a few more minutes to comb his hair. I looked up from my task to see him watching me closely in the mirror. I smiled and leaned forward to kiss his bare shoulder. He moaned softly and closed his eyes.

"I love the way we look together," he said in a gravelly voice. "We complement each other in so many ways, I think." We sat staring at our reflection for several moments before he made a face at me. I laughed and ran my fingers through his hair one last time to be sure I got all the tangles.

"As much I love what you're doing, I'm seriously fucking starving."

I ran my hands around his front and squeezed him once more, pressing a kiss against his shoulder blade. "This has been a perfect morning," I whispered. "Do you want me to leave this down?"

He stood from the bed and approached the mirror. "It's okay. I'll pull it back until it dries. Otherwise it gets my shirt all wet and it's going to be a little chilly today." He grabbed some boxers, a pair of black jeans and a cream thermal top and walked into the bathroom. "I'll be right out."

I fell back on the bed and inhaled his masculine scent. Whatever he used to shower with had a very distinct fragrance. I wanted to climb him like a tree and bury my face in his hair. I laughed out loud at myself. If he only knew how much I wanted him—

"Not half as much as I want you, chère."

I blinked up to see him standing in front of me at the foot of the bed. His grin was all satisfied male. "I promise, I don't do it all the time, but sometimes you project clear as a bell."

"Good. Then you'll always know what I want. That will be nice. Okay, what do I want right now?" I couldn't wait to see if he'd speak aloud the thoughts I projected.

Mage's smile fell and his eyes flared.

I laughed. "Relax. I'll settle for some red beans and rice."

Mage ran his hand down his face and swore under his breath. He held his hand out for me. "Come on, ya hussy. We can't stay in bed all day. If we aren't careful, Jade will bring the whole crew down here and then I bet you'd be pretty embarrassed if they caught us doing *that*."

Damn. "I guess you're right. But someday..."

He pulled me in for a dangerously delicious kiss once more before taking my hand and leading me away from "temptation", as he called it. As he pulled the door shut, I had a thought.

"Uh, maybe I should put the 'do not disturb' sign up? The rose petals?"

Mage pressed his lips together and said, "I'll be sure to leave a good tip."

We had a huge lunch at Antoine's and then strolled through the French Quarter like a couple of tourists without a care in the world. I stopped and listened to every street musician, leaving tips each time. My heart felt lighter than it had in years. Mage was the consummate tour guide and was incredibly patient, as I wanted to stop in every shop and touch everything, even if he did tease me.

"Nobody ever told you to look with your eyes and not your hands?" He playfully bumped into me as I was looking at the jewelry on a rack, almost knocking it over in the process. I turned and swatted his ass as he strolled away chuckling.

We stopped by the hotel so I could drop off my purchases from the day and then Mage suggested we take a detour to see the St. Louis Cemetery No. 1, which was just two blocks from the hotel. Stepping through the gates brought a heavy feeling to my chest. It was early dusk, a magical time of night, and I felt the presence of many, many restless spirits. I gripped Mage's arm a little tighter and closed my eyes. I didn't even realize I'd stopped walking until he gave a little tug.

"What do you feel, chère?"

"It's like a million tiny fingers all over me. It's...incredible! Do you feel it, too? And I hear music! Mage! What is that music?"

He led me farther into the cemetery and the music in my head got louder and more jumbled. "Our funerals here? Most folks have brass play and a second line follows the procession here. My granddaddy was involved with a local social club, he and Gran, and they helped organize some of these. I used to love joining the second line as a kid. You're probably hearing the echoes."

"Second line?" I was full of questions once again. Now I couldn't wait to meet his family.

"Yeah. You never seen a parade in New Orleans? That's what we do, how we celebrate. Oncle Joseph's band? From the airport? They play in clubs around the city, but also they do a lot of funerals. Some of our family members are buried in this cemetery, in fact. I used to love to come here and just, I don't know, listen to the music until the bands left, then I'd just listen to the voices. Since tonight is the solstice, I figured you might be even more open today. Tell me what else you're picking up."

I giggled as I felt the fingers start to tickle me. "You hear voices, I feel fingers. It doesn't feel wrong though. It's like...joyful. Yeah. It feels nice." I looked around and took in the night air, cool against my face. The energy in this place was definitely positive, which surprised me. Perhaps the way the New Orleanians celebrated their dead was the right idea.

I turned back to Mage and touched noses with him on tiptoe. "We're quite a pair, aren't we?"

He smiled and gave my arm a squeeze. "I love it, Sammara. I just feel like I can tell you anything. I can say anything and you're gonna believe me and understand. You don't know what kind of peace that gives me."

I focused my energy on him and felt whatever I'd been feeling around me start to dissipate. "I feel that way, too."

He walked me past the crypt where his granddaddy was laid to rest along with his great aunts and uncles. He explained to me that on All Saints Day, his family comes and cleans up the crypts, repairing any cracked plaster or loose bricks. I loved that ritual. I was already making plans to join him next year. That is, if we were still... It was such a foreign concept to me, but it sounded better and better every moment.

"Mage? How did your family fare with Katrina?" Immediately I worried whether I should have asked. "You were in Houma, right? With your mom?"

He nodded and looked off into the distance. "My gran left town with Oncle Remy's family and stayed in Baton Rouge with her friends until they could get a place. My oncles LeRoy and Albert, they went, too. Only Oncle Louis, Oncle Moises and Oncle Joseph stayed here, and they faced some hard times. My daddy was in New York, where he lives most of the time.

"It took a couple of years, but they slowly came back and fixed up Gran's house. We didn't lose anybody, but they lost they houses. Only Gran's remained with very little damage. I think everyone has finally moved out of Gran's except for Moises and Louis. It was hard, but they had each other and they had music. I would come every chance I got after Gran came back, just so I could help folks out in the neighborhood. The band, we really got our start and things happened for us in two thousand seven. I almost didn't leave with them, did you know that?"

I shook my head, shocked.

"Yeah, I didn't want to leave my gran with work still to be done, but she told me it was what I was meant to do, that I was meant to leave and chase the muse, you dig? So when the guys were ready to move to L.A., I went with. It was hard, but I was ready to have some adventures."

"I guess so. So now you're kind of between places."

"Yeah. I'm okay with it. Hollywood and New Orleans both feel like home to me. I was so pissed at my daddy when he left, even more so when Mama took me away to Houma. I hated being away from the music and my family, but now I understand it. He was meant to go to New York. He had much more success there. I was meant to be with my crazy boys making 'that screamy racket', like Gran calls it."

"I can't wait to meet your gran," I said, nuzzling his shoulder. The sky was really getting dark now and the chill was starting to get to me.

"I almost forgot," Mage said suddenly, reaching into his pocket. He pulled out a small gift-wrapped box.

Oh.

"Now, no freak-outs. I see you. I just wanted to give you something for when I can't be there."

"Mage!" I exclaimed, shaking my head at him. He handed the box to me and ordered me to open it.

"It's not what you think," he said, his voice wavering a bit. "I just wanted you to have a piece of me, of this place, to take home with you. For when we're apart. That's all. It's not..."

Inside the package was a small silver ring with a fleur-de-lis engraved in the center of a circle. It was carved so intricately. You could see the artist's work was done very lovingly.

"It's beautiful," I said. I slipped it onto my right hand. It was too big for my ring finger, but it fit my middle finger perfectly.

Mage took my hand in his and kissed it, rubbing my knuckles against his cheek. "It's not much—"

"It's perfect. Thank you. I feel better." We kissed softly and I could feel relief coming off of him. He had been really nervous to give me this gift.

"Mage? Can we pray? I always do, on my birthday."

"Absolutely." We knelt on the stone walkway by his family's tomb. Mage held my hands while I prayed to the Mother my thanks for the path she'd guided me on, and for her protection for our fledgling love for each other. I heard Mage suck in a breath.

"Blessed be, dear Mother, for placing my heart in this man's loving hands. If this is my fate, I embrace it with all that I am."

When I opened my eyes, Mage's were wet and shiny. His lip quivered as he spoke. "I am not a perfect man. I am impatient, moody, and stubborn as all get out. With your heart in my hands, however, I will strive to be all that you need and more. I've waited for you for so long, chère. I wasn't always on that good and righteous path, and I will make mistakes along our journey. But know that I will always, always, be by your side if you need me. I won't fail you."

"And that is why I came to you and your home."

He squeezed my hands and pressed his forehead against mine. "Happy birthday, chère."

*Best. Birthday. Ever.*

We stood together and he brushed off my clothes before taking my hand.

# Nineteen

We reached Frenchman street later that evening. Mage pointed out some clubs where Maggie's Bones had played in their early days. He kept his arm around me the whole time and gestured with his free hand.

"We're a bit heavy for most people's tastes around here, but we always threw in a few local favorites each set. Mr. Daryl's friends and associates always filled the places to capacity to support us."

"Mr. Daryl? Is that the guys' uncle?"

Mage nodded. "He is that. He's also the president of a local motorcycle club and an unofficial mayor of the Quarter. He's been our greatest patron. Really. Maggie got us the record deal, but Mr. Daryl gave us the start-up cash we needed and had the connections to get us gigs. My uncles helped, too, but it took them a while to warm up to the fact that we weren't playing traditional music. Anyway, and he introduced us to Jaylene, who changed our whole lives. If it weren't for her, I think the band would have split very soon after we lost Maggie."

"She's pretty special, that's for sure. I talk to her a lot. She's been more helpful than the therapist I'm paying, I think."

Mage squeezed my shoulder. "She came to both of us at a crucial time. Fate." He smiled mischievously at me and then pointed to a building coming up on the right. "Behold. Pins and Needles."

Walking through the doors of the tattoo shop was like stepping out of the history of the town and into the present with a slap in the face. Iron Maiden blasted from the speakers as people milled about the lobby, looking at flash on the walls. Several more stood at the counters flipping through portfolios of tattoos I assumed Jaylene was responsible for. There were three small stations and all were filled with the buzz of tattoo rigs. A guy and a girl worked the first two, and Jaylene had a more spacious spot in the back. Her hair was piled up on her head and she was bent over a woman's abdomen tattooing in a very tender spot. I winced.

"Holy...I hope that chick isn't planning on having babies."

"Why would you say that?" Mage asked, frowning at me.

I rolled my eyes. "Stretch marks? You do know where babies come from, don't you?" I fluttered my eyelashes until he smirked at me.

"I do know. I know how to make them, too." He winked at me and led me to the counter where Mackenzie was filing her nails while two girls argued over whether to get their navels or nipples pierced. Mackenzie did not appear to be amused.

"Nipples, navels, kneecaps, I don't give a fuck, but you two better decide soon because I got a date." She gave Mage and me a salacious smile and licked her lips at us, being sure to show off the stud perched on her tongue.

When I'd first met her, she had teal-colored hair. Today it was black with two bright blue streaks in the front. She was dressed in a leather halter top that barely contained her ample cleavage. For bottoms, she wore Lycra leggings with colorful skulls all over. She held out her hand to Mage, who kissed it and then stepped in to kiss her cheek. She pulled his arm around her back and waved for me to join them.

"Yes, indeed. I've got a date with these two. Damn, girl, you just get hotter every time I see you." I could tell she was playing with these two sorority girls so I let her keep up the ruse. I hugged her close, making sure our breasts pressed together. I gave the girls a wink as Mackenzie nibbled on my ear. Mage reached around and we made a Mackenzie sandwich for a moment until Star approached. He wrapped his arms around Mage's waist and bit him on the neck.

"Do I get to join in on the fun?" he asked, thrusting against Mage's backside.

I couldn't keep the giggles in any longer. It got totally out of control at that point. Mackenzie kicked a leg up on the counter and moaned as she pulled my face down to her chest. Star pulled on Mage's ponytail and they started grunting. The girls had no idea what to think of our display that was getting louder and louder by the minute.

"Alright, kids," Jaylene hollered. "How many times do I have to tell you? No group sex on the counter!"

Mackenzie whined as we all untangled ourselves. Star came over to greet me and kissed me on the cheek before heading back to watch Jaylene work. Devon came in from the back of the shop.

"What did I miss?" he asked, leaning down to kiss Jaylene on the head.

"Oh, just some soft-core action. No tits came out."

"Damn," he said, shaking his head as he walked over to Mage, giving him a bro hug. The girls went all wide-eyed staring up at the rock god with mouths hanging open. Mackenzie wasn't done having fun.

"Devon, these girls can't decide where to let me stick my needle. Do you have any suggestions for them?"

He raised an eyebrow without smiling. "Nipples are my personal favorite."

Jaylene snorted loudly from the back of the shop. Devon winked at me and went to huddle with Mage over on the couches by the window.

"I've always been curious," I asked Mackenzie, who was so much damn fun I couldn't help myself. "Do they really add sexual pleasure?"

I heard Jaylene cough and I turned around to see her choking on a sip of water. Her face was red and I wondered how much of that was from lack of oxygen or from embarrassment.

Mackenzie laughed loudly. "They absolutely add to the pleasure. Enhancing one's erogenous zones with a piercing definitely improves the stimulation." She flared her eyes at the college girls, who started whispering to each other. Mackenzie stepped around behind me, towering over me in her heels, and whispered in my ear. "I'm being totally serious. How about I give you and Mage a matching pair?"

I looked over at him and wondered how he would feel about it. I didn't have any tattoos. It's not that I didn't think they were lovely, but I hadn't felt strongly enough about anything to have it permanently etched onto my skin. Piercings were sexy, though.

"I'll have to ask him," I whispered back. She clapped her hands together and bounced her boobs right near my face.

"Oh goodie! Let me take care of these two and I'll be right out." She leaned her elbows onto the counter and rested her chin in her hands, giving them a clear view right down her top. "So what's it going to be?"

"Um, can we..." The girl pointed at the barbells Mackenzie had labeled "great for nipples" and giggled. Mackenzie took their money, had them sign some forms and explained the process and aftercare to them. They followed her to a curtained-off area of the shop and their voices became muffled. I walked back to watch Jaylene at work.

"Hey, girl," she said, pursing her lips at me for a kiss. I laughed as I leaned down to give her a peck. "When Mage told us you were coming to town, I made him promise I could see you. Pull up a chair."

I sat on the opposite side of the table from her and sucked in a breath. "That looks incredibly painful. Gorgeous, but ouch!" I looked up at her client and it was clear she was struggling with the pain.

"Just a few more spots to shade, Courtney, and then we're done. You can hang in there?"

The woman nodded and blew out a breath.

"How's the visit been so far?" Jaylene asked.

I looked over to find Mage watching me with a smile while he and Devon talked. I gave him a finger wave and sighed.

"I'm mentally packing up my condo to move here," I said and barked out a laugh.

Jaylene just smiled down at her work. "Best move I ever made," she said quietly. "Of course, I fell in love with the city before the man. You've done the opposite."

She was so right. "I think Mage could live in Bakersfield and I'd still want to move there."

Jaylene cracked up at that and had to stop her work for a moment to collect herself.

"Ok, maybe not Bakersfield. Did you hear he had a whole brass band meet me at the airport?" I couldn't get the damn smile off my face. My cheeks hurt but I wouldn't have it any other way.

"His uncle's band? I'm not surprised. I think he wanted to throw you a parade, but he didn't have enough time to get the permits." I hoped she was joking. When I didn't say anything, she looked up at me. "I'm only mostly kidding. He's been talking about your visit nonstop. He wasn't going to share you either." She pouted at that.

"After that welcome I just had, there's no way I'd want to miss seeing your shop. I'm guessing she's always like that?"

Jaylene looked toward the curtain and shook her head. "Best friend a girl could ever ask for. And if she offers to pierce your nipples? Take her up on it."

Star was tinkering with a tattoo machine across from Jaylene's station and he jumped when the first girl screamed from behind Mackenzie's curtain.

"Gets them every time," he chuckled. "Hey, Jay? I'm pretty sure I can get this running again. Next time I run out to Houma, I'll work on it with my uncle. He's a genius machinist. I know he'll have what I need." The second piercing must have occurred because we heard an equally loud shriek. Most of the others in the shop ignored it.

Jaylene smiled at him. "That would be great. It's always nice to have a couple of spares. That one is finicky but it does great shading for black-and-gray pieces. I got it from my old shop."

Girl number two got her piercings with only a few f-bombs. What a trooper. Mackenzie showed them out and then returned to her station presumably to clean up. Star watched her movements with a dreamy smile on his face.

The three of us talked for a while until Jaylene finished up the woman's tattoo. She'd designed a lotus flower opening with rainbows coming from the top. It was kind of cool, I guess. Not exactly my style.

"I love it, Jaylene!" The woman thanked her profusely as Jaylene bandaged it up, handed her a sample tube of antibiotic gel and gave her instructions.

Mage came to stand behind me. "Hey, chère? Devon and I are going to go pick up Jade. He's over at Mr. Daryl's. Then we'll get some dinner?" I beamed up at him as he leaned down to kiss me softly.

"I'm fine. Oh! But Mackenzie—"

"I know. She told me. I'm always game for new experiences, but it's up to you. She kinda scary with that needle. You should have seen those girls when they left! They's white as ghosts. Well, whiter than when they came in here."

"I'm already the whitest," I laughed. "I can take it." His eyes dropped down to my red long-sleeved t-shirt with the Hard Rock Café logo on it. I could feel him mentally caressing my breasts. My nipples hardened from the images flashing through my mind from last night. He'd certainly had fun feasting on them then.

"Dude, quit eye-fucking your girlfriend and go get Jade. Geez! I'm surrounded by perverts," Mackenzie said, exasperated. The whole shop laughed at her statement, fully aware she was, in fact, the biggest pervert.

The guys returned with Jade a half hour later, just in time for Jaylene and Mackenzie to finish cleaning up their workstations with Star's help. He was their unofficial shop boy whenever he was in town. The other two artists were going to continue to work through the night.

I followed the girls up to their apartments so they could give me the tour and get cleaned up. Jaylene came out wearing leggings and a Metallica t-shirt that was huge on her, and then slid into a black zippered hoodie with devil horns on the hood. Mackenzie joined us in a more sedate outfit than before. At least on top. Her black leather pants and thigh-high lace-up boots with four-inch heels were quite intimidating.

The three of us were on different areas of the spectrum, to be sure, but were becoming fast friends. A shared love of music—and musicians, apparently—tied us together. I hoped as we got to know each other more, our friendship would continue to grow. It wasn't often you met women in life you could really connect with. I felt like I'd found that connection with these two. We were only missing our fourth.

"No Sherry and Marcus this weekend?"

The girls shrugged and looked to each other for answers. "I guess they're in L.A.? I don't know," Jaylene said sadly. "We haven't heard much from them lately." I hoped wherever they were, they were both okay.

. . .

We ate dinner up the street at a restaurant run by one of Mage's cousins and I had the best fried chicken I'd ever eaten in my life. I tried gumbo, which was yummy, and fell in love with the alligator sausage. I never gave much thought to food, only really eating when I needed to or felt hungry. I had a feeling I'd need a much larger wardrobe if I made this place my permanent home. I said as much to Mage after we left and were walking towards one of the many clubs we'd visit that night. He looked me up and down and smirked.

"Eat as much as you want, chère. More of you to love is just fine by me."

Again with the awful lines, but man did they work for him.

We heard all kinds of music that night. It seemed as if each bar had a different genre, but it was all good. The Sunset Strip was never this consistent. Frenchman Street had a great vibe. I loved the blues players the most. One club we went to had these two guitarists that were dueling with solos that had me bouncing in my seat and clapping like crazy. Mage just smiled at me. It was hard to carry on conversation, but I knew he was enjoying watching me.

No one ordered any alcohol, which surprised me until I remembered what they'd told me the first night we met. They all toasted me with their non-alcoholic beverages for my birthday and I was even brought a small ice cream sundae at one place, which no one would take any of. I ate it all, barely stopping myself from licking the dish clean. Everything was better in New Orleans, even the ice cream.

In between sets, they were all so easygoing with each other and told stories all night that had me in stitches. Jade was just plain adorable. He flirted and danced with different girls at every stop, thanking them graciously, but never staying too long with any one of them.

Mage explained that Jade was behaving because the ladies were out with them tonight. "Usually he'll find one or two he finds interesting and then he'll put on his charms until they beg to leave with him."

"Or with both of you, you mean?"

He looked nervous, like he wasn't sure how to answer.

"Mage, it's fine. I know the two of you were, ah, partners in crime."

He rubbed his hand down his face and tried to hide his flushed cheeks. "Now, chère, that was a long—"

"Did you enjoy it? The chase? What was your favorite part?"

"You're seriously asking me about this?"

I nodded, but before he could tell me more, the music started; this time it was a funk band complete with horns. Everyone jumped up and danced together, passing us girls around until the three of us ended up together, bumping and grinding. The guys stopped and stared hungrily.

Around midnight, we trudged back to the shop, where we accepted Devon's offer to drop us back at our hotel. I'd worn comfy boots with my wool slacks today, but my feet were still tired. We said goodnight and laughed the whole way up to our rooms, out of breath. I threw my arms around Mage's neck while he struggled to get the door open to my room.

"In you go, tired girl. Let's get you tucked in, shall we?"

"I am so in love with this place," I mumbled, as I fell face first onto the bed.

# Twenty

"Good morning, Sammara," he whispered against my cheek, his lips kissing me gently.

I opened one eye and saw he was fully dressed, and not in the clothes from last night. His hair was wet and down around his shoulders.

"I wanted to let you sleep, but we need to do breakfast."

I sat up, gripping the sheet to my chest. I looked around, trying to clear the fog.

"What happened? You..."

"I let you sleep. You were so relaxed, I just watched you. I went next door after a bit to give you some peace and then I came over when I couldn't stand to be away from you anymore." He sat on the edge of the bed with his hands under his legs. He made no move to touch me.

"Then why are you away from me? Come here," I said, reaching my arms up for him. He blew out a breath and shook his head.

"I can't, chère. I—"

"I know. It's not fair of me to keep asking either. I'm sorry."

He took my hands in his. "Did you have fun yesterday?"

I smiled up at him. "So much. Did you?"

He kissed my hands. "I did. And I want to have so much more with you. But the more time we spend in these rooms, the more—"

"I know. You don't have to say it. I'll get ready." He stood from the bed and started for the door. "You don't have to leave! I'll just be a few minutes."

He smiled nervously, his hands in his pockets. He looked towards the window. "I'll just be out here."

I hated the awkwardness this morning. I was determined to make it go away. Yesterday I'd had the best birthday with him and his friends, and I had been given the best gift ever. Someone to love me who I could love back. I intended to treasure every second I had with him.

I must have spaced out in the shower because I heard a knock at the door.

"We really need to get a move on, chère. I've got plans for us."

I laughed at his persistence. I could imagine him pacing outside the door. I hurried up for him, just putting some quick product in my hair and the minimal of eye makeup. I had brought my clothes into the bathroom, so when I emerged I was completely ready to go.

"What's on the agenda for today?" I asked on the way to the breakfast spot Mage had picked out.

He said, "There's a whole lot I'd like to do today, if you're up for it. And tonight, I'm taking you to meet my family."

I gulped. "Your *whole* family? And what will you tell them about me?"

Mage frowned and cocked his head to the side. "What do you mean, what will I tell them about you? I told my gran I was bringing you to meet the family. That you're with me. What was I supposed to say?"

"I don't know. This is all so...I don't know. We never—"

"I know we never talked about it, but you know what is in my heart, chère. Do you have any objection?"

"No! It's not that. It's just, what am I—"

"You need a label put on it? I don't want to scare you."

I took a moment to think about what he was saying to me. Did I have any misgivings? I knew I was falling in love with him, and if I trusted my instincts with him, I knew he loved me, too. I just knew he was planning our future, and I was used to living in the present. I barely planned what I was going to do each day, much less whom I was going to be with for the rest of my life. I wasn't raised with the best examples of family. For the Mother's sake, I didn't even know for sure who my father was!

"Mage, you just have to give me time. You're so far ahead of me. Let me catch up."

He nodded and looked down at his feet. "I know. I'm trying."

"I know you are. I'll get there."

His smile was so bright and contagious. I couldn't help giggling.

"Why are you laughing at me?"

"Hey," I said, gently. "I'd never laugh at you. Know that." We'd shared enough with each other that I knew he would be just as sensitive as me about feeling ridiculed or humiliated.

I reached up to touch his face and he pressed his cheek into my hand, closing his eyes. We stood like that for a long time. Unspoken sentiments passed between us. I wished we could just hold each other for this entire weekend. If I was being honest, I didn't ever want to let him go.

How had I gone from never wanting the touch of a man on my skin, to wanting to attach myself to this man for good?

Breakfast consisted of French toast made from the hugest pieces of bread I'd ever seen at the quaintest little place I'd ever seen. Mage also ordered me grits and bacon and potatoes and eggs.

"What are you trying to do, fatten me up to serve as the main course?"

He snorted. "You know I'd keep you all to myself, me. I don't share." One more thing to love about him. He wasn't being possessive, or at least I didn't take it that way. He just made his feelings known. Frequently.

"Good. I don't either." I took a bite of sausage off his plate and he stopped my fork with his as I was pulling back.

"Woman, I just said I don't share." He smirked at me as he slid the piece of sausage from my fork and started lifting it to his mouth. I grabbed his hand and redirected his fork to my lips and snatched the piece.

"You better be careful, chère. I'll fight you for it." He knocked my fork with his again and I knocked back. We both started laughing and pretty soon, I flung some eggs at him, he popped a potato off my forehead. It was full-on war.

"You gonna get us kicked outta here, you." He leaned forward and kissed me quickly, grabbing his wallet from his back pocket.

"You started it," I said with a smile. "It was delicious. Thank you. I hope you'll let me treat you for lunch or breakfast tomorrow, though. You're the starving artist here."

He stood from the table and did a very courtly gesture. "Of course, milady. I forget you're the big-time Features Editor."

"Funny," I said, standing up next to him. I slid on my sweater and allowed him to lead me from the restaurant.

We spent the day visiting a couple of museums, one of which was in the old Mint building, and he gave me a full history of New Orleans Jazz. I was fascinated by his knowledge of his heritage. The pictures were incredible and the music...wow. It sounded more like life than any other music I'd ever heard before. The more he talked, the more engrossed I became. I asked him a million questions and he answered them all like a pro.

"How do you know so much? You're like a walking New Orleans encyclopedia!"

He chuckled as we waved goodbye to the docent, who laughed at our exchange. "You haven't met Gran yet. Then you'll know. She knows everything. About music, New Orleans, Voodoo... I told you I was home-schooled. That was my schooling."

"And I got home-schooled by a bunch of hippies. I can tell you a lot about the Civil Rights Movement and free love, but that's about it." We laughed as we sauntered through the French Market and then started talking about books and poetry. My brain was just as turned on by this man as the rest of me.

We shared a late lunch at the hotel before going up to our rooms, separately, so we could clean up. I started to panic about meeting his family, so I took a few minutes to meditate. I'd brought my candle and some chamomile with me to help calm my nerves in case I needed it. Boy, did I need it right now.

When we left the hotel an hour later, he asked if I was still up for walking after we'd walked around for the past two days. He said his gran's was just a few blocks farther. I assured him my boots were made for walkin', which led to him singing silly songs with me all the way there.

It was eerie walking the streets in Tremé. We took Basin Street past the park and down to Ursulines. The house sat on the corner with bushes and trees all around. Mage pointed out homes that were still empty since the storm. "There are fewer now. Some new folks moved in, some old folks came back. Gran's happy with the changes and has a full house most of the time, with family who come home to visit and recharge."

We were the first to arrive. The house had a flight of steps up to the porch, which was obviously well-used. Comfy seats and a bench swing had me dreaming of nights enjoying the outdoors. I could even picture Mage and I sitting there together holding hands. Mage had told me he believed all of his uncles and their families were coming, including the uncle I'd met at the airport. I grew more excited by the minute.

"Saturday night dinner at Gran's is always rowdy, so just stay by me, chère."

"Rowdy noisy? Or rowdy rowdy?"

"Noisy, raucous. Sometimes the brothers get to breakin' each other's balls a bit, but it's never come to blows. Although there was one time, Oncle Louis took a bat to Oncle Remy's car over some girl. Don't worry though. It's more the women you gotta watch. Tante Lulu and Tante Celeste get downright evil with their gossip sometimes. They're all about the 'if you got nothing nice to say, come sit by me' mentality. They're hilarious."

Mage knocked on the door as he opened it. "Gran! Where you at?"

A tall, slender woman dressed in a brightly colored blouse and faded jeans came towards us with her hands outstretched.

"My grandson. I'm so glad to see you! It's been too long you been out there making that screamy racket!"

He hugged her tight, a boyish smile taking over his face.

"Gran, this is my Sammara."

She turned to me with a knowing glance and pulled me into a tight hug. She was very strong, but nowhere near as strong as her energy. Goose bumps rose up all over me at her touch.

"God bless you, young lady. Martín, you come in here and help me with the table, you. Sammara, we'll be right back. Make yourself comfortable, and I'll bring you some lemonade." She kept smiling at me as she led him by the arm to the dining room. I heard their hushed voices as they turned the corner and I laughed. I could only imagine what she was saying to him. I didn't feel any suspiciousness coming from her, not like I did with little Josephina.

Right on cue, the door opened again and in the little girl stomped, as if she owned the place, followed by who I assumed was her mother and Joseph.

"Good to see you again, Miss Sammara," Joseph said, moving to shake my hand. "This is my wife, Lulu."

Lulu appeared to be only a little older than me, although with her flawless skin and jet-black hair—neatly styled in an asymmetrical cut—it was hard to tell. She smiled and raised her eyebrows at me. "So you the one Martín be making a fuss about. Come here, girl."

I started to hold out my hand but she pulled me in for a hug. I felt her inhale deeply against my hair, startling me.

"Mmmmm, he's right."

"I told you," Mage said as he appeared by my side. "She smells just like red roses." He leaned in and kissed Lulu on the cheek quickly before bending down to pick up Josephina. He swung the little girl up and hugged her until she squealed to be put down.

The next hour was insane. The house filled up with people until every seat in the house was occupied by laughing family members. All of the brothers, with the exception of Moises, who apparently had to work, and Albert, who was playing in a band somewhere, arrived. Soon I was on the couch with Lulu on one side of me, Celeste on the other, Josephina on my lap scowling at me, and Mage watching me from the other side of the room as his uncles asked him about the band and living in Hollywood.

"What I don't understand is why he don't move back here and start a band up. I know he misses playing jazz and blues with Joseph. Why would he want to stay out there in Los Angeles anyhow?"

A beat passed before I realized Celeste was actually talking to me. "You mean Mage? I don't know. He did say Maggie's Bones was taking a break next year." Shit. I didn't know what was okay to say. Not being sure what I was to Mage, and what my role was...

"Sugar, you need to relax," Lulu said in my other ear. "That old bitty is just trying to stir up some shit. Lil Martín is my favorite nephew and he's Josephine's favorite grandson. He's special and he loves you. You can say whatever the hell you want, other than the Saints are no good, and everyone here is gonna love you just as much."

I gazed at her, dumbfounded. She and Celeste looked at each other and laughed loudly. I looked to Mage for help.

"Are you going to marry Parrain Martín?" Little Josephina was waiting for an answer with her hands on her hips.

"I...um..."

What the fuck was I supposed to say? This time I sent a mental *HELP* to Mage and he got the hint. He made his way over and sat on the coffee table facing me and took Josephina's hands in his.

"Now, darlin', don't go chasin' her off, you hear me?" He leaned in and whispered to her, "She a scaredy cat. You be careful or she might run away."

Josephina turned on me with a determined look. "She don't go unless I say she go. Come on, Miss Sammara. I'm gonna show you mah dollies and you're gonna play with me."

I was actually relieved to be led away from the couch of interrogation by this little boss. Mage's evil grin had me shaking my head. Josephina had a corner of the living room to herself with a decked-out Victorian dollhouse complete with miniatures and tiny figurines. Josephine followed us over.

"My late husband made this for me when Remy and LeRoy were young. He was just sure I was going to have a little girl next, but then came Lionel, Albert, Moises, Joseph and Martín Sr. I knew I wasn't going to have no little girl, but I loved the house and all the little things he made for it. Now Josephina gets to play with it. You be careful, sweet girl."

I smiled up at Josephine, and immediately her energy surrounded me. I felt a bit more at ease, especially when I picked up on the grilling Mage was getting from his aunties. I listened to Josephina prattle on about her dollies with one ear and held back my laughter at Mage's end of the conversation. His aunties were doing a better job of keeping their voices down.

"Yes I bought her flowers... No, I haven't... No, we haven't! I don't know when I'm moving back for good. I don't know if she'll come with me, damn... Yes, I want to marry her... Will you give me a break? No, I haven't touched nobody... I ain't tellin' you about that... No, I haven't talked to my mama... We don't have time to get out to Houma. I'm about to... Not yet... Yeah, I'm buying it... Yeah, we working it out... I don't know if I'll be here for Mardi Gras. Give me a break!"

He tried to extract himself from Celeste's grip while Lulu sat on his lap to hold him down. He fought them both off as they attempted to kiss his cheeks and howled with laughter. When he finally got away, he came over to our corner just as Josephina was telling me about her conversations with her deceased granddaddy.

"Granddaddy gon' add another room on the house for me. He tell me he didn't know I was coming, so he gon' add it here."

Mage wiped at the lipstick on his face and smiled down at Josephina.

"Granddaddy also tole me you comin' back here with Lil Martín for Mardi Gras. You gon' dance with him on Canal Street."

Mage and I looked at each other. "Phina, when you talk to Granddaddy?"

"All the time," she said matter-of-factly. "He tole me you got nekkid by a fire. You get nekkid by a fire in Caliaforney?"

We both laughed nervously. Mage kissed her head and held out his hand for me. "Phina, you go get cleaned up for dinner. Gran's almost ready." She grumbled under her breath the whole walk down the hall towards the bathroom.

My wide eyes found Mage's and I gulped.

"What—"

"Please don't be afraid—"

"I'm not! But Mage?"

"I know. They're a lot to take. I'm sorry. Maybe I shouldn't have brought you—"

"No. Please. I'm glad I get to meet them. I just... We're coming for Mardi Gras? I've always wanted to." His eyes bugged out and I leaned in to kiss him, then came away scrunching up my face. "It's weird kissing you with another woman's lipstick on your face."

Mage wrapped me in his arms and pulled me in tight. "We'll do whatever you are ready to do, chère. I'm just so glad you're here with me now."

We snuck in a quick kiss before we were all summoned to the table. In the hallway outside of the dining room, there was a small altar with half-smoked cigars, a bottle of rum, some feathers and bones, and other items I assumed Josephine used in her daily practice. Mage told me his gran was a priestess. I wanted to know more, but I didn't want to be the nosy reporter tonight. Instead, I was Mage's—or "Lil Martín's"—guest of honor, and the others had the job of being nosy.

We held hands around the table, Mage on my left and Lulu on my right. Josephine offered a blessing on the food and a prayer for safe travels for her family. The family praying together gave me a warm feeling, totally different from the judgmental fire-and-brimstone prayers I'd heard from my grandparents. Josephine spoke with a combination of Catholic ideology and Voodoo practice.

As we sat down, the front door opened wide and a man dressed in a fancy suit came barreling in.

"Am I too late for Mama's gumbo?" He strolled over dramatically to Josephine and kissed her on the cheek. She looked perturbed.

"I tole you to come on time if you were joining us." She started to stand to set another place at the already packed table, but he told her to sit down.

"I already ate in town, Mama. I just wanted to see my son." He glided over to Mage, who stood up and held out his hand.

"Daddy," was all he said.

The man laughed at his hand and pulled him into a huge hug,

which Mage stiffly returned. He then went around the table, slapping hands and sharing half hugs with his other brothers. He kissed Celeste, made a fuss over Josephina, and then kissed Lulu. He stopped when he got to me.

"Damn! You all kinds of fine, girl. What's your name?"

"She's my girl, Daddy. Sammara, meet Martín Dumas, Senior. My father."

I held out my hand, acknowledging Mage's frown. Martín made a big show of bending to kiss it. I studied him for just a moment and saw the similarities between father and son. Mage had his bright green eyes, but Martín Sr. was darker-skinned and wore his curly hair slicked back and cut close.

"Beautiful. Yeah. Where you from?"

"Martín," Josephine interrupted. "We just fixin' to eat. You grab a chair and let us get on with it."

He bowed to his mother and left the room. There were whispered complaints around the table, which ceased when he reentered. He pulled up a chair next to his mama and proceeded to talk to Joseph, Remy and Lionel throughout our meal. I ate quietly, watching the family dynamics. Josephine glanced at me from time to time with a smile that was warm, if not a little sad, which I returned. When the meal was finished, I followed her into the kitchen with the intention of helping, but Celeste and Lulu assured me they had it covered.

"Come walk with me," Josephine said. Mage had already followed the men out to the front room, so I stepped out back with her. She pulled on a sweater and took a cigar from her pocket, lighting it with a match. I'd never seen a woman smoke a cigar before. I was intrigued.

"Bad habit, you probably think. It's just my way. I used to share a smoke with my husband after dinner. I still honor him by continuing the tradition." She offered the cigar to me and I took it hesitantly.

"I've never—"

"Just take a puff, hold it for a second, and let it go. Let it all go, chère. All that stress you got going on."

I smiled and did as she said, glad I didn't launch into a coughing fit.

"My grandson is nothing like his father. My son like to think he know what's best, but being the baby, he done picked and chose what he learned from what his daddy and I taught him. The music he embraced with a passion. Love, not so much. He likes to spread it around, if you know what I mean. He wanted kids but didn't want to be tied down, so he split. I don't blame Rachel for taking Lil Martín away from here when she did. I liked her a lot. Still do. We talk. She did the best she could with Martín and he grew up to be a fine young man. Them Cajuns he hooked up with is good people, them. I'm glad Marie moved here to New Orleans. She and I became great friends when the boys left. That gal can cook!

"Anyway, I just didn't want you to think bad of my grandson after meeting his father. That son of mine, he a looker and always had women after him. Lil Martín, too. But he got too deep of a soul to play too long." She puffed on her cigar for a moment, closing her eyes as she blew out the smoke. "He tells me about his dreams."

She turned her gaze on me and I flinched a little, which caused her expression to soften.

"You spook easy, chère. I understand. I see what he can't see. He won't never understand what it's like to be violated like that, how it makes it nearly impossible to trust your instincts about people."

She saw right through me. Somehow I knew she had a little experience with it herself. I took another puff from the cigar and tried to relax, although I was afraid of what else she could see.

"I do trust Mage," I said quietly. "He's the only one I trust. But I don't know if I can give him what he wants. He deserves more than that."

"*You* deserve more than that, chère. You are not what your circumstances have made you become. You have so much more to offer than you even know. Your gift is strong, but you let the negative spirits influence you too much. Being with my grandson will help you bring the positive to you. The negative ones want you because you are pure of heart. That's why they find you and hurt you. It doesn't have to be like that, Sammara. Your mama doesn't have the gift like you do, so she couldn't ever tell you, and your grandparents, well... That a whole other story.

"But your daddy... Yeah, I know about him, too. Once Lil Martín tole me about you, I could see it all. He a strong witch, your daddy. You should spend some more time with him and his hippie friends, you.

"Now come on. I want dessert and my boy is getting antsy in there. He prolly worried I have you out here cutting off chicken heads or something." She laughed at her own words and took my hand to lead me back into the house.

I felt better. I did. The fact that she could so easily accept everything she knew about me floored me, but also made me feel more at ease. Mage's dreams were important to him. While I didn't know if I believed in them as he did, I knew in my heart I wanted to be with him, wanted us to build a life together.

As we entered the front room and I saw him with his family, tears welled in my eyes. Tears of joy.

He hurried to my side as soon as he saw me and took my face in his hands. "What's wrong?"

I smiled and took his hands in mine. "Absolutely nothing," I whispered with a smile. "Your gran wants dessert."

"Come on, everyone!" Josephine shouted as she slipped on a sweater. "I want to go to Kermit's."

Everyone jumped up and slipped into coats, except for Celeste and Lulu.

"We'll stay here and get Josephina down for sleep. We got cards to play." They kissed their husbands and then swooped up the little girl and carried her protesting into the back of the house.

"You up for this?" Mage asked me, a worried expression on his face.

"How do you say? *Laissez les bon temps rouler.*"

He threw back his head and laughed. "You got it right, chère." He kissed me softly as the others headed out the door. Then he paused. "I was trying to hold back, but dammit. I love you, Sammara. I love that you're here."

My sweet man. I cupped his face in my hands. "I love you, Martín. Lil Martín, is that what I should call you?"

He scoffed. "You know better."

I gasped in mock disgust and slapped him on the ass as he walked towards the door. He was right. There was nothing "lil" about him.

"I hope them boots were made for dancing as much as they was for walking."

# Twenty-One

We brought up the rear of the Dumas family. Martín was rambling on and on about his latest album and his regular club gigs in New York and Chicago. I rolled my eyes at the amount of name-dropping he was doing with his brothers. They seemed impressed, to a point. Occasionally I'd hear Josephine put him in his place.

The walk was short and the men laughed and joked the whole way. Remy and Joseph let loose a little without their wives around, although it was obvious that they loved them very much.

Kermit Ruffins' Tremé Speakeasy was jam-packed with people dancing and laughing along to some great music. The crowd was so thick, I was glad we were with Mage's uncles, who all surrounded us as a sort of barrier for me. Everyone seemed to know each other in the club, and there were lots of hugs. The band that was playing had a full horn section and an older African-American woman was singing a saucy blues number.

Mage put his hands on my waist and guided me away from the bar and towards the dance floor, which had no clear dividing line from the rest of the restaurant. People sat at tables and bobbed their heads along as they ate what looked to be decadent dishes of Creole food. Josephine headed to the bar with Remy and Lionel at her side. The others joined Mage and me, and I found myself dancing with him, his father, and Joseph and Moises, who had been here already. He apologized for missing dinner.

"It's nice to meet you, Sammara. I hope you don't mind, but we gon' steal yo man for a minute or two." Joseph and Moises stood at my sides while Albert grabbed Mage by the arm and dragged him up to the stage.

"Make way, make way," he shouted. "Hey Tom! This here's my nephew, Lil Martín. Let him stand in on bass for your next number." The bandleader shook hands with a smiling Mage, who graciously accepted a stand-up from a member of the band. I glanced at his father, who was talking to some women in front of us.

"That's my boy! He probably forgot how to play the standards, though, Tommy! He might need some help."

Mage shook his head. He leaned the neck of the bass against his shoulder while he pulled out a hair tie to tame his mane, and then he adjusted his grip. The musicians talked to each other and, I assumed, agreed on a song. The number they launched into was a vaguely familiar tune. When the singer began crooning, it came to me.

"*La Vie En Rose*," I whispered, bringing my hands to my chest.

I just knew Mage had chosen this song for me. He played with such concentration that I never caught his eye, but the small smile on his face let me know he could tell just how much it affected me.

Their next tune was a fast one and I was quickly swept away with the others. I danced with the uncles, I smiled so hard my face hurt, and I fell in love with this place, this atmosphere that Mage loved so much.

I had a colleague at the magazine where I worked before *Feedback* who once went to New Orleans on a story about a cooking school. She never came back. Apparently that was a thing. People just up and moved. I could feel the temptation. There was so much positive energy in this bar, I was drunk on it. I spun around and stumbled into a really large man.

"Oh, I'm so sorry." I was mortified. He just laughed and patted my shoulder before turning back to raise his beer to the band.

Mage glanced up a few times but he was completely absorbed in his task and was grinning like a fiend. I couldn't believe he could keep up with these guys so naturally. There was a lot more to learn about him and his musical education. I would relish every minute of it.

I'd always loved jazz and the blues, but there was nothing like hearing it live. One song morphed into another and another. Before I knew it, it was two in the morning and I was about to drop. The band finished their set and they all shook hands and hugged Mage and each other. He made his way over to me, and his uncles all hugged him.

"Boy, you can play that thing. Ever think you'll quit making all that racket and get back to your roots?" Albert asked him.

Mage shook his head. "Nah. The Bones aren't done. But you know I love this place. Imma come back. I am. I want to open a club here. The guys in the band and me? We're putting in an offer on the St. Germaine in the Quarter. Can you imagine what we could do with that? You guys could cook, we'd bring all our favorite musicians in—"

"Oh, you think you gon' come back here and just fit right in, you? Damn, son. I thought *I* had big balls. You sure got a pair if you think you can come back—"

"Simmer down, Martín. You know we need all our people to come home. If folks got a place to play, maybe more of our musicians will come back." Joseph reached for Martín but he yanked his arm away.

"Man, he don't even play right. You think you stand up there once with Kermit's house band and you da man?"

It was obvious Martín was drunk and feeling combative. Mage put his arm around me and led me away from the men, who were trying to calm his father. We made our way to the bar and Mage spoke in his gran's ear. She raised an eyebrow and pursed her lips. She shook her head and pulled me close so I could hear her.

"I tole you my grandson was not like his father. You two enjoy the rest of your trip here, darlin'. And here," she said, reaching into the pocket of her coat. She pressed a small satin bag in my hand and closed my fingers around it. She leaned in and kissed me on the cheek.

"Gris-gris, child. To help you make the decisions you got before you. I'll be seeing you soon."

I thanked her heartily, kissing her on the cheek as though I'd known her forever. Mage chuckled at my exuberance.

"Come on, ya lush," he said, tugging me down the street. Josephine was cloaked by her sons, minus Martín, who'd stayed behind with the ladies. They all sang songs as they walked the opposite direction back towards her home.

"That was amazing! *You* are amazing! I love this place," I shouted, ending with a hiccup.

"I didn't see you with no drink, chère. What's got into you?"

I shrugged. "My only explanation is that all the energy in that place made me a little—"

"Drunk. Got it. Come on, *ma cherie.* Let's get you to bed."

I stepped in front of him and put my arms around his neck. "Will you take me to bed, Martín? Please? I want to be with you tonight." I think I batted my eyelashes at him and probably did the whole biting on my lip thing.

Instead of having the desired effect, he frowned at me. "I can't do that, chère. Not like this." His voice cracked a little and his green eyes looked so sad.

"What did I do? I'm sorry."

He shook his head and tugged me to keep walking, which we did without speaking the rest of the way to the hotel. I wanted to cry at the fact that I'd possibly ruined our perfect night together. We entered the hotel and went up to our floor. I started to pull my key out, but Mage stopped me.

"Let me explain," he said in a low voice. He opened his door and gestured for me to step inside. "I don't want to say this in the hall," he said by way of explanation. He shut the door and made sure to step away from it so I had a clear exit if I needed. Oh, he was so thoughtful. He was so good to me.

Why could I barely keep my balance? There were two Mages in front of me.

"Sammara," he began. I tried to focus on his words but it was tough. "I promised you that nothing would happen on this trip, and I have to keep my word. I want everything to be perfect, chère. When we make love... Jesus, I sound just like D. Ha! Wow. I thought he was an idiot. Now, I understand."

"Understand what? What are you talking about?"

He held up his hands as he tried to get his laughter under control. "Jaylene told us that the reason Devon waited to, ah, be intimate with her, until they were away from the St. Germaine, was because he got all mushy and wanted it to be perfect when they had sex. See, it was her first time... Shit. I shouldn't be saying all this."

"Mage, you can trust me. I wouldn't ever—"

"I know, it's just... Anyway. I get what he meant. It's almost three in the morning. You had some sort of something happen to you tonight at the club. I just can't, chère. I have to keep my word. When we are together again..."

"And when is that going to be? Are you staying here? What are you going to do, Mage?"

He shoved his hands in his pocket and frowned again. I didn't like that look on him. "I'm here through the holidays, I suppose. I don't remember exactly when we go back on the road. Sometime in January. I'll be here for Mardi Gras. That's all I know. It ain't much."

I hugged myself where I stood, coming down off that high from the club. "Ok. Tell me about Christmas in New Orleans. Talk to me. Please. I don't want this night to end."

He smiled and kicked at the bed frame. I bent down and unlaced my boots, clumsily slipping them off. I reached under my top and unhooked my bra and did that complicated move us chicks do to get out of our contraptions without taking off our shirts. Mage started to speak, but I held up a hand.

"I don't want this night to end, but my feet are tired and I hate wearing a bra. You need to get over it. Can we sit down? Or lay down? I'm feeling kind of woozy."

He moved to take me in his arms, just as I kind of fell against the bed.

"You sure you didn't have nothing to drink?"

"No! I'm telling you! Between the tickling fingers in the cemetery yesterday, the psychic overload at your gran's, and then all the crazy energy in that club, I just feel kind of loopy. Will you hold me, or are you going to keep yelling at me?" I hiccupped again and he cursed under his breath.

"You a mess, you. Come on." He helped me crawl into bed. He

went around the other side, took off his shoes and got out of his suit coat and button-down shirt. He was wearing just a tank undershirt beneath, which he left on, along with his slacks. He flopped onto the bed next to me and pulled me into his arms. I shivered a bit, so he got up and pulled the blanket out from underneath me, grumbling about my crazy ass, and then covered us both up.

"Christmas. You were going to tell me about Christmas."

I know he said something, but I just remember how much I loved the sound of his voice and the way his lips moved when he spoke. I might have touched them a bit. I don't remember anything else about that night. It was so full of goodness, and a bit of insanity.

It was not only my bestest birthday weekend ever, but the greatest life of my night to date.

# Twenty-Two

My last day went way too fast and before I knew it, I was on a plane back to Los Angeles with Mage's iPod in hand, full of New Orleans music he insisted I needed to listen to. The other hand clutched the gris-gris from Josephine. I'd dreamt of her sometime that night while asleep in his arms. She looked much frailer and she was speaking to her sons about a second line for a funeral. I didn't mention it to Mage. My dreams weren't always about what they seemed, so I kept it to myself. I knew she had to be getting older, but I wasn't about to ask how old. I guessed her in her mid to late seventies. She could still have many years left.

I'd left my car at the Burbank Airport and didn't hit much traffic on the way back to Hollywood. My first thought when I stepped in my condo was that I missed Mage already.

My second thought was that I'd forgotten to take out the trash and clean out the fridge. GAWD it was awful.

I spent the late hours cleaning my kitchen, taking the time to remove everything from the fridge so I could clean all of the shelves. I sometimes processed shit this way. There were times I'd be down on my hands and knees cleaning grout for hours with a toothbrush while pondering some issue.

I arrived at my appointment Monday morning with only seconds to spare as I'd forgotten to set my alarm. Brantley and I discussed my article more and he decided that it should be a series of articles, so we outlined the material I'd cover over the course of the next several issues. The first part, which I'd written about my experiences, would serve as an introduction. I could feel my vision start to go fuzzy around the edges a few times and had to ask him to repeat himself. He seemed frustrated with me, but overall I thought the meeting went well. I came to an understanding that his gruff way of dealing with me was more his discomfort at discussing this issue. His emotions were not angry, just helpless.

I threw myself into working on the articles, but I made sure to call Mage every night before bed. That was the deal we struck before I left New Orleans. Sometimes he'd text me and say he couldn't talk, but he said knowing I would call him every day made it easier to be away.

My mother and I spoke the day before Christmas and she asked me, if I didn't have other plans, if I would please come out to the ranch for dinner. She said Oliver wanted to talk with me. I called Mage with the news, and he was really happy for me. He said if I wasn't with him, the desert was the next best place to be.

I drove out to the ranch Christmas morning, singing loudly in the car to the tunes on Mage's iPod that I'd had on repeat nonstop. I parked and pulled out the small gifts I'd picked up for Mom, Oliver, Laramie and Robin: candles, some special oils I liked to pick up from my local herbalist, and some succulents for them to add to their garden. Oliver and Mom greeted me at the door with a big group hug. I worried I might get panicky without Mage here, but I could feel him, almost as though he were standing beside me.

"Thank you for making the drive, Sam."

"Thanks for having me! I was prepared to eat SpaghettiOs and Corn Nuts on a TV tray while watching a *Twilight Zone* marathon."

"No way! Man! Sometimes I miss having TV." Laramie pouted at Robin, who shook his head.

"It's too distracting, honey. We'll never get any work done."

I had so many questions about the studio portion of the ranch that I spent most of our meal talking to Laramie and Robin. Mom and Oliver had prepared a quasi-typical meal of tofurkey and mashed potatoes with all of the trimmings. I made eye contact with Oliver a few times. He was watching me with fascination.

After our meal, we went out back to sit by the fire. The weather was a perfect seventy degrees, and the sun was just about down behind the mountain range. Laramie and Robin asked Mom to help them with something, leaving me blatantly alone with Oliver.

"They really need Mom to help them choose the towels to hang up in the bathroom?"

Oliver chuckled and stroked his beard. He seemed so huge, with his tree-trunk legs jutting out from his hips. He had his belly distended, exaggerating its size to a comical level.

"They're about as subtle as a fox in a henhouse," he joked. Then his smile faded a little.

"It would take a blood test to be sure, but after meeting you, Sammara, I know you're my daughter. How do you feel about that?"

I pulled up my knees and rested my chin on my arms. "I don't know. Curious? Confused? Relieved." I said the last with a laugh. Thankfully he smiled.

"I can relate to the first two. Relieved?"

"Yeah. There were a few guys I remember that I really don't want to think about my mom sleeping with."

Oliver barked out a laugh at that. "I guess you're right. What sort of things do you remember from that time?"

I tucked my hair behind my ears. "Just flashes, mainly? Sort of like pictures, or like an old home movie without any sound. Then I have music that plays in my head that I know I had to have heard here. But I don't remember you. Like at all. Did you look different?"

"Yeah," he said. "I guess I haven't aged gracefully."

"No! That's not what—"

"I'm kidding. I didn't have a beard back then and I probably weighed about a hundred pounds less. My hair was blonde then." It was dark reddish-blonde now. The only similarity I really saw between us was my freckles. I had my mother's black hair and gray eyes.

"I used to have a lot of questions when I was younger, when I started real school and learned that other people didn't live like us. Kids would ask me about my dad. It didn't bother me until I started church with my grandparents and saw the families together. But I didn't dwell on it. I was just trying to make sure I had a way out when I was old enough."

He leaned forward, resting his forearms on his knees. His gaze burned right through me. "Sammara, I won't pressure you. I love your mother, and I want to know you, whether you're mine biologically or not. You're important to her, and that's important to me. I don't want your mother to be alone anymore, or afraid to be who she wants to be. I'm going to take care of her. I want you to know that."

"I know," I said, surprising myself with the surety I felt toward his words. "I know how you feel. As long as you can be patient, I'd like to know you, too."

We held each other's gazes for a few more moments, smiling at each other over the fire, and then the others rejoined us. I stayed and talked for a while, but graciously declined their invitation to pray with them. I missed Mage too much.

I called him on the drive home and made him stay on the line with me until I got into bed. It was late in New Orleans, but he stayed up for me. His voice was so damn sexy over the phone, it was difficult to concentrate on the dark roads. Once I was inside my condo and curled up in bed, I sighed happily.

"Thanks for seeing me home, my love. Merry Christmas."

"Merry Christmas to you, too. Thank you for sharing your drive with me. If I can't be there..."

"Soon. I love you so much."

"I love you back."

# Twenty-Three

Two days before New Year's Eve, I treated myself to a day at the spa. It had been way too long. I finished up around seven that night and went to a nice dinner. I realized I hadn't checked my phone all day, so before driving home, I looked and cursed. Mage had been trying to call me for hours. I dialed his number frantically from my contacts.

"Hey you," I breathed when the call finally went through.

"Where are you, chère? I tried...I couldn't...I need—"

"I'm coming, love. I'll be there soon."

I prayed I wouldn't run into any police on the way up to the mansion, but something in Mage's voice had me rushing to see him. We spoke on the phone as I drove. He said they'd had to come back to town suddenly this morning to work out some things with the label, and that they'd all gone out to a club.

"I had dinner with them," he'd said in a shaky voice. "I just feel off. Something's wrong. They all wanted to stay. I just need to see you."

I pulled up and barely made it up the steps before he threw the door open. We collided on the top step and hugged each other tight.

"I'm sorry, chère. There's just something wrong. I haven't felt this bad since the night—"

"Let's go inside. I know. I'm sorry I didn't get your message earlier."

The emotions from the house were strong tonight, but Mage's were stronger. I pushed aside all that didn't come from him. He led me up to the ballroom, leaving it dark, the only light coming from the large windows. He stopped in the middle of the floor.

"The most peaceful time I've had with you was dancing together in front of the fire. Can we do that again?"

I looked around and saw a gas fireplace at one end of the room. "Does that work?"

He nodded. We started the fire together. He left for a moment and came back with a tube of lipstick that probably belonged to Mackenzie. I recognized the color. He drew a five-pointed star on the floor as I located pillar candles on the mantle of the fireplace. I lit them and placed them at the five corners. Wordlessly, we undressed outside the sacred space. We stepped in together and joined hands. I felt a rush of love from him, followed by uncertainty. I wanted to wipe that away tonight.

I stepped into his arms, looking up into his eyes. "You have been so patient with me and so much has happened since we met. I'm grateful for you, Mage. I just needed to tell you that. Whatever you're feeling..."

His eyes searched mine for a moment, and then he closed them, pressing his forehead against mine.

"I can breathe again now that you're here. Anytime I get a bad feeling now, I just can't help but worry something's happened to you."

Our bodies were pressed together, skin on skin. He was so warm and the flames did such lovely things to his eyes. They were studying me intently. I made myself remain quiet while he put his thoughts into words.

"I've always had a clear view of what was going to happen, the good and the bad. Then I dreamed of you and I kinda went a little bit crazy. I haven't felt right being away from you and I wasn't able to see what was going to happen. I thought the worst. I needed to trust you. I knew you had things to work out, but I couldn't just accept it. I didn't mean to freak out, but I had this bad feeling... When a man finds the woman who is meant for him, it's not easy to just let nature take its course. I can't help how I feel, Sammara. I love you and I want you. All of you."

This moment felt important, like the moment I first walked through this door. As though greater forces were at play.

"Then take what I have to give you, Mage. You can have all that I am. I just hope you can find it in your heart to be patient as the rest of me knits back together."

"We're going to make it happen together, chère."

His lips descended on mine, but our eyes remained open. We kissed as though our souls were fusing. Our hearts beat as one. Mage's hands slid down my body as he whispered a gentle prayer. I answered him with a prayer of my own as we slowly lowered to the floor. Mage took me onto his lap, his eyes never leaving mine. Outside the winds rattled the windows and rain began to pelt the glass. The storm brewing was nothing compared to the one inside of me. All of the anger and fear I'd felt over my past left my consciousness and was replaced by a need for him, for the love and desire he had for me.

Greedily, I drank it all in as I took him into my body.

We both gasped, surprised at the power we felt at our connection.

"Sammara, are you sure?"

I moved against him, his cock pressing against my womb, and I dropped my head back. "Completely. I want all of you, too, love."

Mage's hand grasped the back of my neck and he forced me to look at him. "Sammara, I love you. You're the love I've been looking for my whole life."

Thunder clapped loudly outside as he pulled my hips down hard, impaling me. It had been a really long time since I'd had a lover, one I'd chosen to be with. Mage erased my pain with his loving. Each stroke from his powerful body felt as though it was cleansing my spirit. I took him all in, I let myself go, and he loved me again and again. We didn't speak, just let our bodies speak for us. I felt him inside my thoughts. He was slowly letting go of his worry for me, determined to make me feel whole again.

When an image of me pregnant flashed in my mind, I stopped him.

"Mage? Are you..."

"Sammara, I can't help thinking about it. I want children. I want babies. Lots of them. I want little freckled girls and crazy-haired, green-eyed boys running around. I want a family. With you."

I put my hands against his chest. "I don't know if I can give that to you. I'm not sure I'm ok with babies. I'm sorry..." I started to move off of him, but he held me to him.

"It will happen if it's meant to. I just want you, chère. Whatever that means for us."

We made love playfully, frantically, and finally, tenderly, on the ballroom floor in front of the fire for hours. My heart was so full of love for Mage. We'd opened some kind of connection tonight and he said he could feel it from me stronger than before. We experimented with reading each other's thoughts and laughed hysterically at the ones we got wrong.

"Face it, silly. Whatever we have, it's spotty at best. Hit or miss. Sometimes we're going to know, and others, well..."

"Yeah, but if we practice, maybe we'll be able to do it when we're apart."

"Mage?" We were lying next to each other on the floor and he grabbed my face between his hands.

"Hold on. You're thinking...we should go to my bed because your ass hurts."

I burst out laughing and slapped his ass, which got him so hot, he flipped us over, knocking one of the candles over.

"Oh shit!" We scrambled to put out the small fire that had started on my t-shirt. Mage put it out with a throw pillow from the couch and I grabbed a bottle of water from behind the bar. I ran over and started to pour just as Mage leaned forward.

"Fuck me, that's cold, chère!" The fire was out and the two of us fell apart laughing.

"What's so damn funny up here?"

*Oh Shit.* The others were apparently back from the club.

"Hold up a second," Mage called out. That led to whoops and hollers from down below and boots pounding up the steps. Mage had just pulled up his pants and I'd pulled his shirt on over my head, barely covering my ass, before Jade came busting through the doorway.

"What in the devil's name are you two doing up here?" He laughed until he saw the pentagram on the floor. "What's this? Is this devil shit? You brought devil shit into our home?"

"What the fuck, Jade? You know I don't worship the fucking devil! What the fuck's wrong with you?"

"Well what is this?"

"It's a five-pointed star, Jade," Star said as he and Mackenzie came wandering in, followed by Devon and Jaylene. Star put his arm around Jade. "Remember? Mage and Maggie explained it before. It's the five points. Water, earth, fire, air, and the ether. It's Wiccan, dude."

I was hiding behind Mage, not very well, but hopefully covered up enough.

"Hey, Sammara," Jaylene called out. "Boys, why don't you let them clean up? Let's go down to the kitchen and they can join us when they're ready."

Thank the goddess for Jaylene. She mouthed "sorry" to us and pushed the guys out the door. Mackenzie turned around and winked at me before she and Jaylene followed them.

"I am so sorry, chère." Mage wrapped his arm around me and walked me down the hall to his room. "I hope you weren't in love with that shirt."

"Actually, I got it at my first Foo Fighter's show. I met Dave Grohl for the first time that night. That shirt is priceless to me."

He turned on me with a look of horror. "Sammara, I'm—"

"I'm just messing with you! I got it at the third show I went to. I interviewed Dave and Pat afterwards at a bar in Kansas City. It was a blast!"

"You little..."

I loved his way of getting me back.

We made it down to the kitchen almost an hour later. The gang was still up playing cards. Mage fixed us burritos, we had some sodas and laughed and talked as a group. Jade told us about the evening at the club, how it had been super packed, and how Marcus had been surrounded by women all night.

"I don't know if he'll make it back here. He said he was going to stay at his apartment tonight," Star offered, taking a bite of Mage's second burrito. Mage slapped at his hand but he'd slowed down already. I told him his eyes were bigger than his stomach, to which he gave me a wicked smile.

"I saw him talking to Sherry before we left," Jade said. "Hopefully he went home with her. I want them to work things out. I can't stand it when people don't get along. Especially folks who love each other." He seemed a little down and worried about something. I reached over to touch his elbow and he visibly flinched.

"What was that?" he asked in wonder.

I shrugged and looked at Mage. He grinned proudly.

"She's strong, isn't she? She's just sharing her energy with you, trying to make you feel better. You feel better, my brother?"

Jade blinked a couple of times and looked between us. "I do. I don't get it, but I do. Everything's fine, right?"

Mage nodded at him and Jade stood from the table.

"Everything's fine. I'm going to go to bed. Good night, Sammara."

I couldn't help the giggle that slipped out. He blushed and gave a nod to the others. Jaylene had fallen asleep on Devon as we talked and Mackenzie was whispering in Star's ear that she wanted to go to bed. They made their way upstairs, Devon carrying Jaylene in his powerful arms. I watched them with a smile on my face, basking in the love in this house. I barely felt the negative energy after the night we'd had.

"Let me take you to bed, darlin'. I want to hold you all night."

"I love it when you say that," I whispered, taking his lip between my teeth. "I love you."

"I love you back, *mon chère.*"

# Twenty-Four

Shouts roused us from sleep the next morning. We hurriedly dressed and ran down the stairs, me close on Mage's heels.

"I told you! I went home with Sherry around midnight. What the fuck is your problem, Star?"

"My problem, you son of a bitch, is this!"

We entered the kitchen as Star was pointing angrily at his laptop.

"What the hell, Star?" Marcus looked as if he'd rolled out of bed, just like the rest of us, and come straight over.

"This woman is all over the fucking internet saying you raped her last night! This is bad, dude. Like some serious shit." Marcus looked shell-shocked. He stepped forward and leaned over the table to read what was on the screen.

"That's the Metalwire site. They're one of our affiliates," I whispered to Mage, who stood in front of me. He moved closer to the table to read over Marcus's shoulder.

"What... She's saying I raped her? Shit! I talked to a bunch of women last night. I don't even remember this girl. I left with Sherry around eleven. This little bitch said it happened after the bar closed. I wasn't even there! I was at Sherry's."

"Watch your fucking mouth, Marcus." Star was really pissed.

"She'll have to corroborate that," Mage said matter-of-factly. "If this chick goes to the police, will Sherry back you up? I know you haven't been on the best of terms with her."

"What the fuck do you mean? You think this chick is telling the truth? You'd actually believe I'd do something like that?"

Devon spoke quietly. "Calm down. No one's accusing—"

Star interrupted Devon. "Yeah but we all know how you get around the girls."

"Fuck you, Star! I don't have to explain myself to you! Women make this shit up all the time! I don't have to take what I want. She probably just got more than she bargained for from someone else."

My gasp was heard around the room. Everyone froze, except Mage.

"Motherfucker, you watch your filthy mouth," Mage growled before launching himself at Marcus. They hit the table, splintering a leg off and knocking Star's laptop to the floor with a clatter. I heard a scream from one of the other girls as wood went flying.

Mage landed several punches before Devon and Jade hauled him off of Marcus. Star stood back staring daggers at Marcus.

"Go to hell, you son of a bitch!" Mage shouted. "I've had enough of your ignorant fucking bullshit!"

Marcus's face was covered in blood. My knees couldn't hold me and I sank to the floor, shaking and crying.

"That's right. Just believe the worst. Go ahead. Anyone else want to get in a few shots? Step right up!" Marcus stood with his arms out, dripping blood from his nose and mouth. He looked pointedly at Star. "After everything I've done for you guys, after all we've been through, you're going to believe some little bitch crying wolf on the internet?"

I gasped again, catching Mage's attention. I couldn't believe the horrible things coming from Marcus's mouth, but then, I couldn't believe *any* of this was happening, especially that Mage had been so violent with his friend.

Marcus looked around as he backed toward the door. "No one? Not anyone gonna ask me my side of the story?"

"Maybe you should just go," Jade said softly from the doorway.

Marcus turned on his brother with fury. He started to speak, but then he threw up his hands and went out the front door swearing. He slammed it shut and immediately the clanging clock started going crazy in the other room. Everyone covered their ears to protect them from the loud sound. When it finished, we surveyed the aftermath.

"Shit," Devon said, finally letting go of a still struggling Mage. The kitchen table was toast, and three chairs were knocked over. Several plates had fallen onto the floor and broken. Star's computer lay on its side with a cracked screen.

"You boys go into the ballroom," Jaylene said calmly. "We'll clean this mess up." The guys all looked around at each other and started to file out. Except Mage. He knelt down in front of me.

"Chère, I—"

"I'm fine. I'm so sorry. Go talk to your boys."

He lifted my chin and looked me in the eyes. "I'm sorry you had to see that. You okay for a few minutes?"

I nodded and offered him a weak smile. "I'm okay. But Mage? That site...If the police...He's telling you the truth." I don't know how I knew this, I just felt it was true.

Mage stood and took in a shaky breath, letting it out to calm himself. "He's crossed the line one too may times. We've warned him. I'm not hearing him talk about women like that ever again." He followed the guys out of the room and upstairs, shooting one last glance my way before he was out of sight.

"Here we go again," Jaylene sighed.

Mackenzie came over and offered me a hand. "You ok, Sammara?"

I nodded. "I can't believe Marcus said all that," I murmured, not sure what to think about what just occurred.

"I can. He's such a prick. He runs his damn mouth way too much."

"Kenz," Jaylene said calmly. "We didn't even hear his side of the story. What if he was telling the truth?"

"You going to believe him? After what he said to you in New Orleans?" Mackenzie stood and started angrily picking things up, not making eye contact with Jaylene.

"That has nothing to do with this," Jaylene replied, trying to stay calm.

Mackenzie moved with quick, jerky movements. Her breath came in and out fast. "'Little bitch crying wolf'. Well fuck him! That's the last time I want to ever see his face! That cocksucker whores around all over and we're expected to believe he didn't—"

"Mackenzie! Listen to yourself! Do you know what this could do? What this means?"

"Yeah! It means..." She trailed off, the anger on her face morphing into fear. "Oh no."

"Yeah, 'oh no'! They can't handle another falling-out like this. I better call Sherry. Knowing Marcus, he's headed straight for her."

I stood and helped Mackenzie finish cleaning up while Jaylene spoke in hushed tones on the phone. The guys filed in about twenty minutes later, just as we'd finished cleaning up the mess, mopping the floor, and doing what was left of the dishes.

Mage held out his hand for me and I turned to see if Mackenzie still needed me, but she was crying against Star's shoulder

The two of them walked out of the room and up to their bedroom. Mage gave them a second and then we went to his room. We sat on the bed, me facing him, Mage with his head in his hands.

"Are you okay?" I asked him. He looked down at his hands and frowned at the bruising and swelling on his knuckles.

"Oh my God. Let me go get you some ice."

"No. Please stay," he said, putting his hand on my knee. "I'm so sorry you saw all of that. That shit has been brewing for a long time. Marcus has a long history of talking shit and bragging about all the chicks he's banged. Well, this is it. We're done with it. Jade and Star agreed. He's out."

"What? You mean out of the band?"

Mage nodded solemnly.

"We warned him. When he talked shit about Jaylene... Sammara he flat out said to her "Just because you're fucking him doesn't mean you have a say." It was ugly. We told him then if he didn't learn some respect for women, we were through. Star and Devon were ready to walk. This time Jade was the one to finally say it. I know it's killing him, but he knows Marcus was way out of line."

"What about Devon?"

Mage frowned. "He said we should all calm down and find out what happened. He didn't believe Marcus would do it, but he was pissed at what he said." Mage flexed his hand and cursed, shaking his head. "He's right. I don't think Marcus could actually hurt someone, not like that, but he was so far out of line with what he said. I just can't handle it anymore. He'll never learn if we don't put our collective foot down."

I pulled Mage's hair back from his face and saw his lip was starting to swell and he had an abrasion on his cheek. "I really should get some ice for you," I said, but he turned to face me.

"Sammara, I will never allow anyone to disrespect you in my presence. You are mine, and I know what he said hurt you. I felt your anger and...I don't know. I just snapped. I don't fight, though. I mean, not really. I haven't in a long time. Not since I used to brawl with my cousins. I don't want you to be afraid of me."

"Mage, I'm not afraid. I know why you did what you did, but think of what you're saying. You guys have worked so hard together. Are you really ready to end your band because he acted like a douche?"

Mage stood and looked out the window. He took in a deep breath and let it out slowly. "I told you I had a bad feeling yesterday. I just never imagined it would come to this. What's done is done. Jade is going to call Sherry and tell her that he's fired. We're a majority rule, so he's gone. I don't know what that will mean for the band in the long run. I guess we'll be taking that time off a lot sooner than we thought."

I stood and wrapped my arms around him from behind. "I'm so sorry. I can feel your pain. I know you love him, and I know what it feels like to be so disappointed in someone you love."

He sighed heavily and his hands came up to cover mine.

We went back to bed and talked for a long time, just trying to figure out what this all meant for him.

"I guess I'll just go home," he said finally. "I still want to buy the St. Germaine. I've got plenty of money to buy it myself if the other guys aren't into it. Maybe I'll get some investors. We'll get it ready to go. I can run the club. That ought to keep me busy. I don't do well when I'm not busy."

"Me neither. I always have to be working. I guess I'll just have to lug all my office shit to New Orleans."

Mage shifted so he could see my face better. I lifted my head off his chest. "What? You think I'm letting you go home alone, after all of this? No way. You need supervision."

His eyes bugged out, searching mine for some clue as to what I meant. "You'd do that? But your home is here, Sammara. I would never ask—"

"Which is why I'm telling you. I know you'd never ask me to leave my home, but what kind of a home is it anyway? My home is with you now, love. Isn't that what we're supposed to be doing? Making a life together? I want to be with you, Mage. I don't want either of us to be alone anymore."

He pulled me so tight against him, whispering his thanks and words of love against my hair before kissing me so deep, I had to tap out for air.

"You gonna love it in New Orleans. I don't know where we'll stay—"

"We'll work it out. We have time. I've got to break it to my bosses that they're going to have to let me work remotely. I can come back here once a month and check in. If they want me, they'll work with me. Otherwise...I might just be ready to write a novel, or go to work for a New Orleans-based magazine."

Mage laughed and held me close, rocking me in his arms. "You can do whatever you want, chère. I'll support you, whatever you want to do. I can't tell you how much this means to me that you'd come home with me."

"Well, we better find a home first! I don't want to shack up at Gran's. I'm going to want our own space so we can continue, you know..."

"Yeah. I see you, Sammara," he said with a chuckle.

My whole life was about to change, and all I could do was smile like an idiot.

"I see you, too, Martín."

He frowned. "Really? Are you going to call me by my given name?"

"It's kind of sexy," I answered, nibbling on his jaw until he shuddered and groaned. "I like being the only one outside of your family who calls you Martín." I ran my tongue up the side of his throat and he moaned. He was so damn sexy when he came apart like this.

"You keep that up, you can call me whatever you want, chère." He pulled me tighter to him. "You're not outside my family. You *are* my family."

# Epilogue

After the fallout with Marcus, Mage met with the other members of the band, along with Sherry and their attorney, and they agreed to start their hiatus early, cancelling all tour dates for 2013.

Sherry completely understood and said she'd work her magic to get them out of their tour without too many fines or financial losses, but she was tight-lipped about Marcus. The official story was that the band was taking time off to care for family, which wasn't too much of a stretch. Marie Doucette Boudreaux, Devon's mother, was diagnosed with early stages of breast cancer in January. Devon and Jaylene returned to New Orleans straight away to take care of her. Luckily the doctors caught it quickly, so her prognosis was excellent. The couple decided to postpone their wedding plans until Marie was well enough to dance at their reception.

Jade, Mage and Star decided to go forward with the plans for Club Haunt, which Devon also invested in. Between the four of them, they purchased the historic building and decided to do a lot of the work themselves. They all had different ideas for how to use the space and were excited about working together on this new endeavor. Star moved in with Mackenzie, and Jade took over Jaylene's apartment while she and Devon stayed with Marie.

My excitement about moving was tempered some by my meeting with Josh and Brantley. They were not thrilled about my plans to work remotely from New Orleans. The first installment of my article on sexual assault did so well for the magazine, however, that they agreed to give it a six-month probationary period on the understanding that I would work in L.A. at least one week a month.

Mage said we'd make it work. "I'll come with you as often as I can. I don't want you out of my sight, woman." Thankfully, I didn't want to be out of his sight either. We decided keeping my condo was a good idea so we'd have a place there we could both use whenever we needed.

The guys moved out of the mansion, ready to be done with that chapter of their lives. Mage was sad to leave it, but having me home with him in New Orleans had him so jazzed, he got over it quickly. He was determined we'd find an equally haunted house to buy when we were ready. In the meantime, we agreed to move into the St. Germaine.

*Maggie's Bones Falls on Tough Times Again*
*Josh Freeman*
*Feedback Magazine*
*February 2013*

*Just when it appeared the band was ready to reclaim their throne as the kings of metal, tragedy and discord struck again. The band has returned to New Orleans to care for family members and to pursue other business endeavors. Marcus Lambert could not be reached for comment, but D Boudreaux stated for Feedback, "The Bones need this hiatus. We need to get healthy and get our heads back on straight before we can determine where this band is headed. None of us are finished making music, and we appreciate our fans for supporting us through this difficult time."*

*Rumors abound as to the whereabouts of Mr. Lambert, as he apparently did not return to New Orleans. His manager, Sherry Jordan, claims he has asked for privacy. As for the matter of the sexual assault accusations as first reported by Metalwire, surveillance from the Key Club shows Mr. Lambert clearly leaving with his manager two hours before the alleged assault took place. Police have cleared him of any wrongdoing and have dropped the case on the grounds that there is no evidence to back up the story of the young woman who claimed she was assaulted.*

*Stay Tuned for More...*

# Final Thoughts

I have known many people who have been assaulted in their lives. Whether it was by a stranger or, as in my case, by an intimate partner, physical, emotional, and sexual abuse will have lasting effects on that person's life.

Recently, a person in my inner circle was sexually assaulted and even in 2024, they were encouraged by a health professional not to call the police, and when I spoke to a close friend about the assault, there was victim blaming involved.

We have to stop. As a society, we need to ignore our instincts to lecture victims. We need to support people who come forward so they may get the help they need. Even if the assault occurred in a situation you feel you would have handled differently, you owe it to the person you care about to support them.

We also need to create a culture where predatory behavior is not tolerated, where EVERYONE, but specifically male-identifying folks, needs to speak out. We need to make predators feel that they are not entitled to take what they want from others without consent. There needs to be real consequences for their actions. Unless we do that, unless we stop making excuses and rationalizing abusive situations, we will never be able to feel safe. We will never be free.

Everyone deserves to have autonomy over their own body. No one deserves to be assaulted.

My intention with this story was to portray a character that went through a horrific experience and came out on the other side a strong, confident woman. Just as Sammara sought help to deal with her trauma, I would encourage any of my readers to do the same. Here are places to start:

https://rainn.org/get-help/national-sexual-assault-hotline

http://rapecrisis.org.uk/

# Prequel: Bated

Chicago
February 2012
Valentine's Day

Being the front man for a colossal band like Maggie's Bones can be a hardship at times. Not when it meant I got laid whenever I wanted, or received VIP treatment at the swankiest joints in town. But when it came to babysitting my four band mates and trying to keep our business afloat, there were plenty of things I'd rather do on Valentine's Day than taking a stupid fucking bus tour through Chicago at night in the freezing cold.

"But come on, bro. This will be epic! Just think of all the freaky shit we will learn about," my brother said as we boarded the bus. Jade was like a persistent puppy most of the time. Annoying as hell, but so damn cute you couldn't stay mad for long. He'd been like that since we was kids and I never could resist him.

I wrapped my coat around me even tighter, wishing I'd worn a thicker pair of pants. My balls were shriveling up from the fucking cold, which sucked because I had plans later that required blood flow to that particular area.

"Jade, it's not freaky shit," Mage scolded. "This is real history, feel me? There are some amazing stories about this town. People have experienced otherworldly shit here. For example, I read that Oprah's studio, Harpo? That building was where they took all the bodies after a ferry capsized on the river that runs right through town. Like eight hundred people died and they stored the bodies where she films her show, man. People have said there's all kinds of paranormal activity in that building. Just think of all the lost souls. You gotta wonder."

Mage was always carrying on about supernatural shit. No lie, he really did have some extra sense going on a lot of the time. One time he told me before a show to avoid the front left area of the stage. I almost brushed him off because that's how I connect with the fans, you know what I mean? But for some reason I listened and thank God I did. Halfway through the set, the front risers collapsed and one of the security guys almost got trapped underneath. A cabinet fell over and barely missed hitting the audience members clamoring to get over the rail. I would've been... Let's just say ever since that, even if I thought he sounded full of shit, I listened because he was right when it mattered.

So that's why we were sitting on an old school bus that was painted black and had fairy lights strung along the inside taking a haunted tour of Chicago. Some chick was up front giving us her credentials as a Medium, and I was replaying my earlier argument with Sherry in my head.

"*You going to come with us, or what?*" I'd teased her. "*You know you want to ride the bus with me. You can sit on my lap and I'll show you how to make the wheels go 'round and 'round.*"

Sherry had growled at me. "*God, Marcus, do you ever let up? I don't have time to go play with you boys. I've got to get the riders approved for the next three venues. I've got people screaming at me that tickets aren't selling out on the European leg... And your damn cousin won't do anything except play his guitar! That last interview you guys had, with the guitar magazine? He totally blew it off when they'd asked specifically to talk to him. This job is killing me,*" she'd shouted.

"*I fucking know you've got shit to do, Sherry. I'm doing my best to keep these fools from self-destructing. Did you know I found Star passed out in a pool of vomit last weekend in Denver? Or that I found pills in Mage's guitar case? They're driving me fucking crazy but someone has to keep them moving forward!"*

I hadn't even mentioned to her that I'd been having heart palpitations and pain in my gut. I even pissed blood last week for a day or two. I figured it was just a kidney stone because I'd had them before, but it had taken all of my strength to get up there and keep singing my ass off. All I wanted to do was get lost in some pussy and forget about all the bullshit, forget I'd lost my best friend when Maggie died. Just thinking about her made the chest pains worse so I pushed it to the back of my mind. The show must go on.

"*Marcus, you've got to keep them going. Get their shit together! We can't fuck this up,"* Sherry said.

I'd wanted to tell her to go fuck herself, but I would never disrespect her like that. I needed her. I needed her to keep propping me up or I was going to take my finger out of the dam and Maggie's Bones was going to wash down the fucking drain.

"Since tonight is Valentine's Day, we're going to have a special tour for you featuring tales of doomed lovers and heart-wrenching tragedies, just to stay in the spirit." The woman was wearing a black velvet dress that was low-cut and clung to her ample hips. Jade licked his lips and figured he'd found a conquest for the night. She was somewhere around late twenties, early thirties. Jade loved his women curvy. He especially loved the ones who were sensual without just hanging their twats out there for the taking. I could see him plotting his next move as we drove towards the first destination on the tour.

I glanced back at my beloved cousin, Devon, and heaved a big sigh. Devon had folded his huge frame into a bench towards the back and was looking out the window, not paying attention to the stories. He'd been mostly silent since his sister, my cousin, our manager, died in December.

Star was sitting near Devon sipping from his always present flask. The guy was wasted more often than not these days. He'd smile and play and pretend everything was okay, but I'd heard him crying at night on the bus. Poor bastards. It sucked. I was in pain, too, but we had to be strong and move on.

I looked around the bus at the rest of the people we had to be strong for. Our crew members had joined us tonight and it was good to see everyone, well, most everyone, having a good time: Charesse, a gorgeous fucking chick who sold our merch dressed in leather, Jason, Tommy and Knuckles, our guitar techs who chased as much tail as my brother, Adam, who ran our sound board like a boss, and lastly Keegan, our drum tech, who I intended to replace when this tour was up. He was decent, but Star was never satisfied with how the guy set things up, not to mention I was pretty sure he was Mage's connection for the fucking drugs. We'd also invited the guys from our two opening bands, Hush and Obsess, who we'd brought out with us on this series of Midwest dates. These people were all counting on us to keep it together and bring it. If we fell apart, the tour fell apart, and all these people would be up shit creek. Mage and Jade were trying their best, but Star and Devon could fucking go off the deep end at any time. Although if Mage was taking pills, and Jade didn't keep his dick in his pants...

Oh, *shit*, bro. Jade moved toward the front of the bus and kept asking Madeline, the Medium, questions about her stories, and damn if she wasn't blushing and getting all flustered. We Lambert men had that effect on women, what can I say? Jade just had to flick his long black hair and grin with that dimple of his and panties were left strewn about his wake. I had to try even less.

I tried to turn off the thoughts in my head and listen to the stories this woman was telling...

"Many lovers have found each other in Chicago, but it's the tragedies that define our haunted city. Besides the ferry disaster and the Great Fire, we've had everything from the Devil Baby of Hull House to the beautiful young women who haunt a lonesome stretch of road. And of course there is the St. Valentine's Day Massacre. We'll see many of these haunted places tonight."

We drove down Archer Avenue and Madeline told us about Resurrection Mary, a ghost who apparently did things like jump in front of cars and accept rides from strangers.

"Several men told stories from the nineteen thirties and forties of meeting a woman at a dance hall, spending the evening dancing with her, and then driving her to the directions she'd give which would take them to the Resurrection Cemetery."

As we were passing the cemetery, Mage jumped in his seat. "Did you feel that," he shrieked. The rest of the group just laughed at him.

"Mage, you dumbass," Jade said. "No one is going to fall for that—"

"Oh, shit!" One of the guys from Hush actually jumped to a standing position and shuddered. The bus driver told him to sit down and started to slow the bus. Everyone totally started laughing except Mage and this guy. The two of them started freaking out and telling wild tales.

"You may have just been visited by Mary. She certainly loves young men," Madeline laughed. She wasn't creepy or anything. She just shared the history of her city. I could appreciate that.

My brother was appreciating her on another level. I couldn't help but chuckle at him putting on the moves for this woman. It was subtle but I could see him trying to work a little magic on this Medium.

"There's also a tale of a young flapper girl who hitchhikes along this road."

I shook my head and just watched out the window for a while, tuning everyone out.

I must have dozed off for a bit, because next thing I knew, we'd pulled up in front of an old stone building. Madeline was talking about people coming to this place, the Hull House, which kind of rang a bell from middle school history class.

"There was rumored to be a baby born with horns and cloven feet. Jane Addams wrote about the old women who came and shared their stories of misfortune with their own children along with thousands of people from the nearby towns and other parts of the city. Whatever the reason may have been for this child to appear the way he did, which we know now was likely due to explainable birth defects, these thrill seekers wanted to explain his presence as caused by the wrongdoing of husbands or wives who spoke out against each other. Perhaps one should be careful what they say to their spouse."

We got out of the bus at the Hull House and took a leg stretch break. She mentioned that people had often had paranormal experiences in the courtyard we were standing in. The only thing paranormal was the fucking temperature. I missed home in Louisiana. This Midwest winter shit really sucked.

Mage and the guy from Hush were still telling each other stories and I smiled to myself.

"Hey, brother," Jade said, bumping me with his shoulder. "You doing okay?"

"Yeah, man. Just tired. You seem to be making some progress. Where's your Medium?"

Jade looked over to where Madeline was in a heated discussion with the bus driver. He didn't seem to like it that some of the guys were drinking on the bus.

"She's hot, that's for sure. We'll see how the night progresses," he said with a grin. But then his smile dropped. "I'm worried about D. What can we do?"

I sighed and we looked over to where Devon was having a smoke. Star was trying to talk to him, but it looked like he was only getting non-verbal answers.

"I don't know, bro. I don't know what to do with him."

Jade looked so sad, I needed to do something before he got off focus.

"Don't worry. I'll think of something. You have other things to be thinking about," I said with a wink and looked towards Madeline, who was reapplying lipstick. She had dyed red hair, but otherwise was a true natural beauty. I loved women of all shapes and sizes, as did my brother, and ladies like her often proved to be the most fun. She was safe from me tonight, though. As we climbed back onto the bus, my thoughts were on a fiery woman with dark skin and eyes who had me in knots. *Damn.*

*"Sherry, whatever you are thinking about Maggie, don't. You are doing just as good a job taking care of us. She always had trouble with those guys from the label. She just didn't let it get to her. You're so much like her, you know?"*

Some of her anger had bled out then.

*"But I'm* not *her, Marcus. I know you guys miss her. I miss her, too. But we have to get these guys, especially Devon, moving forward. We have to do something."* She'd looked at me accusingly like I had all the answers and was just not doing anything about it.

*"I know, chère. I know. I'm trying."*

She'd just huffed and gone back to her table, telling me not to let the door hit my ass on the way out. Ouch.

When the bus finally pulled back up at our hotel, the Standard, we piled out and trudged through the lobby, desperate for warmth. Jade had his arm slung around our tour guide and Mage was following them. I'd heard him tell Star "he wanted to watch." Devon stormed off to his room, probably not to be seen again until we left for sound check the following day. I was beginning to think taking a night off was a bad idea. Star headed to the bar with the guys from Obsess and was chatting up their female lead singer, Scarlett. She was not exactly my type, too mouthy, and not the kind of mouthy a man really enjoys. She could sing her ass off, that was for sure. She liked to get into verbal sparring matches with the guys, though, and talked a good game about her skills in bed. I just hoped if Star tapped that, that he didn't get sucked into her play. He was pretty good about getting what he needed from a female and then moving on. He wasn't a dick about it. He just liked sex. Like the rest of us. Well, except Devon.

Now, Devon was a phenomenal lover. He had a natural sensuality that he never had to amp up. The few women I knew he'd been with were loath to let him out of their beds. The dude was a straight up stud. We'd had some fun in Europe, including one night with these eight women who...Let's just say I could barely keep up, and that's saying something. I thought I'd seen it all, experienced it all, but I'd seen things that night that blew my mind, and Devon just went with it. Watching him make these women scream over and over was quite educational. Damn, I'd never come so many times in one night.

Thinking about all of this just made me angrier with Sherry and I couldn't quite figure out why. The woman was a knockout, for sure, and I liked strong women... to a point. Not the ones who were all in your face about it. But Sherry was different. She took my shit and didn't let it get to her like some of the other women from the agency did. Sherry was a lot like Maggie, and that's why I felt so comfortable with her. But it was different. Sherry got me. She saw through my ego, and I let her. I didn't know why, though. She was no easy conquest. Hell, I didn't even think she'd ever be interested in me. But it was fun to try.

I didn't like how we'd left things earlier, so I picked up a bottle of champagne from the bar, told Star to make sure he was rested up for tomorrow night's show, and left just as I watched that singer chick stick her tongue in his ear. It was pierced. *Damn.*

I took the elevator up to the eleventh floor where we had a block of rooms. I figured I'd see if Sherry wanted to have a drink to relax with me and then I'd head to bed. After all that haunted shit, I didn't feel like trying to track down some pussy. I wasn't feeling great, anyway. Sherry's door was a couple down from mine and Devon's was in the middle. I stopped in my room, dropped off my heavy coat and then knocked on his door.

"D, it's me. Open up." It took a few moments and then he opened the door in just his boxers. His huge blue eyes were bloodshot and wet like he'd been crying. His nose was red.

"Hey, man, want me to come in?"

He just shook his head and looked away.

"D, man, I'm here for you. I wish you would talk to me, something! You—"

He tried to shut the door but I stopped it with my hand.

"Listen, dick, I'm just trying to keep things going. You don't want to talk to me, fine, but D, man, you can't keep—"

The pain in his eyes when he looked up at me, the tear running down his face... This was a man barely hanging on by a thread. My heart ached for my cousin, the man I'd tried to emulate my whole life. I loved him like I would an older brother, like a best friend. He had always been there for me, the jerk. Why wouldn't he let me be here for him now?

Devon shook his head at me and closed the door a little less forcefully.

I blew out a frustrated breath. If he insisted on keeping it all bottled up, fine. I intended to let off a little steam, hell, maybe even tie one on. Sherry and I could both probably use a little drunken revelry to lift our spirits... Or at least forget what the hell we had weighing on our shoulders.

I knocked on Sherry's door and I heard her cuss on the other side of it. Sherry's cursing made me chuckle. She didn't do it often. She opened the door to the chain.

"What do you want, Marcus? It's late."

*Damn!* Another member of my little family was crying. Seeing Devon cry hurt my heart, but seeing Sherry's tears brought out a whole different emotion.

"Open the door, chère," I said firmly. No way was I leaving her like this.

"Marcus, go away. I don't want to talk to you. Don't you have some—"

"Sherry, open the fucking door or I'm going to kick it in."

That at least got her pissed off. She shut the door and I heard the chain slide back. Then she was standing before me in a caramel colored silk nightgown. I couldn't stop to dwell on how fucking gorgeous she looked. I backed her into the room and shut and locked the door behind me. My hands came up to her shoulders.

"Why are you crying, chère? What can I do? Whose ass do I need to kick?"

That made her bark out a laugh. She wiped at her tears and then pressed her hands to her face.

"Why don't you just go, Marcus? I'm fine, okay? Just...I'm just tired."

I led her over to the bed and sat down. I pulled her down onto my lap and held her in my arms, shocked that she came willingly. She must have really been down to let me touch her like this. We hugged and stuff, sure, but she was always so rigid. She wasn't an affectionate woman, not touchy feely like Maggie was.

"What is it, Sherry? Please, talk to me." I lifted her chin with my finger and instantly knew I was in big trouble.

Her big brown eyes were so vulnerable, it kick-started some damn protective instincts I'd never really had for women. I was done for.

She took in a shaky breath and let it out. "I don't think I can handle all of this, Marcus. Maggie had an iron grip on everything. I can't get these assholes to deal with me like she did. That guy from PR? Chaz? He's giving me all kinds of shit about you guys not doing enough press and he wants to book another photo shoot and it just won't fit. He told me he's going to complain to my supervisor if I don't do what he says and get me dropped from working with you. I've worked too hard for this, Marcus. I can't just let—"

"I'm not going to let that happen. We've made enough money for these people. I'm not going to let them push us into any more shit. Besides, we asked for you. You're our manager now, and that's not going to change." I held her face in my hands and whispered, "You're stuck with me."

That worked. Sort of. I got a half smile. "Did you bring champagne, Marcus? And just who did you think was going to drink that with you?"

*That's my girl.* The fire was back in her eyes, however she wasn't moving out of my hold. I ran my finger along her cheekbone that stood out so elegantly from her perfect face. I wanted to...

"You're going to drink it with me, darlin'. In those lame-ass plastic cups from the bathroom. We're going to toast to a lame-ass Valentine's Day in freezing-ass cold Chicago."

She barked out a laugh and stood from my lap. "Fine, but it better be good champagne at least."

I watched her lithe form sashay into the bathroom. She closed the door for a moment and I heard her run the water.

"What the fuck am I doing?" I whispered to myself. I had no idea what to do with a woman like Sherry. She was like supermodel perfect with balls almost as big as mine. I'd never admit it to her, but she intimidated the hell out of me. And the thoughts entering my brain right now were certainly hot enough to thaw me out after that bus ride.

She came back in looking a little less raw and she had two plastic-wrapped cups with her. "You going to pop that thing, or what?"

For a minute I thought I was misunderstanding her. Did she really want to—

"The bottle, Marcus? You going to pop it?"

Fuck me, I was blushing. Why did I lose my shit around her? I needed to turn this little interlude back to my control.

"Was just waiting for you, chère, before I popped my cork. It's always important to let the lady go first."

She full on snorted at me.

"Boy, you really think that shit works? I mean, I know you can rock a stage, but with come-ons like that, I have serious doubts you could rock the bedroom without all that ego." Fuck me, but did she have my number.

"Are you issuing a challenge?" I asked her as I stood and approached her. I gripped the champagne bottle by its neck and towered over her. She looked mildly perturbed. "Because all you gotta do is say the word."

She jumped a little when I let that cork go and then squealed when the spray headed towards her. She laughed and held the lame-ass cups out to me.

"You couldn't handle me, boy," she said, sounding a little less sure of herself. I wondered what a few glasses of bubbly would do to unravel her resolve a little. But what the fuck was I doing, I asked myself again. Sherry and I needed to work together, but just how close could we get without destroying everything we'd built?

"Is that so," I teased as I sipped the champagne. It went down smooth and it was only after finishing my first glass and pouring a second that I remembered I hadn't eaten dinner. I was kind of a light-weight when it came to booze. I figured I better slow down, but then she was finishing her second cup. She lay down on her side on the bed with her head in her hand, a mischievous smile on her face.

"Say you were to try to woo me, Lambert. How would you try to seduce me?"

Was she for real? I rubbed at my soul patch and tried to read her. She seemed a lot more relaxed but she was challenging me. I wasn't going to let that challenge go unanswered.

"Well, Miss Sherry, I reckon I'm not sure I could ever woo you," I murmured. I was sitting in the armchair at the end of the bed. "I might *sing to you,*" I began, carrying a husky note high up into my falsetto.

Her eyes went wide as her smile and she placed a manicured nail against her lips.

"You would sing to me? What, some Heavy Metal power ballad or something?" She threw her head back and hiccupped, which made her laugh even more.

"I'd sing whatever you desired. What song would it take to woo you?"

Her laughter died down. She gave me a taunting smile. She looked like a damn lioness lying in wait for me.

"Hmmm... What song. What song would make Miss Sherry's toes curl? Would she like something like," and I sang a few bars of Marvin Gaye's "Let's Get It On." Her eyes flared, but she kept a straight face. "No? Are you more of a..." I sang a few bars of "Poison," by Bell Biv Devoe.

She cracked up at that.

"Please! You think with your white boy swagger you can pull off something like that?"

But she was squirming. Lord, her body was incredible and the way that satin nightgown clung to her hips...

"You're going to have to help me out," I murmured, standing from my chair. I swung up the bottle of champagne, walked over to fill her glass and then finished off the bottle in one long swig. She laughed as I tossed the bottle onto the carpet and then walked back over to the foot of the bed. "What do you want, chère?"

She sighed deep in her chest and stretched out a little more. "How about something a little more classic? What you got, rock star?"

I remembered hearing once that Sherry didn't really like much rock, nor was she a rap or hip-hop fan. There was that one time in her car that I gave her shit about her easy listening station... I took a chance on "Lady" by Kenny Rogers.

Sherry sat up on the bed while I sang to her. Her left leg was curled under her and her hands were resting on the bed in front of her. Her corkscrew curls fell in her face and her eyelids drifted closed. She was picture perfect. Beyoncé never looked this hot. Sherry was beyond compare.

I leaned forward against the bed, waiting for her to say something. It seemed an eternity before she moved, crawling forward on her knees until she was right in front of me.

"I never...Where did... How did...?"

When she couldn't get the words to come out, she resorted to a more physical response. She reached up fast and pulled my face down to hers, stopping with just a half inch between our lips. She stared at them hungrily then looked up into my eyes.

"You better be as good as you say you are," she whispered a split second before her lips pressed insistently against mine.

I froze wondering how the hell...

I grabbed her hips hard and pulled her against me and her head fell back in a gasp. So many times I'd studied her long neck and wondered how it would taste, and here I was. I intended to sample it and so much more.

"God, Marcus, don't make me regret this, but I want you."

I left her throat long enough to use my height to an advantage. I moved her closer to me and looked down into her determined eyes. I could see hesitation in her gaze.

"Whatever you want, chère. Whatever you need, you take it from me."

I kissed her long and deep, praying she wouldn't come to her senses before I got to feel her luscious skin rubbing all over my body. Her kiss was like falling into a vat of pure honey. She was sweet and tart and she dragged me under into her trap. She yanked at my shirt and I let her lift it over my head. She bit down on her lower lip as she ran her cafe au lait hands over my pale white skin. She leaned forward and feasted on my collarbone. I let out a groan. I couldn't believe she was touching me, or letting me touch her. There was a good chance this would be our only night together. She'd feel differently in the morning, but tonight, I was going to experience her in ways I'd only ever dreamed about.

Once again she turned the tables on me. She somehow managed to use some grappling hold to flip me onto my back on the bed next to her and straddle me, her nightgown riding high on her hips. If my cock hadn't been thawed out before now, all the blood in my body was now making a mad dash for that lucky area that was right where I wanted to be.

"Before this happens, you have a condom, boy? Because there's no way—"

"Of course, no, I understand."

I was a little miffed at her tone. *Boy?* This boy was going to love her harder than any man she'd ever had, that was a guarantee. I kept the cliché condom in the wallet just because... well... being prepared and all that shit. I didn't want just one, though.

"Let me run to my room. And don't even think about changing your mind." She laughed and moved to get off of me. I hated that I had to put a stop to this, even for a moment, but I was going to make the most of my night with Sherry.

With superhuman speed I dashed out the door, fumbled with my room key, then ran right for the bathroom and my toiletry bag. I took a minute to glance in the mirror and see that I could use a shave, my eyeliner was smeared a tad, and my hair was flat from the weather outside. *Fuck it.* I didn't smell, that was the good news. I grabbed a handful of condoms and I swear I was back at her door before it had a chance to swing shut.

Sherry lay on the bed and I covered her with my body before she had a chance to protest. I had to stop myself before I turned all horny teenager and mauled her. Instead, I gripped her hips and brought her back on top of me.

"I liked this view," I said when I had her back straddling me.

She threw her head back and laughed.

"You're kind of cute when you let me have my way with you." She leaned her head to the side, studying me. "You're really something, Marcus." She smiled gently down at me and I could see her changing her mind about me behind her playful expression. She'd told me more than once I had too much ego, that I was an asshole, but then she'd laugh and say, "guess I can say the same for myself."

Maybe tonight she'd see me as more than my punk-ass attitude. I wanted her to see me as a worthy male. I slid my hands up under her nightgown and delighted at the feel of her smooth skin.

"Please tell me I can touch you, Sherry."

She nodded slowly and I sat up beneath her, dragging her nightgown with me as I went until I pulled it over her head. She was naked beneath it. She was so beautifully naked. All I could do was stare at her perfect skin, her dark nipples, her exquisite form. She watched me carefully, and then cocked her head to the side.

"Okay, pretty boy. Let's see what you've got going on underneath those clothes. I'm dying to feel all that creamy skin and silky hair under my hands."

She leaned back to yank on my belt. She slid it out of the loops quick, making it snap. I must have appeared startled because she threw her head back and laughed.

"Oh, you think I'm going to hurt you?" She folded it in half and snapped it again. The look on my face had her cracking up. "Baby, you're so damn cute. Get these pants off, lover. Then you better get to work."

I loved this side of Sherry. Once she had me naked, she proceeded to inspect all of me. I'd never felt shy or embarrassed before, but the onceover she gave me was unsettling. She made a few approving sounds as she traced my tattoos first with her fingers, then with her tongue. She moved to the side so she could roll me over.

"I love a nice back on a man. You've got an excellent back. Those wide shoulders of yours, this narrow waist and those hips... Damn. You're so pale, honey. Don't you ever go sunbathing?"

I laughed and turned over. "No way, chère. I burn like crazy. Besides, when do I ever have time?"

I didn't want to bring up any thoughts of work or the like. I wanted this to be about forgetting our troubles. I pushed her back and opened her wide, creating access to every part I wanted to explore. Sherry was completely uninhibited and showed me exactly what she liked. She didn't hesitate to tell me what was making her hot, and she got so wet for me. It was the best time I'd ever had going down on a woman. Most of the sex I had with women was just intercourse. I didn't take chances with my health. I was careful. And thank God I had been, because I wouldn't have wanted anything to ruin this experience.

Eventually our oral odyssey went both ways and she had my whole body tied in knots. The woman did things to me that I'd probably never recover from.

"God, Sherry, I don't want—"

"If you pull away from me, Marcus Lambert, I will hurt you!"

"*Fuck*, okay, whatever you say."

We both gave orders and we followed each other's wishes. She rolled a condom on me and practically made me lose my shit when she once again straddled my hips. She ran her hands over her small breasts as she slid down my length.  I wanted to be everywhere. She was strong, so limber, and so incredibly hot. I touched where we were joined and groaned at the feel of her body tightening around me. She cried out and begged for me to send her over that delicious edge. I couldn't wait to watch her fall. I sat up suddenly, pulling her down hard on me, and with one slight flick of my thumb against her clit, she fell. The strength of her orgasm shook her whole body and completely did me in. Mine took me by surprise. I was so frustrated that I cursed against her throat.

"You will be doing that again," she stated firmly as soon as she'd caught her breath.

I laughed and gently laid her next to me on the bed. Neither of us spoke as we panted and processed what exactly we'd just done. I pulled off the condom and dropped it in the wastebasket next to the bed without getting up. I was still breathing hard and was trying to work up the nerve to ask her how she liked it.

"Marcus?" she finally spoke. I turned to find her looking unsure. No, she couldn't. She couldn't possibly have enjoyed that as much as I did.

"Just trying to decide if that really happened or if I'm dreaming."

She laughed and pulled my face against her chest.

"Does this feel like you're dreaming?" She brought my hand up to her lips and sucked in a finger. "Does this feel like you're dreaming?"

I started to nibble her nipple but she pulled away and got up on all fours, her ass my undoing.

"How about this? Are you dreaming now?" She wiggled a little and gave an evil laugh. That's all it took for me to be ready for round number two, which was even more intense than round one.

"How did you know to hit that spot?" Sherry groaned. She had her arms stretched above her head on the mattress, still on her knees with her lovely back there for me to caress. Her hips pressed up against me as the jolts continued to, make me twitch inside her.

"I don't know, chère. I think it had more to do with how you moved against me. Goddamn, you are unbelievable, you know that?"

I wanted to stay right here forever. I'd gone beyond thinking I was dreaming to believing I'd died and gone to heaven. It was like Sherry was made just for me. I was kind of long and had a little upwards curve, which had apparently been giving her G-spot some good loving based on how many times she'd come.

When she pulled away, I fell forward on my face and she laughed as she rolled me over and disposed of condom number two. I closed my eyes just for a second while she went to the bathroom and when she returned, she straddled my hips to sit on my ass.

"You made me relax. Now it's your turn."

I jumped when she touched me with hands covered in cool lotion.

"Oops," she said, taking a minute to rub her hands together for a moment before she made another long stroke along my spine.

"You don't have to do that. I'm not going to stop you, but you really don't have to."

She chuckled to herself and hummed a little as she worked the muscles around my shoulder blades.

"You feel like you need this, baby. I know you've been working so hard."

Why was she all of a sudden taking care of me? No, no, no, no, this was not good. I needed her to boss me around, to yell at me, not to use her nimble fingers and make my tension go away. I needed that tension.

She slid them along my spine and then she dug her thumbs in just above my hips—

"Ah *fuck*! Damn, that's sore," I tensed and tried to unseat her, but she held me still with her thighs.

"Marcus! I barely touched you! What's wrong?"

"I don't know."

She ran her hands gently along my lower back. "Am I hurting you? Are you okay?"

I sighed and patted her leg to have her lift off of me, which I hated to do. I pulled her down and kissed her, then tucked her into my side.

"I think I passed a kidney stone but I'm fine." She started to sit up, but I held her to me. "No, please. I'm fine with you right here. Just stay right here."

She only relaxed a little. When I looked down into her beautiful face, she was frowning.

"Marcus, if you aren't well, let's get you checked out. You can't mess around with this."

"If it happens again, I'll tell you. I'll see a doctor, I promise. I've had this happen before, so I knew what it was."

She pulled tight against me and whispered, "Please be okay, Marcus. I can't do this alone."

"You won't. We're partners in this insanity, right? We'll get through this tour and then figure out what comes next." I kissed her hair and let myself enjoy the feel of her pressed up against me. I fantasized about having this every night with her. What would that even be like? To live a life where you weren't sleeping on buses for months at a time? Where you came home to a perfect woman like Sherry who ate dinner with you and asked, "how was your day?" For some reason that reality sounded perfect, especially when I gazed down at Sherry's luscious body. I could never get enough of her slight curves, her perfectly natural breasts, her shapely ass...

My heart swelled with the thought, then deflated when I realized this just might be it. The fantasy might just be over soon, and I wasn't done with her. My emotions kind of got the best of me, and before I knew it, I had her on her back underneath me and was kissing her for all I was worth. This time I did lose control. I barely stopped in time to put on condom number three before I was driving into her forcefully. She gasped in surprise, her eyes going wide. I needed her, wanted her, and was desperate for her like I'd never been before. I was insane. I gripped her hips and pounded into her like a madman, ignoring the thought that I should slow down, until her hands came to my face.

"Marcus."

Her voice brought everything into focus. I stilled, my body wound up so tight. Her eyes held me still for several beats. Something passed between us, something powerful. I moved slowly this time. Slow and deep. Long and strong. I don't know how long we made love like that, but that's what it was. No more fighting for dominance, no more challenges, just love passed between us. Or maybe it was all my imagination. But I was going to pretend that was what was happening. Something I never thought would happen to me, something I'd never had any interest in. Until now. Now? I was insatiable. There was no way I would be able to live with just this once.

Sherry was completely wrapped around me and the friction of our bodies moving together made her come again, one last time. This time, she called my name. She moaned it, like a prayer. Her expression was one of absolute bliss and I was grateful I'd brought her there.

"Come for me, baby. Say my name, Marcus."

If I hadn't said it out loud already, it had been all I could think of, all I could focus on. She was everything as I let go and came inside her, shouting her name, and wishing all the while I could be marking her as mine. In that moment, it was as if she snatched my heart right out of my chest. And that scared the shit out of me.

When I caught my breath and my courage enough to look into her eyes, she paused in her stroking of my hair.

"You were every bit as good as you said you'd be, baby." She laughed and kissed me one last time. Then she pushed out from under me and walked naked across the room. She got herself a water from the mini-fridge and held another up, asking if I wanted one.

"I might need you to hold the bottle for me," I joked, really just wanting to tuck her into my side and hold her all night. I was going to experience cuddling for the first time, dammit. I wanted it with her.

But she shook her head. "Uh uh, you are not falling asleep in my bed, Lambert."

I loved the way the French pronunciation of my name rolled off her tongue, but then I realized what she was saying.

"What, you going to kick me out?" I smirked to cover up the pain her words caused me.

"Hell yeah I'm kicking you out! I need sleep and I certainly don't need everyone else knowing what we just did."

Ouch. *Fuck*, lady, could you sound any more ashamed?

"Then I'll just be out of your way then, darlin'," I drawled sarcastically. "Wouldn't want anyone to think you lowered your standards." I pulled on my pants in one angry yank and went searching for my shirt.

"Marcus, don't be like that. You know what we have at stake. I had fun, didn't you have fun?"

She had no idea what she'd just done to me, and damn if I was going to tell her.

"Sure. Fun."

If I acted like a dick now, there was no way this would ever happen again, and I had to appreciate the position she would be in with the stuffed shirts if they thought she was slumming it with the bayou rats from Houma. "I'll stay your dirty little secret." The smile on my face was incredibly forced. She saw through it.

"Marcus? Are you okay? With this? I mean, you know it was just to scratch an itch, right? Relieve some tension?"

"Yeah, chère. I feel you. No, it was great. Just what the doctor ordered, right? I'll scratch your itch anytime."

I laughed but inside she was ripping me to shreds. I took her in my arms and thought maybe I'd leave her with a lingering kiss. She let me, but she was holding back. I could feel it.

"We should both get some sleep," she said. "You need to look your freshest tomorrow night. The limo will be here to pick us up at noon. We're have dinner catered and—"

"Yeah, I get it. I'll see you then. I hope you sleep better."

I floated out of the room before she could say anything else to kill my buzz. And I intended to take my buzz back with me to bed. I didn't even want to shower. I wanted to keep her delectable smell on my body, her sweet cream on my face. I wanted to bask in Sherry for as long as possible.

I got into my room and collapsed on the bed. I was feeling it, the travelling, the pressure to perform, the stress... It had gone away for the several hours I'd just spent inside Sherry.

"My happy place," I snorted. Oh well. If she was going to treat this like a casual affair, I was going to have to suck it up and put up a front. I drifted off to sleep with the memories of her sweet thighs wrapped around my face.

STAY TUNED...

More Bated stories with Marcus and Sherry will be out soon...

The correct reading order of the series is as follows:

*Haunted*

*Bated*

*Fated*
*Minded: A Paranormal Haunted Story*

And to celebrate the tenth anniversary of *Haunted*, check out *Feuds and Interludes: Road to Rocktoberfest 2024* and catch up with the band Maggie's Bones. The *Haunted* series finale is coming soon...

# Chapter Two

"MARCUS! MARCUS!" The banging on my door at four in the morning yanked me out of my beauty rest. I was still in my pants, thankfully, as I flung the door open. Star was out there with Sherry, who was trying frantically to get a key card into Devon's room.

"He's screaming in there," Star said, looking worried. Sherry's hands were shaking terribly.

"God, I can't get this to work!"

"Here, let me." I took the cards she had in her hands, one for each of our rooms, and tried two before the door clicked open. Devon was on the floor at the foot of his bed with the sheets balled up in his hands screaming and crying. Sherry clicked the lights on and I saw glass around him on the floor.

"Holy shit! He's bleeding!" Star and I heaved his heavy ass up onto the bed and Sherry tried to calm him.

"Devon, sweetie, it's us. Wake up."

His eyes were open but glazed over, like he was sleepwalking or something. "Star, get some wet towels. I need to see how bad this is."

Sherry took control of the situation while I tried to help her wrestle the sheets out of his grip. He pulled away from me and threw a punch in my direction then screamed "MAAAGGGIIEEEEE" once more before falling into whole body sobs. I caught Sherry's eyes and she was crying. I touched her hand once and she squeezed mine, then turned her attentions toward Devon. She smoothed his hair back off his face while Star and I went to work cleaning the blood off of his knees and hands. He must have fallen off the bed onto some beer bottles, which had broken. Luckily most of the glass was kept from his skin by the thickness of the comforter. He did have some cuts on his knees and hands, though, so Sherry told Star to call down to the front desk and have them bring up a first aid kit.

"Marcus, will you go get my makeup bag out of the bathroom? I've got some tweezers. I need to get this glass out."

I stuck my hand out for her card, which she handed to me without looking, and I went in search of her lady stuff. The front desk dude and I got back to the room at the same time.

"Do you need me to call the paramedics, sir?"

I shook my head. "He'll be fine, but you might need housekeeping to get up here with a vacuum. Later though. I want him to get some sleep. We'll call down when we're ready."

"Very good, sir. I'm terribly sorry for your friend."

"He's my cousin," I said, feeling my heart start jumping around in my chest.

I could have lost him tonight. If he would have fallen and cut himself worse? And not woken up? From now on, if he wasn't going to talk to me, I was going to fucking share a room with him on the road. I needed to know he was safe. I couldn't take a chance with him.

Star looked like hell when I got back inside. He helped me bandage him up after Sherry cleaned out the wounds and picked out two pieces of glass from his knee.

"His hands look fine, just scratches. Think he'll be okay to play tomorrow?" she asked me quietly.

I shrugged. "Probably not, but that has nothing to do with these cuts. How many more shows do we have?" I asked her.

She thought for a minute. "We're out through mid-March. Then back to L.A. where you guys should have a couple of weeks before we start working on the next album." I blew out a breath.

"He needs time. I don't know. I just don't know if he can keep this up."

Star had passed out in the chair while we were talking and dropped his flask on the floor. Sherry and I looked at each other. Frustrated, I walked over to him and shook him hard. He came around, but he was pretty wasted.

"What the fuck did you take, man?" He tried to focus on me but his eyes weren't working right.

"What? Just booze, man. And I think, I don't know, but I think Scarlett may have slipped me some E. Fuck, I'm going to be sick." Star stumbled into the bathroom and started hurling into the toilet.

Sherry dropped her head in her hands and groaned.

"Jesus, Marcus. What are we going to do?"

She and I were sitting on either side of Devon on the bed. She looked all rumpled and sleepy, which was sexy as hell and exactly how I wanted her to look, but upon further inspection, she was beyond sleepy to exhaustion. She needed to rest.

"Chère, go back to bed. I'll stay with these two clowns in here. I'll make sure they get sleep. You need rest."

She raised an eyebrow at me.

"So do you!" She tried to sound indignant, but I could see the faint lines around her eyes. I reached out and cupped her cheek.

"I've got this. Let me handle this. You're going to have to prop me up eventually so you better rest now. You already took care of me tonight," I murmured with a wink and I swear she blushed a little. She stood from her side of the bed and walked around to mine. She wrapped her arms around me and kissed my forehead.

"Good night, lover," she whispered and then she did that sashay thing out the door. I sighed, feeling blissfully happy for a split second. Then Star flushed the toilet and started hurling again. I went to check on him and offered him a bottle of water from the mini-fridge.

"Drink some of this if you can, alright?"

He nodded, his face green.

"I think I'll just sleep here," he said, lying down on the floor. I pushed him over onto his side and placed a couple of towels under his head.

"Get better, bro," I whispered.

He moaned and nodded his head.

"I'm so sorry, Marcus. I'm going to stop. I swear it."

He sat up quickly and retched into the toilet until all that would come out was bile. I gave him a wet rag and left the water bottle close to him. When did I become the mother hen of this group?

Back in the room I stretched out on the bed next to Devon, who was sleeping fitfully. I stared at the bloody sheets for a long time, reliving the night Maggie died. Thankfully they had her taken away before we got to the scene, but when Devon saw her blood and her purse strewn about Sunset Boulevard, he fell to his knees and screamed, just as he'd done tonight. I figured I should call Uncle Daryl tomorrow and see if he could come ride with us for a few days. I hated to take him away from Katie and the girls, but if anyone could get through to Devon, he could.

I lay there for hours thinking about Sherry lying in her bed next door and wished I could just wrap myself around her. I started humming that damn Kenny Rogers song and thought I should record it for her or some corny shit like that. Maybe we could re-arrange it and sing a heavy version on the road. I fell asleep next to my cousin and didn't wake up until he rolled over around eleven. His punch to my chest was what woke me.

"What the fuck?" I shrieked.

Star came running out of the bathroom and for a moment I was relieved to see he was still alive and with us.

"I guess cousin dear didn't expect to have a bedmate. How are you feeling?"

Devon sat up and rubbed at his hair. He winced and then looked down at his hands, puzzled. Then he pulled the blanket up and saw the bandages on his knees.

"You fell on some beer bottles, man. You could have been really hurt."

He frowned at my scolding and I figured that wasn't the right approach.

"Do you remember anything?" I asked in a calmer voice.

He shook his head. Star told him what happened and his eyes got a little wider, but that was the only response. He stood up and went to the bathroom, shutting the door behind him. Without saying a word to either of us.

"Marcus, man, what are we going to do?" Star was shaken up.

I sighed heavily.

"We keep doing what we're doing until I can figure something out. I'm going to call Uncle Daryl."

Star nodded, chewing at a nail.

"I need to get cleaned up. I feel like something died in my mouth."

I snorted at him.

"That's probably because it did."

He took one last look at the bathroom door and then waved as he walked out.

I figured I could wait for Devon to come out and not talk to me, or I could leave him alone to process what happened. I had no answers. I stood from the bed and walked to the bathroom, careful of the glass, and knocked on the door.

"Hey, D. I'm going to have housekeeping come clean up this glass. I'll be in my room if you need anything." The door opened a crack and those haunted blue eyes stared back at me. He nodded, and then shut the door. Fuck me, he never said a word.

Two hours later we were all dressed up and ready to go rock the venue. The House of Blues was a cool place to play. We'd sold out the show and would be leaving after on our bus to drive all night and then play in Flint, Michigan at the Machine Shop tomorrow, then another overnight to play in Columbus... Thankfully we only had a couple more weeks. Then we'd go back to L.A. I just hope the Bones made it in one piece.

Mage and Jade chatted happily about their conquests of the previous night. Well, Jade's. Mage had adopted a hands-off policy recently. He said something about having a vision of his wife.

"She's out there. She just don't know she's mine yet." So he was kind of saving himself, but he still loved to watch. Jade liked to be watched so it worked out. I wondered about those two.

Star was sitting with Devon trying to talk to him and not getting any response.

I was just about to call up to Sherry's room to make sure she was okay when she came stalking off the elevator with a purpose. Dressed in a tight grey suit with tall pink heels, she looked like a boss. I wanted her to boss me some more. It took all of my limited acting skills to stand up when she arrived, kiss her hand, and lay on the lothario.

"I sure love what those stilettos do to your ass," I whispered to her. It got the desired effect. She wrinkled her nose at me, but she didn't get pissed. She actually smiled. I was hopeful.

"Alright, boys. We have a couple of stops before we get to the venue. I was able to arrange the photo shoot this afternoon with the photographer you guys worked with before from Feedback Magazine. He happens to be in town and has the afternoon free. We'll do the shoot, maybe take you shopping? Mage, did you still need some more pants?"

"Yes, Mom," he snickered and Jade started cracking up.

"Yeah and he needs a new G-string, Sherry. His other one snapped last night." The two of them started slugging at each other until she had to whistle loudly to break them up.

I chuckled to myself watching my brothers being playful. It gave me hope.

"Star? What about you?"

He shrugged. His face was really pale and the circles under his eyes were massive. "I just need to get there early tonight to make sure Keegan doesn't fuck up my drumheads again. I might need a new earpiece, too, Sherry. I'm sorry."

She nodded, tapping some notes into her smart phone.

"Devon?"

He shook his head and looked down at his hands. He'd put fresh Band-Aids on the palms of his hands. Luckily his fingers weren't damaged.

"You going to be okay to play, bro?" I asked him in a low voice.

Without looking up, he nodded. Sherry and I met each other's worried gaze before she spoke.

"Alright then. Let's get this show on the road."

The guys all stood and grabbed their shit. The techs had all gone over earlier to get everything set up for us tonight so it was just the six of us in the limo. The other guys all piled in, but I stepped in front of the door before Sherry could enter.

"Marcus?" She frowned up at me, a little closer in height with those heels on.

I rested my arm on top of the car and blocked the door. I leaned in so I could whisper to her.

"Last night was more to me than just scratching an itch. I promise not to get weird or anything, but I needed to tell you."

"Marcus," she whispered harshly, looking around nervously. She smiled despite her attempts to stay cool. "We can't do this now."

I raised an eyebrow at her.

"I wasn't going to suggest we do it here," I joked, still speaking so the others couldn't hear. That made her giggle.

"What do you want me to say?" She was all kinds of flustered. That made my heart swell again. I took a deep breath for courage.

"Say we can do this again. For fun. Because we want to. No pressure."

She crossed her arms and that challenging expression was back. "No pressure. Just fun. Can you do that? Can you handle that?"

I nodded enthusiastically. I so wanted to pull her in my arms and remind her just how good we were together, but I had to protect her.

She stepped a little closer until our bodies were almost touching. She licked her lips and gave me a wicked smile. I waited with bated breath for her response...

# Chapter Three

New Orleans
April 2012

This day couldn't get here fast enough. I knew I should've had my head completely in the songwriting game, but all I could think about was her.

It had only been three weeks, but that was too long. My last night in L.A. with Sherry before coming back to Louisiana was perfection. I'd been ready to say, "fuck it," and never leave if that meant I could hold her in my arms that much longer. What the fuck was wrong with me?

It was a good thing Devon was driving right now. I could barely contain my excitement, not to mention stay cool in front of my cousin. He'd come out of his near catatonic state after meeting Jaylene Charles, the tattoo artist their uncle Daryl recommended. I'd been at a loss for what to do with the band now crippled with grief after losing our manager, my cousin Maggie. Now Devon was talking, playing, and it appeared, falling in love with the tattooed beauty.

"Those roses were a nice touch," I said, trying to hide my envy. Sure I missed Sherry, but it was hard not to be disappointed that I'd never have my way with Jaylene. She was pretty, different. I knew the first moment I saw those two together looking at each other with fucking puppy-dog eyes that something was brewing. I should've been happy for him, but something had changed in the band dynamic. That could work in our favor. Or not.

Devon shrugged his broad shoulders and I think his lip even twitched. Not quite a smile. "I just want her to know, man."

"Know what? That you've got major wood for her? I can see it, you can't hide it from me."

Devon's forehead gathered in that disgusted look he often gave me. "Shut the fuck up, Marcus. You have no fucking clue what you're talking about."

Feeling conciliatory, I prodded him to tell me. "It's not just wood? Okay, a little curiosity? She's definitely intriguing. I'd love to see where else she's got ink."

"Cousin, I am not your little brother. You fuck around with this woman, and I will kick your ass up and down Frenchman Street. She's not like that, asshole."

"Relax! Man, calm down. I'm just fucking with you. I merely want to know what your intentions are with this one."

Devon took in a deep breath and let it out slowly. His eyes never met mine. Those aviator shades he'd taken to wearing completely blocked his blues so I couldn't get a read on his mood.

"You wouldn't get it even if I explained it to you using small words and hand gestures. I just feel her, man. She's like oxygen. Much needed oxygen that I've been without for a long time."

I knew what he said was true. He'd only started talking once she showed up. He'd been playing his guitar more, coming up with some brilliant shit. Sadly, the songs he was writing were going to have to grow some balls if we were to record them as Maggie's Bones. Our fans expected a heavier vibe, one with aggression and heat, not some forlorn lovesick 'I'm dying inside' shit. I had to be focused for all of us. We had to deliver this fucking album and get the label off our backs so we could move on. If I could just keep it together. Keep them together.

It had been such a rough ride. Star was freshly out of rehab and hanging in there. Mage and Jade were more focused than they had been in months, no longer sitting back and letting D and I come up with everything. I knew they both had talent when it came to making music. They were finally starting to step up. Good thing. My muse was all tangled and twisted. Which brought me back to thoughts of Sherry.

"I hope we get there before her flight lands," I spoke out loud unintentionally. Devon frowned at me.

"Who, Sherry? She knows we're coming, right?"

"Yeah, but I don't want her to have to wait."

I couldn't wait either. I almost wished I could have made this trip alone, but I needed Devon involved in the conversation. We turned off the interstate and Devon drove toward the airport in silence. It was going to take all of my shitty excuse for self-control to keep my hands off of Sherry. I just wanted to get her alone...

"Do I need to remind you that getting involved with our manager might not end well for either of you, not to mention the band?"

Caught. *Great.* "It's not going to be a problem. She wants things strictly play. No attachments." I couldn't keep the bitterness out of my tone.

"You don't sound happy about that. What would be so wrong with falling in love, man?"

"There's everything wrong with it, dude! Look at my mama and how fucked up her life was after my daddy left. Look at how devastated Aunt Marie was when Uncle David died. Or Uncle Daryl when Aunt Lila died. I don't need any of that, thank you very much. All I need is a little up close and personal time with a beautiful lady, and Sherry happens to fit that criteria beautifully." And I was totally full of shit.

Devon snorted at me and shook his head. "She will eat your ass alive and feed your bones to the gators. Just don't fuck up, Marcus. She's good for us."

Devon let me off in front of her terminal and I hurried to the monitors to see where she'd be coming out. Devon said he'd circle around and grab us when we made it outside. Even though it was a warm day, I'd covered up my tattoos and left off the guyliner. My clothes were tame and businesslike; black tailored suit and a maroon dress shirt. I didn't want to call any attention to myself. I couldn't do much about the hair, though. It had its own life that I rarely attempted to interfere with.

Once inside, I located her flight and went to wait by the correct baggage claim carousel. I didn't think she'd have a checked bag, though. She was very efficient when it came to traveling. I thought I was good at packing light, but the woman bested me.

I saw her lime green blouse first. Her curls bounced as she walked with a purpose towards me. She had her phone out and was reading something as she moved that had her frowning. She didn't look up until she ran into me and bounced off. I grabbed her arms to steady her.

"Hello, gorgeous."

She tried to be mad, but then she smiled. I had missed her so much. Without thinking, I pulled her to me and laid a demonstrative kiss on her. She went stiff in my arms for a minute and made a little squeak.

"Marcus," she scolded. "We're very much in public."

"Exactly. That's why I'm not divesting you of those clothes, lover. But I want to. Promise me you'll share my bed tonight."

She pushed her curls back out of her face. "Marcus, we talked about this. This trip is business."

I pulled her closer and pressed my forehead against hers. "I know it is. I'm sorry. I just can't stop thinking of you. Three weeks is a long time, chère."

She gave me a crooked smile that sent a jolt of lust right down to my cock. God, I loved it when she looked at me like that.

"I guess we can have some fun, as long as you don't let me get loud like last time. Lord, my neighbor will not stop giving me shit about it. That thing you did, with my vibrator—"

"Fuck, Sherry," I groaned. I was so fucking hard right now. I'd make it so good for her she'd never want to leave New Orleans. She was the kind of woman that made me want to be a better lover. I'd never really given a shit before. But something about making her get loud, making her lose her business-like attitude and say the most erotic things. She was becoming my obsession.

She giggled and pulled back. I reluctantly let her go.

"I'm starving. Feed me, lover," she purred and I thought there was no way I was going to get through dinner with her and Devon.

Sherry took my hand and led me out the doors. I took her stylish tote from her, marveling at how she was able to fit everything in one bag. We had to wait a few minutes for Devon to arrive, so I wanted to fill her in a bit.

"You'll be pleased to know that my beloved cousin is smitten with our Tattoo Girl. A brilliant plan. He's smiling, he's talking...He's playing a mean guitar once again. I think there's hope."

Sherry sighed loudly. "What a relief! I was afraid we'd never get him back. Now what about the others?"

"All squeaky clean. I've even been checking their rooms and where they'd usually hide shit to make sure there are no drugs. Nothing. Just D's smokes, but that's the least of our worries."

Sherry nodded grimly. "It's progress, that's for sure. How about the album?"

Devon pulled up just then and I took Sherry by the elbow to navigate through the throngs of people and cars pulling in and out, the sea of drivers not even paying attention to the pedestrians. I helped her into the front seat and I took the back, being all gentlemanly and shit. All I could think about was what she was wearing under that suit.

God, she smelled like heaven.

# Chapter Four

"Shhhhh," I teased as I reached for Sherry's second hand. The first was already lovingly tied to the bedpost. Devon had chosen well with this bedroom and I was grateful he'd given it up for the night. The wrought iron bed frame, while a tad squeaky for my taste, suited my needs well.

Sherry was wrapped in a silky kimono that slid across her skin deliciously with every movement. I'd already untied the belt, but I wanted to take my time tonight. As much as I'd missed her, I couldn't just dive right in. Sherry required foreplay, and for the first time, I was thoroughly enjoying giving, probably even more than receiving. Even a selfish bastard can change with the right woman.

"You can't expect me to be quiet when you do that," she purred. I was having so much fun exploring the beautiful brown skin covering her long legs. I actually didn't care much if we were discovered. It wasn't like Devon didn't know. The other guys? Well, they might suspect, but I'd been pretty convincing when I said I was sneaking out to meet Uncle Daryl.

"Then I might have to gag you, because I'm just getting started, dahlin'."

Everything about Sherry excited me. It was as though she kept everything so tightly wound to do her job, that when I put my mouth on her in strategic locations, she melted into a puddle of happy. Her moans were so damn sexy, it was tough to take it slow, but I knew how sweet the payoff would be if I pushed her a little more. Just a little more.

I took each of the fingers of her free hand into my mouth and sucked them, one at a time, very slowly. She watched me closely, her breath coming in small gasps now. Oh, this was delicious.

"Marcus," she whispered. "Make me come, baby. I need it."

"What you need," I spoke against her breastbone, "is to let me take care of you."

I reached for another tie and crawled up on the bed closer to the headboard. Her eyes grew wide as I lifted her head from the pillow gently, placing the tie over her eyes and reaching around to tie it.

"But Marcus—"

"Do you trust me?" I asked her quietly.

I knew her answer would be no. She didn't trust anyone.

"Not any farther than I can throw you," she said with a smirk.

I wouldn't let myself get too disappointed. Her trust would come in time. I was determined to earn it. The fact that she was allowing me to have her in such a vulnerable position meant we were making progress.

"You won't be able to throw me at all once I get this other hand tied up, now will you? But first," I said, sliding her kimono open to reveal one perfectly formed breast. "I have a job for you. See, what I'm about to do is going to require the use of both of my hands." I licked her index finger and brought it to her exposed nipple.

Her back arched as she gasped loudly when her finger came in contact with her sensitive flesh, which pebbled nicely.

"I want you to keep this," I said, bending over and licking her nipple and finger at the same time, "and this," I said as I exposed the other breast and licked her nipple, "standing at attention. If these lovely bits start to relax, I'll stop what I'm doing, no matter how much you beg me to continue."

"You're an ass," she said with a laugh. I bit down gently on the nipple she wasn't currently toying with and she gasped again. "Fuck, Marcus!"

"Not yet. Now you better not lose your concentration. Come now, get busy or I won't get busy."

As she twisted her nipple, her hips began to undulate beneath the silky fabric. It slid to one side with her movements, revealing her lace panties.

"Mmmmm, are these the ones I love so much? The ones with the ruffles across the ass?"

"Yes," she said, biting down on her lip. Her hand travelled to the other breast and I watched her movement, my cock throbbing in time with my pounding heart.

"I'm gonna want to see those later so perhaps..."

The cream colored lace hid my happy place from me, but I love the way they looked. I could see her trimmed vee clearly through the fabric and my mouth watered anticipating her taste. I ran my hands up her thighs and spread them for me, with her eagerly helping, and I slid one finger along her panties, exposing that sacred place I was dying to be.

"Marcus," she cried out, her free hand gripping the sheets.

"Ah, ah, ah," I whispered, rising above her body, my lips hovering over hers. "You can't stop your task, sugar. I need you to keep these hard for me. Now I'm going to go to work. Do I need to gag you?"

Sherry shook her head, licking her lips. "Please, baby," she whimpered.

I grazed my lips across hers and she lifted her head to keep us connected. I wanted to give in, plunge my tongue into her mouth and possess her as thoroughly as she'd possessed my every waking thoughts, and even my dreams. Instead I bent down, licked both nipples for good measure, blowing cool air across them, then continued down to the juncture of her thighs.

"Keep those gorgeous nipples standing at attention for me. I'm going to be watching, dahlin'."

She nodded and pinched at them frantically as I honed in on my happy place.

Her hips bucked wildly, forcing me to use one hand to press them down into the bed. The other hand...well, being blessed with long fingers didn't only help with playing guitar. I used one hand to hold the panties to the side as I found that spot she loved right away, causing her to bow up off the bed. Over and over again I used my tongue, inside and out, to bring her closer and closer to that blissful edge, only to back off just slightly when she'd start trembling. I knew I couldn't keep it up, that I needed to let her come, but knowing I was responsible for making this carefully crafted woman break apart before me was such a head trip.

I'd gone too far, though. She cursed and grabbed a handful of my hair, holding me in place as she worked herself into more of a frenzy. I just smiled and tried to hang on, giving her just a little more finger before her legs clamped around my head and she came with a violent shudder, the bedframe groaning as she pulled at it with her tied hand. I rode it out with her, the strongest one I'd managed to bring out of her to date, and couldn't wipe the proud smile off of my face.

I extricated myself and kissed my way up her body, loving the way she writhed beneath me. I kissed her mouth softly and she returned my kiss eagerly, moaning into my mouth and biting my tongue and lip.

"I want to see you," she said reaching up to untie her blindfold and I let her, wanting to see her eyes as well. They were filled with lust. That was just the warm up. We had plenty more to do tonight.

"I love it when you pull my hair," I confessed. I'd almost blown my wad when she'd yanked on it, pulling my face closer to her luscious hips.

"Yeah," she said breathlessly. "Sometimes you just need to be reminded of what you're supposed to be doing. I had to get your attention, pretty boy."

"You always have my attention."

I smiled wickedly at her and sucked a nipple into my mouth. She had small breasts, but damn did they feel good in my hands, against my lips. Her body was made so perfectly for me. She was a gift, and not only physically. Sure, she kept me completely sated and there was always more to explore with her, but mentally... I could talk business with her in a way I'd never been able to with anyone else, even Maggie.

Maggie treated us all equally, and outwardly Sherry did, too. But I could tell her anything, and she would be on my side when it came to the band. Unless I was being a dick, then she'd tell me so.

It killed me earlier tonight when we'd been discussing the lack of progress we'd made. Devon was so furious, he shouted at her when she brought up Thomas' name. Thomas was Maggie's husband, the one who killed her while driving under the influence. I knew if I didn't stand up with Devon against the label, the rift between us might never mend, but I knew even as I said the words, *"if you can't stand behind our decisions, then perhaps we need to hire a new manager,"* I'd find some way to keep things together. I'd prayed in that moment that she understood where I was coming from. I'd never fire her. I was never letting her go.

"You know if you untie me I'll have better access to you," she murmured, using her free hand to caress my throbbing cock. It hurt so good. I wanted in her desperately. But not yet. I hadn't worked hard enough yet, hadn't made her feel worshipped enough yet.

"Tonight is about you," I said, my voice serious. "You came all this way and I know tonight—"

"Forget it, Marcus," she said, looking down. "I understood. If it was best for the band, I'd step back."

"No! Absolutely not. You are *it* for me. The band. I mean, you're our manager..."

She looked at me suspiciously through narrowed eyes. "Yeah, huh. The band. Marcus, you know we can't keep doing this. Sooner or later it'll get out, and you guys are already on unsteady ground."

Her words stung me like the cold hard slap of reality they were meant to be. "Yeah, well, it'll continue as long as I have you tied up," I went the playful route. No sense arguing with her tonight. Tonight, I was going to love her so hard, so deep, she'd never forget my name. She'd never be able to be with another man and not think about how my cock was so at home inside her, I could make her orgasm on command. She'd made the mistake of telling me that, and I intended to drive that point home as often as I could. Like now.

I sat up and rolled her over, careful not to wrench her arm that was still tied. "As long as I've got you right where I want you, you can't run away from me, dahlin," I teased, running my cock along her folds.

She sighed. "You better have condoms, boy."

I grabbed for a roll and smacked her ass. "I told you if you called me boy again, I'd have to punish you." I tore open the package with my teeth and hurriedly rolled on the condom, yet another reminder that she didn't trust me. "Are you going to take your punishment like a good girl? Or like the naughty one you know you are?" I spanked her once more and she rolled her hips, pressing her perfectly rounded ass towards me.

"Which one is it going to take to get you to stop talking and fuck me?"

"Oh," I shuddered, my cock straining towards her. I yanked her hips back, spreading her legs a little more until I had everything I wanted on display. I caressed her drenched panties with my fingers, teasing her until she was groaning into the pillow. Without warning, I slid home, burying myself deep inside her as she cried out.

"Marcus!"

"That's right," I said thrusting hard against her. "Take it, dahlin'. Take it all. Take all of me." I used her shoulder for leverage as I drove deep into her, so deep she had to brace herself against the headboard. Our skin slapped together, the lace from her ruffles teasing me with every meeting. I ran my fingers under the material and explored the contours of her ass and the skin between them. As my finger brushed gently against her rear, she gasped and tightened around me. God, that felt good.

"Does the naughty one want attention? Does she like that?" I stroked her oh so lightly and she cried out again. Oh, now didn't this make things interesting? I leaned over her back, slowing my strokes as I pressed my lips to her ears.

"You can have me however you want, chère. All you gotta do is ask, you. I'll be so gentle with you. I'll make you feel so good, Sherry. But you gotta ask me."

I felt her tighten around my cock and knew it was time for some of that on-demand action. I tilted my hips a little more upwards and she froze, her whole body clamping down on me as she came hard.

"Marcus! Baby! You're so gooooooood."

I wanted to hear her say that again and again. So I made her. Somehow I held it together to slow down and bring her to that peak twice more before she sat up, yanked on my hair and told me to finish. I was good at following her directions.

Later when I rolled over to dispose of the condom, she hurriedly dressed in her kimono and went into the bathroom. She stayed in there for a long time. I was exhausted, but I didn't want to sleep until she was tucked in next to me. We still hadn't spent a whole night together, she always kicked me out when we were finished. She was on my turf now, though, and I intended to spend the whole night next to her.

She came back in and sat on the edge of the bed with her back to me. Her shoulders were curled in. I reached out to touch her and she moved away.

"Sherry?" I asked, very concerned at her body language.

"Marcus? You might be used to girls just letting you do whatever you want to them, but that's not me. I might like to have fun, but I don't want you treating me like one of your groupies, or like some whore."

"What?! Chère, what did I do? I would *never* disrespect you. Come here," I said, hoping I could coax her into lying with me. She refused to make eye contact. I sat up and moved behind her, placing my hands on her incredibly tense shoulders. I tried to work a little magic with my fingers, but she was too tight for me to get any purchase.

"Sherry, what did I do? Did I hurt you?"

Finally, she shook her head and I felt her take in a deep breath. "No, of course not. It's just...I've never...I mean, I've been with other men, and I love sex..."

She trailed off. What was she trying to tell me?

"So, what did I do wrong? Did I push you? Did you not like being tied? What is it, Sherry? You can tell me anything. I'd never do anything to hurt you."

The thought that she'd left this bed feeling vulnerable did something really ugly to my insides. I couldn't stand the thought I'd made her feel bad.

"That's the problem, I guess." She wrapped her arms around her mid-section. I couldn't have her closing off to me. I wrapped my arms around her and pulled her back against my chest, cradling her with my body. I smoothed her hair back and kissed the side of her head.

"Tell me, darlin'."

She sighed and let her head fall back against my shoulder. "It's just that I know you've been with a lot of women, different kinds of women, and I'm fine with that. In theory. But I don't want to *feel* like one of them, you know? You make me feel things and do things I've never allowed myself to do before."

"And you don't like it?" I asked, feeling like a total ass.

But then she shook her head.

"That's just it. I *do* like it. A lot. And I don't know what that says about me." She laughed humorlessly.

Now I was confused. "Did I do something or say something to make you feel that it was wrong?"

"No! You were... No, it's just... Marcus, I don't want to be one of your hoes. I don't. I saw those women lined up outside and I know they'd do anything you wanted, they'd beg for you to take whatever they had to give, and sometimes? I feel just like that. Like I'll do anything you want, that I'd beg you to do something that's totally out of character for me, and then I wonder if I should still have any respect for myself. You make me feel things I never thought I would and you make me want things that a woman like me never should."

I had to tread carefully here. I didn't know whether to be offended, flattered, or proud. The fact was, Sherry was uncomfortable and that was not okay.

"Can you tell me what specifically I did, or we did, that was out of character, or made you feel bad?"

She squirmed again. I tried her shoulders and this time found them a little more pliable. I knew if I could get her to relax she'd open up and then I could figure out what the hell just happened.

"Being tied up, for one. And touching myself in front of you." Her voice was so quiet, I knew it had taken a lot for her to admit that.

"Did you like it?" I asked, afraid of her answers now.

"I did. I liked it when you told me what to do. No one has ever—"

"Good," I said, cutting her off before she did any more of that comparing me to other men, because then I might have to commit murder. "That's good. Was it when I asked you whether you wanted to be good, to accept your punishment?"

She shrugged, her shoulders loosening a little bit more. "I don't know. I've never let anyone spank me before you, Marcus. That's a big deal."

It was a *huge* deal. I'd remember that in the future. If there were a future. *Please let there be a future.*

"And when you touched me..."

I knew where she was going with this. "Did you like that, chère?" God help me, I was already hard again just talking about it.

Her breathing grew somewhat ragged, her voice lowered to a whisper. "I wanted more. But that scares me, Marcus! That's not something I've ever done, ever wanted. Why do you make me want things I've never wanted before?"

She turned on me with confusion on her face. And vulnerability. I pushed her curls back from her eyes and hated the discomfort I saw there. She was about to yank a confession from me that could go either way. She'd either finally understand what I felt for her and we'd be okay, or she'd get up and leave and that would be that. I paused with bated breath awaiting her reaction.

"I have never thought about another woman when in your presence. I only see you, Sherry. I only want you. I haven't been with anyone else since our first time, on Valentine's Day. I haven't even thought about anyone else."

That was a slight fib. I'd entertained the idea of Jaylene's company for a split second before I started comparing her to Sherry in my mind. In that moment, I'd realized Sherry was it for me. I didn't want another woman's company. Ever.

Sherry rested her hand on my bare thigh and she looked down at it, likely observing the differences, which I'd come to love. I loved the way her skin felt, and watching our bodies come together gave me a rush. She was fucking perfect. I loved... I loved her.

"You know I don't trust people, Marcus. But for some reason I trust you. I want things from you...But this can't ever go anywhere. It would ruin my career, probably mess things up for the band. It can only ever be sex between us."

I swallowed hard, praying the fear didn't show on my face. "I heard you when you said that before," I said, trying to fight back the emotions that were filling my chest with lead. "I want whatever I can have with you Sherry. Things may be different some day—"

"How? No matter what happens between us or in our professional lives, one thing that will never change is that one *really big* difference between us."

I snorted. "What? My cock?"

She rolled her eyes and socked me in the shoulder. "No, you fool. How is it going to look for me to be seeing a white guy? From the South? What the hell will my family say?"

Another cold hard reality slap. Sometimes I could kick myself for wanting her to tell me what she was feeling. It just seemed to get worse.

"I may be from the South, Sherry, but things are different in Louisiana. In my family. Look at Mage. He's my best friend. One of my first girlfriends was his cousin, and don't you ever tell him I told you that."

"Marcus, just because you've banged a sister before don't mean—"

"Banged a sister? Do you think I just don't have any heart? That I'm really that much of a manwhore that I don't care where I stick my dick?"

"No!" she said, her hand coming up to my face. She scooted closer to me on the bed. "I'm sorry, Marcus. I didn't mean that."

I was afraid to open my mouth. "Sherry, I love women. I love all kinds of women. I love them for their differences, and *because* they're different. It's exciting to me. In all the places we've been, all the women I've been with, I've loved that they all had something unique about them. With you, your color, your culture, all of it is a part of you. And I love it. I love—" *Fuck.* "I love it that you share yourself with me. Look, I'm a poor white kid from Houma. I never had nothin' but family and music. And I didn't care. I wore fucking Devon's hand me downs, that were handed down from other cousins. My mama even made us shirts sometimes. She worked hard, but my daddy took off and left us with nothing. We had food and we had a house. That was it. Now? I've got everything material I could ever need and I could give a shit. I'm still that poor white kid from Houma and that's all I'll ever be. And I'm okay with that. But if that don't work for you..."

Sherry moved fast. She wrapped her body around me and kissed me hard. Before long, our tongues were plunging into each other's mouths. We scratched and pulled at each other trying to get close. Sherry started to straddle me and I stopped her, my sanity flickering in at that precise moment knowing she'd hate me if I didn't use a condom. I rolled it on with one hand while kissing her. I thrusted my fingers into her heat, stroking her until she was crying my name into my mouth. I tore away from her lips, wanting to look her in the eye as I pulled her down onto my lap, sliding back into her until our pelvises met and ground together.

I cradled her face in my hands. "I only see you, Sherry. I only want you."

She gasped as I hit that spot she loved so much. "I see you, too. Marcus. You're beautiful to me. You make me feel so good. Make me feel it, feel so good."

She yanked my hair back and bit down on my neck until I groaned so loud she started giggling.

She was in for it then. I hoped she'd been doing her yoga, because I bent and twisted her body in all kinds of crazy contortions trying to get closer, to drive her higher, until she was screaming into the pillow. I pulled her legs over my shoulder and slammed into her so hard we were both swearing and grunting. When she came that last time, she nearly wailed with her release. I fell forward to muffle her cries with my mouth and thrust into her with so much force I worried I would break her.

"I'm gonna come, Sherry...I can't...I love...I need...I, FUUUUCK," I shouted, my release thundering through me until I saw spots and could only hear my blood rushing through my ears.

Sherry sighed and moaned as I rocked against her, our bodies slick with sweat and arousal. She stroked my hair and my face and murmured in my ear, "that's it, that's it, give it to me baby, give me all of you. I want all of you."

I knew she never would have said that if she were in her right mind, but hearing it made my heart sing. She could say this was just sex all she wanted. I knew she was afraid of all the external factors, but what mattered was that when I was inside her, she knew I belonged there and she wanted me, too. I'd have to hold onto that for now.

# Chapter Five

The next morning Sherry woke me in a particularly delightful way. She rolled over and threw her leg over my waist, her hand tangling in my hair. Her curls covered her face, but I could see her lips parted just so. The sheet was down far enough I could see her breast lovely against the white sheets. I loved the contrast of our skins together. It made us seem so different, but complementary.

I reached over to run my fingers down her spine and she made soft noises against the pillow. Our feet rubbed together and I had to fight not to laugh out loud when she caught just the right part on the sole of my foot to tickle like crazy. Then she rolled over and backed that beautiful ass up to my side and wiggled. It was invitation enough for me to drape my arm over her and pull her close. After a moment, she rolled over and she actually snuggled against my chest.

A warm feeling spread through my chest. This is what it felt like to share a bed with a woman you loved. This is what it felt like to be loved in return, or at least what I imagined it would feel like. Sherry might be into me, but I'd never fool myself into believing she could love me. I wanted to bask in her warmth, in the sunshine coming through the uncovered windows. I wanted to spend eternity at rest with her. I realized that I was actually relaxed for the first time since Maggie died, maybe even before that. I bet the same was true for Sherry.

"Mmmmmmm you going to bring me some coffee, lover?"

Her sleepy smile was my undoing.

"I'd bring you the Statue of Liberty this morning if you asked for it. Did you sleep well?"

She nodded, still not opening her eyes. "You make a very nice bed partner, Mr. Lambert. But tell me, what had you giggling in your sleep early this morning?"

I moved my head to the side and frowned at her. "Giggling? What are you talking about? I don't giggle."

She rolled onto her back, her gorgeous breasts standing at attention. "You most certainly do! Something had you giggling in your sleep around three a.m. I tried to wake you and all I could get was 'paint balls.'

Marcus smiled. That had been a good memory.

"If you want more of my love gun, you just gotta ask."

She groaned but I knew she wanted me. She didn't have to ask.

# Chapter Six

Los Angeles

April 2012

A few days later...

"You said *what?*" Sherry's question was not one I wanted to answer. After the dumbass move I just pulled, I was lucky she'd let me in the door. I'd called her from the cab after I landed in Burbank to tell her there'd been some trouble back in New Orleans between me and the guys. My feet were on some unsteady ground at the moment. I stood before the woman I loved more than anything in my life with bated breath, waiting for her judgment.

"I know," I answered her in a low voice. "It was stupid. I—"

"Stupid? *Stupid?!* Stupid," she shouted, jabbing a finger into my chest, "is riding a motorcycle without a helmet. Stupid," *OW*, "is parking next to a fire hydrant. Stupid," *Ow FUCK*, "is having unprotected sex with one of your fucking groupies! What you just did? That wasn't just stupid, it was hurtful! How could you say that to a woman who has given up life and livelihood to take care of you spoiled brats?

How could you disrespect her, and your beloved cousin? Sometimes, Marcus, I have no idea what goes on in your fucked up head."

After Sherry'd left the St. Germaine building in New Orleans where the band had been staying, I'd gone back to being uptight. I wanted to go back to L.A. as soon as possible to be with Sherry. Watching Devon and Jaylene being so lovey-dovey just made it harder. At breakfast that morning, Jaylene had gotten all protective about her man, *my* fucking cousin, and I'd put her in her place. We didn't need a Yoko Ono in our midst. But I'd known better. As soon as the words left my mouth, *"just because you're fucking him,"* I'd wished I could take them back. I took off, went to Uncle Daryl's where I'd gotten a ration of shit. Then Devon came over and we had it out. I was tired, feeling like shit, and I thought Sherry would have my back.

Sherry paced in the kitchen of her condo, shaking with anger. Her eyes darting back and forth like the weight of the situation was hitting her like it hit me. Hard as fuck. Right in the sweet spot. She turned on me again with her finger out. I recoiled, praying she didn't poke me again. I was definitely going to have a goddamn bruise.

"You have to apologize. You have to make this right. The whole band, your future depends on this. Devon loves this girl, Marcus! How could you be so—"

"Stupid! I know. Fuck. I said I was sorry."

She shook her head, her corkscrew curls bouncing in her lovely face. "That's great. But you have to say it to her."

"I will! *Damn*. But Sherry, I don't think—"

"That's right, you don't think. If you thought ahead one split second, you would have clamped down on that big mouth of yours and not fucked things up with your brothers." She crossed her arms over her chest and stuck a hip out.

This was actually worse than I thought. I figured she'd bitch at me for being rude to Devon's girl, but she was furious. I'd been on a plane for hours, I hadn't eaten anything since last night, and my back was killing me. All I wanted was to fall in her bed with her and love her until the pain went away. Apparently, my plan was seriously flawed.

"Well, you're just going to have to figure this out, aren't you? Otherwise you can kiss your career goodbye. What the hell are you going to do without your band, huh?"

Okay, that was a low blow. "What the hell does that mean? You think I'm nothing without them? That's bullshit and you know it. They are nothing without *me.* I'm the one that dragged their sorry asses out of the bayou and into the big time. If it weren't for me—"

"Mr. Big Fucking Ego! Would you listen to yourself? How can you stand it?"

So that's what she thought of me. Yeah, that ego was demanding I dress her down for that remark, but inside my wretched heart, something cracked. Talk all the shit I wanted, this woman was going to break me.

I pulled myself up to my full height and looked down at her, trying to keep my damn voice from cracking.

"You saying my big fucking ego isn't welcome here? Fine. I won't sully your doorstep one moment longer, chère. Or your damn reputation."

I stormed out her door and slammed it behind me. I couldn't let her see me break down. I just couldn't. She'd been the one thing going right in my life, the one person who I thought would understand me. Hell, even forgive me. Guess I really was alone on this one.

I walked for blocks that night, hungry, exhausted, and in pain. I finally sat down on a sidewalk bench someplace in Hollywood and tried to breathe. My chest felt as though I had bricks being piled on one at a time until the weight would crush me. I read about that once, how they used to kill witches or some shit like that. I began to think perhaps there was really something physically wrong with me when I woke up to a cop kicking my foot.

"Son? You don't look so good. Too much partying?"

It was dawn. The Hollywood sky was grey and pink. The sun rising on a new day should have had me feeling relieved and hopeful. Instead I felt like death sucking on a Lifesaver.

"No, I didn't...I..." I couldn't form the words. My head pounded in time with my rapid pulse. I tried to stand and collapsed at the cop's feet. I vaguely remember hearing him call someone on the radio and curse his luck.

# Chapter Seven

"Mr. Lambert? I have your test results if you are ready."

The ER staff was cool. They whisked me in, jabbed me with needles, took blood, ran an IV...The real VIP treatment. The nurses fought over who would take my blood pressure and my temperature. I signed autographs but wasn't in the mood for chitchat. I wanted to find out what the hell was wrong then get the fuck out of there.

"What's the deal, doc?"

He studied my chart, made some weird clicking sound with his mouth and then looked up at me gravely.

"For a young man your age, you've got a helluva lot going on here. Blood pressure is dangerously high. You're severely dehydrated, your iron is low...All of these are serious issues, but the real worry is that it appears you've got the beginnings of kidney disease. Mr. Lambert? How much alcohol do you drink on a regular basis? Drug use?"

I shook my head, used to people assuming this of me. "Doc, I ain't had a drink since February. My cousin was killed in an accident."

I choked. I had to catch my breath. Every time I talked about Maggie it still hit me hard. "My band, we all decided to quit. Other than the occasional joint when I was younger, I don't touch drugs."

The doctor pulled at his goatee and frowned. "Well, that's good to know, because you definitely can't touch the stuff anymore. You're going to have to start monitoring your system better. You need to get in with a specialist and start taking better care of yourself or you're going to end up on dialysis before you're thirty."

He rambled on for a while, but I was done listening. Sherry's words played through my head until I wanted to scream.

"Doc, if it's all the same to you, I'd like to just go home."

Home. *Shit.* I kinda didn't have one of those. Sure, I could go stay with Ma in Houma, but what the hell kind of life would that be for a guy like me? All I'd ever known was music, making it with the four men I called brothers. I grew angry thinking about Maggie leaving me to deal with all of this shit. Then I got pissed at myself. I only had myself to blame for my current predicament.

"I'd like to keep you overnight for observation and to get some fluids back into you. You're not in any shape to be out and about. Why don't you just relax? The nurses will get you into a room and we'll keep you until tomorrow. Then you can get back to rockin' and rollin'." He chuckled to himself, shaking his head as he left the room. Guess everyone knew who was here.

"Hey, doc," I called out to him. He stuck his head back in the door.

"Yeah?"

"Any way you can keep this out of the news? And no one was called, right? I don't want—"

"I think they tried to call someone named Meg? Her card was in your wallet, said she's your manager?"

Hysterical laughter is a creepy thing. The laugher doesn't really get how creepy it is, but someone hearing it will become alarmed.

"I'm sorry," I said, leaning forward to stop the stomach cramps, which only aggravated the pain in my back.

"It's alright. Do you need anything for the pain? Your kidneys are really pissed at you right now."

That just made me laugh harder. "Kidneys? Pissed? Get it?"

He gave me a sad smile and waved as he left the room. The gravity of the situation hit me hard. I had no one to call. I'd just managed to alienate my entire family and my lover in just over twenty-four hours.

That had to be a record. Figuring I had nothing better to do, I stared at the ceiling of my hospital room until they came and wheeled me into another room to spend the night, and I promptly began staring at that ceiling as well. It's amazing how many ways you can berate yourself while staring at ceiling tiles. I came up with ways I was a loser for each square above my head, then I started over again when I ran out of tiles. I know I slept a little, but I felt every hour I spent in that damn hospital bed.

What the fuck was I supposed to do now? Sure, Jaylene would probably forgive me because she was a nice person. Devon would forgive me eventually because he always did, even if I didn't deserve it. Uncle Daryl was so angry, I'd never seen him lose it like that, not even when we was kids and got into trouble. Mage and Star, they weren't blood, but they'd been friends for so long...

Jade. He was probably the one person in the whole world who had no reason to ever forgive me. I'd done that baby brother of mine so dirty so many times, yet he was always there. Would he be there this time?

All this time since Maggie died, I pushed and pushed and treated them all like shit, screaming about how it was all for them, all for the band. The reality was just like Devon accused me...I was looking out for number one because I knew without Devon, there would be no Maggie's Bones, and where would I be? Well, someplace like this. Up shit creek without a paddle stuck in a hospital room with no one to call. Pathetic.

The next morning around nine the doctor came to see me and gave me discharge instructions.

"Mr. Lambert, it is imperative that you see a specialist immediately. I can refer you—"

"Thanks, doc. I'll have to find someone back home in New Orleans. There's nothing left here for me."

STAY TUNED...

More Bated stories with Marcus and Sherry will be out soon...

. . .

For more Rock 'n' Romance News, go to www.rlmerrillauthor.com and sign up for my newsletter-y thingie!

# Chapter Eight

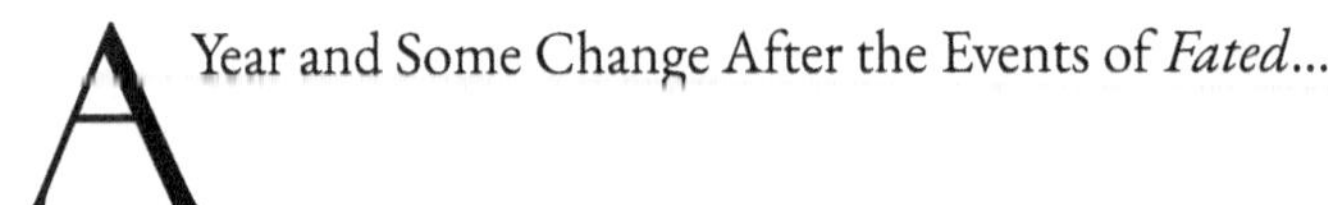

A Year and Some Change After the Events of *Fated*...

Marcus

"Please tell me we can go home now," Sherry moaned into his mouth. They stood beside her car in the parking lot behind The Roxy, where Marcus had just performed the first show of his new gig.

Marcus Lambert...Solo Act.

Marcus pulled back and kissed her forehead. Then he shivered. "Yeah, let's go. Something feels..."

He looked around with a frown on his face. He pulled Sherry closer to him, feeling safe in her arms like nowhere else since he'd been on his own. She'd really been his rock this past year.

His brothers had turned on him, but he couldn't bring himself to be angry anymore. That time had passed. Now he just felt empty, unless he was with the woman he loved.

"What is it, babe?" Her big brown eyes gazed up at him, worried.

She took such good care of him. He would be forever grateful that she'd believed in him when the rest of the band thought the worst.

Being accused of sexually assaulting a woman at a club had seemed ludicrous at the time, but now? It was just the chickens coming home to roost. He'd been a player for so long, he'd forgotten how to just be himself. Sherry was the only one he felt totally comfortable with, and once she proved she'd stay by his side, he'd made peace with his fate.

Sometimes you aren't forgiven, aren't given a second, or third, or twentieth chance to prove your worth. He didn't blame his friends and family for their reactions to the accusation. He only blamed himself for not making changes sooner.

He took Sherry by the hand and led her out the back door of the club. She kept asking him if he was okay, but he was starting to feel that tightness in his lower back, which often meant he was too rundown or stressed out. His health was precarious and Sherry was always worried about him.

* * * *

Sherry

"Hey," she said, holding his face in her palms, which was sometimes the only way she could get through to him. "What's wrong, baby? And don't tell me nothing, please? You seem so sad." Her hands came up to cup his face, forcing him to look at her.

"I don't know. I'm just...I miss them. I miss them all. I love these new tunes, but it's—"

"It's not the same," she finished for him. It nearly killed Sherry to see this once proud, cocky-for-a-damn-good-reason man feeling so much pain. Literally. She could see the tightness around his eyes that meant he was hurting. She'd learned to recognize the signs after several ER visits and trips to the doctor over the past several months.

"Maybe you just need some rest," she said, pressing her face against his chest. After spending a year denying Marcus and pretending she wasn't involved with him, she relished his affection. She now had endless opportunities to have him however she wanted. He was usually up for anything.

It had taken her a long time to accept how she felt about him, and to realize that he really did love *her*. That she wasn't just a conquest. Since then, they'd been inseparable when she wasn't working and he wasn't in the studio working on his solo project.

He'd moved in with her after the fiasco at the mansion, which she still got angry about. How dare they turn him away after all he'd done to keep the band together? He'd explained to her time and time again that they were right to jump to conclusions about his relations with women, that he'd done too many wrongs to expect anything else. But thinking about it just got her hackles up. They were her friends, too, and she'd remained civil for business reasons, but she wanted to fly to Louisiana and slap the whole bunch of them for how much pain they were causing her lover.

Sherry felt Marcus breathe against her hair and his hands slid down and gripped her hips. He leaned down and kissed her neck, biting down just the way he knew would drive her crazy. She moaned at the sensation, linking her fingers behind his neck and tilting her head to give him more access. He trailed his lips, his teeth, and then his tongue down the sensitive column of her throat and over to her collarbone. Sherry could feel her tension slip away and wished desperately to have her hands on his skin.

"Let me get us home," she murmured, giving the back of his hair a tug the way he liked it. He grunted and yanked her pelvis against his, then he swiveled his hips to give her a taste of what he was feeling.

"I don't think I can make it home, chère," he breathed. His fingers slowly gathered up the material of her dress. "I can't wait."

Sherry gasped as he hooked his fingers over the strings holding a thin piece of lace in place. She'd never been so adventurous before, but Marcus made her feel so alive, so wanton, that she'd become much more accepting of his advances in what previously had seemed such scandalous places.

"Are you really trying to fuck me right here in this parking lot, Mr. Lambert? Is that what you think you're going to do?" It got him hot when she challenged him. Letting her fingers do a little walking proved that to her. His erection was so thick, and so eager to get to its happy place.

"Why, *Mrs.* Lambert, I do believe I *will* fuck you right here in this parking lot, just because I can't wait to be buried up here..." His fingers found her core and slid home with ease. She was so ready for him, excited by this little scenario.

"Mr. Lambert! But what if someone sees us?" She went for demure, but he always knew better. He spun her around so quickly, she barely caught herself with her hands on the hood of her brand new Mercedes, a gift from Marcus. She felt him rip the sides of her panties and quickly do away with them. Pity. She liked those ones.

"They'll see me making love to my incredibly hot wife." He slowly slid her dress up over her hips, causing her to arch her back. He fell to his knees behind her and began to worship her. Thoroughly. She only gave a slight thought to their surroundings as he pressed his lips against her.

Sherry wobbled on her heels, but didn't dare move. Marcus on a mission was an experience she'd never deny herself, especially when she knew he'd make her come like a tidal wave. He held her in place with his strong hands and licked and sucked until she thought she'd scream so loud she'd get them caught and arrested. Just when she thought she couldn't take any more, he did this thing where—

"Marcus! Oh, baby, you can't—" She let out a squeal just as Marcus stood and clapped a hand over her mouth. He chuckled in her ear as she panted through a 9.0 on the Richter scale of insane orgasms.

"Come on, chère. You can't get us caught now. I've still got more work to do," he whispered as he entered her, not quite gently. He was beyond that. Sherry held on for dear life as he thrust so hard against her, her feet lifted off the ground. He kept his hand over her mouth to keep her from screaming her ecstasy until all of Sunset Strip came running.

"You know when I get you home you're going to get more of this, don't you, wife? You know I'm going to be in you until you can't walk straight tomorrow. I wouldn't be doing my husbandly duty if I didn't keep you more than satisfied." He thrust even harder, until she stumbled, only his arms keeping her from face planting on the car.

"You won't be if you mangle my face, now get back to that husbandly duty— OH!" He hit that spectacular spot that always brought her right to orgasm. Every time. It was like his cock had some sort of homing beacon. Damn, was he good to her.

Marcus whispered that he didn't think he could stay in control any longer after he felt her core grip him tight...oh so tight. He came in a rush, holding her against him as he cried out the words that made her swoon. "I love you, my wife. Love of my life."

Marcus told her he still planned to have a ceremony in front of their friends and whatnot, but after everything they'd been through over the past year, he hadn't wanted Sherry to go another second without knowing how much he loved her, how much he owed her his life. They'd had a civil ceremony at the courthouse and made it official. He then took steps to make sure she'd always be taken care of, no matter what happened to him.

They stood together, panting and laughing for a few moments before the back door of the club opened and a large party spilled outside. They righted their clothes and kissed once more before Marcus opened the driver's door for Sherry and then let himself in on the passenger side.

"You still planning on continuing your duties," Sherry asked her voice husky. Her heart hadn't returned to its normal pulse rate yet. Depending on his answer, it might not.

She waited with bated breath for his response...

***STAY TUNED...***

More Bated stories with Marcus and Sherry, as well as a long-awaited series finale, will be out soon...

For more Rock 'n' Romance News, go to www.rlmerrillauthor.com and sign up for my newsletter-y thingie!

# And now, a paranormal adventure from the Haunted universe...

## MINDED: A HAUNTED STORY

When landing in Purgatory, no matter the cause of death, a soul must experience an awakening, establish awareness, and ultimately achieve acceptance of its circumstances.

For Maggie Stone, none of these options were ideal. She had always been a woman in control of her own destiny. She was not thrilled about becoming a pawn in some afterlife game. But in order to move on, she'll have to complete her task and accept help from an unlikely source dressed in black denim and pissed off at the world. Will she be able to work her magic and mind her kin who are still struggling with her death?

Louis Sheffield has spent an eternity in Purgatory for reasons somewhat beyond his control. When he's given an opportunity to earn his ticket out of his holding cell, he's irritated to learn he'll have to hold the hand of a pretentious, know-it-all party girl whose every action grates on his last nerve. But Maggie is not what she seems, and once he's exposed to her world, suddenly he's tempted to finally accept his destiny and embrace hope.

These two lost souls work together against the clock to complete a seemingly impossible task. When their charges refuse to cooperate, Maggie and Louis must resort to unorthodox methods to create harmony from bitter chaos. In the end, it all comes down to choices and consequences they never imagined possible.

Revisit the band Maggie's Bones and find out if, once again, love can cure the haunted.

# Acknowledgments

My family members are my biggest supporters and have made it possible for me to share my brand of crazy with all of you. Thanks to my husband, children, Mom, Dad, and sister for always being there when I needed a kick in the ass or a big hug.

My amazing partners-in-crime, Ellay Branton and Kimberlie L. Faye, kept me sane while I worked to get this book out. Their encouragement, knowledge and patience are invaluable in my writing process. I don't know which of the Fates decided to put them in my path, but I'll be eternally grateful.

Thank you to my friends in the Indie Author community for your continued support. I consider myself blessed to have you all in my life.

To my beta readers, those who have been with me from the beginning, and the new ones I've recently come to call friends, thank you for the use of your eyes and for allowing me to corrupt, I mean, entertain you with my tales of Rock 'n' Romance! Thank you for always being available to check over some crazy idea no matter the time frame or task. Without you I'd be nowhere.

# Connect With R.L. Merrill

I would love to connect with you! Here's where you can find me lurking: Facebook at www.facebook.com/rlmerrillauthor

Instagram @rlmerrillauthor

Twitter @rlmerrillauthor

And my groovy website: www.rlmerrillauthor.com
where you can find my newsletter-y thingie and stay up-to-date with the latest from my world of Rock 'n' Romance! You can even pick up passwords to unlock short stories set in the Teacher, Haunted and The Rock Season worlds.

# Reviews

Reviews are incredibly important to authors. If you enjoyed Fated, please leave your review for others from whichever rooftop you'd like to shout it from!

# Other Books By R.L. Merrill

**Haunted Series:** (Contemporary Romance)

Haunted

Fated

Bated

Jaded – (Coming Soon)

**Minded Series:** (Paranormal Spinoff of Haunted Series)

Minded

Blossomed

Father F'in' Christmas

A Peculiar Prom Night

**Magic and Mayhem Universe:** (Funny Paranormal Romance in the universe created by Robyn Peterman)

Shifted

Ghoul Me Once

Gator Me Twice

Magic and Mayhem/Shifted Collection

Fang Me Three Times

Fangtastic Four

Five Fanger Witch Punch

**Hollywood Rock 'n' Romance Trilogy:** (Contemporary Romance)

Teacher

Teacher: Act Two

Teacher: The Final Act

**Contemporary Romance Series:**

The Rock Season

Road Trip

You Fell First

The Heart Knows (Re-Releasing Soon)

A Match Made in Spain

**LGBTQ Romance**

Pinups and Puppies (Originally in Love Is All Vol. 2)

I Want, More – Bolder Breed Studios #1 (Originally in Love Is All Vol. 3)

Love and Pride – Bolder Breed Studios #2 (Originally in Love Is All Vol. 4)

Everything's Better With You: An MM Sports Romance

All I Wanna Do — Bolder Breed Studios #3 (Email Ro for your copy)

Under His Sheets: Accidentally Undercover – Out April 9, 2024

Feuds and Interludes: Road To Rocktoberfest 2024 - November 2024

**The Banes of Lake's Crossing** (Historical Horror Romance)

The Fourth Man (The Banes of Lake's Crossing) (Historical Horror Romance)

The Redemption of Nathaniel Bane

The Absolution of Jonah Bane

**The Gifted Series:** (Supernatural Suspense/Paranormal Romance)

Healer

Connection

Protector

**Sundowners** (M/M Paranormal Romance

Sundowners Book One

Moonwish: Sundowners Book Two (February 13, 2025)

**Forces of Nature Series:** (Gay Contemporary Romance)

Hurricane Reese

Typhoon Toby

Earthquake Ethan

**Summer of Hush Series:** (Gay Contemporary Romance)

Summer of Hush

Brains and Brawn

You Can Do Magic: Carnival Of Mysteries (A Summer of Hush Tie-In)

You Can Save Me: Carnival of Mysteries (Season Two, Book Two)

**Anthologies:**

Thanksgiving Day Parade From Hell (Worst Holiday Ever) (Gay Contemporary Romance

Valentine's Day From Hell (Worst Valentine's Day Ever) (Gay Contemporary Romance)

Salty and Sweet (Summer Fair) (Lesbian Contemporary Romance)

The Fourth Man (The Banes of Lake's Crossing) (Historical Horror Romance)

A Piece of Him (Gone With The Dead) (Horror)

Breaking Bread—Dark Divinations from HorrorAddicts.net Press (Horror)

Exchange (Renewal) (Science Fiction)

Tap-Tap-Tap (Impact) ( Horror)

Human Sacrifice (Innovation) (Horror)

The Sitter (Clarity) (Horror)

Joy Is A Phone Call Away – A More Perfect Union (Lesbian Contemporary Romance)

The House Must Fall – Haunts and Hellions from HorrorAddicts.net Press – May 2021 (Horror)

A Kept Woman – BAQWA Presents: Horror Show 2021(Lesbian Horror Romance)

Gods of Rock 'n' Roll (Free on Wattpad)

How Bittersweet is Karma? Free on Wattpad)

Let Me Stand Next To Your Fire (Queer Cheer)

Midnight in the Renaissance Elevator

**Holiday Romance**

A Peace Offering (Re-release)

Love and Pride – Bolder Breed Studios #2

Once Upon A Goth Dog Solstice (December 2024)

**Audiobooks**

The Rock Season (Kiss App)

Brains and Brawn (Kiss App)

Teacher (Kiss App)

Hurricane Reese (Kiss App)

A Match Made in Spain (Audible)

Healer: Gifted Book One (Audible)

Under His Sheets (Audible Coming Soon)

You Can Do Magic: Carnival of Mysteries (Coming Soon)

Road Trip: A Rock Season Novel (Coming Soon)

**Non-Fiction**

Horror Addicts Guide To Life Volume 2 - Edited by Emerian Rich

Death's Garden Revisited - Edited by Loren Rhoads (Out Fall 2022)

www.ingramcontent.com/pod-product-compliance
Lightning Source LLC
Chambersburg PA
CBHW030318200626
46816CB00006BA/1835

* 9 7 8 0 9 9 6 2 8 0 3 5 8 *